THE SAVAGE WARS OF PEACE

THE SAVAGE WARS OF PEACE

Soldiers' Voices 1945-1989

CHARLES ALLEN

MICHAEL JOSEPH
London

MICHAEL JOSEPH LTD

Published by the Penguin Group
27 Wrights Lane, London W8 5TZ, England
Viking Penguin Inc., 40 West 23rd Street, New York, New York 10010, USA
Penguin Books Australia Ltd, Ringwood, Victoria, Australia
Penguin Books Canada Ltd, 2801 John Street, Markham, Ontario, Canada L3R 1B4
Penguin Books (NZ) Ltd, 182–190 Wairau Road, Auckland 10, New Zealand

Penguin Books Ltd, Registered Offices: Harmondsworth, Middlesex, England

First published in 1990

Typeset in Linotron 11/12½pt Times by
Wilmaset, Birkenhead, Wirral
Printed and bound in Great Britain by
Butler & Tanner, Frome, Somerset

A CIP catalogue record for this book is available from the British Library

ISBN 0 7181 2882 6

Library of Congress Catalog Card Number: 89–64335

Contents

Why do you have this comradeship
and brotherly love? It comes from
the fact that you are prepared to
die for the man on your right or
on your left, and you know that he
is prepared to do the same for you.

John 'Patch' Williams, DCM

Photograph Credits

The Author and Publishers would like to thank the following organisations and people for permission to reproduce the photographs in this book:

Section I. Between pages 98 and 99
Page 1 Royal Marines Museum. Page 2 Imperial War Museum. Page 3 *top left* William Hewlett; *top right* John Frawley; *bottom* E. Lillico. Page 4 *top* Imperial War Museum; *bottom* Gurkha Museum. Page 5 Royal Marines Museum. Page 6 *top* Brigadier E. D. Smith; *bottom* Airborne Forces Museum. Page 7 Gurkha Museum. Page 8 *top left* Colonel J. Williams; *top right* E. Lillico; *bottom* Royal Marines Museum.

Section II. Between pages 130 and 131
Page 1 Imperial War Museum. Page 2 *top* Royal Marines Museum; *bottom* Airborne Forces Museum. Page 3 *top* Royal Marines Museum; *bottom* Captain W. P. Pringle (courtesy of the *Daily Express*). Pages 4–6 Colonel R. E. Blenkinsop (courtesy of the *Daily Express*). Page 7 SAS Regiment. Page 8 Private Source.

Section III. Between pages 226 and 227
Page 1 *top* Imperial War Museum; *bottom* Royal Marines Museum. Page 2 *top left* Press Association; *top right* Private Source; *bottom* Private Source. Page 3 *top* Private Source; *bottom* Airborne Forces Museum. Page 4 Royal Marines Museum. Page 5 *top* Royal Marines Museum; *bottom* Ulster Defence Regiment. Pages 6–7 Army Information Services.

Preface and Acknowledgements

The Savage Wars of Peace of my title are the counter-insurgency campaigns fought by the British Army between 1945 and the present day. It is said that since the 1680s, when a standing army was first created to deal with the 'present troubles in Ireland', only one year has passed that has not seen British troops involved in one theatre or another. What is certain is that since the Second World War British forces have been on active service every year except 1968, the so-called year of peace.

This active service came in two forms: there were the full-scale military engagements of Korea, the Suez Invasion and the Falklands War; and there were the lesser conflicts that in service jargon are classified as 'low intensity operations'. The latter are the little wars of our times, the 'Savage Wars of Peace' in which the aggressors have engaged in armed insurgency against the state and where British troops have been called in as 'an aid to the civil power'. In most cases they have arisen from Britain's shedding of her colonial role and the enemy has been – not always but almost always – the same: the shadowy figure of the gunman and the bomber, what those in the armed forces would unhesitatingly call the 'terrorist'.

What follows is not a formal history but a perspective of this form of warfare as seen principally from a foot-soldier's point of view; an oral history, in fact, assembled from the spoken recollections of some seventy military men and women, the great majority of whom served – or are still serving – in infantry battalions. Their collective experience covers all the main theatres in which the British Army's 'Savage Wars of Peace' have been played out: from Indo-China and Palestine in 1945, by way of Malaya (1948–60), Kenya (1952–60), Cyprus (1955–59), Brunei (1962–63), Borneo (1963–66), Aden (1964–67) and Oman (1958 and 1970–75), through to Northern Ireland (1969–).

In selecting my seventy military 'eye-witnesses' my main criterion has been experience, so that most of those whose recollections make up this book have an average of twenty years' soldiering and two or three campaigns behind them. Articulacy and chance also played a part in deciding whose voices should be heard and whose should not. Some interviews were snatched, others were spread over several long sessions. Some were missed and there are entire regiments and corps that ought to be represented here and are not, so that in no way should my seventy voices be regarded as a representative cross-section of the British Army's experience of fighting insurgency since 1945.

Taken together as a group these seventy 'eye-witnesses' would be seen by their comrades-in-arms as sharing outstanding qualities of leadership and courage. Ideally, I should have liked to have set out in cold print their decorations for bravery along with their names and their commands – but circumstances do not permit this. For reasons of security or personal safety a number of 'eye-witnesses' have not been identified by name: one or two high-profile figures recently retired, as well as many more still serving, likely to return to active service or – as in the case of members of the Ulster Defence Regiment – on continuous active service. If these occasional lapses into anonymity mar the flow of the narrative I hope the reader will understand and excuse.

This is not a book that glorifies war. It is about soldiering at the sharp end evoked by those who have been there through their own words and feelings. 'I never did glory in what I did,' remarks one of the seventy, a man who in his own time was renowned for the cold-blooded skill with which he pursued and killed Communist terrorists in the Malayan jungle, 'but I wasn't paid to go to the place of battle and turn away from it. I have lived a life where I have seen aggression, seen indigenous peoples willing to slaughter their own friends, and I like to think that the fighting I've done has been to try to prevent that kind of thing.' Another of my 'eye-witnesses' reinforces the point: 'We don't go to war to self-glorify our profession of arms. Our chosen profession is to stop war, not make war. We are servants of the people in exactly the same way as anyone else (in government service) is a servant of the people, and we do *your* bidding, not our own.' Perhaps it is worth remembering, too, that this profession is, as a third contributor puts it, 'one of the few which is prepared to put its life on the line for its country and, indeed, for its politicians.'

Some of those whose voices are heard here have been fortunate enough to get to the top of the tree in their profession, some are on their way to the top – and others have not been quite so lucky. Their testimonies were all given off the cuff and are set down here as spoken, warts and all, with only the minimum of tidying up. My own contribution has been that of listener and editor. Having asked the questions, I have confined myself thereafter to setting down only what has been said to me, recounting the experiences, feelings and opinions of others without – I hope – allowing my own views to intrude. Some of the events recalled go back over forty years. People forget, omit, exaggerate, make mistakes – as we all do when talking about past events. This has to be allowed for without, I trust, detracting from the sheer authenticity of what they have to say. Theirs is an extraordinary story, as real-life experience so often is, and in every case I am deeply indebted to every one of my seventy 'eye-witnesses' for their kindness and candour in talking to me so freely and so frankly.

I should also like to record my thanks to the many good people who helped in one way or another to get this project off the ground and who helped to keep it going. Many of these cannot be named or would not wish to be named, and I think in particular of the brave and good-hearted people whom I met in Northern Ireland. My thanks, also, to the unsung custodians of regimental history dotted up and down the country in various offices and barracks, acting as keepers of museums or as honorary secretaries of regimental associations. Without their support and guidance this book would have been infinitely the poorer.

One institution that I can name without qualms is the Imperial War Museum, where I should like to thank Dr Margaret Brooks, Keeper of the Department of Sound Records, and her staff – Alan Morrow, in particular, who was always available to help me with recording equipment and facilities.

Some part of what follows was broadcast in 1988–89 in the BBC Radio series, *The Savage Wars of Peace*, produced by my old friend and sometime mentor, Helen Fry, who has just retired from the post of Chief Producer Archives Features after a distinguished career in BBC Radio. My special thanks to her – and to our fellow-collaborator on that series, Major-General Sir Jeremy Moore, also recently retired after an outstanding career in the Royal Marines that culminated in his command of the British Land Forces in the Falklands War. A small part of his own experiences before the Falklands – in Malaya, the Canal Zone, Cyprus, Brunei, Borneo and Northern Ireland – is included in this book. However, my particular thanks go to him for providing advice, encouragement and very constructive criticism.

Only someone who was there can ever know what it was really like. My hope is that this drawing-together at second-hand of what Jeremy Moore, his fellow Marines and other soldiers experienced at first-hand not only approximates to the truth but also does some small justice to their achievements.

CHARLES ALLEN, AUGUST 1989

INTRODUCTION:
One of the Boys

I remember very well in Northern Ireland passing a sentry who was in a very dangerous position. He was a kid from the backstreets of Liverpool, not very bright, and I said to him in a rather disconsolate way, 'Are you happy?' With a big smile he said, 'Yes, sir. Fine!' And I almost turned on him enraged and said, 'How the hell can you be happy in this situation?' But he was a child of the slums, from a broken home, adoptive parents, who'd changed schools so often he could hardly read or write. He'd been shoved around and rejected all the way but he was bright enough to get into the Army – and here he was, a member of Number Six Section. Okay, he was the most junior member but he was one of the team, and to this boy who had been at the end of the line all his life it was worth being shot at or blown up to belong to that Number Six Section, to be one of the boys.

The General walks with a limp that makes him wince. 'Parachutist's hip,' he grins. His name, rank and number are missing from this year's Army List. A photo shows him being armchaired – quite literally – out of his old regiment, trundled past ranks of cheering soldiery in an armchair attached to a fork-lift truck. Caught off-guard by the camera, the General looks glum and bewildered. A second photo shows him on guard, as one of seventy grim-jowled, crimson-tabbed, gold-peaked blimps in khaki massed on the forecourt of the Staff College, Camberley, for the Chief of the Defence Staff's Annual Conference. *Mars et ars in excelsis.* A fearful sight.

Seen in retirement in his new home in Yorkshire the General resembles nothing so much as a genial human being. He talks with gusto of his plans as he leads a lightning tour of the tumbledown smithy that he has rebuilt to his liking. In every room the walls proclaim the mysteries of his craft: plaques, crests and shields; prints of battles ancient and modern; groups formal and informal; framed letters, signed cartoons, mementoes of almost forty years of soldiering. Finally, the General pulls down a series of scrapbooks numbered by year. More photos, many from newspaper clippings. One shows the new commanding officer of the battalion, youthful – 'just before my thirty-seventh birthday' – and hearty, smiling from ear to ear. Another shows the same man, careworn and troubled. Eighteen months separate the two photos but the place is the same: Belfast in late 1969 and again in 1971.

The Army – and the Navy – made the General: 'I had come from fairly humble beginnings. My father had been killed in the War and my mother was eking out a living in my home town. I was lucky to go the way I did thanks to the Royal Navy.' Sent away to Christ's Hospital on a naval scholarship, he was encouraged by his house-master to try for the Army and 'once I'd made up my mind to go into the Army I became extremely enthusiastic'. First there was a compulsory spell in the ranks, where 'you had to learn parrot fashion all the details of the 75-pounder, and I can sit down now and write them out without even thinking. That was a lesson I learned, by going over these things, getting it wrong and having to carry a hammer spike above your head round the square or other little penalties, which the sergeant-majors had a habit of pushing. It was a lesson that remained with me, that if you get the training right at the beginning of a soldier's career it stays with him for the rest of his life.'

After the basic training came eighteen months at the Royal Military Academy, Sandhurst, where the General-to-be was taught to be 'an officer and a gentleman, in that order. The old gentleman-soldier bit had died out in the War but what was important was that you learned good manners and how to behave with your friends.'

The British Army that the General-to-be joined as a professional in 1950 was made up largely of conscripts doing a two-year period of National Service. At its core was the infantry battalion and the infantryman:

> The basic infantryman is much the same as a Roman legionnaire who used to travel across Britain and Europe. Although he has to master more technical weapons now, he has the same basic skills to maintain in field-craft and cunning and thinking. Also in the organisation of our army very little has changed in principle, because of the capabilities of the individual. A section commander is happiest when he has got between seven and twelve men and a good strong section is about eight or nine, which you can fit into the back of an APC [armoured personnel carrier] now. Then the platoon commander will take up to thirty men and, if you look back again at the Roman legions, you have the centurion who takes a

hundred men. That's your company commander now. Then a
battalion commander has between six hundred and up to a
thousand men and this, too, is a number that hasn't changed over
the centuries. It's a number which a group of people can identify
with and an individual leader can identify with, too, because you
cannot expect anybody to know more than between six hundred
and a thousand people well in a team.

A battalion could be a single regiment in itself or it could be one of
several battalions in the same regiment, depending on the defence
requirements of the time. For the great majority of soldiers it was the
battalion that became their home and the regiment to which they
gave their loyalty. Like so many of his contemporaries – both officers
and other ranks – the General-to-be joined his local 'county'
regiment: 'I'd grown up in B . . . . I was very proud of that town, all
my family were there and I lived not far from Victoria Barracks, the
old . . . shire regimental depot. As a boy I used to watch them come
down to church every Sunday with the band so I had an affinity, and
your county regiment is quite important to you. I joined the . . . shire
Regiment in 1952 when they were just about to leave for Malaya.'

The Colonel, by contrast, joined one of the 'smart' regiments – the
'best regiment you could get into without private means between the
two world wars' – one that has acquired some notoriety in post-war
years on account of the number of 'thinking generals' it has
produced. The Colonel would certainly have been one of them – had
he stayed on.

The Colonel now works from an office overlooking the main street
of one of those quaint little towns that straddle the upper reaches of
the Thames. He took early retirement from the Army twelve years
ago. When he joined his regiment in the mid-1950s he expected to be
part of the military establishment of a major world power but 'all that
happened, of course, was that one was engaged in a series of well-
conducted but minor withdrawal operations, and by the time I'd
twigged this it was really too late to get out. I was very happy for
years and years but, in fact, one was looking backwards. It was
managing withdrawal and decay.'

The Colonel was born to Army service, 'born in barracks in India
and my birth certificate is an Army form.' He was the sixth
generation from father to son to serve as an Army officer, with his
son making a seventh generation. 'I can say with confidence that my
family, as a family of regular officers, has never to my knowledge
engaged in an advance. Right from the American War of Independence we, the regular officer families, have conducted retreats. I

added it up once and as a family it came to 17,000 miles of retreating.'
The extraordinary fact in all these 'endless apparent disasters' was
that the British Army remained a fighting force. 'What is it that holds
the Army together?' asks the Colonel. He believes that leadership is
the answer:

> The one fundamental in this is that the other ranks know that the
> officers will never intentionally let them down. We, the officers of
> the Army, may let them down because circumstances are against
> us. We may even let them down through incompetence, but it is the
> basis of our ethos that the first duty of an officer is to get shot first.
> For the first month of my first tour in Northern Ireland we had a
> man a day hit, either wounded or killed. Now in terms of major
> wars this is not a high casualty rate. Nevertheless, it *is* a casualty
> rate but there was no sense of a collapse of morale or anything. The
> system held together and it held together because the officers were
> there to be shot at, too.

Another strength of the system is the way that it moulds officers
and men to fit into the system:

> It's not that the Army with its class system excludes people. What it
> does is to retype them. It recycles them and they come out looking
> as if they were born to it, but actually the percentage who weren't
> born to it is very high. And the reason for this is to produce the
> homogeneity that you require if people are going to live together
> for very long periods. Now the way Army officers conduct them-
> selves in the mess and so on is the most masterly way to get on with
> other people year after year without quarrelling. It was developed,
> I suppose, when regiments used to go for years and years to live in
> the Punjab or somewhere, where if you allowed everybody to do
> their own thing you'd be shooting each other before long. So you
> had to produce rules.

The exact nature of the Colonel's present business is never made
clear, but it is something to do with transporting sensitive goods. 'For
twelve years now,' says the Colonel, 'I've lived with risk-taking and
decision-making in business in a way that is impossible for an Army
officer in peace-time service – and I would now be a vastly better
Army commander for my business experience.'

Also retired from Army life – but a life seen from a very different
perspective – is the ex-Warrant Officer Second Class who owns a
bungalow near the Welsh border alongside his old regimental
barracks. Its perimeter fence cuts across the bottom of his garden.
He and other former comrades-in-arms provide a *cordon sanitaire*

round the base. 'No one moves around here without us knowing about it. Anyone comes asking questions, they'll know about it.' He nods towards the barracks. He, too, comes from an Army family:

> My father was in the 9th Lancers and, of my three uncles, one was in the naval division and two were in cavalry regiments that went through the First World War. We go back to a great-great-grandfather who was a battery sergeant-major stationed on the island of St Helena when Napoleon was held prisoner there. I joined the Army as soon as I was able when I turned eighteen years of age in 1951. I joined my county regiment, the Royal North-umberland Fusiliers, as it was then, but to my surprise when I'd finished my basic training, expecting to go with a draft to Korea, I couldn't find my name on the Northumberlands' drafts list. They'd cross-posted me to the West Yorkshire Regiment.

This rebuff led the WO2-to-be into joining the Parachute Regiment, from where he made his way into a Special Forces unit that worked in squadrons and troops rather than in companies and platoons. Here it was leadership from the non-commissioned officers rather than from the commissioned ones that most deeply impressed him as a young soldier; the sergeant and corporal instructors who were 'dedicated to the regiment' and whose enthusiasm 'rubbed off on us'. It was the sergeant, in particular, who provided the working link between officers and other ranks:

> The Army really is a process of teaching and passing on lessons. The lessons that were passed on to us we are duty bound to pass on to the blokes who come behind us, and so on ad infinitum. And so a new officer was more or less on probation and relied on his troop sergeant for guidance, which is right because this new guy can be the best bloke in the world but unless he's got the relevant skills under his belt, he wouldn't know what the score is. And so officers over the first twelve months, more or less, used to take all the advice of the sergeant. Did blokes take advantage of it? You got the odd one or two who, maybe lightheartedly, would throw in the odd crippler but you always had the restraining hand of the sergeant who made sure nobody ever got out of order.

As the young officer developed his skills so in all good regiments there grew a mutual respect between the men he commanded and himself. When this was combined with interdependence on the battlefield or in a testing environment it helped to unite officers, NCOs and men into one extended hierarchical family:

For thirty-three years I went through this happy state of affairs and in that thirty-three years I've only ever fallen out with two officers and that wasn't a major falling out, just a difference of opinion on certain minor tactics. But once you've been with a bunch of blokes through the rain, living in the field, sharing your rations, sharing your last drop of beer, you know, and especially when you've been through combat with them, it certainly bonds you in, because you know you can turn around and trust that bloke behind you. If you're ever in trouble you know you can drop back on them, or if you're too proud somebody will notice the straits you're in and alert the boss of the regimental association. We had one bloke who'd lost both his legs and it was through the association they got him a little motor car to give him a bit of mobility. Another good lad who in his day killed about eight CTs [Communist Terrorists], known as 'The Whispering Leaf', he was living on his own and too proud to admit it but the association found out about the state he was in and he's now at an Old Soldier's Home at R . . .

The regiment means a great deal to the ex-WO2. 'Once you're in the regiment you're always in, regardless. The comradeship is something rather special.' As the years pass his loyalty and his enthusiasm remain undiminished. Over the mantelpiece in his sitting-room is a painting by a friend showing a four-man patrol in the Borneo jungle. The ex-WO2 details the weapons the men carry: 'The pump-action shotgun normally had the barrel sawn down to make a perfect lead-scout weapon' – his eyes glint with enthusiasm – 'You always had one up the spout and four in the chamber, loaded with SG9, maybe a quarter-inch size ball and nine of those in one round so, say, at a distance of about fifteen to twenty metres it would give you a spread about the size of a dustbin lid. The tactic evolved by the regiment was the double tap, to get one shot off, which used to freeze them, and then the second shot was an aimed shot to kill. It was the old, old business of the two kinds of soldier – the quick and the dead.'

The Company Sergeant-Major has an office in one of the many bitumen-painted shacks that surround half-a-dozen parade grounds outside Colchester. His conversation is punctuated by the ringing of telephones, the slamming of doors and the crashing of boots in corridors. There's a crackle of light arms fire from the ranges, even the wail of a bagpipe. The rifles are being zeroed. The battalion is on the move.

Unemployment is high in the CSM's home town but that wasn't why he joined his Highland regiment. 'I wanted to join the Army,' he declares. 'My father was in the . . .s so that seemed the natural choice. I joined straight from school. I went to the recruiting office, which was in Stirling, and I joined the regiment in Edinburgh in 1973.' He belongs to the modern generation of professionals who run the slimmed-down, new model, post-1967 Army: soft-spoken, articulate, hair short but not too short, fashionable NCO-type moustache, seemingly too young to have earned a crown on his sleeve. So young, in fact, that he was still at school when his regiment did its first Northern Ireland tour. He's done three since; twice as a private and once as a section leader, when 'the soldiers look to you all the time for advice and you are the directing force. It's down to you as a corporal to go out there and do it – and you've got to have the confidence, otherwise it just doesn't happen.'

The new unit that has emerged from Northern Ireland is the brick: 'a brick is a part of the section, possibly four men in an eight-man section and commanded by an NCO. For that brick to function every man in the brick must think, must act together; otherwise a small unit like that can go to bits. So now every private soldier has to be a thinking person out there. He can't just be a guy who tails along at the back and thinks nothing, because if he is then that brick is in danger. So it's the private soldier himself who has a lot more responsibility on him than he ever had before.'

The CSM faces the prospect of a fourth tour with equanimity. It's the wives who find it a strain.

So, finally, to the Private, who was seen on television scrambling in dark green Number Ones over the rubble in the aftermath of the Enniskillen Remembrance Day bomb in November 1987. The Ulster accent is unmistakable, but this Private is a wife and mother as well as a part-time soldier who's never really been off-duty since the moment she joined her regiment. In ten years she's attended more funerals than most will ever do in a lifetime.

She joined her regiment for the most basic reason possible: 'I was born in Northern Ireland and as far as I'm concerned it's my country and I'll fight for it.' She, too, has a military background – 'I can trace back both my mother's and father's families and they've always been Army people who served in the wars' – but her own chance came in 1974. 'Things weren't getting any better,' she remembers. 'I had worked all my life until after I was married and my son was born. But I can't sit at home at all, so I was looking for a job. I saw the advert in the paper and I spoke to my husband about it and I thought, well, at least it will be doing something worth while for my country.'

At the time the notion – without parallel in the rest of the British Army – of women soldiers serving alongside the men did not go down

well in the regiment. 'At the start the men thought we were more of a
hindrance than a help but after a wee while they got used to us.
Initially, we trained as radio operators and female searchers and that
was our main role for a time, but we also went out at night with the
men on the ground. The first time I went out on patrol obviously I
was nervous but the more you got to know the men the more you
grew in confidence, knowing that they are there to back you up if you
get into trouble just as you are there to back them up.'

The Private began her soldiering as a part-timer and right from the
outset found that sex was no impediment so far as the terrorists were
concerned:

> I don't think I'd even had my training done when the first woman
> soldier was killed in Northern Ireland. They fired mortars at our
> base and she was dashing to safety and got hit. It was traumatic. I
> had just been sworn in and I suddenly realised that that could
> happen to anybody and it could happen anywhere, anytime. She
> was the first servicewoman to be killed but I had actually never met
> her. My first low moment was when an old friend and comrade was
> shot dead down the road a bit from here. He had been like a father
> to me. I done guard of honour at his funeral and I was hardly able
> to stand I was that upset.

Many other deaths have followed in the regiment, which have
served only to draw its members closer together. 'Speaking for
myself personally now,' says the Private, 'I will not be browbeaten by
anybody, I don't care who they are. As long as I can keep doing this
job I will do it.' She and her comrades are now locked into a special
kind of courage: 'Over here we call it crack and it's that crack that
keeps you going when things get rough. It's like a little flame that's
handed over to you when you join and it's that flame or spirit that
keeps you there, made up of loyalty between soldiers and officers,
between one soldier and another.' Her talk is punctuated by the
clatter of helicopters taking off and landing outside the window. A
couple of days later some home-made mortar bombs are lobbed into
the base from the back of a lorry, causing minor damage but no
casualties. The incident passes unreported by most mainland papers.

Private and General; Colonel, WO2 and CSM. Combined with the
voices of other servicemen and servicewomen their stories represent
the experiences of the British soldier through the last four and a half
decades since the end of the Second World War. The ending of the
war in Europe and the Far East is where that story begins.

Britain entered this post-war era desperately weakened by five
years of total war, with all the responsibilities of a major world power

but with a shattered economy and without the means to resume her pre-war role. Her combined military forces numbered almost five million men, the bulk of whom were conscripts enlisted 'for the duration' and whose days of military service were numbered. These were men trained to 'shoot and kill and defeat the enemy', hardened in conventional warfare in which uniformed soldier fought uniformed soldier. They expected to be swiftly demobilised and returned to civvy street. Instead, many found themselves taking on a new role as 'peace-keepers', either in clearing-up operations arising out of the immediate aftermath of the war in such places as French Indo-China or Dutch Batavia or, in the case of Palestine, returning to tackle an earlier problem that had been put on ice during the war years. Although not perceived as such at the time, both situations heralded the break-up of Europe's colonial empires.

'We were told for the first time in my memory of a thing called "Imperial Policing" or "Aid to the Civil Power",' explains Henry 'Todd' Sweeney, then a young officer who had taken part in the airborne landings at Pegasus Bridge on D-Day and the Rhine Crossings in March 1945. This 'Imperial Policing' was part and parcel of the British Empire whose legitimacy most soldiers simply took for granted. To all outward appearances British authority seemed as complete as it had been before the war, fully justifying the self-confidence of those who exercised it. 'We were still very much cock-a-hoop from the war years,' declares Todd Sweeney. 'As we sailed through the Mediterranean, everywhere we stopped you saw the Union Jack, because at that time the British controlled the Middle East and all the way down the Suez Canal. In fact, if you'd sailed on out to Malaya every port you'd have stopped at would have had a Union Jack.'

But this confidence was misplaced. Britain's days as a great imperial power were over and in every British colonial territory brave new ideas about nationhood, adult suffrage and liberation were finding popular support. British Palestine was no exception, as Todd Sweeney discovered when his regiment, the Oxfordshire and Buckinghamshire Light Infantry (known to themselves as the '43rd and 52nd', to others as the 'Ox and Bucks') landed at Haifa in the autumn of 1945 to join with the 6th Airborne Division in restoring British authority.

Although the Union Jack flew in Palestine it was not a British colony but a mandated territory, governed by Britain since 1923 under special mandate. The rights and wrongs of their being there meant very little to the troops on the ground. 'Most people were simply looking forward to the day when they would be demobilised,' admits Sweeney. 'You just wanted to get back to your wife and children and, quite frankly, I don't think we cared a hoot about the political situation. We couldn't see why the Jews and Arabs shouldn't be able to share this lovely country and live together.'

Here was a situation that had already revealed its ugly side in communal disturbances and riots both in India and in Palestine itself before the war and was to recur with dreadful familiarity in later years in other territories: that of two communities struggling for power over the same territory while governed by a third. In Palestine troops called in to aid the civil power were involved initially in containing civil disturbances between Jews and Arabs. To start with, their sympathies lay with the Jews but this changed as the Jews began to back up their demands for a separate Jewish state in Palestine with increasingly violent demonstrations directed against the British authorities. One of those whose views changed was John Stevenson, then Regimental Sergeant Major of the Ox and Bucks: 'We had to be fair and seen to be fair to both sides, to the Arab and to the Jew. I sometimes felt a bit sorry for the Arabs. It seemed not quite right that so many settlers should suddenly descend on top of the Arabs in Palestine, and talking to some of our young soldiers I gathered they were a little bit sympathetic towards the Arab, too, but they knew they could not express that openly, particularly not to a newspaper-man and, God knows, there were a few of those about.' The flow of Jewish refugees mainly from Europe into Palestine had to be stopped and illegal immigrants rounded up, which led to the troops being compared in local Jewish newspapers to the SS: 'What could you do about the propaganda, which was poured out in the newspapers in English and in Hebrew? You were accused of being murderers, you were accused of this, you were accused of that, and yet you were probably the very men that had released some of the Jews from their awful concentration camps in Germany.'

By the end of 1945 a pattern of behaviour had been established by Jewish extremists in Palestine that was to become a model for subsequent insurgencies in other colonial territories. This involved, in the first place, the banding together of a relatively small number of extremists prepared to use any means at their disposal to draw attention to their cause, to force waverers over to it and, ultimately, to secure their aims. In Palestine it found expression in the *Irgun Zvai Leumi* and the Stern Gang, strengthened by the much larger Jewish underground army known as the *Haganah*. All three organisations depended on the politicisation of sufficient numbers of their own community to provide them with shelter, funds and political support, achieved through political and armed propaganda. While the *Haganah* organised disturbances and acts of sabotage against strategic installations, the two hard-core terrorist groups concentrated on shootings and bombings.

British troops like the Ox and Bucks spent much of their time reacting to incidents of one sort or another. 'You'd get what they called a "flap" on,' remembers Todd Sweeney, 'when you'd be brought out at all hours of the night or day to go and get your rifle and ammunition, your small pack and weapon equipment. Then on to the trucks and, if the East Yorks got there first – because we used to work pretty well with them, like two battalions – they'd surround the place and we'd go in and search. We used to take it in turns.'

Such cordon-and-search operations were to become standard procedures in all counter-insurgency operations and almost inevitably they brought the Army into conflict with the local civil population, as Sweeney experienced on his first such operation:

> Some illegal immigrants had been landed and had been rather swiftly arrested, but some had got away and so we carried out a cordon-and-search of a village to see if there were some of the illegal immigrants there. We were faced by a horde of angry women who I remember took off their shoes, which had high heels, and began trying to beat the soldiers over the head. It didn't amount to very much but it was just enough to give us a foretaste of what internal security operations might be like.

Breaking up demonstrations and orchestrated riots soon became routine, with the troops following a riot drill developed in India that included verbal and written warnings being given before controlled shots were fired. 'I remember the banners,' states John Stevenson. 'Several of them were put up and the words written on them in Hebrew, English and Arabic were, "Disperse or we fire." But I certainly don't remember having to fire on anyone there.'

Increasingly, these disturbances were backed up by actions that the British security forces were unable to counter so easily. These took the form of deliberately lethal and often callous acts of violence directed against British targets. Such 'terrorism' had been employed before – notably by Bengali terrorists in India in the 1930s – but here in Palestine it was employed with greater sophistication and impact. Todd Sweeney remembers the bitterness among his men when two British sergeants were 'caught in a village and found hanged, not only hanged but their bodies were booby-trapped. This caused a revulsion of feeling against whoever had done it, whether it was the *Irgun* or the Stern Gang or the *Haganah*. And then the King David Hotel was blown up. The Officers' Club in the King David had a bar and I happened to be there on the Sunday, leaning up against the wall where the milk churns were later parked. If I'd been there on the Monday I'd have been blown up with the rest.' Ninety-one British servicemen died in the bombing.

Attempts to come to grips with the terrorist organisations were largely unsuccessful, due to the absence of an effective intelligence network – a situation that was also to repeat itself time and time again in other theatres. The one police undercover unit that did have some success fell foul of the authorities when it began to take the law into its own hands. Its leader was an 'irrepressible character' named Roy Farran, a major in the recently-disbanded Special Air Service Regiment, whose wartime successes behind enemy lines in France and Italy had led him to argue – unsuccessfully – that 'a unit of the SAS type trained to operate individually with the minimum support' should be a part of a peacetime British Army. Farran's attempt to operate a counter-terrorist undercover group in Palestine ended in disaster with his court-martial for 'what was then said to be the murder of a Jewish terrorist'. However, before his disgrace, Farran was obtaining excellent intelligence, as Todd Sweeney experienced when Farran came to him with information that Menachim Begin, the leader of the *Irgun Zvai Leumi* terrorist group, was hiding in a certain village: 'I had this Stand-by Company and he asked me if I would turn out my company and surround the village, while he would bring in Palestine policemen and search. So we went racing to the village and surrounded it and he brought in his special sniffer dogs and the police. They searched and they didn't find Menachim Begin, but afterwards he learned that Begin had, in fact, been hiding there all the time. So history might have been different if that afternoon they had managed to arrest the head of the *Irgun* – who later became the Prime Minister of Israel.'

Unable to penetrate the terrorist organisations or to cut them off from popular Jewish support and faced by ever-increasing demands from both Jewish and Arab political groups, Britain could only react by sending out more troops. However, it soon became obvious that the situation could not be contained by police and military action alone. By mid-1947 Jerusalem had become a beleaguered city, divided by barriers of barbed wire into zones. A degree of demoralisation had also set in, exemplified by one incident that Sweeney remembers from this period:

> One of the areas that was very difficult was the Meer Shareem
> Quarter. I had a company guarding that and in it what we called a
> Lightning Platoon. The idea was that when an incident occurred

this platoon went racing out in three vehicles, and cordoned the whole area off so that the police could then come along and investigate the incident and search the houses. So one night the alarm went off because a vehicle had been blown up somewhere nearby and the leading vehicle of our Lightning Platoon, a white armoured scout car with a sandbagged floor, went racing out of the gate. It got about three hundred yards down another road, so as to get round to the back of the incident, when it too was blown up. Then a police car coming down a third road towards our headquarters was also blown up, so clearly the terrorists had blocked every exit. The roofs of all the buildings were manned either by the Arab Legion or by paramilitary forces who were very trigger-happy and as a result of this banging one of them fired. Somebody on another roof immediately responded by firing back and so a gun battle then went on for about twenty minutes, entirely a gun battle between the security forces.

In September 1947 the British Government to all intents acknowledged defeat by announcing that it would be relinquishing the mandate and handing the Palestine problem over to the United Nations. In May 1948 the last British troops pulled out, many leaving with considerable regret. Some, like Todd Sweeney, were to look back on their Palestine years with a feeling that it was a job that had not been handled well: 'The United Nations came in and made the plan for the partition of Palestine and we left quite happily, feeling, "Well, that's settled the problem. They don't seem to get on so they've been separated. They've each got their territory, they'll now all live quite happily ever after." Partition is supposed to be the answer to all these problems. It's never worked – but at the time it's a let-out.'

Palestine provided an ominous example of how armed insurgents supported by a civil population could make a territory so ungovernable as to force an occupying power – whether legitimate or not – to withdraw. It showed that armed propaganda in the form of acts of terrorism paid off, however morally offensive it might appear to those on the receiving end. 'A terrorist', explains a British soldier who has twice been wounded by terrorist acts in two quite separate theatres of conflict, 'is the worst kind of animal that's ever presented itself to the modern world because he's indiscriminate. His bomb and his bullet take the innocent as well as the professional and in the name of terrorism kill innocence.'

But outrage is not enough. From Palestine onwards the British soldier had to accept that one of the chief roles of a peacetime army is dealing with local insurgency in the form of terrorism or armed propaganda; a thankless, bitter task in some instances, a rewarding experience in others but, in any event, an inescapable fact of modern soldiering. By trial and error combined with a great deal of hard graft and good soldiering the British Army learned how to come to terms with terrorism. But it took time.

Palestine was an early lesson – and a warning. So, too, were events in Indo-China and Batavia. Here the situation was very different from that in Palestine in that local nationalist forces had moved in to fill the vacuum created by the sudden surrender of the Japanese in August 1945. In the absence of Dutch and French troops, British and Indian Army forces were flown in to these two territories to help the French and Dutch to restore their colonial administrations.

Among those flown to French Indo-China were the British officers and Nepalese soldiers of the 1st Battalion of the 1st Regiment of the Gurkha Rifles (1st/1st Gurkhas), who were almost immediately involved in heavy fighting against 'a well-armed and very tough and ruthless enemy'. These were the Annamites, forerunners of the Vietminh and Vietcong, who soon made it clear to them that they were not welcome. John Cross, then a young subaltern, recalls a note being delivered to their camp near Saigon which began, 'To our friends the British, a warning. We are about to start an armed struggle against the French. We have no quarrel with the British', and which ended, 'Be prudent. Never ramble about with the French.' A brother-officer, Edward 'Fairy' Gopsill, also remembers the intense hatred of the local people for their old colonial masters: 'The Japanese had proven that they could chase us and the French out of places like Burma and Indo-China and I suppose the Vietnamese said, "Well, if that can be done why should we hand it back to the French?" – and I can quite understand their feelings.'

For those involved in the fighting in Indo-China there were valuable lessons to be learned, both about the nature of armed insurgency as a form of warfare and about the difficulties of waging a counter-insurgency campaign without the support of the local population.

From Indo-China the 1st/1st Gurkhas moved south in February 1946 to Mocassa in the Dutch East Indies: 'This again was a colonial situation. The Dutch had been there and the Indonesians didn't want them back after the war.' But resistance to the return of Dutch rule crumbled as British, Indian, Australian and, finally, Dutch troops were brought in. Almost the last foreign troops to leave were the 1st/1st Gurkhas, who arrived back in India in the summer of 1947 to find that country also in turmoil.

Here the situation was more or less out of British hands. Independence had been fought for as part of a political struggle in which non-violent civil disobedience had played a major part and violence only a minimal and counter-productive part. However, the real threat of impending violence had forced the Hindu political leaders to accept the partition of the country into the two separate states of India and Pakistan. Outbreaks of inter-communal violence in a number of cities between Hindus and Sikhs on the one hand and Muslims on the other had already stretched the security forces to the limit, forcing the Viceroy to speed up the time-table for Independence. In Ahmedabad, where the 2nd/7th Gurkhas were deployed, Captain Eric 'Birdie' Smith was commanding a company with his own section of the city to look after. 'As partition approached the tension got worse and worse,' he remembers. 'The two communities were beginning to go at each other's throats.' Much of his time was spent policing his district, trying to keep sectarian gangs from attacking isolated minority communities and, occasionally, using the well-tried Internal Security Drill to break up a riot:

> It entailed drawing a line across the street, and the magistrate warning the crowd that if anyone crossed that line they would be shot, and attention was drawn to all this by bugle blowing. It was all clear-cut and laid down. I duly put my company in position and drew the white line, the magistrate warned the crowd and everything seemed to be going according to the text book until one of the ring-leaders left the crowd, crossed the white line, shook his fist in my face and said, 'Go home, you filthy British!' I suppose theoretically I could have ordered someone to shoot him but the situation was saved by my company second-in-command, an old, experienced Gurkha officer, who grabbed hold of this chap, kicked him up the bottom and then chased him back. It not only got rid of the leader but because a lot of the crowd thought it funny the tension disappeared for a bit as well.

When Partition became a reality following Independence in August 1947 many hundreds of thousands – possibly a million or more – men, women and children caught on the wrong side of the new border became the victims of a double genocide as Sikhs and Hindus massacred Muslims and Muslims massacred Sikhs and Hindus. Too few in numbers to be effective, the security forces could do little to stem the violence. For the 1st/1st Gurkhas, moving down by train from Peshawar in Pakistan to Allahabad in India, there was a nightmare journey that 'Fairy' Gopsill remembers all too well:

Every hundred yards down the track of that railway journey of some hundreds of miles there were never less than two bodies in sight. We did pull into Amballa station and there I noticed a train standing in the siding full of dead people. Every one of them had been slaughtered. The Colonel ordered me with my company out on to the track where there were thousands of Sikhs, who had just perpetrated this carnage. So I told the Sikh leader – I said, 'You will clear this railway station.' And he told me in Urdu that I could go to hell. I thereupon lined my Gurkhas up, told them to fix swords – because in the Gurkha Rifles you talk about 'fixing swords' although it is actually the bayonet – and I then said, 'Unless you do clear the station I will clear you at the point of the bayonet.' They held their ground for a moment until I gave the order: 'Two paces interval advance.' Down came the bayonets into the on-guard position and the men started to move forward – and there is no doubt we'd have had to fight if they'd fought. However, they turned tail and left the station. We went down the train. The stench was appalling and there was nothing we could do at that stage with those people. One or two were alive but so terribly mutilated, with limbs hanging off, that we did in fact give them so much morphia we knew we killed them.

Partition also meant 'the end of that wonderful Indian Army, when regiments that had served us truly and well all those years were left behind to we knew not what'. As for the ten Gurkha regiments, it was decided that six should go to India and the remaining four transfer to the British Army. Once the decision had been taken regiments, officers and men were quickly divided. 'Those were terrible days,' declares Gopsill, whose regiment was one of those selected to remain in India:

> The saddest day of my life took place at this time when the men that I'd known and fought with were being kept behind in the Indian Army and we had our final farewell together. We had one dinner as officers and we had a *nautch* with the men, a Gurkha dance where the men dance for you. But at our dinner somebody drew the commanding officer's attention to all the Gurkha officers who were looking in at the window, and the Gurkha Major, Ram Sarun Pun, whom I would consider possibly the finest Gurkha I ever knew, said 'I just wanted to bring my Gurkha officers down to see you at your last dinner.' So they sat down with us and we drank and talked and we all got a little too drunk, and we parted the following day covered in garlands and tears on every side.

'Fairy' Gopsill and John Cross were among those who transferred to the 2nd/7th Gurkhas, which was reduced to a core of about fifty experienced soldiers. Then they, along with the 2nd, 6th and 10th Gurkha Rifles, left India for good to find a new home in the British Army. Malaya was chosen as their first destination, for no better reason than that it was the British territory closest to India.

The Gurkhas' departure from India did indeed mark the end of an era. A united India, like Palestine, had been a British creation and ultimately it was the British themselves who had allowed its bloody division in their rushed disposal of power. But all that was now over, as were the dark years of the war and its aftermath. The last British troops sailed from Karachi on 26 February 1948 and from Bombay on 28 February. Eleven weeks later, on 15 May, the last British troops to leave Palestine sailed from Haifa. In Germany, too, the British Army of the Rhine was in the process of being reduced from an army of occupation to a modest military presence of two divisions and two brigades. Demobilisation had at last become a reality.

In the four British Gurkha regiments a 'terrible backlash of resentment remained', but they could at least look forward to a more peaceful future as they settled down in Malaya to rebuild and to retrain. Or so they thought. 'We arrived in Malaya on 12 January,' recounts John Cross. 'We'd left tribal territory on the North-west Frontier in October 1947, we'd left Pakistan in November 1947, we'd left India in December 1947 and we'd left Burma in January 1948. Four months on the trot during which we'd seen nothing but our flag pulled down and being spat at etcetera, and it had all been very nasty. So we were delighted to get somewhere that was peaceful. Ha! Ha! Because in June 1948 the Emergency was declared!'

I. WAR IN THE JUNGLE

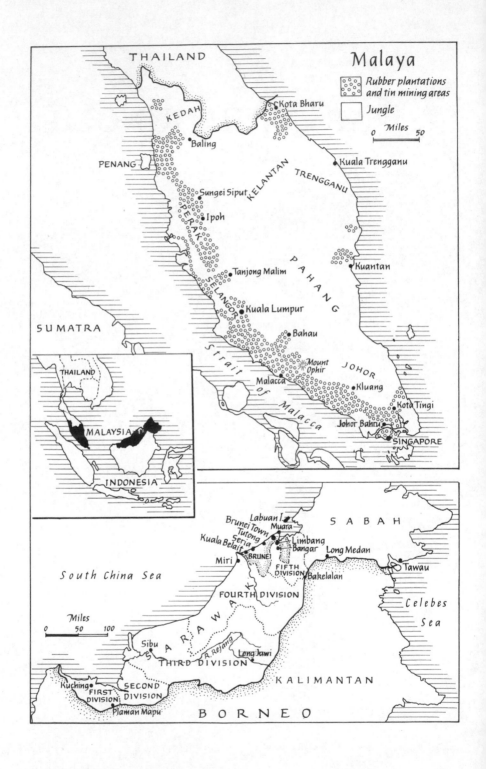

Malaya

Rubber plantations and tin mining areas

Jungle

0   Miles   50

THAILAND

KEDAH

Kota Bharu

Baling

PENANG

Kuala Trengganu

KELANTAN

TRENGGANU

Sungei Siput

Ipoh

PERAK

PAHANG

Kuantan

Tanjong Malim

SELANGOR

Kuala Lumpur

SUMATRA

Bahau

Strait

Mount Ophir

JOHOR

Malacca

Kluang

Kota Tingi

of

Johor Bahru

Malacca

SINGAPORE

THAILAND

MALAYSIA

INDONESIA

South China Sea

Labuan I.

Brunei Town

Muara

SABAH

Tutong

Seria

Limbang

Kuala Belait

Bangar

Long Medan

Miri

BRUNEI

Tawau

FIFTH DIVISION

Bakelalan

FOURTH DIVISION

Celebes Sea

Miles

0   50   100

SARAWAK

Sibu

R. Rejang

Long Jawi

THIRD DIVISION

KALIMANTAN

Kuching

SECOND DIVISION

FIRST DIVISION

Plaman Mapu

BORNEO

Chapter One

MALAYA:
The Gurkhas Bear the Brunt

I remember in Malaya when we walked out after one operation through the ruins of an abandoned village, abandoned because it was so far into the jungle that it was not possible to protect it from the terrorists and so the population had been resettled. And there were the ruined huts and the discarded implements gradually sinking down into the ground again – and I remember thinking as I walked through that village, I wonder what the Romans felt as they headed for Dubris in 410 and walked through the villages of Roman Britain. I wonder if they thought this is the end of the Empire.

When the first killings of planters and tin miners began in mid-June 1948 the British colonial government of Malaya was caught on the hop. Warnings that the Malayan Communist Party (MCP) was planning to seize power had been ignored. During the Japanese occupation of Malaya the MCP had formed a guerrilla army of resistance in the jungle, armed and supplied by the British. Military intelligence reports that it had reformed as the Malayan Races' Liberation Army (MRLA) with the aim of liberating Malaya from the colonial yoke and had organised itself into ten district regiments consisting of some five thousand armed men, supported by perhaps a quarter of a million local Chinese, had been ridiculed by the then British High Commissioner. The result was that, initially, the guerrillas outnumbered the local forces.

Six Gurkha battalions made up the core of Malaya's defence forces, each ridiculously under strength, so much so that odds were very much on the Communists: 'If the bandits at the beginning of the Emergency had known as much as they did at the end or if we had gone across later then Malaya would have been lost without a shadow of a doubt.' The 2nd/7th Gurkhas had arrived in Singapore about sixty strong: 'We moved to Kuala Lumpur next door to the 2nd/6th Gurkhas and between us I shouldn't think we could have raised a hundred and fifty men.' Each battalion grew as men re-

enlisted and as new recruits arrived, but in the meantime its officers
and men had to make do with what they had in taking on the major
defensive role in what was quickly declared to be a State of
Emergency. 'Many soldiers hadn't completed their recruits' training
but had to go into the jungle and take on active roles because there
was no one else to do it,' recalls 'Birdie' Smith. 'They were
inexperienced and untrained in jungle warfare and this was also true
of British units as well because, although these skills had been learnt
in Burma, most of these units had either been disbanded or gone,
and so really all the British Army in Malaya had to learn from scratch
and from bitter experience.'

To make matters worse there was a shortage of arms and
ammunition, so that to begin with the initiative lay firmly with the
Communist terrorists, who 'knew when and where to strike. The
Police Special Branch was tiny and there was no real Army
intelligence organisation either, with the result that we were reacting
to the Communists rather than taking the lead and going back at
them, and this continued for about two years. They would attack
rubber estates, attack managers' bungalows, attack railways, and
road ambushes were quite common during this period. We'd get
information that the Communists were mounting an ambush somewhere or likely to attack a rubber plantation. We would dash there and
sometimes it would be based on rumour and the effort would be
completely wasted.'

Smith's own introduction to the Emergency was pretty dramatic:
'Although I'd heard that things were going badly I learnt that lesson
very quickly on my first day. I was going back to rejoin the battalion
in a scout car and we went up the hill to Fraser's Hill Rest House. On
the way I heard over the scout car wireless that a convoy of three
vehicles consisting of Gurkha soldiers who were married and were
going on two weeks' leave with their families in Kuala Lumpur were
making their way towards me. At the Rest House I stopped and I
waited for this convoy. It didn't come, and I was beginning to get
worried when I heard a lot of firing.' As Smith and his driver set out
to investigate, a British civilian drove up at speed, ran past him into
the Rest House and telephoned Smith's commanding officer with
news that he had just driven through an ambush on the road with
three military vehicles under fire. To Smith's amazement the civilian
then rushed back to his car and drove away at breakneck speed to
Kuala Lumpur. He turned out to be a civilian judge who had decided
that fighting was the concern of the security forces and not his
business. Smith then got into the scout car and made his way
cautiously towards the sound of firing:

As I rounded a bend I saw a jeep which had come under heavy fire. The windscreen was smashed, there was a Gurkha driver slumped over the wheel, very dead, and there were two bodies in the back. I then moved further down in the scout car and went round another bend. Some fire was directed at the scout car which I returned and that was the end of the engagement. The two vehicles had around them quite a few bodies but they weren't all dead. From behind the last vehicle emerged two grinning but bedraggled young Gurkha soldiers and it was these two who had stopped the Chinese terrorists getting on the road and taking all the weapons from the dead and the wounded. I put them in for a decoration. I'm not being cynical but it is true that when the British Army has a reverse, gongs and decorations are not easily forthcoming. One got mentioned in dispatches, which to a Gurkha doesn't mean a lot.

The 2nd/7th Gurkhas had got off to a bad start in Malaya. 'Somebody had had the bright idea that one regiment of Gurkhas should become gunners, the 1st and 2nd/7th were selected and they had an influx of gunner officers. But gunner officers do not make good infantrymen and they do not know Gurkhas.' In 'Fairy' Gopsill's view at least one of these officers should never have been allowed into the jungle: 'I remember going on one operation with him when he turned around as we were going through an open area and said, "The buggers are following us, the buggers are following us." Then he turned around and said to this Gurkha Bren gunner, "Fire some bursts into that grass." So the Gurkha did as he was told, but there was nothing there. On the second operation that I went on with this man my best friend was killed.' This was one of the many occasions when the security forces were reacting to incidents, in this case the killing of six planters in the Sungei Siput area:

We had come into the hills from south of Sungei Siput to see if we could flush out the enemy. And as we were approaching through the jungle a number of shots rang out and Pickin was killed instantly. I followed up and we killed three there, and then we carried on into the hills, but were called off to start another operation. I felt that this was wrong, but of course these were early days. We hadn't got air supply, we had no tin rations. The rations on our backs were fresh ones stuffed into socks and we had to make fires in the jungle from old wood. We had no hexamine lighters or anything like that and there were no compo rations, so it was quite right that we should have come out after three or four days, because we couldn't support ourselves for more. These were the lessons that were learned very rapidly.

The isolated rubber planters and tin miners formed the terrorists' main targets, and they, too, had to learn a harsh lesson when it came to protecting their families and employees: 'They asked for small groups of Gurkhas to be put on their estates where they felt safe. Now, fortunately, the higher command would not agree to this and if we had we'd have become totally defensive. People like Colonel Walter Walker and the higher-ups in the Army at that time, Brigadier 'Bum' Skone, and people like Colonel Philip Townsend, these were men who had fought war and they knew all about it. They said, "No, there's no way that you're going to sit in defence. You get out and beat the enemy on the ground." And their tactics proved absolutely right in the end although the planting community couldn't see the effect of what we were doing.'

Sometimes it was possible to help the planters, although not always with quite the result that might have been expected, as Gopsill discovered when he went to the aid of an elderly planter named Geering: 'He'd been shot up quite a number of times and so one night I slipped out with four Gurkhas long after dark and I didn't even let him know that we were going. We lay up near his house and, of course, we heard the enemy coming, chatting away in Chinese. Then they opened up fire, and so while their firing was going on we crept closer to them and then in a mad rush we killed four of them. And when we took them up to Mr Geering's bungalow the following morning we found out two of them were his adopted Chinese sons.'

Despite the lack of support the planters proved to be staunch allies of the troops, who learned to appreciate their courage – and their eccentricities. One well-known character was Mr Puckeridge:

> I remember coming out of the jungle in almost the centre of Malaya near Jerantok to an estate that had no roads out. If you had to get out of that estate you had to go by train. In my filthy state I asked one of the Chinese labourers to take me to the bungalow where the *tuan* [master] lived, and I arrived to find a ceremony going on conducted by Puckeridge; the lowering of the flag. The Last Post was being played by Puckeridge on his trumpet and his Chinese labourers were lowering the flag as we would at sunset in the Army. He greeted me and said, 'You must come to dinner.' I replied, 'Well, I'm like this and I've got my Gurkhas just tucked up in the jungle.' He said, 'Bring them on to the estate, old boy,' so I sent a message back with my runner to come closer in and bivouac for the night near the bungalow. They dressed for dinner. He was there in a dinner jacket and Molly, his wife, was there in her evening dress and he said, 'One has to keep up standards, old boy.' Then after

dinner Molly played the piano and Puckeridge played the banjo and both sang wonderfully well, and they entertained me for a couple of hours. They lived in total isolation and when I asked him why he didn't move off the estate he said, 'Why should I?' Nothing was going to budge him.

It wasn't only the civil population that was taking casualties. In these early years of the Emergency when the Communist terrorists were operating from positions of strength they could – and did – mount their ambushes and raids with devastating effect. 'Fairy' Gopsill had transferred to the 1st/6th Gurkhas and was with his new company up near the Thailand border when news came in of a disastrous ambush on another Gurkha company: 'I had just come back from another patrol when Colonel Philip [Townsend] said to me, "You're ready to turn out, aren't you?" Now I had a system that when we came back from an operation, we sat down outside our barracks and we completely cleaned our weapons, we completely packed our packs, we completely did everything ready to go back on operations and then – and only then – would I allow the men to bath and hand their dirty clothes in for washing, so that we were ready to go out. He said, "Fairy, there is trouble." There had been the most stupendous ambush on 'A' Company. Tulprasad, a marvellous Gurkha officer, and Major Ronnie Barnes had been killed and so had many of the men.' Gopsill and his company hurried to the scene of the ambush:

> As we were going up we found another boy slightly wounded, not demoralised but very badly shaken, only a young soldier, and he said, 'I'll come back with you, Sahib,' and I said, 'You're a good man.' So off we went. This was very rough, hilly jungle and the going was very hard with full packs. However, we made good going and got there at about two o'clock in the afternoon. It was a scene of utter destruction. Ronnie Barnes's body was on the path and Tulprasad had got right up almost to the enemy but the enemy had dug in along a ridge and there was no way that any man going up that ridge would have lived and certainly there were many bodies there. We then started the awful task of carrying back the bodies with about ninety men. I know I was carrying two Bren guns and three packs so as to release two men. However, we got back at about eleven o'clock at night and we laid the bodies down and some British soldiers came up with transport to take the bodies back and one soldier refused to touch them. And I'm afraid that was the only time I struck a British soldier in real anger. I struck him and I told him, 'Pick him up! He was a good man.' I remember saying it and he looked at me in the dark and then he said, 'I suppose he was,

Sir,' and he picked him up. I don't know who that soldier was but I felt very sorry I had to do it. Then I said to the men, 'Eat.' And they said, 'Sahib, we'd just like a cup of tea.' So they took up their positions for all round defence and the following morning before first light we were on our way.

The men in Gopsill's company were in very low spirits, understandably so, since 'these were men from their own villages and they'd seen them shot to pieces'. However, their determination to exact revenge overcame their fears as they set out to pursue the enemy: 'All that day and the following day and the next we moved down the Badak River – which had been ambushed on both sides, there was no doubt about it.' Then they came to an area in the jungle that had been cleared by squatters:

> I said to Partap Singh, my marvellous Gurkha officer, 'We'll bivouac for the night, Partap,' and he said to me, 'Sahib, I think we'd better get up the slope a bit. We couldn't lift our heads here.' I said, 'Yes, Partap, of course we must.' I had been guilty of making the first mistake. I was tired and I just wanted to stop and rest. This wasn't just the physical tiredness, it was the mental tiredness coming through, and so we moved up the slope. Now we were living like animals, don't make any mistake about it. We could smell the enemy. We used our nostrils and our ears far more than we used our eyes. We could sense the presence of defecation, a scent, something different. The intonation of, say, a monkey in the jungle would give us a clue. You were alert all the time and if anybody ever says that people who've been in the jungle a long time can smell the enemy, they can, I assure you. I then said, 'Come along with me, Partap. We'll just go and look round the side of the river to see if we can see anything.' And I suppose we'd gone half a mile, just the two of us, when suddenly the stream went cloudy and these are things you notice instantly. It was only a small stream coming into the Badak River and, of course, we had to use sign language and I waggled my hand as much as to say 'What is it?' and he did a thumbs down which meant 'the enemy', and I waggled my hand again and looked as much as to say 'How do you know? Is it an animal?' and he shook his head and we withdrew. Then he said, 'Sahib, one animal would have gone across. That's been coming down for quite some time.' So we knew there were enemy there.

Gopsill then briefed his men on a plan to attack the enemy camp at first light the next morning. While most of the company moved in the dark to take up positions on high ground behind where they believed the camp to be, Gopsill took a small party of four men up the stream and then along a track that led them directly into camp:

> As we were going up, very cautiously, as you can imagine, the firing started at us and came zipping across over our heads. We couldn't see anything at that stage but we started to move forward, firing as we went. We came across this little sentry post, which by then had been abandoned, and then quite a broad track going up into a huge camp for about a hundred and fifty men. It actually had a basketball ground in it and this is where they'd made a base camp, way out of the area in which they'd done the ambush on 'A' Company. We only got eight out of them but at least we got Tulprasad's map case and Ronnie Barnes's shoulder tabs. And then we harried them for five or six weeks all along the border and I suppose we took a toll of very nearly thirty-five of them in little actions because they split up into smaller parties. On one of them I remember we were coming down off a spur and Partap was just behind me and suddenly he pointed – and there was a mark, wetness on this tree trunk. I said, 'Rain', but he pointed and there was the odd bubble on the ground. Somebody had peed there – and then up on the breeze came the distinctive smell of a Chinese cigarette, which is made from very dark, sweet-smelling tobacco. I had six men with me and we crawled down and there were four of them sitting round – and, of course, they were dispatched straight away.

Even in these early years the MRLA guerrillas – known to the Gurkha riflemen as *daku* or dacoits but referred to by most British troops either as 'bandits' or 'CTs' (Communist terrorists) – rarely operated in groups of more than thirty or forty. The MRLA's policy was to avoid pitched battles with the security forces in favour of hit and run raids. The only major MRLA force that 'Fairy' Gopsill ever encountered was one that had ambushed a large rice convoy on the Kuala Lumpur-Kuantan road and was in the process of retiring back into its headquarters deep in the jungle. He and a platoon of Riflemen had been sent out after it in hot pursuit:

> I asked the trackers how far we were behind them and they said about five hours. So I said, 'Run!' Now this is not the kind of thing you do in the jungle but the men, fully loaded with ammunition and rations, ran – and we ran until nightfall. Then I said, 'Right, tomorrow morning we'll have a cup of tea and we'll be on our way by four o'clock,' which was done. The men were as eager as I was because, after all the patrolling you do, when you hear that first shot the first thing that goes through your mind is, 'We've met

them, good!', because of the awful frustration of going on endless patrols and not meeting anything. Anyway, we went charging on through the jungle for about half an hour and then, naturally, caution took over because we knew we were getting close. However, at just about first light the first shots were fired at us by the sentry and we charged and killed the sentry and eight people in the first *basha* [rough thatch hut]. Then the fighting started and there were bugles blowing all over the place. Now this was an indication that there was a lot of people there because they were giving their instructions by bugle, so I kept on shouting, 'Charge for the bugle.' As we fought our way forward I kept shouting something like ' "A" Company go left, "B" Company go right', so that they had the impression they were being attacked by a large force.

In the rush we overwhelmed the first line of *bashas* but we could see hundreds of people flitting away. Their camp was alongside the river and a lot of bodies fell in the river and then we had to fight our way round the hillside. I had one or two marvellous sergeants and Gurkha officers there who were doing their stuff wonderfully well and we seemed to be no time at all in the fight and yet when I looked at my watch it was twelve o'clock and the enemy had gone. I think it was sixteen that we'd killed, but there were many more who had gone in the river. Our job was not to search for bodies, though; our job was to get on after them. But there were over four hundred packs there and the bugle and the weapons – and we'd got all the food that they'd stolen.

In accordance with classic Maoist revolutionary theory, the first aim of the MRLA was to force the Malayan authorities to abandon the countryside and withdraw into the towns. The security forces countered with a programme of intensive activity that combined swift responses to terrorist incidents with sweeps and patrols on the fringes of the deep jungle, often conducted on a random basis. In Pahang, where the 2nd/7th Gurkhas were initially based, the battalion area was subdivided into company areas many miles apart. However, operations were often conducted on a battalion or even a divisional level. 'A lot of the major operations were sweeps organised by headquarters above,' recalls 'Birdie' Smith. 'These were, in the main, a waste of time. Map squares were supposedly cleared and a pin would be put on the map in the operations room but, of course, what was really happening was that the men on the spot usually knew whether there had been any Communist terrorists in that area and after a bit, when they were told to move to another map square, it became a very frustrating business and morale went down.'

One of the battalions most seriously affected was the 1st/6th Gurkhas and to counter this its commanding officer was replaced. The man who took over was Colonel Walter Walker:

> On my way up to its base in Bahau I was told by the Divisional Commander, General Hedley, to call on him at Seremban where his headquarters were. And he said to me – and a lot of people won't like this – he said, 'You are going to take over one of the smartest battalions in the Gurkha brigade, but they can't kill Communist terrorists – and I don't know why. Their kill rate is very low, and yet their men are bloody good. You have got to find out the reason and you have got to make them as good in the jungle as they are smart in their appearance.' So I went out with each company in turn to see what was wrong and I found them too noisy. I found their tactics were shoddy and we missed a lot of Communist terrorists in the ambushes, which we had laid down as a result of good information.

Walker was no newcomer to jungle warfare. He came to 1/6GR with a reputation as a ruthless disciplinarian and as a man who got results. In Malaya he was to become the supreme exponent of the ambush, using skills that he had first acquired a decade earlier in Waziristan on India's North-west Frontier. 'I suppose I really learned the technique on the North-west Frontier,' he asserts. 'When we went out of our perimeter camp to ambush the tribesmen who were sniping at our camps at night, you had to be an absolute adept at concealing yourselves and making certain that if they entered your ambush they were killed.' These skills had been further refined in Burma:

> I tried them out in training to see why was it that the Japanese did not walk into this ambush? Why was it that when the Japanese did walk into this ambush they were not all killed? What were the mistakes? And I therefore laid down the technique of how an ambush should be laid, so that you didn't fire until the enemy had entered your ambush, that you had stops to get the people who might not have been immediately in the ambush, and stops to make certain that those who retreated from the ambush were also killed. And this technique, which I learned and taught in Burma, I carried forward to the Malayan Emergency.

On taking over command of his new battalion Walker set about retraining it to his requirements, which were set out in the form of a series of 'Golden Rules' that had to be learned and followed to the letter. After two months of so-called rest and retraining – 'mighty little rest and a helluva lot of retraining' – 1/6 GR went back into action. 'We were then sent down to Johor where we started to knock off Communist terrorists,' Walker recalls. 'I went out with my troops and I don't suppose the company commanders particularly liked me for being there but I was determined that my soldiers would be led in the way I wished them to be led. And I was determined that my company commanders would adopt the policy I had laid down.' Walker's methods worked and 'when we were eventually sent from Johor elsewhere the Brigade Commander, Brigadier Pugh, had me up and said, "You have killed more Communist terrorists in my brigade than any other battalion and I am very sorry to lose you." '

It had very quickly become obvious that the only way of stopping the MRLA was to destroy their bases, hidden deep in the Malayan jungle. A number of British civilians had worked alongside the CTs during the war years, many of them as members of Special Operations Executive or Force 136 who had parachuted into Malaya in the last stages of the Second World War. These civilians were brought in to act as leaders in a special unit known as Ferret Force: 'The idea was to attach some Gurkhas to them and use their expertise in the jungle to go and search out the camps that they had known.' Volunteers from other units besides the Gurkhas were also brought in, but Ferret Force enjoyed only limited success: 'It wasn't lack of endeavour. It was lack of time and, of course, the enemy was very, very wary.' In fact, the men of Ferret Force were outclassed by an enemy who had had years of experience in how to live and hide in jungle.

One happy outcome of the Ferret Force experiment was the setting up of a Jungle Warfare Training School with Walter Walker as its Commandant. 'General Ritchie came up from Singapore to see me give a demonstration to this Ferret Force,' recalls Walker. 'Most of them were extremely bolshie and did not want to be taught by a whippersnapper like me when they had been working behind the Japanese lines. But they were commanding my soldiers, my Gurkhas, not themselves, and I wasn't going to have them killed because of slipshod methods. General Ritchie saw me give this demonstration and the next thing I knew was to be told, "Report forthwith Singapore and you will raise the Jungle Warfare School." So I raised the Jungle Warfare School and there all the techniques that I had used when commanding my battalion in the jungle were put into operation.'

The priority at the Jungle Warfare Training School was to get soldiers used to what was still widely regarded as an alien and even hostile environment. In this respect the Gurkha Riflemen had a natural headstart. 'Every time a British officer walked with us in the jungle at night I saw they believed in the eye,' declares Purna Bahadur Gurung, who had followed his father's and uncles' footsteps in joining the 2nd/6th Gurkhas in the early 1950s. 'I believe in my feet and my hands, and I feel first, but they believe in their eyes so they just walk and fall down. Anyone who lives in an advanced country, who has a car, metalled roads, electric lights from the beginning, finds it very difficult in the jungle without washing, without shaving, without lights, without making noise. Living in a village in Nepal is like a jungle, so we have early practice in walking up and down in the jungle and living without lights or running water. In Malaya I enjoyed the jungle because it reminded me of home.'

British officers and soldiers lacked this natural affinity with the jungle which could, according to 'Fairy' Gopsill, 'have a very strange effect on some people. It is dark, it is damp, there's nothing there except wild animals and snakes of all kinds and it's an alien environment to most people. The jungle is oppressive if you let it be. This was particularly so with the British soldiers.' Even the bravest men could lose their nerve in the jungle: 'I know a regular officer who came to join the 1st/6th. I was on patrol when Colonel Townsend got on the [radio] set to me and said, "Move to such and such a river and pick up this officer. He can't take the jungle." And when I got to him the following day he was a gibbering idiot. He had been a brave soldier in the desert but the jungle had got to him.'

With his innate advantages the Gurkha who was trained in jungle warfare became the 'supreme fighting machine' that his officers believed him to be, always ready to take on what was required of him. 'Generally, there was no warning,' declares Purna Bahadur Gurung. 'We had our packs ready with four days' ration and kit. We had a mosquito net in the pack, so that when the duty officer came everyone got up ready to be taken somewhere.' On the patrol itself all orders were given with hand-signals: 'We had to be alert, listen to every noise. We were so unhappy if our own friends made a noise in the section. Someone would complain to the second in command that they did not want to take him out. Even in patrol base we had to be quiet, signalling or whispering – and it was very boring, very tiring, not knowing what was going to happen next.' Making camp in the jungle was also a very strictly controlled routine:

> We normally camp at three o'clock. First the operation commander sends a patrol round the camp to check nothing is around. Then he checks the ground and the trees. The ground could be muddy and if it rains it could be under water. Until the patrol comes in we make

no noise, everybody is sitting on their packs or on guard. Once the patrol reports the area is clear the commander or the second commander signals 'unpack'. No sound, just 'unpack'. The second commander will post out sentries in three different areas with their Bren guns aimed in three different directions, about four hundred metres from the camp. We have our tents, two men sleeping in one poncho, even the commander sleeping with one Rifleman. One carries the poncho and blanket, one carries ground-sheet and mosquito net, so they live together and cook together. One does the cooking and one is on duty, so we have to eat before dark. At night there is also a sentry in each section to man their own posts and before dark there is stand-to to make sure your position is safe in case of trouble. Before dawn it is done again for half an hour or until the commander thinks it is clear. Immediately after, he will again send out the patrol to check round the area.

From an officer's point of view the Gurkha Rifleman's effectiveness in the jungle was dependent on good training. 'You can't give a Gurkha too much training,' was 'Fairy' Gopsill's view:

I used to practise with my men almost to distraction the drills that we would take up once action was joined. I never said to the men, 'If we meet the enemy'. I always used the word, 'When we meet the enemy this will happen. So many shots will be fired, the leading group will do this, the centre group will do that, the rear group will do this.' And it all depended on where the high ground was. They knew if the high ground was on their right the centre group would go for the high ground and the left hand group would follow them round. It was a question of constantly training so that they knew exactly what they were doing without giving it too much thought.

Once the patrol had entered the jungle there had to be constant attention to detail:

When you're crossing a river you've got to have the men spaced out. You've got to make sure that if you're going along a track there are men above you on the high ground. You must get to the top of the hill before you can stop and have a smoke, and some of the hills are half a day long. You must have all round defence. Men must clean their weapons. This is second nature to a Gurkha but, even so, when Gurkhas get tired they can be just as fallible as anyone else. I had the reputation of being a hard man and the men used to call me *Korop*, which is 'hard', but I wouldn't let them get themselves into trouble. I used to say to them, 'You'll draw your pension if you're with me.'

Supporting the British officer in every Gurkha company or platoon was a Gurkha officer who had worked his way up through the ranks: 'There was no substitute for their length of service, their knowledge of terrain and their ability to seize a point quickly.' They were there to advise, often to guide the younger and usually less experienced British officer: 'It is too easy to allow slipshod methods to creep in, out of tiredness. At Baling some British soldiers went for a swim in a mining pool and twelve of them were killed. The enemy knew they went there regularly. It was doing something you do in England – but they didn't come out of the water.'

Since the four Gurkha regiments were to be on operational duties in Malaya virtually throughout the full twelve-year duration of the Emergency – unlike the British infantry battalions or the Royal Marine Commandos, who came out on two- or three-year tours of duty – they inevitably became masters of jungle warfare, operating against an enemy who was quite as tenacious and courageous as themselves. John Cross remembers one particular CT who 'had his guts shot away. We shot this man up and he ran about two hundred yards with his intestines held in his hand. And then, when he lay down to die, he hid himself and lay on his rifle so that it wouldn't be discovered. We only found him because his intestines started smelling next day.' Another wounded terrorist was also spotted in very similar circumstances:

> The only reason we found him was that the Gurkha in front of me
> bent to feel some ashes and realised that the fire was still warm.
> Suddenly, he saw out of the corner of his eye this man in the
> undergrowth. When we pulled him out the maggots were actually
> eating him and he was in a bad state. We gave him a tot of rum and
> I said in Chinese, 'Have a tot of rum because it'll do you good.'
> And he turned round and said in immaculate English, 'I say, have
> you no whisky,' which rather knocked me off my perch. By and
> large, our soldiers didn't think of any bandit as an individual. He
> was just a man who had to be eliminated, but there the Gurkhas
> realised that man was an adversary who had failed in his task
> because they were better than he and they treated him
> extraordinarily well.

What was less easy to accept was the ruthlessness and the cruelty shown by the CTs, sometimes towards their own people. 'Fairy' Gopsill recalls capturing a woman member of a terrorist group – 'she

had been firing a Bren gun at me' – who turned out to have a baby
with her:

> She was a toughie. She refused to feed the baby and it sat in my
> pack for about five days until we could get a helicopter to pick them
> both up. We had to get an Auster to come over and drop Glaxo, I
> think it was. My orderly made a teat from an old oil bottle, which
> we used to keep our *ghee* [clarified butter] in, with a bit of plaster
> over it and the baby fed from that. I think my orderly actually gave
> the baby a little tot of rum to put it to sleep at night. The mother
> was tied to me at night, one arm tied around a tree and the other
> arm to me and when she went to the lavatory two men held a long
> rope and she went behind a bush.

As the battalions gained experience, more initiative was given to
individual company and platoon commanders, so that officers of the
calibre of John Cross and 'Fairy' Gopsill became extremely adept at
playing and beating the CTs at their own game. 'If you were going to
smoke, then the answer was to smoke something that the bandits
smoked,' explains Cross. 'And their answer was to smoke something
that we smoked. Some of our superb operators would brush out their
tracks with leaves or branches, but there were cases where the
bandits would use our jungle boots so that we would think that what
we saw were the footprints of our own troops who had strayed from
another area. I even remember one case where the bandits walked
over half a mile while the end man formed exact replicas of tiger pug
marks with his fingers in the mud, because there happened to be tiger
in the area.' Sometimes, however, even the good operators could be
too clever. John Cross once heard some bandits talking to each other
using bird calls: 'I had laid down with my people that if they heard a
cuckoo call – I can make a cuckoo noise pretty realistically through
my hands – they were to close in on me. Well, I did make a cuckoo
noise and we never got the bandits because the bandits knew there
were no cuckoos in Malaya. But that was during phase one in
Malaya, the learning phase.'

In learning to 'outbandit the bandits' with skills of their own, the
Gurkhas became master-craftsmen in such matters as laying ambushes and fire discipline. John Cross remembers an instance when
he and his men laid an ambush in a rubber estate where 'we only had
about six inches of cover crop – the low foliage that the rubber estate
would have to stop weeds growing up. The soldier who was three
from my left was lying in ambush and a woman rubber-tapper came
along and squatted down, took down her knickers and piddled, and if

the man hadn't turned his face away she'd have piddled on him. She never knew she was in the middle of an ambush.'

Cross also recalls a particularly nerve-wracking encounter that took place just a few days after two patrols of the Queen's Regiment had run into each other in the jungle, killing several of their own men:

> I was with four or five men near a swamp and so we crossed this swamp which was full of very tall, thick, prickly, noisy leaves. We got halfway, moving terribly slowly and quietly, and suddenly we heard what the Gurkhas thought were Chinese voices and we froze. We came into the standing aim position and five men walked in front of us. They didn't see us and I was in a terrible quandary because their uniform was almost issue but the insignia on their hats was a star, a red star, and that was unknown to me except in a context of the bandits. And I whispered, 'Wait till I say fire,' and the man on the left of me whispered, 'Don't fire.' And as he said that these men turned around almost in unison and saw five men aiming at them and their immediate reaction was to aim at us and there we were – tense. I had to make a lightning decision – whether they were Gurkhas dressed as Chinese or Chinese dressed as Gurkhas – and my immediate decision was to take my hat off, put my rifle down, walk up to them and say, 'For goodness sake, don't shoot,' in Gurkhali. And they happened to be Gurkhas from a neighbouring battalion who had come by mistake over the boundary that they had been given. I learned later that the insignia they were wearing was not what they wore in the lines, but had been worn to baffle the bandits. But the relief was something indescribable and I turned to the man who had been on my left and said, 'Why did you say don't fire?' He said, 'I recognised my brother.' And the lesson comes out loud and clear that fire control and rock-firm discipline is what is wanted to overcome one's immediate instincts.

The improvement in jungle skills was being matched by other advances that were effectively robbing the Communists of the initiative. 'I went away on leave and, by the time I came back in 1951, we had definitely left what you might call the first phase,' recalls John Cross. 'We were entering the second phase when we were much more aggressive in the jungle itself, learning how to live and fight and move through the jungle. And that coincided with the Communist terrorists themselves not being so beastly to the public as they had been hitherto and going further back into the jungle to fix up bases and gardens or jungle cultivation. This next phase, from 1951 virtually through to 1956, was a time when I was a company commander, when we went deeper and deeper into the jungle. We went in at the start for three days and three nights thinking ourselves heroes, and at the end, two or three weeks was no trouble.'

Chapter Two

MALAYA:
The Poxy Green Hell

A poxy green hell, that's what the jungle is, there's no doubt about that. All right for Sakais and Ibans, I suppose, and all right for Europeans as a novelty for about a month, but that's about the limit of the jungle, about a month. You come out of that jungle with so much relief. You'd sort of say, 'Please don't let me go back in there for a little while' – and we'd be back in the following day.

Over the twelve years of the Emergency more than thirty British infantry battalions as well as Royal Marine Commandos, artillery, armoured and engineer regiments, signals squadrons and other specialist units such as the Special Air Service went out to do their tours in Malaya. At the start only three of the eleven understrength battalions in the peninsula were non-Gurkha British infantry but within three years their numbers had risen to ten, whose ranks were very largely filled by National Service conscripts, mostly teenagers aged eighteen and nineteen.

The Devonshire Regiment had enjoyed a fairly uneventful beginning of its tour as part of the Singapore Garrison before the violence began. It was then very quickly despatched by companies to various locations up-country. Initially, eighteen-year-old Philip Longbon found himself guarding rubber plantations near Klang, where he very soon came face to face with the CTs. 'People don't seem to know that in the first six months of the Malayan campaign it wasn't a question of us going out and hunting the Communists,' he declares. 'It was a question of defending yourself against them.' His first action came when a large group of bandits attacked the rubber plantation that he and four other Devons were guarding together with a fifteen-strong detachment of Malayan police: 'To be quite honest about it, the first thing the Malayan police done, they all slung their rifles down on the floor and run down the road, which left just myself, a cook, the corporal guard commander and one of the chaps, who sort of threw a fit – and we had to tap him on the head with a Sten gun magazine.' There then followed a fierce firefight – 'you're talking about a shoot-out at the OK Corral, that's exactly what it was like' – before the enemy pulled back.

Other incidents followed as the Devons were switched from one crisis point to another. The strains soon began to take their toll:

> The thing that shook me so much was the lack of reinforcements. We was going out as platoons on our first patrols, say thirty strong. After about two months we would be round about twenty strong and eventually we was going out – a platoon, mind you – a dozen people. We was simply getting no replacements. And then, lo and behold, we got another regiment come out there. What were they? The 8th Hussars, who rode up and down the road on armoured cars, you know. So nobody give us a hand. Then the Grenadier Guards come out. They was only out there for about six months – and my mob was still left out there. People said, 'There's no way we're going to get home. So-and-so's gone. He had malaria, lucky so-and-so.' It didn't kill him but he went. One of my own friends, Ben, got shot off the road. The driver in his vehicle – his head got cut off. I was a pall-bearer. I carried Ben on my shoulders when we buried him and I remember the flies round his coffin, the flies trying to get at Ben inside. We planted him at eight o'clock in the evening and they put us in shorts and white gaiters so we got eaten alive by mosquitoes. We was sick to death. We was gutted!

There was also tragedy of a different kind when Longbon's patrol in hot pursuit of three CTs chased their quarry into a hut in which a family of Chinese squatters had also taken refuge: 'It's a terrible story to tell because we assaulted the *basha* with grenades. Two young kids ran out flaming. Terrible. We hadn't known they were there. I mean, they talk about My Lai, but there's been My Lai gone on for ever. There always will be.'

Increasingly, the Devons found themselves operating in what to Philip Longbon, at least – 'born in Bermondsey, an out and out Cockney' – regarded as an utterly alien environment:

> If I was to say that the jungle seemed to sort of open its arms to greet you it wouldn't be an exaggeration. You could imagine all the creepy-crawlies saying, 'Look, here's a lovely tender little European. Let's eat him!' So many insects out there liked the human body. The leech was the worst. People can't reckon that a leech can get through the eyeholes of a boot and then go in through the tongue and then through your sock and your undersock and then get through your trousers that you've got rolled in under your socks and then get to your skin. But they do it.

On average, you'd have thirty leeches on you and it was very rare for a leech to drop off sated. A leech would find your blood so easy to take that he would burst himself and then you would have a dried leech with his head stuck in your skin and all the blood that he'd taken out flowing down your body. If you stood up after a patrol and worked your feet inside your jungle boots you could pump the blood out of the eyeholes of your boots. That sounds incredible but it's true.

The troops were also fearful of other perils, because the Communist terrorist was a 'wonderful booby-trap merchant. He used what we called a *chola* branch, which was a water vine with spikes, and bamboo stakes in the ground with razor-sharp edges that would give you a terrible wound.' However, it was the stress of being in the jungle itself and of not knowing what might happen that the men found hardest to bear. One of their biggest complaints was that they were never told anything. 'We could have been three minutes away from a big bandit camp but the officer would tell us nothing,' Longbon declares. 'We'd be climbing all over the place and never knew what we was doing or why we was doing it. And we used to say to ourselves many, many times, everybody, you know, "What the bloody hell are we doing here? How can anybody want to live here?"' Yet, quite remarkably, Longbon and his fellow Devonshires learned by hard and often bitter experience to come to terms both with the jungle and its inhabitants: 'We never really knew what to do, but for sure we cured that by the end of our time, 1949–50. We done a bloody good job – and nobody ever gave us credit for it.' One of the last operations that Longbon was involved in was a night ambush on a bridge: 'We took two slats out of the bridge. The first bandit fell down the slats as we knew he would in the dark because he didn't know they was missing, and as they bunched up, we let them have it with a Bren gun on a fixed line. I mean, there we had seven kills in one night.'

Other infantry regiments followed the Devonshires. While there was the view that, 'by and large, the British troops in Malaya hadn't got the patience to mould into the background and to have standards of personal survival that were of a harsher, stricter nature than those of the bandits', many of these British regiments did extraordinarily well. 'The Suffolks got a tremendously good name for themselves,' remembers one Gurkha officer. 'Another battalion that I can think of didn't. The aboriginal home guard had a higher figure of kills and captures than they did after a whole tour.'

Statistics based on kills were very misleading but running totals were published and became a source of competition between units. 'It was used as an incentive but it was unfair', observes one officer, 'because it really depended on which area you were operating in. In some areas there were many more Communist terrorists, the intelligence organisation was probably good and it was possible to achieve a lot of successes. In other areas where there were few bandits around, it meant hours of searching and very little success and after a while the morale of those battalions who were in those sorts of areas inevitably dropped.'

Whether or not it was an accurate yardstick, the Suffolks undoubtedly produced an impressive tally of kills. 'I'm not sure of the exact number, but I think we lost twelve blokes and fifteen wounded in three and a half years,' avers John Frawley, who joined the Suffolk Regiment in Malaya towards the end of its tour. 'But to come out with the highest number of kills of any British battalion – I think it was virtually on two hundred – that is good. And the climax to it all was that after chasing this Lu Kong Kim for three and a half years, Second-Lieutenant Hands of 5 Platoon "B" Company, he chased him through the southern swamp and shot and killed him.'

Even in a battalion like the Suffolks, which was largely made up of conscript soldiers, comradeship was a vital unifying force. It inevitably brought distress and shock when friends were wounded or killed, but it played a major role in holding the group together in moments of stress, as John Frawley experienced when taking part in a sweep through secondary jungle where three terrorists were believed to be hiding out:

> I was Number Two to this chap Humphrey on the Bren, which meant that I carried a certain amount of magazines for the Bren gun and he carried the Bren. We were doing the sweep through and this guerrilla had got himself down into the scrub facing us with a sawn-off shotgun, as we found out afterwards. He fired and the next thing was my Number One had gone back. He shouted, 'Oh, I've been shot in the back', and with that down he went. In fact, he had got shot in the front and it had come right through and killed him. Then everyone just opened up on this particular area where this guerrilla was lying. Humphrey would have walked on top of him actually. I mean, it was only a matter of less than two yards from me. Well, we had to take Humphrey back up on to the road and put him up on to the jeep ambulance, which was always there just in case anyone got wounded. Everyone was upset about it. I mean, to see someone like that, one of your mates. He'd joined the

Army with us, you see, done all his basic training and everything else with us and he'd finished up lying dead.

So, of course, the company commander, Major Martin, he sort of rallied us around and back we went in again to flush the others out. I mean, with the Suffolks they always said they were like a family regiment, as you might call it, and that went right the way through the whole battalion when somebody got killed. So there was no way you could turn round and say, 'Well, I don't want to go back in there. There's still three or four [CTs] sitting in there somewhere and we've just lost one of our chaps.' No, you've got to go in. I mean, we were there to do a job and although we were only National Servicemen – well, I say *only* National Servicemen but I think it speaks for itself, what a good job the National Servicemen done, especially the Suffolks, anyway. I mean, you were there and you were serving King and Country and it was your job. It's only afterwards that you think, Oh dear, oh dear, poor old Humphrey is not going to come home with us.

It was very important for the troops to be able to relax away from the stresses of the jungle in the bright lights of Singapore or Kuala Lumpur, but for operational reasons this wasn't always possible. 'If you were lucky you'd have what was called a recreation period every month,' remembers John Frawley. 'We'd go down to Wardiburn, which was battalion headquarters, arriving there perhaps at midday and then you'd have the evening to go down into Kuala Lumpur and the NAAFI club and have a few beers. The first place everyone used to head for was Nanto's bar for steak and chips, having had compo rations for six weeks or what we used to call jungle stew, which was all the compo rations that each member of the section was carrying put in the brew together. So we'd have a nice steak and chips and a few Tiger beers. Then we'd come back and spend the night at Wardiburn and rejoin our company the next day.'

Only very rarely could the men escape the 'absolutely unbeliev-able' humidity and heat: 'I mean, there were people going down with heat exhaustion and tinea and prickly heat. To save you dehydrating they gave you salt tablets. Tinea you just couldn't get rid of, so they used to send you up to the Cameron Highlands where it was a lot cooler. Once you got up there they'd carry on with the treatment, then you'd probably come back cured and after a while back it would come again, you know.'

In John Frawley's eyes, the key to the Suffolks' success could be put down to 'magnificent leadership' from officers whom young National Servicemen like himself – 'about seventy per cent of us were eighteen-year-olds' – looked up to: 'You knew you was with the officers and you felt quite confident being with them. You looked to them and there never was any fear that you might get lost or that something could go wrong.' And for their part the officers were 'sort of amazed how eighteen-year-olds from the Home Counties, you know, Suffolk, Hertfordshire, Essex, could go out there and adapt to that type of warfare in a matter of weeks really, having done their ten weeks' training at Friday Woods in Colchester and then three weeks' jungle training.'

The Suffolks were perhaps fortunate in that their tour in Malaya lasted rather longer than most, since there was always a marked improvement in standards as a tour progressed. 'Normally, in their first year a new British battalion was clueless,' declares one officer who did two tours in Malaya:

> During that year they'd make all sorts of mistakes and shoot each
> other or somebody else and all kinds of things would go wrong. But
> also during that year they'd weed out some of the bad operators.
> Fat company commanders who weren't up to it would be removed
> and other guys put in who were. And then in the second year with
> the weaker brethren sent home the battalion would be learning,
> learning, learning. They'd get more contacts and more success and
> then in the third year many of them were very good and worth
> operating alongside, you know, because you had some confidence
> in them. I remember some battalion that had sacked all three of its
> rifle company commanders in its first year and when the battalion
> returned from Malaya in its troop-ship back to Southampton there
> were all these guys on the dockside waiting to rejoin the battalion.

Not all regiments were blessed with high calibre leadership. One that 'didn't have all the successes that some of the regiments had' and which 'took rather a long time to get its act together' was the East Yorkshire Regiment. Mike Gray, then a young lieutenant, puts this down in part to a lack of guidance from above, finding a 'gulf between the older members of the regiment, who seemed very unsure, and the young firebrands, some of whom had served in Korea and were exceptionally good soldiers'. As a platoon commander in what was widely regarded as a 'platoon commander's war', he enjoyed his independence – but not the absence of control from above that went with it:

> You are on your own as a platoon commander or as a sergeant.
> There is nobody following you, all you are doing is reporting back
> once every night. There was no company commander breathing

down your neck – and that was what I missed. What we wanted wasn't guidance in loyalty or in the niceties of regimental soldiering. What we wanted was guidance in the field. I only once went out with my company commander on any operation in eighteen months. I can remember seeing my commanding officer twice or three times but never in the jungle. When you weren't achieving anything, when you went out month after month after month and there weren't the signs of terrorists which you had been told were there, and when you weren't actually getting results, you began to wonder whether it was you or the war or what. That was one of the problems, I think, in the county regiment.

Peter Field, who spent a year in Malaya as a subaltern in the Queen's Royal Regiment, found himself in much the same position. Malaya was 'a platoon commander's paradise' yet he felt frustrated by the 'steady life within a good regiment like the Queen's, a good regiment but, in terms of military operations, with limited capabilities. We did simple things and we did them well but, to be fair, the majority of the Queen's officers and senior NCOs were Second World War veterans and zest and enthusiasm weren't particularly noticeable among them and certainly it wasn't a very popular thing to do for anyone to show particular keenness.'

Both Lieutenants Field and Gray had begun their tours in Malaya by attending the by now well-established Jungle Warfare Training School at Kota Tingi. Peter Field had gone as one of a sixty-strong advance party from the Queen's whose job it was to 'learn how to live and how to operate in the jungle' from the experts and then to pass it on as best they could to the rest of the battalion. Their instructors at Kota Tingi included 'hoary old warriors from the Australian Army who had fought in the Second World War in the jungle and had been very successful in countering the Japanese in New Guinea. You learned from them not just how to survive, but they then developed it into the tactical skills of ambush, patrolling, attacking and so forth and you went through this meticulously.' Above all, 'myths were destroyed', including the notion that 'you can't move at night in the jungle. Kota Tingi explored the possibility and taught you a lot about how you do it, because you did have to move at night to surround an enemy encampment.'

Once the jungle training was over the battalion moved directly on to active operations. 'We went out and based ourselves on the jungle fringes in small camps,' Field explains, 'sometimes a company strong, sometimes just in platoon strength, and from there we operated into the jungle. The normal duration of the patrol would be about three or four days unless something happened – if we discovered something or got a message on the radio that something had happened elsewhere.' In his platoon the sergeant was the only regular soldier besides himself: 'Everyone else involved – corporals, lance-corporals and private soldiers – were National Servicemen.' Nevertheless, there developed a 'wonderful team spirit' within the platoon as its individual members learned to work together. 'Your affection grew for the men you were privileged to command,' Field explains. 'One didn't have to pretend that one liked them, one felt it in one's heart. It was a very natural thing to evolve, the little show that you ran totally on your own.'

However, not every National Serviceman in the Queen's Royal Regiment felt the same way about team spirit. William Hewlett was one conscript who developed a rather jaundiced view of officers taking their duties too seriously. 'The thing that got you down were the officers,' he declares. Both he and his fellow conscripts did their best to avoid them:

> When we had an officer who did come out with us on patrol I realised that he was only interested in one thing: killing as many people as possible, that means bandits, and getting himself a name. So you learned to wear a new officer down. When you went out on patrol you'd lift roots and, when he got used to falling over half-a-dozen times, then you'd bring back those attap-type palms that had great spurs on the end, hooks. You'd catch one with your rifle and you'd bring it all the way back and then you'd let it whip back in his face. If you did this for one or two patrols eventually you'd wear him down to the state you were in.

Hewlett believes that 'the men were pushed too far and too hard. You were never in a fit condition to fight and there were times when men did not carry out orders en masse.' If an opportunity came to duck a particularly onerous task it was often taken:

> They'd send you out on five-finger patrols from your main camp in the jungle. This was as if you laid your hand down with the fingers pointing to different points of the compass. You'd take two or three men and off you'd go. Now the idea was that you'd go out for half a day and if you saw anything you would come back and report it. Now, in the end, we tacked on to the idea that this was rest for the officers and damn hard work for us, so we got to the point where the regulars and everybody would go about fifty yards out, sit down and have a smoke for about four or five hours, get a water bottle out, splash it all over your arms and face, and then, after studying the map, come plonking back in and give your report.

For all the training, it was asking a lot of a peacetime conscript to expect him to operate in a tropical jungle full of unknown dangers – 'scorpions the size of lobsters' – against a hidden enemy:

> There was no training you could have that could set you up for what you were going to be faced with. You had to learn as you went along – and a good man learnt quickly. You see, you'd have to go through swamps. You'd come out of the swamp and the sun would dry you in a couple of seconds, then down comes the rain. You'd come through the downpour, you begin to dry off again, then you're sweating through the sun, so once again you're soaking wet. Then you find that the easiest way through the jungle is along a river, so once again you're up to God knows what height of water. And the thing was, the whole effect was on your feet, because your feet were lacerated, absolutely terrible. Everyone had foot-rot, everyone had *tinea pedis*, and you were wet literally all the time, one way or another.

For Hewlett, the Malayan jungle exercised a strong hold on his imagination:

> It was terribly dark, almost lifelike. You had these tall trees going up hundreds of feet into the air and with every tree was a vine, as thick as your arm. And for every little tree that you saw starting to grow, there was the little vine that would choke it to death. You saw the old trees that had tumbled, the trees that had been struck by lightning and other trees that had come down and I'd think to myself, this is almost like a pattern of life. Disease sets in and the minute you're born you're being killed, gradually being choked, and everybody's fighting for the light.

Philip Longbon, too, remembers the jungle as a very special place, 'like a tropical St Paul's Cathedral, completely quiet during the day like a cathedral. You maybe hear once or twice a hornbill but other than that you never heard anything at all.' Then as the afternoon turned to dusk the 'jungle orchestra' would start to tune up:

> You'd get, first of all, the little crickets and the little frogs and the cicadas – and what we used to call the wood-cutter beetle because it was just like a plank of wood going through a saw-mill. You'd get all these insects that we couldn't name – at least, we assumed they were insects. But there were other animals like the bullfrog, big bullfrogs and little bullfrogs. I always imagined them sat in circles in the swamps. They all had their different tones. And then you got some of the major participants in the orchestra. One of them, we

was told, was crocodiles, but we just didn't know what was making
the noise, including a bird or an animal that used to turn your
blood cold.

Night in the jungle was always pitch-dark but Longbon remembers
how once when he was 'under the Bren waiting to get relieved', when
the night started to light up:

> It was unheard of. Nobody ever carried a light. But I see a light and
> I was terrified because there was something strange about the light.
> I'm talking about haunting now, because you've been in this
> element so long you're beginning to think native. I mean, you can't
> remember Savernake Park Road and the fish and chip shop. That's
> the other side of the globe. That's a different life entirely. You've
> become jungle-happy now. But what it actually was, it was about
> ten million, trillion fireflies. I don't know whether it was the
> breeding cycle or whatever but they had all gathered together and
> formed this massive ball in the trees. And as they was going
> through the upper strata of the jungle they was lighting it up, like
> an ethereal light, and I tell you honestly, it turned my stomach over
> because it was the most ghostly sight I ever saw.

Equally unnerving to the men were the snakes – 'as God's my
judge, it was the longest snake in the world' – and creepy-crawlies of
every shape and size – 'because everything was larger than life' – that
sometimes delighted and sometimes terrified. Peter Field has vivid
memories of the first time he experienced 'total fear' when out one
afternoon in the jungle scouting for a river:

> I thought I'd look for a suitable place for the company to 'basha
> up', that's to say, put up *bashas* [thatch shelters] and camp for the
> night. Along the water's edge the undergrowth is very much thicker
> and when I parted it there, within six feet of me, moving from right
> to left was this huge snake, a python about the thickness of a
> telegraph pole. Well, I absolutely froze with fear. I experienced on
> the back of my neck the hair standing up and I was terrified. Then I
> saw it was a trick of the light. In fact, it was a very tall, straight tree
> that had fallen and was covered with a million soldier ants all on
> the march, and in the gloom it was as if it was a giant snake.

Hewlett, too, had an encounter with a 'snake' that gave him some
bad moments. He was walking through the jungle when something
hit him hard on the shoulder 'like someone throwing a stone at you'.
Pulling off his pack he looked at his shoulder 'and there, sure
enough, is two marks'. He had just attended a lecture on snake bites

and knew the drill: 'So I said, "Medic! Medic!" and down came the medic pack and they brought out a rusty razor blade. I said, "Right, sharpen up the knife. Slash me!" Then down came the Iban tracker who was with us. He looked at it and said, "Ornet." I said, "What?" "Ornet." What he meant was that one of the marks was an ordinary spot and the other was a hornet sting.'

A more pleasant encounter with the unknown took place when Hewlett's patrol was operating on the slopes of Mount Ophir:

> I was walking at the front because at this time I was leading scout, and suddenly I see this paper dart whizzing past me. I thought, what flamin' idiot did that! You can't take risks like that! And the next thing was, another dart shot down the other side. I looked round to see where it had come from and I could see quite a few of them coming down – and everyone was behaving quite normally. They weren't paper darts at all. They were, in fact, butterflies of some sort with about a six-inch wing-span, no flapping, just gliding. But, there again, there were so many weirdies that you had never seen before that this was just another one of them.

In fact, the Queen's Royal Regiment acquitted itself very well during its tour in Malaya. 'Our battalion had a terrific name,' Hewlett insists. 'We had seven kills in no time and, when we did used to shoot them, the first thing we did was whip their boots off, because that's where they kept their money. They didn't wear socks, just a bit of cloth wrapped over the foot and stuffed into a little hockey boot. The lads there before us, they had to bring back just the head and the hands, so we were told. We weren't allowed to do that. We had to bring back the whole body. Then we'd have a big booze-up to forget it.'

Yet the strain was there and it did begin to show:

> Well, it was a war of nerves, there's no two ways about it. The snap of a twig would make you jump, would make you spin. Anything would. You could be asleep as sound as a bell and the slightest noise would waken you. In fact, on one occasion I woke up grabbing my own arm. I had my rifle resting behind me always ready for immediate action and I was lying on my arm. I put my other hand up in my sleep and caught this hand, grabbed it thinking it was a bandit going for my gun. My nerves were completely shattered. I was physically exhausted and mentally I was absolutely a wreck. Some went down a lot quicker than me. Officers and sergeants and God knows who committed suicide – and some just died.

Yet for Hewlett himself the jungle itself became almost a place of refuge: 'Going into it was always very dicey and coming out the same thing applied again. You were in both cases exposed. But once you were in the jungle you weren't. You were then in your element, doing the thing that you had been trained to do, and so when you went out in the open you felt naked. You felt as though someone had taken away your armour, and this is possibly the reason why I developed agoraphobia.'

Suicides, like negligent discharges and accidental shootings of the sort that came to be known in Army terminology as 'blue-on-blue contacts', when one unit fired on another, were taboo subjects that 'people don't talk about much', something to be hushed up or glossed over in regimental journals. But the plain fact was that 'our biggest enemy was ourselves' and even the best-disciplined battalions had their share of avoidable accidents, often with fatal results. 'We killed a lot of our own people and rubber tappers,' Mike Gray admits, 'but you have to get people used to using their weaponry and you have to teach them the hard facts of life.'

The Queen's Royal Regiment, too, had its share of disasters, as when an 'up and coming young sergeant' commanding a platoon sent out two patrols, one of which had a Chinese Civilian Liaison Officer (CLO) acting as an interpreter: 'They weren't particularly good at compass reading and they both moved in a semi-circle. They both saw each other in a glade and the group that didn't have the CLO in it presumed he was a bandit and opened fire and killed four or five of their own men. It's too easy and one doesn't blame them, but the sergeant has to live with that for the rest of his life.'

With every soldier on active service carrying a loaded personal weapon day in and day out, accidents were inevitable. 'The first thing you learn as an infanteer is that your best friend is your rifle,' explains Ron Cassidy, who came to Malaya as a sergeant in the Rifle Brigade. 'It is the thing that you look after most. You clean it more often, certainly you fondle it more often than you'll ever do your wife. But, when you're dealing with Riflemen, NCOs and officers who are always keyed up for something to happen, always carrying weapons and live ammunition, even the most arduous training never stops people, who wouldn't dream of firing accidental shots or letting off machine guns without being told to, from doing the stupidest things when they're tired, wet, hungry. It does happen and it will go on happening.'

Even in a very experienced unit like the 1st Battalion, the Rifle Brigade, which came to Malaya directly from combating the Mau Mau in Kenya, there could be discipline problems with National

Servicemen who 'were not keen to be soldiers, didn't want to be there and wanted to get back to the life that they had been dragged away from'. Christopher Dunphie remembers how quickly an outbreak of petty pilfering undermined the morale of his platoon until the thief was caught and disciplined by a pair of corporals. But more often it was the conditions themselves that put a severe strain on discipline. 'We'd been out on an operation for about five days, flogging an area of jungle in which it was thought there were terrorists,' recalls Christopher Dunphie of one particular incident:

> Like so many operations, nothing had come out of it and when the time came to pull out the commanding officer decided to leave one of the platoons in the area. Mine was selected and so when we went to the pick-up point where we expected to be bundled into transport and taken back, there was my company commander with a fresh set of rations turning us round and pointing us straight back into the jungle. It was deluging with rain and what one used to do, perhaps unwisely, on the last morning was to put on the dry clothes in which one used to sleep. Well, on this occasion, therefore, our dry clothes were wet when we were turned round and sent back into the jungle for another five days – and morale took a dip. It deluged all day, we flogged our way to a different part of the jungle and we had to move at some speed.
>
> When we got there it was getting dark rather early because it was still raining. We were absolutely soaked, we had no dry clothes and there really wasn't time to conduct the security patrols, which were part of the routine of forming a base. So I told everyone to settle down for the night, there would be no smoking, no cooking and no noise – and one Rifleman threw his rifle down and using some good English language declined to soldier further. I was conscious of the boys looking at me to see how I'd react. In fact, I put the Rifleman in the charge of a corporal and said that if he did anything stupid the chap was to bash him and that he was darned well staying with us for the rest of the operation and that he'd go into jail when we came out. And he sat morosely on his pack while the rest of us got underneath our bivouacs, but about halfway through the night he decided that he'd had enough and he crawled into somebody else's bivouac and soldiered with us for the rest of the time. However, he did have certain discussions with the company commander after that operation was over. The British soldier is nothing if not a realist and when he can't actually change the conditions and he's there he has a marvellous ability to buckle down. He can see something funny in the worst possible conditions and even the

National Serviceman, who didn't want to be there in the first place
and who probably never stopped grumbling for much of the time,
did it in a light-hearted and amusing way and really put his back
into it in a thoroughly professional way.

Discipline and good leadership combined with training could see a
soldier through most situations but in a sudden and usually fleeting
encounter with the enemy even the most experienced soldier was
faced by fear and surprise. In such moments instinct often overcame
training. 'The soldiers were all frightened,' recalls Mike Gray of the
one ambush that he was involved in:

> When it happens, it happens so quickly – a face coming towards
> you. You can see it, its head is moving, rolling almost, moving very
> slowly and cautiously, and behind it are others, and they just
> suddenly appear. You are absolutely certain that individual has
> seen you and he is looking straight into your eyes, you think. What
> you had to do was to wait until the whole of the [enemy] patrol had
> got through to a certain point and then I, the platoon commander,
> would spring the ambush. But the soldiers who had been told to
> stay there and wait until you open fire must have felt they were not
> going to get away with it, because the other man has a weapon and
> if you can see him, he is going to be able to see you. So it was a
> very nerve-wracking business.
>   Now I thought I had an efficient platoon, but what happened was
> that one of my young men opened fire. Well, immediately they
> scattered. They just disappeared and it was all over in a flash. I can
> remember firing at this fellow who was running away. I was hitting
> him, but I was using an American M2 carbine, low calibre, and it
> didn't appear to have any impact. I was not reacting quite with the
> skills I had hoped I'd find or my platoon would find, but one of the
> things I did learn was that you never let soldiers go to ground in a
> situation like that because you can't get them up again, particularly
> the National Servicemen. Once they get down in long grass you've
> got to find them and kick them up, because they won't get up if
> somebody is firing at them. I did not have the control that I
> wanted, although the lessons I learned about commanding soldiers
> paid off dividends later on.

One young officer who had more luck in his first serious brush with
Communist terrorists was Jeremy Moore, a young Royal Marines
subaltern. The Commando Brigade of the Royal Marines had been
brought over to Malaya in 1950 as part of a general build-up of the

security forces. Acting in a straightforward infantry role, they took over responsibility for the northern state of Perak, then believed to have one of the largest concentrations of MRLA terrorists in Malaya, probably in excess of six hundred guerrillas. Moore joined 40 Commando in Malaya with no more experience of jungle warfare than an exercise in North Devon called a 'jungle exercise without trees'. He found himself 'very much flung straight into it', having to learn as he went along from the more experienced troop to which he was attached as half-troop subaltern. In 1950 'operations in Malaya had not yet reached the pitch of – one might almost use the word – perfection that was later achieved, but I don't think it would be fair to say that we were thrashing about in the dark. We were better informed than that.' However, it was still very often a case of reacting to events or acting on the strength of 'pretty sparse' intelligence: 'I remember spending many weeks developing an operation on to what we were pretty sure was a main enemy communication line, but we had no idea how often they came or at what intervals or in what numbers and it was very difficult to pin it down. There was a long, long period when we didn't get any contacts.'

In fact, when the contact did come it was as a result of hard information from a surrendered terrorist:

> We followed up some of this information with him going with us to guide us on the way in order to set up an ambush on a place where food was placed for the bandits to collect. On the approach march as it was getting dusk he took us to an area that I just didn't like the feel of. Because I felt this was a very uncomfortable area I stopped the patrol and moved off to one side and then, having established from the surrendered chap that they did use a route across this area, I laid an ambush on it myself. Funnily enough, within ten minutes and before we were even properly prepared they did come. The enemy came out of the edge of the jungle and down across this patch of rubber where we were setting up the ambush. The leading group of three got part of the way across it when they suddenly spotted my light machine gunner and that sprang the ambush. We killed two of them and though we hit the other one he managed to scramble away over the hill. Then there was a follow-up and a firefight with the remainder of the enemy out on the edge of the jungle.

The twenty-year-old Moore's first experience of action left him 'reasonably satisfied'. His troop had suffered no casualties, nothing had seriously gone wrong – and he learned some vital lessons: 'It is

the most common thing in war that it just doesn't follow the pattern
you've laid down for it to happen. Nevertheless, I had at least
thought about it beforehand so that when the time came my mind
was running along the right channels, so it gave one a lot of
confidence for the future.'

Since 'one of the basics of being a Marine is the necessity for
adaptability', the Royal Marines reckoned themselves well-suited to
the Malayan environment. They also considered themselves more
fortunate than other units in that the National Servicemen who came
to them were more highly motivated than most conscripts: 'There
was always competition for places in the Royal Marines so that the
guy who was doing his National Service in the Marines did intend to
do his best and contribute.' However, with hindsight, it could be said
that the three Commandos which served in Malaya in the early 1950s
were 'much more amateur' than they supposed themselves to be:
'We were much more inclined to rush at things and less effort went
into careful preparation and training. For example, we hadn't got
around to all the detailed little things one used to do later to lighten
one's load. One went into the jungle with a tube of toothpaste and a
toothbrush and a bar of soap. Later on we wouldn't have dreamed of
using soap, because it would wash downstream and give away our
presence. We didn't go in for all the detailed analysis of the rations
you needed, of only taking exactly what you had to have or reducing
it by half. That only developed out of experience.'

Following the Royal Marines to Malaya in 1952, Mike Gray and
his fellow infantrymen in the East Yorkshires also learned by
experience:

> You had to teach soldiers to take the right things into the jungle
> and this sometimes meant not cooking, because we always used to
> cook with those little hexamine blocks, which have a distinctive
> smell that hangs even more than tobacco smoke. The water bottles
> in those days had metal tops and, when you were in an ambush
> position lying quietly waiting, if you get a soldier who was thirsty
> and he opens his water bottle it will squeak and so we used to put
> Vaseline on the inside, until someone had the idea of making
> rubber tops for the water bottles. There was no plastic, everything
> you carried was in rubber bags or canvas with rubber linings or hard
> Bakelite. All the watches you had weren't waterproof, so you had
> to keep your watch in a little rubber bag.

Right to the very end of the Emergency, however, the British
serviceman's addiction to nicotine remained a serious impediment,
which was not helped by the fact that smoking received official

encouragement: 'People loved to smoke because they said it kept the mosquitoes away. You were getting fifty free-issue cigarettes a week in those days given to you by the NAAFI. They were dropped to you in the jungle by parachute and that encouraged people to smoke. It was always very, very moist in the jungle and the smoke would hang in that damp atmosphere at about ten feet above the ground. The terrorist could so easily pick up that smell, just as he could smell British sweat.'

Ron Cassidy, too, remembers the quite remarkable way in which the Riflemen of the Rifle Brigade, 'this battalion of Londoners', adapted themselves to living in the Malayan jungle:

> We learned how to sleep on the jungle floor. You wrapped a piece of parachute silk around you and, over that, you would wrap a piece of waterproof material. That kept you warm though it didn't necessarily keep the mosquitoes out. We learned the art of carrying hammocks with us, really a piece of rolled canvas with two loops at the end and some parachute cord. When you got into base you quietly cut two small, thick branches and poked them through the two loops of the canvas. You then found two trees with the right amount of space between them to sling your hammock. We learned the art of finding out where the CTs lived, because anybody that lives in the jungle has got to base themselves on water, and so we walked along the river banks and looked for tracks down to the water, because it is terribly difficult to hide tracks coming in and out of water. Then you patterned your patrolling on a pattern. If you can imagine a draughtboard, walking up one line and down the next.

Through this constant patrolling in and on the fringes of the jungle the security forces were gradually able to deny the CTs the security of their home ground. In this respect even the clumsiest operators were able to contribute to what was 'a war of attrition' as much as anything else: 'Bad or indifferent troops weren't a particular menace to the enemy, but the enemy didn't want to walk into them particularly and, after swamping the area for the length of time that we did, gradually the enemy really never knew where we were.'

Chapter Three

MALAYA:
Hearts and Minds

We were very young and longing for action of some kind. We had spent hours and hours and hours in the most boring patrolling and lying in night ambushes, bitten to pieces by mosquitoes. It sounds bloodthirsty, but we were longing to make contact with these terrorists and we were completely motivated. They were the baddies and there was nothing we could think of to support the campaign they were waging. They were just brutal and they were ruining the country and I'm afraid to say we wanted to kill them, and when we did get some action we thought of it as thrilling, exciting. Boy's Own Paper, *if you like; immature, if you like, something to think about in later life rather more deeply and carefully; but at the time that was the mood.*

For the first three years of the Emergency it had seemed to each side in the conflict that the other was heading for victory, but in October 1951 two unconnected events had signalled a significant change. The first was the decision by the Malayan Communist Party and the MRLA to abandon their initial aims and to concentrate instead on a protracted guerrilla war that would wear down the British forces. The second event was the unplanned ambush and killing of the British High Commissioner, Sir Henry Gurney, which shocked the British Government into sending out as his replacement a military commander who combined the jobs of High Commissioner and Director of Operations, with 'powers that no British soldier had ever had since Cromwell's day'. This was General Sir Gerald Templer, whose appearance in Malaya was like 'a breath of fresh air'. John Akehurst, who arrived in Malaya some months after Templer's appointment in February 1952, remembers the 'quite staggering' impact of the man: 'He'd been there, I think, four or five months and already the whole country, from top to bottom, knew exactly who was in charge. He'd pop up in all sorts of places, and I must admit that everybody was terrified of him because he was the most frightening man. He had a rasping, acid voice and didn't seem to bother about diplomacy to us lesser mortals at all, but he said exactly what we wanted to hear.'

John Akehurst had come to Malaya on secondment from the Northamptonshire Regiment to help build up the local forces: 'Templer had seen the Malay Regiment's great potential for expansion on the very good principle of using local forces to fight their own campaign, but with few officers to carry out this expansion, and I believe he sent a signal to the War Office saying he wanted sixty officers with quality straight away.' Akehurst was one of three officers from his regiment who volunteered 'with a twinkle in the eye, seeing some possibility for action and excitement'. The Malay Regiment was reckoned to be 'badly officered, largely by people on their last tour in the Army, in Malaya for a bit of fun and a bit of extra money'. Templer changed that, with six battalions of the Malay Regiment eventually taking their place as equals alongside the most professional infantry regiments to become 'a powerful influence on the eventual success of the campaign'.

There already existed a 'perfectly good plan for co-ordinating the civil and the military war effort', but it was the dynamic Sir Gerald Templer who 'put the whole thing together so that it made political sense and forced it through'. This was the Briggs Plan, drawn up by an early Director of Operations, General Sir Harold Briggs. It was a food denial policy that called for the resettlement of the six hundred thousand or so Chinese squatters who had settled illegally on the edges of the jungle and who were feeding the terrorists with supplies and information. They were to be moved en masse into what were termed New Villages, where they could be guarded and isolated from the CTs. 'Briggs's policy of picking up people and resettling them seemed, I'm sure, in the British Press to be a pretty repressive kind of thing,' admits 'Fairy' Gopsill. But he believes that such a drastic step had to be taken:

> You must understand that these people – the squatters, as we called them – were very poor farmers living on subsistence farming and they were at the mercy of the Communists. The Communists would come into their little areas and take everything they had, their cattle, their pigs, everything, and leave them destitute. Now they had no chance because if they resisted they or their wives and children would be shot. I can think of places like Broga, a village where the enemy went one day. Apparently, one man said, no, he wasn't going to give them any food, so they slaughtered every man, woman and child in the village. General Briggs felt that it was the

food supply that he had to cut off but he was going to make sure that there was protection for these small farmers, so we had the uplifting of all these people and they were put into the New Villages. They had a police post and protection and wire round the village and they were able to get on with their farming and live at peace at night.

Resettlement of the Chinese squatters had begun under Templer's predecessor but the new High Commissioner speeded up the pace so that by the end of 1951 more than two-thirds of all the squatters had been rehoused in some five hundred New Villages. Each of these settlements had to be guarded, which meant that every unit had to do its share of this unglamorous and tedious duty, including the 1st Battalion, the Rifle Brigade. 'Our role was containment and that meant denying them any assistance from the villages,' explains Ron Cassidy:

> Among a village of, say, five hundred people you're bound to get at least ten who are bad'uns who belonged to the Communist Terrorists. So we used to search all the buses that were going in and out, search all the cars, search all the bicycles. Then because Malaya was a great big rubber plantation really, people used to go daily to work into the rubber plantations. So we had to search all the rubber cans that they carried out. Even then, I can remember a company commander, a very astute, good man, who was taken in by a pretty Chinese girl. We'd stopped her and wanted to strip her bicycle. The British soldier was never allowed to search a woman and never did – we used to get Malay policewomen to do that – but we wanted to strip her bicycle. She burst into tears and said, in her pidgin English, she was in a hurry. Generally, we like a pretty face, any soldier does, but you get hardened to the job you're doing after a while and the pretty ones have got to be searched as well as the ugly ones. But not this time, because the company commander was taken in and said, 'Let her go. She can't possibly be carrying anything.' Of course, she was carrying all the messages out to the Communists, as we found out later when we captured somebody. Mind you, she was a dolly!

This drastic policy soon began to have an effect, because 'the locals got so fed up with being mucked around by authority and it was so difficult for the bandits to get what they wanted. For instance, buckets of night-soil were meant to go to the vegetable plots on the edge of the New Villages. These buckets would have false bottoms and it was in that sort of container that the bandits' sugar ration went out to the jungle. Now after a while that sort of cocktail doesn't go down with a helluva swing.' From 1952 onwards MRLA membership, which had climbed to a peak of over seven thousand hardcore members, began a rapid decline.

Templer was equally determined to involve every community in winning the war. 'He was the first person who really banged the drum about winning the hearts and minds of the local people,' Akehurst declares. He was able to witness this at first hand when escorting the High Commissioner on a visit to one of the New Village areas set up as part of the resettlement programme:

> Suddenly the convoy stopped and Templer jumped out of his car and across a ditch and went over to a small group of Tamil men who were swinging the scythes with which they cut the grass in those days – we used to call them the 'swing sisters'. He went up to this chap who looked in absolute terror as this fearsome General with piercing eyes glared at him, but he then said, 'I should like to congratulate you on the work you do to help to keep this country beautiful. You are the sort of person who is making this a country that is worth fighting for.' This was duly interpreted and the Tamils grinned from ear to ear. He then ran back, got in his car and drove on. Now it was an incident that lasted perhaps two minutes, but those people would have told everybody in the village and by nightfall everybody in the area would have known. It was just an exercise of leadership and personality.

Backed by quasi-dictatorial powers General Templer was able to direct his attentions at every level of society in British Malaya, including the civilian administrators in Kuala Lumpur who were thought by some in the military to be dragging their feet. 'My God, they wanted a kick up the arse,' declares Walter Walker. 'All they could think of was the club, and the Emergency was a long way away. Templer stood no nonsense from them. He very soon formed a Home Guard and had these people on road blocks searching convoys and people going through until he had made them part and parcel of the whole operation.'

If Templer thought it necessary to exceed his powers he did so. After a particularly serious incident at Tanjong Malim in which two senior administrators were killed along with seven policemen, Templer descended on the town in a fury: 'He slapped a curfew on and said to the headmen, "You won't have this curfew lifted until you give us the names of the men responsible for these murders. You will be let out for only two hours a day until such time as you reveal the names. I am going to do it by sending round leaflets to each house and you will write the names on a piece of paper and put it in a box. And to see there's no hanky-panky those boxes will be flown to Kuala Lumpur and opened by me in front of your headmen." He got results.' Thirty-eight arrests were made on the basis of information received and the CT unit that was operating in the area was forced to withdraw. Within weeks several thousand men in what had been a notoriously 'black' area had enrolled in the local Home Guard.

These high-handed methods were coupled with major political concessions that undermined the MRLA's claims to be a liberation movement when 'the Government took the main plank out of their manifesto by giving the Malayans self-determination, so that no longer could they say that the British were keeping the Malayans as slaves'. In fact, Independence did not come to Malaya until 1957, but the promise of self-government and the holding of elections in 1955 were a clear indication of the way things were going.

As far as directing the progress of the war went, Templer's main contribution was to lay great stress on the setting up of War Executive and Security Committees at several levels: 'Prior to Templer's arrival we tended to work in our own watertight compartments. This changed and at battalion level we had the district officer, the local policeman and the battalion commander, and by meeting regularly information was exchanged. The district officer, of course, was a source of information from his own work, the police had their own Special Branch and the Army had their military intelligence officers, and information was shared which wasn't before and this inevitably had a great effect on morale and on the way operations were planned.' And if the High Commissioner thought a local committee was not doing its job he had no hesitation in sacking its key members. 'Once he realised that you were doing a good job of work you got praise,' recalls Walker. 'But I remember so well just before I finished command of the 1st/6th when we were down in Ipoh. The policeman there was bad, the Security Committee there was bad. I was riding with Templer in his car coming down when he said quietly to me, "Walter, what is wrong?" I said, "They're all dead wood." They just hadn't got that grasp of the situation that one was accustomed to having. And that very evening he called them together and he absolutely blasted them to pieces.'

John Akehurst used to attend one War Executive Committee regularly as Battalion Intelligence Officer:

> I used to sit on the sidelines behind my commanding officer and I went to one meeting where Templer himself came at about two hours' notice. Of course, everyone was petrified and you could see

all these great men shaking as this fierce General listened to what was going on. One of the problems was that, in order to protect themselves, planters in outlying rubber plantations were being encouraged to get radio sets so that they could call for help, but the Government wasn't going to pay for these radio sets. The committee was discussing how they could persuade planters to pay up for these radios and Templer said, 'I can't think what you're all arguing about, this is a perfectly simple matter. You just send out a section of the Malay Regiment here, dead of night, cut the telephone lines to the recalcitrant planter, fire a few bursts of Bren over his roof and let the bugger sweat till the morning. He'll buy a radio.' That was the sort of practical, stylish way which he managed business!

As a former Director of Intelligence at the War Office Templer was also very conscious of the importance of information-gathering, building up the local Malayan Police Special Branch and placing much emphasis on intelligence in a way that was to have far-reaching consequences in this and in other counter-insurgency campaigns: 'The secret of our success was the garnering of information from all kinds of people from informers and police observers to any bit of tittle-tattle. There were Joint Ops rooms manned by police and military personnel and they monitored all information. They started to collate it into a picture. There were Chinese, Malays, Indians, Pakistanis, people of every race working together and over a couple of years the picture came from nothing to something that was quite vivid. We suddenly realised that there was a picture emerging.'

What greatly helped this information-gathering was the success of a system of rewards offered to terrorists who surrendered and gave information. Coupled with the severe penalties exacted for those caught engaging in terrorist activities, this produced remarkable results as surrendered terrorists – known as Surrendered Enemy Personnel or SEPs – began with increasing readiness to inform on their former comrades. 'I never despised them,' declares 'Fairy' Gopsill. 'When you've got poor people, some of them very poor subsistence farmers, and you're offering big rewards for information, it's a strong man who can hold out against that.' SEPs were often used to lead patrols to enemy positions or sites for contacts. 'We always looked after them and we always made sure that when they'd shown the position to us they'd be taken back by a couple of Gurkhas to the police, so that they were well out of it before we attacked. The only time I did feel a bit irked was when an officer brought a well-known turncoat into our mess. He had been in the band, I believe, which had killed my chum. He walked over and said in perfect English "Hullo, I'm Lam Sui." He stuck his hand out and I'm afraid I couldn't shake it.'

Learning to trust and to act on information from their local Special Branch officers did not come easily to all commanding officers, but where a good working relationship was established it often paid dividends. By 1954 when Walter Walker took his 1st/6th Gurkhas to Perak he had learned to 'put my faith entirely' in the Special Branch: 'There were those who thought that the Army should be in charge of intelligence and that the police should be subordinate to the Army intelligence. I did not agree with that because the Malayan Police were living in the country, spoke the language, knew the terrain, knew the habits of the people. Some were not as good as others but I had a very, very close liaison and friendship with Special Branch. I trusted them and they trusted me and if I failed to pull off an ambush on their information then, of course, they were very upset and so was I.' There were disappointments to begin with but as the Special Branch began to penetrate the local terrorist network, so harder information began to come in. This culminated in a meeting between Colonel Walker and a 'turned' terrorist at an agreed rendezvous in the jungle at which Walker learned of a meeting of local terrorist leaders to be held at a certain location within a four-day period. Walker was determined that the ambush should be a complete success and drew up meticulous plans involving the full battalion:

> It meant a night march so that no one in the village would know we were moving. These six leading terrorists were due to arrive at this particular hill-top and I got the whole battalion round the camp. I had one man actually on the hill-top hidden in foliage with a light machine gun and orders to fire as soon as he got a target of all six of them, and the signal for the attacking platoon would be that burst of fire. I went round and allotted every company its place and we wiped out all our footsteps with branches and twigs. I remember so well how on this burst of fire the Gurkhas rushed forward – I was just behind the leading six, I suppose – and those who were not killed by that light machine gun were killed when they ran into the cordon. I got a very nice signal from Templer saying, 'Terrific!', because we killed six out of six.

For the 1st Battalion, the Rifle Brigade, too, it became very much a question of conducting ambushes 'on specific intelligence'. It was on such intelligence that Christopher Dunphie received what he describes as 'an early blooding' on the Rifle Brigade's very successful eighteen-month tour, which saw them through what was essentially the last serious phase of the Emergency:

Very early on, information came through that a known terrorist, Fu Siong, was likely to make contact with a rubber tapper in a particular area near the junction between a rubber estate and the jungle and as the duty platoon I was stood to to take out an ambush party. Ambushing in rubber was a difficult operation because, of course, many of the rubber estates are very clean with little undergrowth and it was extremely hard to hide in them. We spent a hectic day of preparation, to make sure one's weapons were working properly and zeroed, and to get one's food right, which probably consisted of one tin of bully beef per day, so it would be three or four tins of bully beef and a couple of water bottles. Your only other amenity was a poncho ground sheet in which you wrapped your food, which you strapped on the back of your belt and in which you curled yourself up at night. Then there was also the problem that the issued jungle boot had a very obvious foot pattern and, therefore, you couldn't move round rubber estates in the wet climate of Malaya without leaving marks, and so for ambushing in rubber estates you wore hockey boots. On this particular occasion I made everyone draw an extra pair of socks and put them on over their hockey boots so that the imprint we left on the ground was less marked.

The ambush was to be in a deep little re-entrant, quite small, only about fifty yards across, and was to consist of a killing party and two cut-off parties. The killing party was to be myself as the commander, one Bren gunner and three Riflemen, and each of the cut-off parties a corporal and two Riflemen. The terrorist was thought to be going to make contact with a particular girl who cut the rubber trees in the area of the ambush. We made our way out by armoured three-ton vehicle and our drop-off point was just north of the village. Our driver practised for hours during the day before we left to see whether he could in fact bring the vehicle nearly to a stop while maintaining the revs at a constant level, so that anybody from the village who heard the sound of vehicles would not think that we'd stopped and dropped people off. At about eleven o'clock at night, we de-bused and made our way through the rubber estate, escorted by a Chinese police inspector and a captured or surrendered enemy terrorist. Shortly before dawn, the policeman and surrendered terrorist having left us, we made our way to the actual scene of the ambush. The village inhabitants would be out in the rubber from about half past six or seven o'clock in the morning so for that first day I kept everybody in one small area of scrub without deploying them further. After curfew, about three o'clock in the afternoon, I did a reconnaissance of the area and deployed the ambush. My own party was sited in a small area of what was called beluka, which is rather like a fern. I was near a rubber tree which a woman rubber tapper used to tap every day and as she stood about eighteen inches from my face I couldn't think why she couldn't hear my heart beating on the ground.

On the third evening, after all the rubber tappers had left and the cut-off parties had closed in, one of the corporals asked why I hadn't opened fire. I told him that I hadn't seen any terrorist and he explained that the targeted terrorist, accompanied by one other, had walked about five yards from his cut-off position in the direction of the killing area of the ambush. The rules we'd learnt on our jungle warfare course was that all the cut-off parties waited until the terrorist had entered the middle of the killing area and then the ambush was initiated by the commander. Unfortunately, our terrorist had not read those rules and he never actually came into the middle of the ambush. He had simply walked past one of the cut-off parties, made whatever contact he wanted to make and walked away. I called the ambush off and returned to my company base bitterly disappointed.

After consultations with Special Branch it was decided to try again, since the terrorist had clearly not realised that he had walked through an ambush. So back Dunphie went, this time with a smaller party and with modified instructions that allowed anyone with a clear target to fire without waiting for orders:

We were there for another four or perhaps five days and then – I remember it so clearly, it was about three minutes to ten – I was conscious of a noise behind me in the small area of beluka fern in which I was hidden. At the time I was lying in a steep slope facing downhill. Very slowly I pushed my head through my cover and looked back over my shoulder. And there behind me was the terrorist, about eight to ten yards away. I can remember him so clearly, he was wearing a blue, short-sleeved Airtex shirt, with large sweat marks under his armpits. He had a brown pork pie hat with a wide band going round it and sweat marks coming through the hat and in his hand was a tommy gun. It seemed to me that for an age we were staring at one another. I was completely frozen, not by any fear as to what might happen to me, but by something much more basic than that. I simply couldn't bring myself to shoot this man in cold blood. Now I don't know how long we were staring at one another, I don't even know whether he saw me, but it seemed to me an age. And then he took a step forward and he must have trodden on my belt and poncho ground sheet, which were tucked in behind me and he turned and ran, and at that stage I got up, turned round and opened fire. I can remember my hands shaking, I can remember the feeling of dampness in the palms of my hands and, of course, I missed him. And once again, bitterly disappointed, I called off the ambush and we went back into base.

This second failure made Dunphie 'so keen for success' that some months later when a chance came to engage a terrorist in 'a private shooting match between us' he almost relished the opportunity:

> I can remember, terribly clearly, shooting wildly, stupidly and suddenly something clicking into place, and bringing my rifle out of my shoulder and becoming, in effect, a rather cold, calculating creature, putting it back in my shoulder and shooting him dead. And I think that's the moment at which I solved my own personal problem and it's also a moment which was of great value to me later on. In fact, we also shot another terrorist and when the operation was called off we went in and collected the bodies. I remember this was the first occasion that I'd actually seen a dead body and my own bullet had hit straight in the middle of the chest. It was a very small entry hole, but as I turned the body over I realised that it had hit the spine and blown the whole of the chap's back out. And I remember thinking what a revolting sight it was. In fact, I think if I'm correct I was violently sick.

In all these operations the role of the police Special Branch had been 'particularly impressive', matching the unusual emphasis that the 1st Battalion, the Rifle Brigade placed on Army intelligence. This was due in no small part to the thinking of one particular officer, Frank Kitson, who in a battalion that was later to provide the Army with ten generals and five brigadiers out of some thirty or so regular officers, was himself exceptional. Major Kitson had become a specialist in intelligence-gathering and its application in Kenya (see Chapter Eight), developing ideas that were to have a considerable impact on Army thinking: 'My actual contribution in Malaya was limited to sorting out a small terrorist remnant that was in the very small area in which I operated, but I tried to devise a system with my own company in Malaya for building up background information into contact information, using the Special Branch officers to get the background information that I needed to build up on and see if it worked. I think I made it work: this idea that it is up to the commanders of conventional military forces to get and use information to get more information – and that, I maintain, is what tactics are in the counter-insurgency situation.'

One of those in Kitson's company who saw this process of exhaustive intelligence-gathering translated into a series of successful operations was Sergeant Ron Cassidy. 'Combining with the local police force,' he recalls, 'we were able to clear complete areas and make them peaceful again' – although he remembers one particular operation that was not quite as successful as Cassidy would have liked it to have been:

> I took a patrol out into the jungle with an Inspector of the Malayan Police, a European. We were successful and managed to shoot and kill the four members of the gang who were there. One of them was the local chief of the gang in that area and we decided to lay an ambush in that camp where we'd come across this gang, to wait for the other members – I use the terminology 'gang' to describe a group of people. Unfortunately, the Inspector of Police decided that his resupply party was coming in and so the dear Malayan Police just bumbled around in the jungle, blowing whistles and shouting and trying to find each other. That, of course, really exposed all of our cover and so we had to call off the ambush.

From 1955 onwards success could be signalled for all to see as, stage by stage, one part of the country after another was declared 'white' and all Emergency restrictions lifted within that area. It was entirely fitting that for the final elimination of CTs in the 'blackest' area of them all, Johor State in the south, the task should be given to 99 Gurkha Brigade, made up of four Gurkha battalions plus two companies of the Cheshire Regiment. Its commander was Brigadier Walter Walker, who devised Operation 'Tiger', starting in January 1958, with the declared aim of eradicating every terrorist within the state by the end of the year:

> There were one hundred hard-core Communist terrorists left and the way I tackled it was to hold this symposium. We had a model, and I made my battalion commanders tell me exactly how they were going to tackle their particular area and I got the other battalion commanders to pick holes in the plan and the police to give their opinion. As a result of this symposium I evolved a plan. And I remember Julian Amery, the Minister for the Army, coming into my Operations Room. I had the names and photographs of the remaining Communist terrorists on the wall and we put a red cross on the face when they had been eliminated. And I remember Julian

Amery saying to me, 'Where are they?' and I said 'They are there
. . . there . . . there . . . there.' He said, 'How do you know?' and I
said, 'I am working on informers, Special Branch information and
my knowledge.' I used to send up my Intelligence Officer, my GSO
3, in an Auster at dawn and ask him to see where any smoke was
appearing in the jungle, because if there was any smoke appearing
there were the Communist terrorists having their morning meal,
and so we worked also on that information. The Chief of Staff came
across to me and said 'How long do you think it is going to take to
eliminate the remainder? We want your brigade desperately in
Singapore because of the elections for Independence and this chap
Lee Kuan Yew, we think he's going to give trouble and the sooner
we can get your troops retrained from jungle warfare to internal
security the better.' I said I would have Johor cleared by Christmas
1958 – and so it was.

An area of some eighteen hundred square miles was effectively
sealed off and ambushes laid on routes said by informers to be used
by the terrorists. Ten-day ambushes, with the teams operating in
two-hour shifts, became the norm rather than the exception, with
one particular ambush party maintaining its position for twenty-eight
days: 'Sometimes my commanding officers thought I was mad. I
remember so well one commanding officer, I told him to lay an
ambush working on information and they had to lie in ambush for
days and days. He came to me on several occasions and said, "Can I
lift the ambush because the troops are flogged?" But I had great faith
in my Special Branch man and I went to him and said they had not
come and he said, "They are going to come. I guarantee they are
going to come." And after twenty-eight days they came and they
were killed in the swamp.'

Mass surrenders by the last few bands of guerrillas operating in
South Johor meant that by the end of 1958 virtually the whole of
Malaya was 'white' and free of terrorists. More than six thousand had
been killed since the start of the Emergency, leaving only about two
hundred and fifty still active, all of them in the jungles along the Thai
border, so that it was at last possible in the rest of the country to lift
the Emergency restrictions that had been in place since 1948.

Long drawn-out though it had been – and another two years were
to pass before the Emergency was officially declared to be at an end –
the counter-insurgency war had ended in the defeat of the Malayan
Communist Party and its Malayan Races Liberation Army.
Although never completely exposed to the full glare of modern
publicity – 'we didn't have the threat of the Press and television and

everything else hovering over our shoulders, which would then dissect our actions within minutes of them happening' – nevertheless the Malayan campaign was very much a war in which both sides were conscious of the fact that it could only be won with public support.

Yet almost from the outset of the Emergency a parallel, hidden war had been taking place out of public sight. This was a war fought by specialists in the very deepest recesses of the Malayan jungle. Up to the autumn of 1953 the MRLA had pursued a policy of active terrorism but then, as their casualties mounted and support for their cause began to collapse, a time came when their leaders sent out a directive to all the remaining cadres announcing a major change in tactics. This was discovered by chance when a Gurkha patrol led by Major John Cross killed a CT who turned out to be a courier:

> One day I woke up with a bit of a headache so I broke my own rule
> and said we'd cook a meal before we left at nine – and at five to
> nine a couple of bandits walked into the camp sentry and we killed
> one of them and found a whole lot of propaganda on him. There
> were little spills of paper that to me in my ignorance seemed pretty
> important, together with a whole lot of propaganda papers and
> pamphlets like the Freedom News and the Red Banner and the Red
> Star or whatever they were. We had to carry them out quite a long
> way, we were quite heavily laden and I thought it was a bore and I
> very nearly ditched the whole lot. But I didn't and got them
> evacuated by a helicopter which came to take a sick man out. When
> I heard that they were useless my heart sank, but a little later I
> heard that in fact the Johor Special Branch had broken the code,
> which was reading every fourth word. And that was the first time
> the new policy was being pushed out by the Central Committee.
> The bandits were being ordered to change their tactics from pure
> terrorism, and told to withdraw and survive in the deep jungle.

Chapter Four

MALAYA:
Into the Interior

During that time, I worked out that statistically, for every million man-hours of effort in the jungle we only saw the bandits for a period of twenty seconds, which gives you a statistic which is horrific. And that's why one could go a whole year in the jungle without seeing anybody at all. The other statistic that sticks in my mind is that for four hundred and thirty-five days I spent a total of five shillings and ninepence and that was buying a packet of razor blades and a bottle of rum in an air drop.

Right from the outset of the Emergency various means had been sought to strike back at the MRLA's headquarters and bases in the deep jungle. Ferret Force had been thrown together using the knowledge of the men who had operated with the Chinese Communists against the Japanese in the last stages of the Second World War. Supported by Chinese liaison officers and with skilled Dyak or Iban trackers brought over from Sarawak, these Ferret Force teams had had limited success. But Ferret Force had been too dependent on civilians whose skills were badly needed elsewhere and it had soon become obvious that another strategy employing a different sort of specialist force had to be found.

The wartime activities of the Special Air Service Regiment, operating in small groups behind enemy lines, had shown how valuable such a force could be. An SAS territorial unit had been raised in 1947 but it required the initiative of a remarkable ex-Chindit, Colonel 'Mad Mike' Calvert, to get the SAS going again as an active service unit in Malaya. One of the first officers to join his team, formed originally in August 1950 as the Malayan Scouts but soon to become 22 SAS Regiment, was John Woodhouse, who had been chafing at his post as a staff intelligence officer in Hong Kong. 'Malaya, where the Communist insurrection was looking very serious, sounded a much more interesting place to be,' he remembers. 'I volunteered to join and I told Michael Calvert that I would only come if he gave me command of a troop or a squadron – and he just smiled. When I arrived in Singapore I found he'd appointed me intelligence officer, which didn't please me too much at the time.'

Another of Calvert's original recruits was Frank Williams, a corporal instructor in the Royal Engineers and a demolition expert. An interview with Colonel Calvert in a tent on a Chinese chicken farm was followed by a more rigorous selection test in Johor, after which Williams found himself rubbing shoulders with a 'real hotch-potch' of characters who made up 'A' Squadron and Headquarters of the Malayan Scouts. Things began badly. Discipline was so lax that the organisation came close to being disbanded, having made 'such a bad impression on the rest of the Army that it was going to take years to live down – and did take years to live down.'

Part of the problem lay with the rank and file recruits, who were 'a great mixture of people from all regiments and walks of life. A lot were misfits, without a doubt, people whom the regiments they came from were glad to see the back of. Some were very good and some were very bad. In fact, the saying was "an excellent man but you can't keep him in the jungle for twelve months of the year", because it all seemed to happen when we were on the outside. Once in the jungle away from the drink or whatever pitfalls there were, they worked well together.' But at least some of the unit's problems stemmed from the complex character of its commander. 'Colonel Calvert was a one-off,' declares Frank Williams. 'He believed in leading from the front and, in fact, he was on the very first operation. He hurled himself into this and planned and took part in everything and, I'm afraid, very little paper work was done. He insisted on being in the field and not only him but all the attached clerks, the adjutant and the quartermaster were also sent into the field, so that you'd find that the first base we had of our own, a place called Dusun Tua, was manned by the sick, lame and lazy who sat in gun-pits with Vickers machine guns to defend their post against all-comers while the remainder were in the field.' Looking back, William finds it 'hard to believe that we did operate the way we did in 1950, but it was all unknown and everybody was learning at this stage. Mike Calvert seemed to think he was still in Burma. A good instance of this was the use of mules. We had ten mules sent down from the mule stables in Hong Kong to carry our kit in the jungle but really all the mules did was to carry their own fodder, so it was an absolute waste of time.'

Calvert was having to set up a new regiment from scratch and was under great pressure to get his troops operational as soon as possible, although few of them had any experience of jungle warfare. Even so, Calvert's working methods were not easy to bear. 'Calvert dominated us in a way which it is rather hard to explain now,' declares John Woodhouse, who found him a 'fascinating and infuriating man' to work for:

> There were times when Calvert and I had the most appalling rows. Discipline was really non-existent. Why Colonel Calvert didn't clamp down hard I've never entirely understood. It was rather thought that because the troops had been in the jungle for two or three months they should have a jolly good time when they came out in the sense of parties and drinking and all the rest of it and this led to some very silly escapades, which really got rather out of control. Other things happened which, looking back on it, were very foolish. Men were allowed to grow beards in the jungle, which was a sensible idea in that they hid the white faces, but when the men came out unfortunately they were allowed to keep them on, contrary to all the traditions of the Army, and the sight of smelly, scruffy, bearded soldiers was one which caused almost apoplexy in the Staff and derision among all the other units in the Army. It was a very bad mistake.

But if Calvert made mistakes Woodhouse never had any doubts as to his value as the 'originator of the post-war SAS', whose ideas on the employment of special forces in counter-insurgency were to have a major impact on Army thinking:

> He was known as 'Mad Mike' in the Army as well as in the Press largely because he was always a bit larger than life himself. Ideas bubbled from him rather like water coming out of a fountain. You couldn't sit down with Colonel Mike Calvert for half an hour without hearing ideas flow in a way which I never heard from anyone else in the Army. I remember my first interview in Malaya with him very, very well. He sent for me and he gave me what I think was a brilliant exposé of the whole Malayan position and then he told me the part which he thought a special unit would play. In the deep jungle there were quite large numbers of aboriginals. They'd had almost no contact with anyone except the Communist terrorists, who had been there since the Japanese war and who knew them well and controlled them. The task of a special unit was to win the deep jungle while the rest of the Army fought the main battles along the edges of the jungle – and the first battle we had to win was to win the hearts and minds of the aboriginals. Until we could break them from the Communists we would never be able to break the Communists themselves. All the business of giving medical treatment to primitive people who previously had had no

medical treatment, all that he described long before I heard it from anybody else, and the idea of the Malayan Scouts establishing bases in deep jungle and then spreading out like ripples in a pond. He described how it would be possible if men were properly trained to let them work in patrols of three or four, living there and staying there, and he emphasised the staying there. He reminded us that the terrorists had been in the jungle for five or six years at that time and they lived there, they grew their food there and, he said, 'we have got to do the same thing'.

Calvert's attitude towards the enemy was equally far-sighted. Woodhouse recalls a European police officer visiting their mess in 1950:

He started talking about how to get information out of terrorists, which included burning them with cigarette ends and other unpleasantness. Calvert grew silent and I watched the volcano in him about to erupt. He said, 'Is that what you really think?' And the man said, 'Yes, that's the answer.' And without a further word Calvert picked him up by one arm, swung him and slung him straight out of the room, and when he'd dusted his hands he asked us why we thought he'd done it. After we'd dithered and waffled away he said, 'I'm going to tell you a story now about my Chindit days when we picked up a Korean who had been reporting our positions to the Japanese. I said to him, "What would the Japanese have done to you if you'd been helping us against them?" And he said, "They would kill me." So I said to him, "And what do you expect we shall do?" "Well, I suppose you will kill me." I said, "That's where you're wrong, because in the British Empire we don't need to behave like that and we don't behave like that. You have been misguided in helping the Japanese and I am going to set you free, so long as you promise not to support the Japanese any more." '

Then Calvert explained to us why he had taken this action, because had the man been shot his family would have hated the British for ever more and now that family would be grateful to the British for ever after. That lesson rather sunk home to me. I always remembered Calvert's words and I believe the SAS have remembered them ever since. Later on one might perhaps have been tempted to use force to get information from terrorists but every SAS soldier is taught that that is not the way to behave, because wars don't end just when the shooting stops. The results of war go on for generations.

Judged purely in terms of 'kills' the success rate of the SAS Regiment in Malaya was to be pretty average: 'Over the period of eight years it was in Malaya the SAS killed one hundred and eight terrorists, probably less than outstanding units like the Suffolks and the Royal Hampshires and some of the Gurkha battalions achieved in two or three years.' Its 'contact to kill' ratio, based on kills arising out of actual contacts, was very much higher but the real success of the SAS was to be in other areas – notably in the 'very gradual, bit by bit achievement' that led to the winning-over of the aboriginals.

Calvert's first efforts were concentrated on getting into the deep jungle in strength and on setting up operating bases that could be strengthened into forts and resupplied by air. 'The first operation the whole squadron went in at night with compasses on the back of our packs,' recalls Frank Williams; 'luminous compasses so that each man could follow the man in front of him. We took in twenty-eight days' rations that we had to carry with all the rest of our equipment, which meant that each man was carrying well over a hundred pounds. It was an awful job to stand up, let alone walk, with all this equipment, so had we met anybody I don't know what would have happened.' After a command base had been set up in an abandoned bandit camp, the Squadron's four troops – the SAS equivalent of infantry platoons – were sent out in various directions to establish their own troop bases, from which three- or four-man patrols could operate. After a month fresh supplies were delivered by air: 'The first airdrop we ever took in the regiment was on a razor-back ridge and it took us a week to get the packs back from the bottom of the valley. On the twenty-eighth day you got a piece of bread and a pat of butter, but for the rest of the two months we were there we lived on sheep's tongue, corned beef and hard pack biscuits that had to be from the Second World War they were so weevily. People subsidised this with things they could forage from the jungle but it was quite difficult in those days.'

The lack of success of these first big operations was certainly not due to any 'lack of determination or will'. Enthusiasm, which was to be the SAS's 'essential ingredient' in years to come, was already very much in evidence – but not the self-discipline that should have accompanied it. On one long march Woodhouse ordered three exhausted men to return to base. Disobeying him, they continued and when eventually the boots of one of the three were cut off his feet he was found to have been walking on suppurating flesh that in places had worn down to the bone. It was also a fact that 'A' Squadron was not up to scratch. In Woodhouse's opinion, prolonged failure to make contact with the enemy led to 'a slackening of battle procedures', the troopers becoming 'extremely careless, very noisy and rather bored, going round the jungle in a slaphappy way with big fires at night, dropping sweet papers or ration tins around the place and not hiding them.'

Yet plenty of good work was achieved. Much of Frank Williams's time on this first tour was spent building airstrips beside newly-established jungle forts:

> I was despatched by myself to live with about two hundred aboriginals and a white police officer. We had thousands of pounds of explosives dropped in and my job during the day would be to ring all the trees with explosives using aboriginals as powder monkeys and then on the appointed day to send the aboriginals into the jungle and blow perhaps a hundred trees at a time. Having got the first Auster down on the airstrip I had a signal from Colonel Calvert to say 'Request turn it into a Dakota strip', which would have necessitated moving a mountain of about a thousand feet. So I sent a signal back to ask him to drop me a bulldozer and an operator, at which stage I got a signal to say 'Return'.

Building this and subsequent airstrips, Williams had plenty of opportunity to get to know the aboriginals in the jungle and to experience their way of life:

> I had an airdrop that probably lasted about a month, so it was all tinned rations and aboriginal food. Fish were plentiful because the rivers were quite simply bombed. You'd take the aboriginals down with their dug-outs and drop a couple of explosives in and you'd have enough fish to last you a month. So we provided them with the fish and they cooked it. I liked the diet and suffered no ill-effects from it. Tapioca or *ubi kayu* I quite liked and *ubi cleevit*, which is Malay for potato. With that and fish who wants English food? I liked the easy way of life, the quiet way of life of the aboriginals and in fact I adopted their way of life, loin cloth and no shoes, and I was more than happy to live with them. I didn't want to come out. I wasn't worried in the slightest by jungle noises or leeches or all the weird things that you do find in the jungle. I met tigers, elephants, snakes, but none of them bothered me. To be honest, I think people settled in quite happily, disappeared into the woods and pulled the green around their ears and were very happy for three months.

The arrival of reinforcements drawn from the Second World War veterans in 21 SAS helped to strengthen the Malayan Scouts but this second unit, which became 'B' Squadron, was also sent 'more or less willy-nilly into the jungle' under the command of John Woodhouse: 'Once again it was a very difficult matter to train them for jungle operations when they were supposed to be actually on an operation. I was the only officer with experience in Malaya in that squadron and in the three months I had with them all I can say is that I did establish the rudiments of battle discipline.'

Hard on the heels of 'B' Squadron came 'C' Squadron, drawn from the then Rhodesian Army, who were also 'let loose on the jungle after something like three weeks' training in elementary jungle tactics'. They were quickly followed by what became 'D' Squadron, made up of volunteers who 'had spent a few weeks at the Airborne Forces Depot in Aldershot where they were not parachute-trained but simply used as heavers of coal and hewers of wood – not the best preparation for joining the Malayan Scouts.' Woodhouse became 'D' Squadron's first commander, leading them for six months before his first tour in Malaya ended. Worn down by malaria, amoebic dysentery and fatigue, Colonel Mike Calvert also left before the end of 1951, leaving behind 'a very weak instrument' with which to carry out his far-sighted ideals and tactical aims.

Fortunately for 22 SAS, Lieutenant-Colonel 'Tod' Sloane, who succeeded Calvert as the regiment's commanding officer, believed in old-fashioned discipline. 'He grabbed the regiment by the throat,' describes Frank Williams. 'A lot of people went and there was applied discipline which there never was before. We moved down to Salarang Barracks in Singapore for retraining. There was a very large [barrack] square at Salarang and we spent some time pounding up and down the square.' It was at this stage that, in Williams's words, 'tree-jumping became the vogue'. 'B' Squadron contained large numbers of trained parachutists so a joint operation was mounted in February 1952 in which some fifty members of the squadron were dropped into a valley close to the Thailand border, where there was a known guerrilla camp, while other troops approached on foot: 'They intended to drop on a paddy field but the aircraft missed and only two or three people landed in the paddy field. The rest of them were up trees with fifty feet of knotted rope.' However, there were few injuries and the operation was judged to be a success, with the result that the whole of the regiment began parachute training.

Between 1952 and 1958 22 SAS carried out a series of parachute drops directly into the jungle. The advantages of direct access to the interior were obvious but it soon became apparent that 'tree-jumping' was a very risky business. 'The drill was to try and hit a tree,' recalls Williams, who made seven operational jumps, 'but having no steerage on the parachutes at that time and being dropped so low you couldn't steer anyway. So you headed for a tree, got yourself tangled in the branches and then came down your two hundred and forty feet of tape that you carried under your arms in a bag.' In practice this wasn't so easy as it sounded. One of the biggest parachute drops was on Operation 'Termite' in the Cameron Highlands, which produced some 'hairy moments' for Williams:

> Three troops of 'A' Squadron parachuted along this river line. One of our people landed on top of a bandit camp and one or two shots were fired at him while he was hanging in the trees, but the next man in the stick came straight through the trees and frightened these people to death and they disappeared. I'd got very tangled up in the top of this tree and, in trying to cut myself loose from the rigging lines in the branches surrounding me, I cut through my lowering tape and it disappeared about two hundred feet below. So I had to come down a water vine, which was a bit hairy at the time. There was one man called Chiggi, who was hanging about a hundred and fifty feet up a tree in a hornet's nest. They couldn't get him down and he couldn't get down either. It took most of the day to get him down and when they finally did he was about three times his normal size.

Operation 'Termite' involved three separate drops and four infantry battalions and resulted in the death or capture of fifteen CTs. However, the next drop that Williams took part in was a disaster. This was Operation 'Sword', which took place in January 1954, in a jungle reserve in Kedah State that had been subject to weeks of saturation bombing by RAF Lincolns:

> The dropping zone that we landed on there was in a terrible state. The trees were all bombed and the spikes were sticking up and remember that there was no steerage with these parachutes. You had to go where God took you. Lieutenant Goulding, who was killed, landed in the tree next to me and I remember watching him. His parachute slipped from the top of this hundred-and-fifty-footer and he fell about fifty feet and then he got hung up again and from there his parachute broke loose and he just piled into the ground. My troop lance-corporal, Johnny Bonds, was killed. He fell two hundred feet from the top of a tree. Also there was a Ground Liaison Officer who was sent with us. He had got himself tangled at the top of a two-hundred-footer. He'd got tangled up in his rigging lines and I got there in time to see this knife being tied on the end of the tape and disappearing two hundred feet up. You couldn't see him from down below and the next thing was a body came down. I

was under the tree, in fact, when he came down. He'd cut his line, obviously not intentionally, and he lived I think until midnight. The worst part of the whole thing was the fact that just about every radio set went U/S [unserviceable]. They got banged up in the trees as we went in so we had no communication with outside. And the net result of this operation was nil. There was absolutely nothing there.

What effectively did away with the need for tree-jumping was the helicopter. In the words of Rob Woodard, who flew Whirlwind Mark Sevens in 1960, during the closing months of the Emergency, with 848 Royal Naval Air Squadron, 'the helicopter revolutionised aspects of jungle warfare. A day's march through real jungle was well under five minutes' flying in a helicopter and we could fly a week's walk in well under an hour.'

Three Dragonfly helicopters had been brought into operation in Malaya in 1950 but they and the handful of Sycamores that replaced them were too few and too prone to mechanical failure to be effective. The linseed oil applied to the laminated wooden blades of the Sycamore made them 'mightily attractive to the voracious appetite of the white ant' while the low blades themselves meant that 'if you didn't duck properly you really could get your head taken off'. One bizarre accident with a Sycamore involved an Alsatian tracker dog that was being carried as a passenger: 'The dog sat down on the fuel cocks between the seats which just turned the fuel off and brought it down to earth rather suddenly.'

It was not until the arrival of 848 Royal Naval Air Squadron in 1953 flying S.55s that the helicopter really began to make its presence felt – although to the very end demands for helicopters were always in excess of supply. Even with the advent of the more advanced Whirlwinds, flying helicopters in Malaya placed just as severe demands on pilots and aircrews as those faced by the infantry on the ground. Rob Woodard saw it as 'a schizophrenic existence. Having spent a few weeks operating in the jungle you found yourself in the wardroom of your carrier sipping a gin and shooting the most appalling lines.' The jungle interior itself was 'a terrifying place to be in' from his point of view. Flying over it was another matter:

> Flying over the jungle at dusk with amazing sunsets or at dawn with equally amazing new days, with the mists just starting to form in the trees, was very picturesque. But you were always aware of the menace, because one minute it was absolutely lovely, all was well and you were on time and you knew you were going in the right direction – and the next minute you could be in total silence after a blood-curdling explosion from the engine and the aircraft was

rushing down into the trees. The thing about flying over the jungle is that if you go into it there is a very real chance that you won't be found. If the jungle foliage has closed over the top of you you won't be seen. I mean, there was an incident that happened to a naval helicopter in the mid-1950s when quite shortly after take-off it crashed into the jungle and everyone on board was killed and they were never able to find it. That gives you some idea of how incredibly dense it was.

Flying helicopters in tropical conditions also presented additional hazards:

Everything got terribly, terribly damp and so wirelesses played up. It was not a good thing to fly through a monsoon shower. One had to occasionally but it could do considerable damage to a helicopter. The engines didn't like humidity and they didn't like heat. Heat also reduced the power available and thus the load one took. On a good day you could carry up to six Gurkhas or four Royal Marines and their basic fighting equipment and on a bad day it was five and three. I remember once sitting for twenty minutes at the bottom of a clearing at high power in the hover until I'd burnt off sufficient fuel to equate to the weight of a man so I could fly out with four Royal Marines rather than leaving one man alone in the jungle. And understand that the jungle clearings were just bigger than the helicopter. They weren't swanky clearings at all. You came down virtually vertically, which is not a good thing for the aerodynamics of a helicopter because you recirculate your own air and it can actually be sucking up disturbed air which comes down through the blades and collapses your lift. So there's quite an art to flying vertically down into a clearing through two-hundred-foot-high trees, which are just off the tips of your rotors.

By 1955 a combination of helicopters, together with STOL aircraft working in and out of short landing strips attached to the jungle forts, had begun to transform the war in the deep jungle. 'The way one operated taking patrols into clearings was that you'd refuel at the forts,' explains Woodard. 'So you would be flying fuel tins into a fort for three sorties and then using them to leap-frog you on to another one for another two sorties to the one where you wanted to get to at the end, from where you could fly in and out of a clearing without refuelling. The jungle forts in the main were used as fuelling bases, which we kept topped up. You would climb out and refuel your own helicopter from the five-gallon drums. They were made out of shiny tin and all the natives adored them. There was a currency in used fuel cans. They made roofs out of them and cooking utensils.'

By this time the SAS had also begun to get its act together. Back in Aldershot John Woodhouse had devised a system of training and selection designed to weed out unsuitable volunteers: 'We put them under great physical pressure, long marching and so on, until they were exhausted, to see whether they were still determined to join the SAS. The other side of selection was to see whether they were sufficiently intelligent, and right from that early stage, too, we emphasised that they had to be self-disciplined. We were looking for men who would act on their own initiative and that right from the beginning was very important to us.' Woodhouse made it a rule that, contrary to standard Army practice, 'no troops were to be inspected before they went on operations. Right from the start the SAS soldiers were told, "That is your responsibility and unless you turn up with all the right kit you're no good to us, because no one's going to be a nanny and run round and tell you what to do. We shall tell you that you've got to be on a lorry at six o'clock tomorrow morning at such and such a place. The lorry goes at six o'clock and if you're not there you'll be left behind and, as far as we're concerned, you're left behind for ever, because we shan't want to see you again." So that sort of self-discipline started at selection and was carried on, of course, in the regiment.'

One of the few out of many hopefuls who survived this ruthless selection procedure was 'Geordie' Lillico, who remembers how the enthusiasm of his instructors 'had us all thinking and breathing Special Forces type tactics and ideas. The sort of screaming school mentality of the line infantry where they treat you all as semi-morons and the attitude that the louder the shouting the more comprehensible it would be, that didn't cut any ice with the SAS. What they were looking for was the ability to comprehend, to be told once without having to be shouted at, to grasp it, and to go ahead and do what was required.' Even after his draft had arrived in Malaya Lillico had to survive the regiment's own jungle training course before he was finally assigned to 'D' Squadron. This took place in an operational area and 'a lot of blokes used to get RTUd [returned to unit] for being caught too far away from their weapons. Your weapon in the regiment always had to be within picking-up distance.'

The situation in the regiment was now very different from that of four years earlier. 'The SAS techniques were being honed to perfection,' declares Lillico. The cult of self-discipline meant that 'within reason the blokes used to be allowed to select whatever weapon really suited them.' The choice was between the lightweight

American M1 carbine – 'all right if you got a clean hit but we had cases where bandits ran maybe several hundred yards with three or four carbine rounds in them'; the Australian Owen 9mm sub-machine gun, which was 'one of the most popular'; the old bolt-action No. 5 Lee-Enfield – 'a perfectly good weapon provided you could get the round in'; and the American pump-action Remington shotgun with the barrel sawn down – 'the perfect lead-scout weapon'. Each troop also had its Bren light machine gun. 'The youngest member of the troop was always lumbered with the LMG,' remembers Lillico. 'I inherited my machine gun when I first joined 17 Troop from a character called Jigger Johnson from the Green Howards.'

Another SAS characteristic that Lillico observed when he joined 'D' Squadron was that 'the men tended to make do and mend as regards their equipment. They used to stitch and make up their own magazine carriers so that the magazines were in a position where you could do a rapid quick change. In all these professional little points they were streets ahead of the infantry.' The pattern now was for each squadron to spend three months in the jungle followed by a fortnight's leave and then ten days' 'rest and retraining consisting of an awful lot of weapons work. You always strove to get the drop on the opposition, so consequently great emphasis was placed on immediate action drills, the contact drills, plus we used to expend an awful lot of ammunition.'

John Woodhouse, too, found that things had greatly improved when he returned, after a four-year absence, for a second spell of active service in Malaya in 1955. Coming back to resume command of 'D' Squadron, he was full of ideas for further improvements: 'I'd had two years to reflect on what had gone wrong and by the time I came back I had a very clear idea of what we should be doing.' With the encouragement of his commanding officer, Colonel George Lea, he set about putting his ideas to the test:

> I was so obsessed by our failures in the Malayan Scouts and the
> necessity of having the highest possible battle-discipline standard
> that I was very ruthless with people who failed to live up to this.
> This applied particularly to the officers. We did, unfortunately,
> have to remove a number of people, and we probably removed one
> or two people who shouldn't have been. If, for example, I went to
> visit a troop and I found some signs of their presence in the form
> of, say, a ration tin lying on the track, I naturally sent for the troop
> commander for an explanation and if this happened more than
> once, unless he had a very remarkable explanation – somebody
> attached to him who was untrained or something – he was out. The

severity of it, I think, did cause people to sit up with a bit of a jerk and realise that only the top standards were going to be good enough or you wouldn't survive in the regiment.

As a squadron commander Woodhouse had his own method of dealing with any form of carelessness, which was to 'send the individual concerned out of the camp some fifty or sixty yards on his own in the jungle, where he had to listen and would be too afraid to just go to sleep again.' It is said that a soldier who had shown carelessness in handling grenades was made to do sentry duty holding a grenade with the pin removed.

Other significant developments in SAS thinking also came into being at this time. 'We had no standard operational procedures in writing and Colonel Lea was very keen to encourage the interchange of ideas between different squadrons and to make sure that this got passed on,' Woodhouse recalls. 'During 1955 and 1956 I produced a whole series of notes under such headings as "A base is to be a hive not a nest", which encouraged people to do what Mike Calvert had taught me.' In between operations Woodhouse would set his squadron tactical exercises on paper that involved the troopers as well as his troop commanders and senior NCOs. He also introduced another practice that was to become very much a Special Forces characteristic:

> Obviously, we had to study Communist political theories of insurrection. I was very impressed by reports from surrendered or captured enemy personnel of the terrorist self-criticism sessions. In the camp of a terrorist platoon the commander would encourage individuals to say where or how they thought operations had gone wrong or right and this was conducted in a sort of circle chaired by the commander. I thought there was much to be said for it and did the same thing in my squadron, where I encouraged troops to sit down and talk freely with their troop commander about what was happening. It was best done very informally, because when we were not on operations we frequently went off to camp on the beach where we did some shooting and minor tactical training. The officers and men in the evening would be sitting drinking beer around the camp fire and it was in that sort of atmosphere that these discussions could be developed.

In more orthodox military units this 'Chinese parliament' system would have led to breakdown of discipline. Even in the SAS it imposed certain strains, particularly for new troop commanders who found themselves up against 'the old soldiers' syndrome of saying,

"Well, we didn't do this in Borneo" or "It was like this in Malaya." '
As time went on young officers who had passed the selection courses
to join the regiment for a two-year period as troop commanders
found themselves commanding troopers who were far more experienced and who often had more specialist skills than they. In
'Geordie' Lillico's experience it took five or six years before a
trooper could claim he was paying his way in the regiment:

> We used to reckon as a thumbnail judgement that a bloke wasn't
> really giving the taxpayer his money's worth in the SAS until he'd
> done at least two tours, because by that time he'd had the
> experience of visiting maybe one or two theatres of operations.
> He'd been 'stress-tested', as you might say. He'd also acquired one
> or two vital skills, whether it was demolitions, communications,
> medics – the main three – plus his troop skills: free-fall parachuting,
> amphibious work, mobile work, mountaineering, Arctic winter
> warfare and so on. Even if on operations officers found themselves
> commanding a patrol with maybe a lance-corporal and two
> troopers, all the moves would be done with the Chinese parliament
> within the patrol. The officer would always say, 'Right, this, that
> and the other is the situation.' And the boys would all throw their
> tuppence-ha'pennyworth in and then they decided on a move. He
> would always consult the other three blokes, so you've got four
> heads better than one.

From the officer's point of view, commanding SAS troopers where
'each man is a strong individualist, invariably a strong personality,
with a mind of his own, who spoke two languages, maybe, could
operate on you and take your appendix out, who could blow up a
very large bridge very economically' was never easy. Commanding
them 'was like a Permanent Regular Commissions Board,' recalls
Johnny Watts, who was to follow John Woodhouse as 22 SAS
Regiment's commanding officer in later years, 'because if you don't
come out with the right answer some joker stands up and says
"bloody rubbish" and tells you where you're wrong. So although it
was a great joy to command them, a band of brothers together, they
weren't the easiest fellows. They didn't suffer fools gladly.'

Johnny Watts first joined this 'band of brothers' in 1955 as a troop
commander, returning for a second tour three years later when he
assumed command of 'D' Squadron. By that stage the guerrillas had
been divided into isolated bands and were living very much like
hunted animals deep in the forest. When Johor State in the south was
declared 'white' in December 1958, only two significant 'black' areas
remained: a small pocket in Negri Sembilan in central Malaya and a

very much larger area in the north where the States of Perak and Kedah adjoined the border with Thailand. This was where 'D' Squadron concentrated most of its efforts in the last phase of the Emergency, following the now familiar routine of intensive three-month patrols which, even when they failed to produce contacts or kills, 'destabilised the bandit infrastructure and always kept them off-balance'. At the same time Calvert's battle of hearts and minds continued to be waged. 'The Government policy was to establish a number of big settlements called forts mainly along the spine in deep jungle where the aboriginals were,' explains Johnny Watts:

> Some were nomadic, others more slash and burn and grow food and move on. They used to be persecuted by the Chiefs in Malaya because they were looked down upon as *Untermenschen*, you might say, so many of them feared the outside world. The bandits used them as a surveillance screen. They gave them protection and support so we had to try and subvert this screen that the bandits had. You made contact with them and persuaded them to come into these settlements where they could get food, medical treatment, perhaps use the schooling or perhaps work of some sort, working for the Forestry Department.

Some of the aboriginals had been 'totally subverted' and were regarded as 'hostiles' – with good reason:

> They had a very effective method of keeping you on your toes by erecting spear traps, which they used for hunting. They would make a bamboo spear six to eight feet long and it would be drawn back on a whippy branch and camouflaged. To catch a pig it would be set at knee height and the first thing you knew was that you had set off the trip-wire and 'Shoogh!' – this thing would come out – and we had a number of chaps transfixed. A friend of mine was, through both thighs. I mean the force of the thing just went through one side into the other and out and he was absolutely fixed, lying on the ground. A hostile aboriginal who didn't like you would set them at chest height and this was terrifying and certainly slowed up your operations. I remember a mountain called Gunong Suku, a huge mountain and I spent one year operating round its base and halfway up. A lot of aboriginals were there and a particular group were very hostile, always setting the spear traps for us. So the answer was to tie a piece of bamboo maybe a couple of feet long to the end of your rifle and if you were the leading scout you made sure this was always in front of you and could set anything off. Suddenly – 'Shoogh!' – and huge spears would whizz past your nose!

One especially antagonistic group of aboriginals that Watts wanted to make contact with was led by a chief named Galla. They proved to be extremely elusive:

> One evening an SAS patrol smelled cooking and crept up thinking it might be bandits. In fact, it was three aboriginals cooking a tortoise over a little fire. There they were, stark naked with blow-pipes, enjoying themselves and so my chaps crept up on them, jumped on them and overpowered them. I suppose the SAS chaps smelt a lot and had beards and these chaps were absolutely petrified because they had never seen a European before. They were shaking with fear. We kept two and let the third one go in the morning with a gift of an axe and said, 'Look, if you've got any friends, you know, bring them in.' Anyway, this chap went off and in the afternoon he came back with three other people. I think there was a woman and a couple of kids.

Over the next few weeks other members of the tribe began to appear, many with illnesses and skin diseases that could be treated, until more than a hundred and thirty had been assembled in a special camp that was being built for them. Finally, Galla himself appeared. Watts remembers him as a 'very dignified individual, a fine-looking chap, absolutely starkers, and when we sat down his first words to me – through one of my own aboriginals who spoke Negrito – were to thank me for looking after his people'. What particularly impressed the soldiers was the way in which the group looked after its weaker members: 'They were the most charming people and I think all of us learned a lot from them.'

The purpose of making contact with the aboriginals was, of course, to win them over to the Government cause, using food and medical care as the principal inducements. And as the aboriginals learned about the ways of the outside world, so the SAS 'hearts and minds' teams learned from them. 'Geordie' Lillico particularly remembers their eating habits, which embraced 'any type of protein. They used to amaze us with the amount of snakes they used to catch. They never gutted them or nothing, they just used to throw them on our fire, burn them till all the scales was gone off it and eat everything, the intestines, the brains, the lot.' Python was found to be pleasantly palatable if well cooked – 'like a nice white meat, really, like a heavily-fleshed fish like tuna'. But the troopers drew the line at eating bats: 'We were taking a breather in this bamboo grove and this abo porter he was tapping with the back of his *parang* the various dead bits of bamboo where there were holes until he detected one where he got a rustle inside. He quickly hacked it open and pulled out these little baby bats and just ate them like sweeties in front of us, you know.'

However, the contact between the two different cultures was not always to the advantage of both sides, as Johnny Watts had to witness when, as part of a plan to keep the aboriginals away from terrorist influence, Galla's tribe was led out of the jungle into a specially-built settlement:

> The sad thing about Galla was that we had orders to send his group out for resettlement and off they went on several days' march and were met by the Protector of Aboriginals and staff. And I had an awful inkling that these people were going to be somehow corrupted by modern life, that it was going to be too much of a shock for them, and very sadly they *were* quickly corrupted. People came along to buy the aboriginal girls for the proverbial string of beads or a looking glass, VD started to spread among the group, they started to steal from each other, which was absolutely unheard of when they used to share everything before, and the whole sort of moral family structure started to break down in the group. And this chap Galla, whom I had always admired so much, one day he realised what was happening to his group and he realised obviously that the Government wasn't going to let them go, so if they wanted to go back into the jungle they had to do a bunk. So one night when everything closed down he called the lot together and gave his orders and said, 'Right, we're off, just carry what you can.' When the administrators arrived at the camp next morning they'd gone and Galla had taken them all back into deep jungle, presumably in his eyes to save the integrity, dignity and standards of his group, and I was delighted when I heard about it.

After eight years of jungle operations in Malaya 22 SAS finally left Malaya at the end of 1958. By then CTs had become very scarce indeed and the last operation that 'Geordie' Lillico's 17 Troop went on in a supposedly 'hot' area produced nothing more hostile than a tiger.

The official ending of the twelve-year Emergency in July 1960 was celebrated with a victory parade through the streets of Kuala Lumpur. The MRLA had been destroyed as a terrorist organisation in Malaya, leaving only a rump of hard-core terrorists still dedicated to the struggle. Under the command of their leader, Chin Peng, they found refuge in jungle camps in southern Thailand, making only rare forays across the border to visit their remaining aboriginal allies in Malaya. Attempts by the armed forces to trap these intruders met with little success, culminating in one final effort made by the 1st/7th

Gurkhas in 1961-62. Here a key role in winning over a hostile Temiar tribe of aboriginals in Upper Perak was played by John Cross, whose exceptional gifts for picking up local dialects and making friends with tribal peoples helped him to convert Chin Peng's leading ally: 'The Special Branch had frozen the area in which this man lived and did not allow anyone else to go in, but I went in and I managed to get him on to my side to the extent that his son, his cousin and his brother acted as my aboriginal screen against Chin Peng, who had made him headman of that area. I asked the man who was the cousin whether he would go fishing with me – for fish with two legs. The answer was "Yes", and the upshot was that I was allowed to go in.' Led by these three aboriginals and carrying only enough rations to allow them-selves six and a half ounces of food per man per day, Cross and ten of his Gurkhas initially spent seven weeks in concealment waiting 'for bandits who had not been seen for five years', only to miss their prey by a hundred yards: 'I was told they were not coming – and after they had gone I was told they had been.'

Despite this disappointment, Cross took a second party into the same area, again using the aboriginals as a screen: 'They set up a pattern of hunting which, in fact, would be patrolling and I would come in and stay in the middle, and if any of the bandits came down from Thailand then we would deal with them. For one period of fifty-three days and nights I lived in a patch of jungle the size of a tennis court. It rained from day nine to thirty-nine and I learned patience then.' Again, his party missed the CTs by the narrowest of margins: 'As we walked out so they came in. It was coincidental, not occasioned by our movement. They had waited in Thailand longer than they would normally have done so as to get a shipment of clothing and weapons still with the Americans in Vietnam.' A third foray, this time lasting eighty days, proved in the end to be just as frustrating – and very unsettling: 'It so happened that we were in an aboriginal graveyard and we were haunted day and night, which didn't help things.' Just as information came in that a party of CTs were on their way over the border the trap had to be abandoned. An emergency wireless message had been received from headquarters ordering all troops of the 1st/7th out of the jungle with all speed.

When Cross and his little party finally emerged they were so weak and disorientated that they were on the verge of collapse:

> When we started walking the mile from where we'd been hiding to where the troops had been helicoptered in it took four hours. I ran out of strength to the extent that I could not get one leg in front of the other. I looked down at my feet from a very great height and

wondered why it was I couldn't get any forward movement and I realised that my right leg was behind my left. It struck me that I had to get my right leg in front of my left before I could move. We were hallucinating and everything was going upside down. It was an extraordinary feeling. Eventually, when we got to where my men were, some broke out crying. Gurkha soldiers don't often cry but I'd known them for ten years. I couldn't stand, I couldn't sit. I just put me down and wept like a child.

In fact, there was good reason for the 1st/7th Gurkhas' sudden order to pull out of the Malayan jungle. A rebellion had just broken out in Brunei and a second jungle war was about to begin.

Chapter Five

BORNEO:
A Flare-up in the Far East

The Borneo campaign was the first real campaign where it was run by all regular troops. There were no National Servicemen there. They were all volunteers and regulars and the camaraderie used to be remarkable. Sometimes you could listen at nights when you were back in base to the voice nets of the various infantry regiments and identify them just by the accents. You know, you could hear the King's Own Yorkshire Light Infantry with their Yorkshire accents, you could hear the Argylls with the Jock accents, the Ulster Rifles with the Belfast accents, the Aussies with their drawls, Johnny Gurkhas and the old Malays chuntering away.

When the Brunei Rebellion began in December 1962 the commander of 17 Gurkha Division, based in Singapore, was five days' march from the nearest airfield in Nepal. Major-General Sir Walter Walker had checked with general headquarters before setting out to visit Gurkha pensioners in the Himalayas and had been told that all was well. 'I was surprised when they said that the coast was clear because my intelligence said the exact opposite,' he recalls. 'There were some people – I was one of them – who believed there was going to be a flare-up in the Far East.' Indeed, intelligence had been received and ignored. At least one senior Special Branch officer in Sarawak was known to have been reporting for months that there was instability and unrest in both Kuching, the capital of Sarawak, and in Brunei: 'This had gone back to GHQ but it had not been terribly well received because at that time the political feeling was that Britain wanted to give independence not just to Malaya but to Singapore, Sarawak, North Borneo and Brunei and to bring about Greater Malaysia. The political feeling was that "We don't want any trouble." Therefore, they were ignoring it.'

With the ending of the Emergency the Gurkhas had found themselves without any role to play in the British Army's future plans. Ordered to retrain his troops for internal security duties in

Singapore, Walter Walker had more or less refused: 'I altered that to read: "On *no* account will the Division consider its primary task to be internal security in a city. Our primary task is to be able to move at the drop of a hat to wherever there may be a conflagration – and the person who will win is the person who can get there quickest with the mostest." ' In the event, while the Gurkhas were prepared, their commander was caught on the hop and had to catch up with events as best he could. 'I had a good wireless set with my ADC and he was listening to the news in the morning and at the same time frying an egg and heard that the Brunei revolt had broken out. So we did a forced march – we did the five days in one day – and a Dakota picked us up and I got to Singapore where the Commander-in-Chief briefed me. He saw me off and said, "See you in three months." I said, "Three years", and he just looked at me as though to say, "Walker's riding his hobby horse, as usual".'

The two British colonies of Sarawak and North Borneo, with the little protectorate of Brunei sandwiched in between, occupied an eight-hundred-mile strip of territory along the north-western seaboard of the huge tropical island of Borneo. The rest of the island belonged to Indonesia, whose President, Sukarno, had ambitions to bring the whole island under Indonesian leadership. When, in 1962, plans were drawn up in Whitehall and Kuala Lumpur to link Brunei, North Borneo, Sarawak, Malaya and Singapore into a Federation of Malaysia, President Sukarno saw his plans threatened and began a policy of what he termed '*Konfrontasi*' or Confrontation. In Brunei the *Partai Raayatt* (People's Party) broadly supported Sukarno's aims and, when their elected delegates on the Sultan of Brunei's Legislative Council were outvoted by the Sultan's own nominees, they turned to armed revolt. Fifteen companies of largely unarmed volunteers were secretly raised and trained under the command of Yassin Affandi, an eight-thousand-strong force known as the TNKU (North Kalimantan National Army). At two a.m. on Saturday, 8 December 1962, Affandi launched his coup with the intention of taking the Sultan hostage, capturing the main police stations and seizing the important Seria oilfield.

In Singapore Bruce Jackman had only just joined his battalion, the 1st/2nd Gurkhas: 'I was the newcomer with no experience and everyone around me down almost to the newest-joined Rifleman was wearing a campaign medal.' To the men he was still the '*Sano Sahib*' or 'little officer', a label that all junior subalterns in the Gurkhas carried until such time as they had proved themselves. Down in Singapore on weekend leave from his jungle warfare training course, he had retired to bed after seeing a film with some of his brother subalterns: 'I was woken about an hour later by the Duty Officer who flew into my room and said, "Get up, Jackers, it's war", and shot out again.' Jackman went back to sleep, believing this to be an exercise in which he had no part to play. A few hours later he was woken by his orderly 'in a high state of agitation, shouting, "Sahib, *larain*", which basically was, "Sir, it's war". I told him to calm down, we were nothing to do with this.'

That very same evening Jackman was being 'as sick as a dog' on board a navy destroyer with eighty equally prostrate Gurkhas as his first command, a company of Gurkhas from the 1st/2nd having already taken off by air for a dawn landing on Brunei airfield. In fact, the Queen's Own Highlanders should have gone in first since Brunei was their area of responsibility but they had been unable to muster enough men at such short notice:

> The extraordinary thing about the Brunei Rebellion was that it came out of the blue – no notice, no warning at all. The Queen's Own Highlanders were unable to raise a company because they were dispersed around the island, being a heavily-married battalion. The Gurkhas, being based within a barrack, were able to respond quickly and we were able to get together 'D' Company in four hours to Changi. However, it wasn't our area, nobody had heard of Brunei, we didn't have any maps, we had none of the operating procedures and even the Ordnance Depot had to be broken into to get ammunition as the man with the key for that was on holiday up-country. So there were a lot of people caught napping.

The RAF, too, was not performing at its best, according to Walter Walker: 'The brigade commander got down to the airfield at Changi where he found each Gurkha being religiously weighed. He knew that the first thing that we had to do at Brunei was to get the airfield and that every second counted so he literally kicked the Air Force up the arse and said, "You know perfectly well that a Gurkha weighs far less than a British soldier and that we've got to get them to Brunei as quickly as possible." And that was achieved by the skin of our teeth.'

Also stationed in Singapore was 42 Commando, of which Jeremy Moore was commanding a company. On the Sunday he was writing Christmas cards in his room when he was summoned to the Colonel's room: 'I went along and was greeted at the door with, "Jeremy, how quickly can you move your Company?" and that was the first I knew about the Brunei Revolt. Once we were assembled the Colonel said, "Right, Peter," referring to the senior company commander. To which the Adjutant said, "Afraid we haven't managed to get Peter yet, Sir. He's up-country with his family but the second-in-command's here." "Oh," said the Colonel. "Well, Tim." "Tim's water-skiing, Sir." "Oh," said the Colonel. "Well, in that case, Jeremy, you will have to be first company to go," which was how I got to be the one who did the Limbang operation.'

Meanwhile, in Brunei, the Gurkhas had swept through Brunei Town fighting a series of sharp skirmishes in which they themselves suffered casualties. 'I remember the stark message that came to me when I saw the first wounded,' Bruce Jackman recalls. 'Suddenly I realised this was no exercise. This was for real. I remember very clearly, too, seeing the prisoners in the cinema. Hundreds of them had been roped in as a result of our sweep through the town. The SIB [Special Investigation Branch] and the Police were in among them carrying out interrogations and interviews, but that was the first time in my life, again, I'd ever seen real prisoners and the looks of anguish on some of their faces.'

The next priority was to recapture Seria, where a large number of European oil workers were being held as hostages. Driving through the night along Brunei's only major road in commandeered vehicles, the Gurkhas came up against a series of ambushes. The next morning units of the Queen's Own Highlanders landed at Anduki Airfield and began to clear Seria town. Soon after the Gurkhas had linked up with them Jackman had his first real taste of action: 'We did the attack on Kuala Belait. We didn't really know what was there and we had a lot of young soldiers in the company, a lot of recruits, so Terry Bowring ('B' company commander) put the assault pioneers, who were all old soldiers, up front and they did a classic one-up advance-to-contact down the only road towards Kuala Belait. When they came under fire their return of fire was so effective that I remember seeing rebels leaping out of these houses-on-stilts because, of course, as they were made of wood an SLR round was going through not just one wall but through several houses, and they were literally flushed out under the weight of fire.' In the house-clearing that followed the Gurkhas received not a single casualty.

The next major action that Jackman took part in was equally free of casualties. This was to be a three-company attack on what was believed to be a rebel stronghold on the shore at Muara, involving a beach assault from the sea:

> The first thing that went wrong was when I tried to use my initiative and took over the driving of one of our commandeered tipper sand lorries that was going to transport the company to the vessel. The local driver had fled and in the pitch dark I selected the wrong lever and pitched the entire platoon out on to the road. After that

blunder we eventually got on board the ferry and took off into the
night. The idea was that we would hit the beach at dawn with a
synchronised, two Hunter air strike going down the beach, so for
me this was a very big attack and I thought of the Second World
War and Dunkirk and that sort of thing. Well, come the moment
and we chugged into the blackness towards the coastline all
crouched down behind this steel plating. The sun rose, the Hunters
came and went and didn't fire anything, and we were still at sea
because the tide was going out faster than we were going in, so we
were making no headway at all. Well, the tide turned and at about
eleven o'clock, a very long time later, we made it to the beach. The
ramps went down and there was a surge forward – which stopped.
The second-in-command screamed at everyone to get going, fought
his way through to the front and threw himself into ten feet of
water. We were actually on a sandbank and the first Gurkhas who'd
thrown themselves in had to be fished out. So we had to wait for
the tide to go out a bit before we could wade ashore. That was our
beach assault. No opposition. We did take a prisoner. He was a
fisherman casting his net into the water and was very surprised to
be frog-marched by me all the way down the road to the police
station. So this huge amount of adrenalin was expended on
absolutely nothing and I remember at the end of it we all felt
terribly flat.

The situation remained very confused for several days, with
reports coming in from all sides of towns seized and British hostages
held. Trouble was said to be brewing in the rubber plantations of
Tawau in neighbouring North Borneo, where the labour force was
largely Indonesian, so 'B' Company of the 1st/2nd Gurkhas were
flown up in a Beverley. 'We drove out of the aircraft looking terribly
fierce,' Jackman remembers, 'with machine guns on Land Rovers
and soldiers running out of both sides, taking up fire positions on the
side of this grass strip that we landed on, terribly professional,
terribly war-like, ready to take on the whole world. And we were met
by the most extraordinary sight: all the residents, the Brits and
everybody, with huge trestle tables of food and drink and a small
band playing.' After five days spent driving around the rubber
plantations 'with the Union Jack flying, bristling with machine guns
but everybody lining the route waving', they were recalled to Brunei.

However, by no means were all the reports that came in exagger-
ated. At Bangar a number of government officials had been held
hostage and then murdered – and in the up-river town of Limbang,
which was only accessible by river, rebel forces had seized the British

Resident and his wife as well as other hostages and were threatening their execution, too.

The task of rescuing them was given to Jeremy Moore's 'L' Company: 'My mission that I'd been given by Brigadier Patterson was "Release the hostages!", but I didn't know how many or where they were. All we knew was that there was a Resident and a number of hostages held by what was thought to be not less than a hundred and fifty rebels. That was it. I had a map that had Limbang marked with a little dot about a millimetre across and one ten-year-old photograph which didn't show all the buildings. The problem was that if I just approached cautiously I feared that the enemy would be likely to use the hostages either by bringing them out or by threatening to shoot them.' Moore realised, too, that he had to 'prevent the enemy from having time to think about what to do with the hostages and that meant getting immediately to the heart of the enemy position and either releasing the hostages or at least separating the enemy commander from them'. His best chance of taking the rebels by surprise lay in making a direct assault on the town from the river at first light, using two commandeered cargo lighters operated by Royal Navy crews – 'the chap who was commanding that little naval group was Jeremy Black and that was the first time we went to war together'. The next time was in the Falklands, where Captain Black commanded HMS *Invincible*.

As Moore had already discovered in Malaya, events rarely followed the course predicted for them. As the two vessels came round the river bend below Limbang town the noise of their engines quickly gave them away: 'When we got about three hundred yards down-river from the police station suddenly the whole town erupted like an ants' nest. Then, of course, the firefight started and at that point the leading craft on which I was drove straight at the bank immediately by the police station and the first two sections, led by their troop commander, went ashore.'

Watching the landing from the second boat was Corporal David Greenhough:

> The full weight of fire from the bank coming towards us – which included a light machine gun – sort of threw our plans into disarray and it was suddenly decided that the leading boat would go in and land the troops ashore, and then the rear boat would give them as acute a cover from the Vickers machine gun as was possible. From where we were I could see the leading boat beach and I could also see people dropping as they got ashore. Then one or two people in our boat started getting hit. A friend of mine beside me, a guy

called 'Scouse' Kearings – most unlucky guy – got hit in the neck and also our commander, 'Soapy' Waters, who was up in the driving seat, he got his and he was shouting a bit. The naval midshipman at this stage was calling for the next Marine commander. My sergeant-major was shouting with the troop sergeants at the time to get their heads down, so without further ado, the middy then said to us, 'Right, stand by, Number Two craft, I'm putting you ashore', and he just aimed the boat and I heard the revs increase and we stood by to land.

The leading assault party had already sustained serious casualties from a single, very accurate machine gun and from a great number of shotguns that proved to be lethal at close range. The second assault party now took further casualties as they came ashore, landing 'in the Limbang "gash shoot", where the villagers threw everything into the river, so we smelt a little during the course of that particular day. One guy from our boat got hit, not too badly, as we got ashore. Also, as I landed, I felt heat in my boot for some reason. I paid no particular attention to this until much later in the day when I realised I'd picked up a couple of shotgun pellets.'

Greenhough's troop had originally been tasked to come in at the bottom of the town to cut off the rebels as they attempted to escape. Instead, they had to fight their way round the edge of the town:

My section and I attempted to clear each house by normal training, going in from the top, working our way down. This was my first experience of close-quarter or house clearing and I felt rather light-headed about it as opposed to fearful – on a high, if you like, with adrenalin running. You revert automatically to the training you've been given and one only notices the odd things as one goes. Initially, one is attempting to fire at anything that appears to be shaped like an enemy and moves and I think we killed two cats in the process, but after a couple of houses you do, in fact, react to what's going on and if people are sitting there with their hands up you don't actually fire at them, until by the end of the row of houses it became almost blasé – although we had a couple of casualties, people going through corrugated iron roofs. It sounds, in the way I've portrayed it, as if it happened in minutes but, in fact, it took us nearly all day, living on one's nerves a little bit.

Meanwhile, in the leading tender Jeremy Moore had been having his own problems. As the craft beached the sailor driving it had been hit and the boat had drifted away from the shore. When it eventually returned to the bank Moore followed the troop that was clearing the hospital area of the town. He then heard a voice from inside the hospital 'croaking a ditty to the tune of *Coming round the Mountain* which ran, "They'll be wearing bright green bonnets when they come, they'll be wearing bright green bonnets, but they won't be singing sonnets." This was the Resident, who'd made up this rhyme in order to make sure that if it was the Commandos he wouldn't be mistakenly shot, and it was amusing to be able to walk into the hospital and to introduce myself and say, "But you were wrong" – and pull a book of Shakespeare's Sonnets out of my map pocket! We discovered afterwards that there had been a plan to hang the Resident and his wife that day, so in that sense we barely arrived in time.'

While rescuing the hostages, however, there had been a 'very nasty little action' at the hospital in which two Marines and their troop sergeant were killed. 'It was very close action and it was all shotgun wounds,' Moore recalls. The troop commander and a corporal had also been injured and so a certain amount of reorganisation had to be done:

> I then gave orders to the two brand new troop commanders to do some street clearing. They looked a little blank and I said, "Have you not done anything about street clearing in your training to date?" and they said, "No, sir." So we conducted the familiar military exercise of a TEWT [tactical exercise without troops] under fire as I ran them through how you cleared buildings in street fighting. Now the Marines were all right, they knew what to do, but their troop commanders didn't! So it was a funny little incident which shows that you can't cut corners on training people.

The death of five Marines, with another eight wounded, was a high price to pay but the speed and the vigour of the action at Limbang, on top of other actions by the 1st/2nd Gurkhas and the Queen's Own Highlanders, 'completely broke the revolt. It took quite a long time for all the rebels to be rounded up but they were on the run from then on.' There was, of course, great sadness for the men in Jeremy Moore's 'L' Company – which became known thereafter as Limbang Company, with the anniversary being celebrated annually by 42 Commando as 'Limbang Day' – but Moore had no doubt that 'it was the right thing to have done and I think it did bring the revolt to an end – and one has got to remember that being prepared to face the fact that you may be killed is, ultimately, the undertaking that a serviceman gives. That is what we are all in it to give if we are called upon to do so.'

The 1st Green Jackets – formed in 1958 from the remnants of the old 'Ox and Bucks' under the Sandys reorganisation of the Army and the first all-regular battalion to be sent out East since the ending of conscription in 1961 – had arrived in Malaya in the spring of 1962. Based on Penang Island, they hardly expected to be drawn into the Brunei operations, but were ordered to move to Singapore with all speed. Within six hours the entire battalion – 'except for four people who couldn't be found' – was on the road. Motoring right through the night the convoy reached Kuala Lumpur by breakfast and Singapore by nightfall: 'We had two drivers per vehicle, one good and one not so good, and on arrival at Singapore we were told to drive straight to the docks.'

This came as a bit of a shock to the battalion. Instead of taking over internal security duties in Singapore, more or less the entire battalion was packed aboard the cruiser HMS *Tiger*: 'The normal scale the Navy allowed was one hundred and twenty-five soldiers, the absolute maximum was supposed to be two hundred and twenty-five. We left that night with six hundred and eighty-nine soldiers on board, several armoured vehicles and tons and tons of stores all over the ship. It was a remarkable effort by the Navy and as he pulled away from the dockside the Captain was heard to say, "For God's sake, let's sail before we sink".'

While at sea the battalion's new commander, Colonel 'Todd' Sweeney, was informed that they should prepare to make an opposed landing at the oil town of Miri, just south of the Brunei border in Sarawak. 'We hit the beach expecting opposition,' recalls Robin Evelegh, then a young subaltern. 'I and all the others scampered up it pretty fast to be met by the Mayor of Miri with a speech of welcome. I've seldom felt such a fool in my life – although we weren't really fools because we'd beaten the rebels to it by four hours.'

Two towns in the area were known to have been taken over by the rebels. Dividing his forces, Sweeney sent a company of Green Jackets off to each town, using two ex-Service landing craft borrowed from the Shell Oil Company, while the third company remained on board HMS *Tiger*. Just as the two companies were leaving, news came in of the casualties sustained by the Royal Marines in their gallant assault on Limbang, which prompted Sweeney to order his company commanders to make the final approaches by land rather than by river, if that was possible. For Robin Evelegh and his company, tasked to recapture Bekanu, thirty miles south of Miri by river, this meant making an exhausting encirclement of the town in the dark. Coming into the back of the town through a pepper plantation, they achieved total surprise:

We surged forward rather like a lot of football hooligans and immediately shot and overwhelmed a few of these people who were actually appointing civil servants as the new provisional government. They had no idea we could move so fast. Some of these rebels were trying to escape in motor boats and, because I was slightly behind the forward platoon, I could see that the shots of our soldiers were missing the river, about a hundred yards away. Therefore, I sat in a little garden, calmed myself by breathing steadily, rested my rifle between the ears of an ornamental gnome – this is absolutely true – and fired a shot at a bloke in one of the boats, who keeled over. This man swam ashore and crawled towards our soldiers. I was behind a very young soldier, very courageous but excited, who said, 'Shall I shoot him, sir? Shall I shoot him?' Anyway, we didn't shoot him and we didn't do anything to the guy except give him medical treatment.

Some of the rebels did succeed in escaping up-river but the merits of 'moving quickly and using your brains' soon became evident: 'They all surrendered that night. I think there was a total of three hundred and sixty-nine prisoners and some dead and that was the end of the revolution in that area.' The helicopter-assault carrier HMS *Hermes* had been steaming northwards, parallel to the Sarawak coast, allowing Sweeney to put the ship's complement of Wessex helicopters to good use: 'I said, "I want you to land here and here, there and there," and we did a series of journeys and dropped off the rest of this company at these areas up the river. And all this time HMS *Albion* was slowly steaming towards Brunei, its passage only slowed down a little bit, moving along while we got the use of this squadron of helicopters.' It was a very impressive piece of inter-service co-operation, leading Sweeney to reflect that 'if we'd had some of these sophisticated means of transporting troops in and out in some of our other brush-fire wars we would have stamped them out right at the very beginning.'

The young Robin Evelegh also learned an important lesson that was to be of great service a decade later when he became Colonel of the battalion. The rebel whom he had wounded proved to be a most useful informant:

He was so overwhelmed by the good treatment that he later gave a full statement of who and what was involved, and again and again in my experience if you treat prisoners well this is the best way to get information. This was also my first experience of brutality, because I and my company commander – now a very distinguished general – we came upon certain people, not actually from the

Army, who had one of these prisoners and were proceeding to kick
him. Of course, we put a stop to that straight away. You could have
kicked that guy and, okay, you would eventually have got
something out of him. If you hit somebody for long and hard
enough, they will give you some sort of an answer to the questions
that you ask them. They will tell you where there's a rifle hidden or
something but what you actually want to know is the answer to the
question you never knew you had to ask. That is the thing that is
totally concealed from you and you will only get this from a
defector by getting his co-operation. Again and again I have come
across this sort of brutal treatment of prisoners – the way of the
bully, the way of the dimwit.

Within a week some three thousand of the original four thousand
or so rebels who had participated in the rebellion as TNKU
volunteers had been captured or had surrendered themselves. Of the
remainder some fled through the jungle towards the Indonesian
border while a few went into hiding. At the top of the wanted list was
Yassin Affandi, the TNKU's military commander, but a lot of effort
also went into the hunt for the man who had organised the
insurgents' defence at Limbang, a former Police Field Force
weapons instructor named Saleh Bin Sambas. Bruce Jackman now
had his own platoon to command and for some time his life revolved
around attempts to track down Saleh Bin Sambas:

> I remember doing an ambush on his house for ten days in the belief
> that he would come back there. There was quite a lot of livestock
> running around free, piglets and chickens and ducks, and I told the
> platoon that in no circumstances were they to try and supplement
> their diet because of the possibility of giving the game away with a
> squawking chicken or a grunting piglet. The platoon absolutely
> obeyed the instructions and I was very pleased with them, but when
> we got back and we de-kitted just outside the platoon barrack
> block, I then heard the squawks and the grunts as the pigs and
> chickens were pulled out of packs and sacks. God knows how they
> caught them and kept them quiet.

Evidence soon came in that Saleh Bin Sambas was with a small
group of rebels hiding out in the swamps on the edge of the Brunei
River. It then became very much a 'cat and mouse game, with two
trained groups up against each other'. Acting on tip-offs, Jackman's
platoon twice came upon campsites that had only just been abandoned. Waiting in ambush at the second, Jackman and his men spent
a week 'sitting in among the mangroves with huge bull leeches and
mosquitoes'. Jackman also provided his men with a moment of light

relief by jumping on to what he took to be a pile of palm leaves and having a brief ride on the back of a crocodile.

The platoon was still deep in the swamps, enduring day after day of torrential rain, when the rivers overflowed and they found themselves in serious trouble: 'When we tried to get out the water was too deep. Fortunately, we hit a rubber estate and the Gurkhas literally chopped down a line of trees, one rubber tree falling into the next, and then we had to go hand over hand along the rubber trees to get out.'

The floods had devastated the whole of the coastal belt of the Brunei region. All ideas of continuing the campaign against the rebels went out of the window as a major relief operation began. 'We became tied up with saving civilians,' Jackman remembers, 'saving livestock, pulling buffaloes out of trees, rescuing whole villages by boat, and one began to get very much involved with the community.'

Equally involved were the helicopters and men of 845 and 848 Squadrons flying support for 40 Royal Marine Commando on board HMS *Albion*. David Storrie, one of two Royal Marine pilots flying Wessex helicopters, was switched from supporting the troops on the ground to 'lifting people out of flooded areas and ferrying them rice and stores'. Fortuitously, the floods gave them a chance to 'use our position not just as the putters down of a rebellion which probably had quite a lot of popular support, but to do a great hearts and minds job'. As a result, the British forces soon came to be seen 'not as oppressors but as people capable of helping the local populace and being very caring'. This, together with the fact that 'the locals were fed up with road blocks, curfews and the mortaring of the odd swamp that we'd been doing just to remind people that we were around', helped to convince the local population that the revolt had had its day. The 1st/2nd Gurkhas were replaced by the 2nd/7th and it was their 'B' Company which had the satisfaction of bringing the Brunei Revolt to its conclusion. Led by an informant, a section of Gurkhas under Major David Cutfield flushed Yassin Affandi and Saleh Bin Sambas out of the swamps. A cordon had been set up which the wanted men tried to rush, firing as they ran forward. A newly-joined Rifleman, Naina Bahadur Rai, shot the first two members of the party dead, wounded both Affandi and Bin Sambas and captured the remaining two. All were brought to Limbang where the Gurkhas' signals officer, Mike Allen, found himself having to donate his own blood to keep Saleh Bin Sambas alive:

> A pint of my blood was given to him while he had an operation on his leg and, I have to admit, I assumed he was being spared so that

he could be brought to court and hanged for murder. However, his crimes had been committed in Sarawak and therefore he was sent back to Sarawak and stood trial in Kuching. I don't know how many years he got but the sentence was subsequently commuted and when I was in Brunei twenty years later I went back to Limbang and he was there – and we had a cup of coffee in a restaurant overlooking the scene where he had manned the machine gun back in December 1962.

General Walker had missed the first week of the Revolt, but when he did arrive in Brunei he was quick to assert his own style of leadership as Commander British Forces, Borneo, stamping his personality on what was to become known as Confrontation very much as General Templer had stamped his on the Malayan Emergency. As far as those who fought under him were concerned Walker was the 'round peg in the round hole'. He always reminded 'Fairy' Gopsill of a bird of prey, with a 'very keen eye rather like an eagle, and like an eagle he seemed to see everything. He was a man of very pronounced judgement and he did not like to be corrected. He was a good friend to us all but woe betide us if we stepped out of line, because he would not accept any shortcomings in his officers.' The General was at all times a stickler for discipline. John Cross recalls stepping out of an aircraft on which General Walker was also on board with his beret tilted rather far back on his head: 'The next day the commanding officer of my unit got a telephone call from the General to say "Why was Major Cross wearing his beret like a coal-heaver's hat?" ' All the same, Cross had a very high regard for the man he looked upon as 'my General', believing that 'some people found his character abrasive merely because he saw the threat so clearly and he didn't mind making himself uncomfortable'.

Right from the start it was Walker's contention that the abortive Brunei Revolt was merely the prelude to something much bigger: 'I had tremendous pressure brought upon me to withdraw my troops and come back [to Singapore] myself, but I realised straight away that Azahari [political leader of TNKU] was working for the Indonesians and that something else of a much more serious nature would occur. The whole time the powers-that-be were underestimating the situation – and that's always the same in war. The powers-that-be will not listen to the man on the ground who can smell the battle, read the battle, who has his own intelligence – because by then I was winning the hearts and minds of the people.'

Throughout the campaign that followed Walter Walker was to contend that his chief enemies were to be found among the top brass at the Ministry of Defence: 'I was the whole time fighting three enemies. I was fighting first of all the Indonesians, secondly the CCO [Clandestine Communist Organisation] who were the internal threat to Sarawak, and thirdly the Ministry of Defence, because their eye was always on the British Army of the Rhine and you couldn't touch what they called their war stocks. So when people came round I said, "What the hell do you think I'm fighting? I'm fighting the Indonesian regular army, there is a war and this is where your stocks should come to!" '

Walker had very clear ideas on how to prosecute the coming campaign. While flying across from Singapore to Brunei he had jotted down five main principles, with 'Jointmanship' heading the list. 'The first thing I did was to set the Army, Navy and Air Force together,' he recalls. 'The Air Force was on Labuan Island, the Navy were on their ships and the Army was in Brunei. I took over the school in Brunei, set up my office in the headmistress's study and formed a new headquarters. And I said, "From now on this will be run as a joint exercise operation. Everything will be joint, with the police as well." ' Another key principle was 'Mobility', a point that Walker impressed on a visiting admiral after the latter had given him a lecture on how best to employ helicopters from an offshore aircraft carrier: 'I said, "I'm very sorry, Admiral. The jungle where the troops are is a hundred miles away and to keep your helicopters on your ship and then fly one hundred miles to operate with the troops means that they cannot answer at the drop of a hat. So I want all your workshops off the ship and in the jungle." He looked horrified, but he accepted it.'

Walker's sixth principle – 'the Need to Win the Local People's Trust and Confidence' – he added to his list about a month after his arrival. During the early months of 1963 part of this vital battle for hearts and minds was being waged by the 1st Green Jackets:

> This was one of those marvellous periods when the soldiers
> absolutely loved it because they were in small groups scattered
> throughout these villages on stilts, longhouses they called them,
> where they all lived together for security, and doing what we called
> the hearts and minds campaign. I would go out and take with me
> my medical officer and stay up in a village and he would look at the
> sick and pull out a few teeth and repair some septic sores and so on
> and then we'd move on to the next village.

It was not, in Walter Walker's words, 'until there was a big Indonesian raid on a police station that people sat up and took notice'. This took place in April 1963, just after the Green Jackets had returned to Penang, when a party of intruders – generally designated Indonesian Border Terrorists or IBT – crossed into Sarawak and attacked a police station. At first the attackers were assumed to be members of the insurgent organisation known as the Clandestine Communist Organisation (CCO), based in Sarawak itself. In fact, the IBTs were a mixed bunch led and trained by Indonesian regular soldiers. They were to develop, in Walker's estimation, into a 'very bright, first-class enemy', some of whom had actually been trained at the Jungle Warfare School that he had helped to establish a decade earlier: 'If they were ambushed, the first thing you could expect was that mortar fire would be brought down by them on to your ambush position – and that was a technique that we had taught them.' In the early stages of Confrontation, however, the sporadic nature of the incursions across the border allowed General Walker to take a firm hold of the situation that he and his successor were never to relax.

All the lessons learned in Malaya were applied in Borneo. State Emergency Committees were quickly set up along Malayan lines, the predominantly Chinese CCO was firmly put down and the support of indigenous tribal peoples of the region, such as the Ibans or Dyaks, was actively sought. 'We had one hundred per cent co-operation from the civilian population,' avers 'Fairy' Gopsill, summoned from the Mons Officer Cadet Training School in England to raise a battalion of Ibans. 'All the Ibans were on our side and gave us every support we needed.' Finding volunteers proved to be no problem: 'I had the privilege of meeting the Temengong Juga, who is the titular head of all Ibans. He lived in Sibu and I saw him there and he gave his blessing to the battalion and of course, if he says "Jump", all Ibans jump. He said "Jump into the Army," and they came in in droves, so that it was not long before I had a first-class bunch of young men with these wonderful instructor sergeants and warrant officers and officers from all regiments of the British Army and for a period of twelve months we trained really hard.'

Unlike Malaya, however, the major threat in Borneo was an external one rather than internal, a problem compounded by the fact that the border between Indonesia and the territories of British North Borneo and Sarawak stretched for almost a thousand miles over some of the wildest country imaginable, where only the rivers offered some means of communication. For administrative purposes Sarawak – which was to become the Indonesians' main target – was divided into five regions known as Divisions. The largest was the Third, which occupied the central portion of the country with two smaller Divisions to the north and to the west. 'It was wild country, beautiful country,' remembers 'Birdie' Smith, whose 1st/7th Gurk-has were, to begin with, the only battalion in that division. 'The border with Indonesia was between three and four hundred miles. We were fortunate in having close and direct support from 845 Royal Naval Air Squadron [based in Kuching, the capital of Sarawak], but even going by helicopter it took over an hour to reach the border.'

Since Walker had only five battalions under his command the only way to police the border was to set up a local surveillance network that could feed back information of cross-border activity. 22 Special Air Service Regiment had at that time been cut back from four squadrons to two. However, its commander, John Woodhouse, was determined to find a useful role for it to play. 'We were still not written into operational planning. I was aware of this and I went to see the Director of Military Operations in the War Office and was presumptuous enough to remind him that the SAS had spent nine years in Malaya. The upshot was that I arrived in Brunei some three weeks after the outbreak of the revolt.' Walker's first thought was to use the SAS as a reserve force that could be parachuted into the jungle. Woodhouse disagreed: 'While careful not to pour too much cold water on such an idea, I did suggest to him that probably our most useful role would be to operate in two-man parties with our new radio equipment, which could communicate from the frontier back to his headquarters.'

Walker was quick to agree: 'I was soon straightened out by John Woodhouse, who was a very shrewd man indeed. He saw that I had this enormous frontier to cover and that the Indonesians could penetrate wherever. It was he who advised me to use his SAS in an eyes and ears role with a sting.' 'A' Squadron SAS was flown out – 'rather clandestinely in an old Super Constellation all in civvies' – and settled into local longhouses near the border in small four-man patrol groups. But there were not enough of them to be effective and soon after the first cross-border raid 'D' Squadron was also summoned:

'A' Squadron would have anything up to fifteen patrols
permanently watching key areas, doing a border watch so as to give
early warning to the Director of Operations. That was one role.
Secondly, there was the usual thing of chatting up the locals and
getting them on to our side and giving them help and medical
attention. Also, rather like the bandits [in Malaya] used the
aboriginals, we used the Dyaks as a screen, rewarding a guy who
came in and said he had seen bootmarks up on whatever hill it was.
It was a very cheap way of controlling large parts of the country

and knowing what was going on and, sure enough, the patrols
reported back if Indonesians turned up and tried an incursion.

After their experiences in Malaya, living and working with the
Ibans proved to be no problem for the troopers. 'They always
reminded me a little of miners the way they used to live in their
longhouses,' comments 'Geordie' Lillico. 'I mean, in Northumberland we used to have mining communities living in rows and they
were very similar. They had the same community spirit and their
hospitality was great.' What was also much appreciated was the
Ibans' fighting spirit: 'They used to be head-hunters long ago and
they'd been allowed to go back to head-hunting Japanese in the war
and they were always looking for an excuse to give a hand. They
naturally took to soldiering and the one regiment we had of them,
later incorporated into the Malaysian Army, was the old Sarawak
Rangers. They were our famous scouts in Malaya, like the French-
American wars with the redcoats using the Mohicans, where we had
used them in more or less the same capacity. They could read the
forest like a book, knew all its signs and they could let us know
precisely what was going on.'

The loyalties of the Ibans were never in doubt: 'They had been
long associated with the Brits through their famous Rajah Brookes
[the family dynasty that had ruled Sarawak] and were very, very pro-
British with pictures of the Queen and Prince Philip in all the
longhouses. In fact, they confounded us one day when we asked
them why their kids weren't at school and they were most hurt and
said, "Don't you know it's the Queen's Birthday?" We'd missed that
one completely.' However, joining in the Ibans' social life could
sometimes require efforts above and beyond the call of duty:

> The trick of getting on with the indigenous population is to align
> yourself with them as much as you can, respect their customs and
> make allowances for them and their shortcomings. I mean, some of
> our blokes even got Iban tattoos on them, because they used to
> partake of the old tattoo ceremonies. You were always invited to
> come to the longhouses and drink with them and they used to brew
> two types of what they called *tuak*. One was like rough cider made
> from a root called *ubi kayu* and the other was rice wine, which was
> preferable because it was much lighter. But the heavy stuff they
> used to brew in big Chinese Ali Baba jars and it was quite potent.
> They used to invite you across and the *penghulu*, the headman,
> used to start the proceedings going. He used to have this bamboo
> straw dangling on a crossbar on the neck of this big jar and it had
> notches carved on it. Now if the headman sipped off three notches

of drink you were expected to do the same, but what used to happen was that the headman and possibly two or three of his oppos, his dignitaries, used to take the first few sips. So by the time they'd drunk they'd got past the neck of the jar and were into the wide part, so you had to drink three times the quantity to achieve a notch. They soon had you plastered.

Eating food on these social occasions could also be a problem:

> They had this thing called a *jarat*. What they used to do was half cook any kind of meat, split a bamboo longways and put this stuff in these bamboo sections, put the top back on and lash it up with *rotang* and then they would bury it in some secluded place and allow it to decompose, a bit like us hanging game, you know. This was their perfect meal for visitors. And you'd be sniffing away, because somebody had gone out and was digging one of these bloody things up. Of course, you had to eat it. They used to eat it with relish but it used to turn our stomachs upside down. We used to make polite excuses and go outside and have a good puke. The things you used to do for Queen and country! But this was all part of hearts and minds, you know.

Following the example of 22 SAS, five-man patrols of the newly-formed Gurkha Independent Parachute Company were also employed on border-watch, but there still huge gaps in the security screen. Walker's solution was to raise the Border Scouts, a new type of auxiliary force made up of local Borneo tribesmen. John Cross was brought in as the unit's commanding officer, but missed out on the crucial early stage when the men were first recruited and trained:

> It's sad to have to say so but they were the wrong sort of people recruited for the wrong sort of job in the wrong sort of way. A number of them were Kuching taxi-drivers and people from the lower reaches of the large rivers. They weren't the people who were the traditional head-hunters or the tribesmen from right way up in the Kelabit highlands, for example. They were put into uniform and they were given a rifle and they wore jungle boots, which crippled them, and really they were no use. Their job was not to be leading scouts of Gurkha or British sections but to be the eyes and ears of the whole of the security forces in the villages along the border and so keep the local people in with their own protection that they would neither be subverted nor succumb to any incursion.

Nemesis for the Border Scouts came in late 1963 when an IBT force attacked the village of Long Jawi in the Third Division. A group of twenty-one Border Scouts together with a training team of six Gurkhas awoke one morning to find that the village they were supposed to be protecting was totally deserted. They were then subjected to a fierce and well-directed attack in the course of which the Border Scouts broke and fled. Those who were captured by the Indonesians were put to death. The Gurkha section commander then conducted a very gallant withdrawal and eventually got the survivors of his party away downriver in a boat.

The Long Jawi disaster led General Walker to restrict the Border Scouts to information-gathering. They were to be disarmed, taken out of uniform and localised as far as possible. John Cross was given the unenviable task of converting the Border Scouts to their new role – and of winning back the loyalties of a number of villages along the border. 'That was the brief I was given,' Cross recalls. 'General Walker told me, "It's up to you, old boy. If you fail the whole of Confrontation will fail. Get on with it." ' This was not an easy task and Cross had a number of tense moments – 'only the *dhobi* [washerman] and myself knew how frightened I was' – but the net result after an arduous thousand-mile trek right the way along the border was that the Border Scouts accepted their new role and the support of the border villages was secured.

With the Border Scouts and the local villagers acting as their screen, the border watch patrols of the SAS and the Gurkhas were able to provide fast and accurate reports of border violations by parties of IBTs. This was to prove crucial to the outcome of Confrontation: 'The Indonesian Army was able to cross the border at will, but because of our information we were able to ambush them on the way out,' explains General Walker. 'Not on the way in but on the way out. That was the way we did it.'

Some years after the Confrontation war had been won Walker met one of his former opponents in London who was now the Indonesian Minister of Defence:

> He said to me, 'What sort of radio did you have, which enabled you to tell exactly where my troops were and when they were going to cross the frontier?' I said, 'We had no special radio or radar system which enabled us to do this. We won the hearts and minds of the people, and by winning the hearts and minds of the tribesmen, they went across the frontier and they told the SAS, who were protecting their villages, unseen and unheard – and you walked into the trap. And so, Mr Defence Minister, the first principle of jungle warfare is to win the hearts and minds of the people, not to destroy their villages by bombing them or their land by scorched earth policies.'

Chapter Six

BORNEO:
'Claret' Rules

Because it was classified as top secret we were not able to tell the Press that we were crossing the frontier and one of the remarkable things is that it wasn't, of course, only the SAS and the Gurkhas who crossed the frontier. There were many other people who knew. I suspect that most of the Army in Borneo knew the frontier was being crossed and it's remarkable that that secret was kept for ten or fifteen years after it took place.

Walter Walker's fourth and fifth 'ingredients for success' in Borneo were 'Security of Bases' and 'Domination of the Jungle'. Success in these two areas was made possible by an ingenious system of defence that broke some of the oldest rules of warfare. Rather than concentrating the limited numbers of troops at his disposal, Walker scattered them in small pockets through the jungle: 'Decentralisation was the order of the day. We avoided tying up troops in static posts.' In Sarawak's First and Second Divisions, which bore the brunt of the Indonesian raids, three lines of defence were laid out. Along the frontier there were few permanently-manned posts, but each sector was patrolled at platoon strength. Behind the patrols in the middle ground were their forward company bases, little forts well dug into hill-tops with clear fields of fire in all directions. The company base that David Chisnall and his fellow Marines in 40 Commando occupied was typical of these strongly-fortified positions:

We lived in a dug-in position called Kujonseng, a very small hill, which was a rabbit warren of what were called Bowen bunkers. These were wooden sleepers built into the sand and clay which we lived in for three months. That was our home. So in some ways, going out on patrols or to the *kampongs* [villages], to do the hearts and minds side of things and to get to be known locally, was a little bit of a relief because it was living out of the close environment of those bunkers where it was, as you would imagine, like First World War trench warfare. Trenches encircled the whole of the top of the hill and from there small compartments were where we used to live, five and six people at a time, and in the centre of all of this was the dug-in CP, the command post. The signals would operate from there, and in the middle again were two mortar pits that were dug in. So that was your localised defences, two-inch mortars for the individual section and three-inch and 81mm mortars for the troops.

These company bases were in turn supported by a third line of defence made up of support companies ready to respond to calls for help by bringing artillery or mortar fire to bear on to preset target points, as well as leap-frogging reinforcements forward in the form of troops, 105mm howitzers or 81mm mortars. This was only possible because air transport was on hand to overfly the jungle and land in forward helicopter pads hacked out of the forest.

'The helicopter was the real battle-winner,' explains Walter Walker. 'A battalion with eight helicopters is worth more than a brigade without – and we had the helicopters right forward with the troops in the jungle. So when the alarm went the troops got into the helicopters and went to the spot where there was trouble. A clever company commander with a few choppers could so block the guerrillas at every turn that they would think an entire army was at their heels.' As well as moving troops about the helicopters were employed in moving heavy guns so as to 'make the artillery as mobile as our infantry. The gunners deployed thirty guns in single gun positions, which could be switched to a platoon post twenty miles away in under an hour, picked up lock, stock and barrel by a Belvedere helicopter.'

The men who flew and crewed the helicopters were the 'air heroes of the Confrontation', especially the naval air pilots, whose 'can do' attitude in making particularly difficult landings to insert patrols or to bring out wounded men made them very much 'the men of the moment' as far as the forward troops were concerned. There was endless variety in the 'lift and shift' roles to which the helicopters were put, as David Storrie recalls:

One went on routine troop movement: taking out and bringing back patrols, some of them SAS. You would drop them in a position right on the border and come back two weeks later to a prearranged site not knowing whether or not they were going to get there, very often right at the end of one's fuel range. We were lifting 105mm Howitzer guns to bring them into position; lifting Land Rovers that were stuck in the mud; lifting stores to build new *sangars* [defensive walls] and keeping them resupplied; dropping in survey parties from the Royal Engineers who were trying to improve the maps; even the rather gruesome task of carrying dead bodies back for identification, sometimes just the head that had been cut off by the Ibans; taking doctors or dressers, as they were known, out to very isolated Iban or Kayan or Kelabit villages, landing right up in the headwaters of the Baram and meeting Punans, a small people almost white in colour because of the way they live under the canopy of the jungle. Most of those I came across had never seen a white man, let alone a helicopter, although they seemed to adjust to the presence of a helicopter without much problem.

Every helicopter pilot had his share of dicey moments. 'I count myself very lucky,' declares Storrie who, in his eighteen months with 845 Squadron in Borneo, went through the most rigorous flying conditions he ever encountered:

> One was continually having to make value judgements and decisions and quite often came out with a bit of a sweat, having pulled off a particularly hairy take-off. I can remember once when the other Royal Marine pilot in the squadron, David Roe, and I went up with two aircraft looking for this lost patrol way up in the country above the headwaters of the Rajang. We finally came near them and we saw, just emanating from the tops of these two-hundred-and-fifty-foot trees, a very small wisp of smoke where this patrol had let us see where they were. They had cut some trees out from the bottom but, of course, the branches spread over and the altitude was quite high, two or three thousand feet in the hills, which limited the amount of weight we could carry. I went down into the landing site first and David Roe was orbiting above me watching my left-hand side because I just had a crewman in the back, a naval photographer called McDonald, who leant out of the back of the helicopter watching the back of my tail rotor. I had to go down and then tuck in to the left under branches before I could go down into the landing site. Then David Roe subsequently went down there and picked up the remainder of the patrol and we brought them back. That was very satisfying.

Equally satisfying was working closely with experienced ground troops, which for David Storrie usually meant Royal Marines or Gurkhas: 'Their commanding officers knew the jungle, they'd cut their teeth in Malaya, they had experience of helicopters – albeit Whirlwinds – and therefore they knew how to use them. But there were battalions that came out that didn't understand the value of the helicopter, didn't understand the flexibility it gave and therefore didn't achieve the results.'

There was inevitably a degree of rivalry between the naval air squadrons, with their younger pilots and their experience of working in close support of carrier-borne troops, and the RAF helicopter squadrons who had to operate under a more 'correct' system that did not allow them to 'cross JSP [Joint Service Publication] standards'. There was the famous story of the RAF helicopter pilot who turned out at dusk to pick up a wounded man and was not only reprimanded but immediately transferred out of the area – and the equally famous story of the Gurkha Colonel who refused to work with the RAF helicopter squadron that replaced 845 Squadron when it sailed off on HMS *Albion* for shore leave in Hong Kong: 'He told the brigadier that either the RAF squadron pulled out and he got the Navy back or he would pull out his battalion. He had got to that stage.' The upshot was that 845 Squadron had to be recalled: 'It was about one or two days en route to Hong Kong – really looking forward to a run ashore there – when the ship did an about-turn and we went back, and didn't get to Hong Kong for about another six months.'

Nevertheless, all pilots and air-crews enjoyed working with the Gurkhas. Used to being regarded as 'taxi-drivers' by their Royal Marine mess-mates, the naval air pilots appreciated the 'sparkle of enthusiasm about our work' that came from the Gurkha soldiers – although Gurkha enthusiasm could be overdone, as on one air flight when 'a hot mug of tea appeared out of nowhere. People were happily drinking it when they suddenly realised that there was no Thermos flask. Looking down the middle of the helicopter they saw this little Gurkha, sat cross-legged brewing the tea in a metal mug over a hexamine block, a most dangerous thing to do.' Rob Woodard always took bags of barley sugar from the NAAFI when picking up Gurkha troops:

> Whenever I had to leave anyone behind I'd throw down some barley sugar by way of apology, and I didn't think very much about it until some months later when back in Singapore several of us were invited to a great gathering at Blakang Mati for the Gurkha Dashera festival. After a very good curry lunch we went out to watch a hockey match. The officers were standing on one side of the pitch with the men on the other, and at half-time someone said something in Gurkhali in a very loud voice and they all came streaming across and carried me shoulder high round the pitch. When I was put down I said, 'What was that all about?' – and they said, 'The barley-sugar man'.

As Confrontation developed Rob Woodard returned for a second tour to Borneo, but this time as a pilot flying Buccaneer strike bombers in 800 Squadron off HMS *Eagle*. As far as he and other fixed-wing pilots were concerned, this was a 'really frustrating business. We were there with considerable weight, two strike carriers and the whole of the Far East Fleet, but whereas our own people were flying sometimes with great hazard over the jungle we were unable to do anything that we felt was really helping them.' In fact, the very presence of the Royal Navy in strength was in itself a deterrent that discouraged the Indonesians from escalating Confrontation into a full-scale war.

No Buccaneer or any other strike aircraft fired a shot in anger during Confrontation in Borneo but there was one extraordinary instance of an interceptor being employed in an attacking role. This happened in the Fifth Division of Sarawak where a platoon of the 1st/2nd Gurkhas in ambush close to the border was attacked by a large Indonesian force. After three hours of fighting the Gurkha platoon commander radioed to his company base that he was in serious trouble. In the normal course of events helicopters would have been despatched to bring up reinforcements and a howitzer or mortars but all the Army's forward-based helicopters had been grounded with engine trouble and the nearest RAF helicopters were at Labuan Island, over two hundred miles away. Bruce Jackman, the company commander, found himself with an appalling situation on his hands: 'I had a platoon surrounded, fighting for their lives, where I could do nothing. It was going to take me hours to walk in and I got to the point of desperation where I asked for an airstrike. Now this had never happened before in the Borneo campaign and there was no suitable aircraft up that end of Borneo to carry out an air-to-ground attack.' About twenty minutes later Jackman was told to get his ground-to-air radio set up because an aircraft was approaching his area:

> To cut a long story short, as clear as a bell over the airwaves came this voice which said, 'Black Four Zero. This is Red Leader. Do you read?' And this was the pilot, loud and clear. I told him that if he flew north to south absolutely belly down he would see what I could see – the ridge in front of him where there was a large tree sticking up above all the others. He should hit with whatever he had got to the left of the tree and not to the right of it, where I knew the platoon would be. He acknowledged that and a few seconds later appeared right over the camp, absolutely flat on the deck. It was a Javelin Mark 1, which is an air interceptor, so I had no idea

what to expect. Anyway, he flew at the ridge and I suddenly saw this triangle of the Javelin's outline stand on its tail against the jungle ridge and disappear into the clouds. A few seconds later there were two terrific explosions and the platoon commander, whom I had warned, immediately came on the air and said, 'He's dropped two huge bombs. They're a bit off to the left but it has stopped all the Indonesian firing and all the Indonesians are shouting at each other now.' So I asked the pilot to repeat and he said 'Fine, but I'm afraid this is the last time I can do it. I have to refuel and, anyway, I think somebody might twig.' And that began to throw doubt in my mind as to quite what he was doing. Anyway, he flew the mission again. Again there were two enormous explosions and this time the enemy fled in total disarray. Some of them threw away their weapons. They discarded their packs, their ammunition and fled, and I had to actually restrain Lieutenant Sukhdeo and the platoon from following up because they were so elated at seeing this lot rush off.

When the helicopters finally arrived there was an orderly follow-up and Jackman was able to go over the battle-ground, with devastation and blood trails on all sides but no bomb craters. The explanation only came later: 'When the Mark 1 Javelin fires its afterburners they go off with a tremendous bang as fuel is injected into them and this was what he was doing just over the tops of the trees – and that's all it was. It was total bluff and I then realised what he had meant when he said that somebody might twig.'

However, there were failures as well as successes. 'Magnificent outfits' like 845 Squadron achieved far more than could reasonably have been expected of them but perhaps their extended tours in Borneo went on too long. 'It was a great shame,' declares 'Birdie' Smith. 'Gradually, the unfriendly climate and the overworked machines combined to produce an inevitable staleness which crept in. Near the end of 845's tour, there were three bad accidents, which was a tragic ending to a wonderful operational stint.' Major Smith himself became the chief victim of the first of these accidents, which happened on a visit to a forward company base:

We took off from Sibu in a Wessex helicopter and, fortunately for me, I had prevailed on our battalion doctor to accompany me. Our journey was relatively uneventful until we got near the border, then the pilot was finding it difficult to find the company. Eventually, they were seen on the crest of a ridge. The Gurkhas had cleared the top and built a log platform; it was sheer on both sides and there was nowhere else for the helicopter to land. When we were about ten feet above the platform the engine appeared to give a loud cough and we dropped like a stone. If both the wheels had landed on the logs, we might have been all right but, unfortunately, one wheel was off the platform and in a flash we turned over two or three times, and would have continued down into the river, three hundred feet below, except that we hit a tree stump. The tree stump that saved our lives smashed into the helicopter and trapped me by my right arm.

By this time, we were in dark, dank jungle and, apart from the horrific pain, I cannot remember hearing any noises or voices. I thought I was the only survivor. Unbeknown to me, the doctor had managed to get the Gurkha passengers out and, with the crew, they had run from the scene as quickly as possible because everyone thought that the machine would go up in flames. As the helicopter turned over the pilot had released the fuel. That action saved us but, of course, I was drenched in petrol. It only needed one little spark for the whole thing to go up. The doctor was the first person back, after they had counted heads only to find one person missing. After a quick look, he realised that I was in a very bad way, hanging by my shattered right arm with my left hand holding on to something. He appreciated that he would have to amputate my arm as soon as possible because I was losing blood at an alarming rate, but he had lost his medical bag in the crash, so there was no question of giving any medication to me. Mercifully unbeknown to me, the only implement that the doctor could find to do the operation was a government penknife borrowed from one of the Gurkha soldiers.

Smith's arm was amputated and he was carried up to the top of the hill and casevaced in a second helicopter to Kuching for further surgery. The battalion doctor – later to be awarded the George Medal – stayed at his patient's side throughout: 'When he accompanied me to Kuching, he was remarkably cool and assured, helping the local RAMC doctor during my first operation. However, later that night he was picked up by the military police in Kuching. He did not know why he was wandering around with blood all over him – my blood. Delayed shock had caught up with him. Fortunately for me, it came after he had saved my life with skill and gallantry.'

Indonesian air power was rarely in evidence on the Sarawak side of the border, but on one occasion an enemy transport strayed across with disastrous consequences. 'The border was on a ridge and there was a pass and then a valley where there was an Indonesian battalion headquarters with an airfield,' explains Mike Allen of the Gurkha Independent Parachute Company:

> We used to get air drops from Beverleys and the Indonesians used to get air drops from Hercules. We were only about ten kilometres apart. We were sitting there in our forward headquarters when suddenly an aircraft came up and an officer attached to us from the Border Scouts said, 'My God, it's a Hercules. It's one of theirs!' It was very low, only four hundred feet above us and there were crewmen looking out of the door waiting to drop. So we opened up on it with everything we had. I mean, people were firing Sten guns, machine guns and we obviously hit it. Then it flew very low over this border pass in the direction of the Indonesian camp. We then heard a report on the radio from our own Gurkha Parachute Company patrol, who lived in the jungle on a hillock overlooking the Indonesian battalion headquarters, that this plane had crash-landed, coming down the hillside where one wing was broken off, pancaking down on this tiny four-hundred-metre strip and running on to the end of the runway, everybody jumping out and the plane catching fire. We subsequently discovered that the aircraft was actually brought down by an Indonesian anti-aircraft detachment which, on seeing this Hercules suddenly very low from our side of the border, had opened fire. In fact, the Detachment Commander, having realised that he had made an appalling error, decided to defect. He walked across the border and surrendered to us the next day!

The mobility of Walker's forces served him well so long as the Indonesians limited their raids, but at the end of 1963 Sukarno stepped up the pressure with a major attack against a Malay Regiment headquarters in Sabah spearheaded by Indonesian Marines, known as the KKO. Despite temporary ceasefires and peace talks this military pressure continued until, in August 1964, the Indonesians made the fatal error of launching two airborne raids on the Malayan peninsula. Both were disasters from the Indonesian point of view but gave General Walker the opportunity he had been looking for to move from the defensive on to the offensive: 'I realised that if we weren't going to get involved in a second Vietnam I would have to knock them off balance, and the only way of knocking them off balance was going across the border, but it took an awful lot of pushing both by the Commander-in-Chief and by myself. The powers-that-be in London resisted because we had declared that we would not go across the border and fight the war on Indonesian territory.'

Hitherto the Indonesian border had been regarded as sacrosanct as far as the British Government was concerned, to the great frustration of many company commanders who felt they were fighting 'with one arm tied behind your back'. Nevertheless, at a higher level battalion commanders had enforced restraint. 'It was absolutely essential that we did not cross the border,' explains John Woodhouse. 'There were those in the SAS who said to me, "Colonel, why on earth can't we go across and hammer the bastards on the other side?" I was conscious that if I took in the slightest way an ambiguous line one of my enterprising young officers would be only too pleased to do a sort of Jameson Raid, and I stressed to them that such an action would be quite fatal to the whole regiment because we would never be trusted again with anything else.'

Initially, at least, the restriction was strictly obeyed – except by the locals. Unknown to General Walker, Ibans serving with his forces did cross the border to gather information. 'Frontiers meant nothing to them,' explains 'Fairy' Gopsill of the men he had recruited for his battalion of the Malay Regiment. 'Whether they were Indonesian Iban or British [Malay] Iban, they were all Iban, so they were able to go down and find out what was going on over on that side from the Ibans who lived in that area. They asked to do it, and carried no weapons; they went with my full permission and we were able to size up the situation pretty well from the information they brought back to us. However, I wasn't a brave enough man to tell the General they were doing it!'

When authorisation to go on to the offensive was finally given, it came with many conditions attached. Cross-border penetration was to be limited to five thousand yards and the operations – identified by the code-name 'Claret' – were to be absolutely top secret. They were also to be strictly limited in scale 'because we did not want Sukarno to advertise to the world that we were going across the border. If we were able to inflict minimum damage to his forces without him losing face then he was unlikely to scream about it. If, on the other hand, we were to do the opposite by wiping out a whole company then, of course, he would screech.' Quite remarkably, these 'Claret' operations remained a well-kept secret for a decade.

To begin with, every incursion into enemy territory was controlled directly by the Director of Operations, Borneo – General Walter Walker until March 1965 and then by his successor, General George Lea. Walker drew up a number of 'Claret' Rules that he made sure were rigidly enforced:

I laid down a number of rules, which were fairly restrictive and which meant that the Commanding Officer himself had to plan the operation in very great detail. I then went down as Director of Operations with the object of picking as many holes in his plan as I could, because I was told quite clearly that on no account could a helicopter go across the frontier to evacuate any wounded and on no account was a dead body to be left behind, which could be photographed by Sukarno and shown to the world, or a wounded man taken prisoner. And so the battalion commander concerned had to make for me a mud model of the place that he was going to attack and show me exactly how he was going to do it in precise detail and I did not allow it to be launched unless I was quite certain it would be a hundred per cent successful. If I felt that it was not going to be successful then I did not allow it. I only allowed Gurkha troops to do it in the first instance and then I allowed British troops to do it on their second tour.

Meticulous and detailed planning that allowed for every eventuality became, in John Woodhouse's words, 'simply a way of life' for all those involved in the 'Claret' operations. General Walker remains convinced it was this enormous amount of attention that went into the 'Claret' raids that ensured their success:

In my time there was not one single failure of 'Claret'. There was nearly a hiccup when a battalion of Gurkhas had two men wounded. It was a Sunday and my Senior Staff Officer rang me up to say that the Royal Air Force refused to give permission for a helicopter to go across the border and pick up these men who were bleeding to death. It was touch and go whether or not the Gurkhas would be able to get them out because they were so badly wounded and because the Indonesians were very close, and the only way to get the Gurkhas out of fighting a rearguard action would have been to lift them out by helicopter. The Commanding Officer came on the blower to me and gave me the exact situation and I authorised a helicopter. I said 'How far are the Indonesians away from your wounded?' He said, 'They're very close indeed but if I can get a helicopter in the next few minutes I can get them out and I guarantee success.' So I said 'OK – let it go, but my God, if you fail and let me down, you've got the chop!'

At first 'Claret' cross-border operations were confined to the two most experienced units, 22 SAS and the Gurkha battalions. For the former Woodhouse devised a 'shoot and scoot' policy whose antecedents went back to the Second World War: 'The SAS had, in general, operated on the policy of surprise attack, tremendous impact and a rapid withdrawal – and hence the shoot and scoot policy. I considered tactical action might result in very heavy losses in a single troop and therefore I emphasised – and probably over-emphasised – that when meeting regular Indonesian forces our action should be to open fire on them and to inflict casualties, but not to stay and mix it in a brawl.' This policy of quick withdrawal had to be modified after an encounter in which a fatally wounded trooper was left behind at the scene of an action. His body was later recovered but the incident forced Woodhouse to rethink his tactics to ensure that no dead or wounded were ever abandoned.

The execution of the more serious 'Claret' raids was handed over to the Gurkhas, operating usually at company strength. Typical of the raids they carried out was that executed by 'C' Company 2nd/7th Gurkhas on an Indonesian Army base at Labang, abutting on to a remote corner of Sabah inhabited by Murut tribesmen. The Indonesians had been raiding villages inside Sabah with the aim of ambushing follow-up parties as they responded to the raids – 'which they did quite successfully on a couple of occasions'. No punitive retaliation had been possible because the Indonesian company base had been built in the heart of a Murut village called Labang. Only when the village headman came to the Gurkhas' company commander to tell him that he wished to move all his villagers out of Labang and bring them over the border could a plan to hit back at the Indonesians be put into effect.

'Labang was a very difficult position to attack because it was on the far side of a very big river,' explains Mike Allen, who acted as signals officer during the raid. 'We decided the best way to do the attack was to take it out by fire, using mortar and machine gun fire.' A detailed plan was put into effect involving a cover story of an Indonesian incursion at company strength into Sabah. 'C' Company was shuttled in by helicopter together with an 81mm mortar section and did a two-day march accompanied by twenty Muruts carrying ammunition for the mortars. While two platoons moved forward to take up positions on a bluff overlooking the river, a mortar base was set up in the jungle about a thousand yards to the rear:

> The village headman was with us and through runners he was in active contact with the villagers. This was the most remarkable thing because we could have been betrayed at any stage during this operation. That night the Muruts gave a party for the Indonesians at which they served them their local *tuak* and at about two o'clock that night the whole village – chickens, dogs, children, treasured belongings, everything – they all upsticked, went down to the river

and were ferried across. And by four o'clock we got the message that everybody was across and it was safe to commence operations at first light. Just after six, when his machine gunners with their GPMGs [general purpose machine guns] could see the Indonesians getting out of bed and forming up on their little parade ground, Geoffrey Lloyd, the company commander, gave the code word.

As the two mortars and the machine guns opened fire simultaneously there was pandemonium at the receiving end, but – 'to give them their full credit' – the Indonesians were quick to respond with their own machine gun and mortar fire. 'They also opened up on their radio shouting for help back to their headquarters,' recalls Mike Allen:

> This was interfering very heavily on our mortar control radio net, which I was operating, making it quite difficult to work through it. Then we discovered that where the mortars were blasting away the base plates were disappearing into the ground because the soil was so soft. We dug them out as fast as we could, put new logs down and relaid them and the extraordinary thing was that the first two rounds that went off went straight through the roof of the Indonesian command post. I'll always remember this because on the radio there was a great bang and at that moment the interference stopped. The forward controller for the mortar jokingly said, 'On target. Drop one foot on adjustment.' We then continued with some prophylactic – awful nasty word – fire all round for the Indonesians who, poor soldiers, were having to run into the forests. I think we got through some eighty rounds of mortars, a mixture of high explosive and white phosphorus, and something like four thousand rounds of machine gun bullets. The whole operation was all over in twenty minutes.

It was judged to be a complete success in that the Indonesians withdrew from their forward position on that sector of the border, 'which meant that the initiative in this particular area was shifting away from the Indonesians to us – as was happening in other areas.'

A very similar situation confronted Bruce Jackman when his battalion took over from the 2nd/7th Gurkhas in the Fifth Division in Sarawak. Here, too, the local tribesmen were Muruts whose traditional way of life had been disrupted by the Indonesians. 'The rapport with the locals was excellent and again we were relying on them to provide us with intelligence,' recalls Jackman, commanding 'C' Company at a base close to the border named Bakalalan:

'Us and them': ABOVE Bandits of the MRLA training in a jungle camp c. 1952 – a photograph found on a dead Communist terrorist; BELOW Marines of 'S' Troop, 42 Commando, with a captured MRLA flag, Ipoh, c. 1952.

Jungle fighters: ABOVE A Gurkha in ambush identified by the crossed kukris worn on the back of his jungle hat; BELOW A patrol of the Suffolk Regiment resting in the jungle.

'England's last hopes': ABOVE LEFT Private Bill Hewlett (far right) and friends in 4 Platoon, 'D' Company, 1 Queens, 1953; ABOVE RIGHT Private John Frawley (third from right) and 'some of the lads from MMC Platoon, Suffolk Regiment, 1951'; BELOW Sergeant Frank Williams (second from left) of 22 SAS Regiment. This team had just returned from the jungle after rescuing the pilot of a crashed Auster.

ABOVE Winning hearts and minds: General Sir Gerald Templer, High Commissioner and Director of Operations, Malaya, inspecting women members of a Home Guard unit, Manjor; BELOW Supreme exponents of jungle warfare and their most potent weapon: a platoon of 1st/6th Gurkhas wait their turn to board a Whirlwind of 845 Royal Naval Air Squadron.

CAPTURED

SALLEH bin SAMBAS

15 yrs T.P.K.

AP 30   Printed by The Govt. Printer at The Brunei Press Ltd., K.B.

Revolt in Brunei: villain and victims. LEFT Salleh bin Sambas, who organised the rebel resistance at Limbang; and BELOW some of the casualties from 'L' Company, 42 Commando, being tended after their dawn assault on Limbang.

Confrontation in Borneo: RIGHT
The 'architect of victory', General
Walter Walker, Director of Operations; and BELOW his opponents,
Indonesian cross-border raiders,
photographed by a CCO insurgent
later ambushed with his escort by
1st/6th Gurkhas.

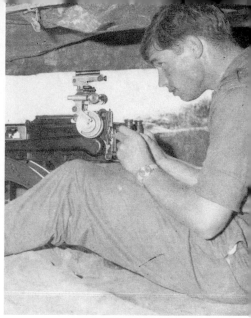

ABOVE LEFT Lieutenant-Colonel E.D. 'Birdie' Smith, commanding officer 1st/2nd Gurkhas, back in command in Borneo a year after the helicopter crash in which he lost his arm. ABOVE RIGHT Major Bruce Jackman, 1st/2nd Gurkhas, manning an LPMG at Bakalalan Company Base shortly before his 'Claret' raid on Long Medan. BELOW A hilltop helipad on a forward landing site in Borneo.

Survivors: ABOVE LEFT CSM John 'Patch' Williams, 2 Para, defender of Plaman Mapu;
ABOVE RIGHT Sergeants E. 'Geordie' Lillico and Ian 'Jock the Clog' Thompson, 'D'
Squadron 22 SAS, back in Borneo after recovering from their wounds.
BELOW 42 Commando mortar section practice at Fort Stassi watched by the local Ibans,
Sarawak, 1963.

Through this intelligence an extraordinary picture gradually built up in my mind of a community that had been divided by an Indonesian force, size unknown, that had established itself over the border at a place called Long Medan and had sealed the border. There was only one proper crossing; that was over a pass through which the buffaloes from the Indonesian side of the border were driven through Bakalalan right up to the coast 250-odd miles away. It was through the sale of buffaloes that this whole community bought their oil, their sugar and their goods and chattels. Also it was the Medan Valley that had the natural salt in the hills which, being rice eaters, the whole community needed. We entered into an enormous airlift every week whereby bags of sugar, salt and soap, all the things that they would normally get from the sale of buffaloes, were provided through our own funds to the locals. They were enormously grateful for this but they were getting very agitated as to how the long-term future was going to shape out for them.

Eventually, a group of headmen asked for a meeting, and towards the end of the meeting my Special Branch Sergeant-Major, who was a local Murut and my interpreter, suddenly said to me, 'You're now being asked by all these headmen to do something about the situation. They're asking you to go over and sort out the Indonesians on the other side to reunite the community.' So with a Murut who knew the enemy camp, my orderly, a radio operator and I went over one night and located the camp and watched it throughout the best part of the next day to get my own ideas as to what it was all about. I identified a mortar and a machine gun, a Browning, and so they were regulars, and therefore I was quite clear in my mind that if I was to do anything it was going to be a big operation.

Jackman reported the situation to his commanding officer. A visit from the brigade commander was followed by one from the Director of Operations himself:

General Walker was convinced, but required more information; distances, nearby camps, what was the reaction time, all sorts of things that as an inexperienced twenty-three-year-old I hadn't really thought of and required a lot more scurrying about on the other side of the border. Then the Commander-in-Chief came down and he seemed very pro the idea and said that it was clearly a good target but I had to convince everyone that it was a feasible one and that there wasn't going to be a nonsense. And so the next three to four months I spent gaining as much intelligence as we could about the place. At one stage I went and sat very close to the camp in daylight with a cine camera and I filmed sentries changing over and activities within the camp and sent the film back to the intelligence boys back in brigade headquarters for them to interpret. We were now waiting for authorisation and all the time we were training. We built replicas of the dug-outs that I could see in the camp. They had no barbed wire but they had bamboo fencing around the camp so we had to devise a way of getting over it, flattening it in an assault. We practised hitting bunkers with 3.5 inch anti-tank rounds and following up straight away with soldiers getting into the bunker. So all this was going on until finally the news came that I was allowed to go. I picked the next new moon, which was ten days later.

A fourth platoon was flown in to act in support and to defend Jackman's mortar base. Then, at the appointed time, his own company's three platoons made their way by different routes up to the border, each man loaded down with ammunition. However, as they waited for darkness a contact was made:

The commanding officer was with us, Johnny Clements, who had walked down with us so that he could actually see us over the start line and while we were sitting there having a bowl of rice, suddenly there was a bang from the left-hand platoon up on the ridge and immediately they came on the radio saying an Indonesian patrol had walked straight into them. A young soldier had waited until the very last minute, so long that when he shot the leading Indonesian the man fell over him. There were four in the group, two were killed, two got away. They were carrying an RPG7 rocket launcher and we assumed they were coming up probably to fire some rockets at the camp. Unfortunately, the Indonesians then moved a mortar out on to the very hill that I wanted to place my mortars and machine gun on and started spraying mortar in the area of the contact. Well this, of course, posed an enormous dilemma. I needed that hill for my mortars, because I'd taken across ranging equipment and ranged in all the information that the mortars and the machine guns needed to put on their dial sights to fire.

Calling up the Forward Observation Officer, whose job it was to direct the fire of the 105mm howitzer that was supporting them, Jackman asked him to clear the Indonesians off the hill. This was done but Jackman now found himself in a terrible quandary over whether to call off the attack now that the Indonesians had been alerted or to go ahead and risk 'going down in history as somebody who led a company into a highly activated ants' nest and ended up with a disastrous attack.' Having made it clear that whatever Jackman decided would have his full support, his commanding officer left it to him to make the final decision:

> In the end I got my Gurkha officers together and I told them that given all the factors I thought the odds were still with us. So on that basis we went ahead. We had the full moon and it was very effective. We didn't go by the tracks, we walked through the jungle going slowly, but I remember my company sergeant-major got a tickle in his throat and he could not cure it. He tried stuffing his handkerchief in his mouth and everything. I threatened to leave him behind and eventually he managed to control himself and I then moved with two platoons [9 and 10 Platoons] around to the flank that we were going to do the silent attack from. There was a very convenient small ridge in the ground and we deployed along behind this little bank, about forty or fifty metres only from the bamboo fence.

While Jackman's two platoons moved into position to make their silent attack, the third platoon was already in position ready to give supporting fire for the attack with four rocket launchers, six M26 grenade-launchers and four machine guns. However, it had been agreed that Gurkha Lieutentant Sukhdeo, commanding this platoon, would open fire with his rockets if his presence was discovered. As Jackman and the two assault platoons stood by to launch their attack at dawn the silence was broken by the 'terrific crunch of four rockets going into the first bunkers, bang-bang-bang-bang simultaneously. Clearly, something had happened and Sukhdeo had been disturbed. Immediately the platoon commanders, without any word from me, whistled the message all the way down the line that it was Plan B. And sure enough, I heard the grenades go in, I heard the machine gun start and then on either side of me I saw soldiers get up and go in at the low crouch for the fence.'

Before the moment of assault Jackman had felt 'absolutely petrified', not on his own account but 'worrying more about what was going to happen, how many people I was going to lose. I never for one minute worried about the fact that I might get killed but I was terrified that it was all going to be an absolute nonsense and go badly wrong.' Once the assault started, however, Jackman's fears were forgotten:

> I seemed to have so much time to think and see things and to take it all in it was quite extraordinary. Every action was in slow motion and very clearly embedded on my mind. The fence was pulled down

by the first soldiers who immediately swarmed over and then the firefight started. I was enveloped in black smoke and cloud and dust from the rocket launchers and grenades, and also section commanders were throwing smoke grenades to provide some cover for themselves. There was a tremendous amount of shooting, a lot of it ours – difficult to say how much of it was the enemy – but there was just a huge amount of noise that will stay with me for ever. The soldiers were quite magnificent. Section commanders had got tremendously tight control within this smoke and confusion and dust and I remember seeing one, Deo Bahadur, immediately in front of me. He gripped his machine gun group and told them to fire at a bunker while he grabbed four Riflemen and ran around to one side and did a classic little section attack on one bunker, all in a very small space because the camp was about seventy-five metres across and about fifty deep.

There were eight bunkers in all, four in the front and four at the back and the mortar pit, and it was quite incredible watching these soldiers diving in. Grenades were thrown in first and you saw the roofs of bunkers just lift off after the grenade explosion and there was shrapnel flying in all directions, and then kukris were out and they were in. And the speed with which it happened surprised me. I thought it would be a fairly sort of deliberate fight through. It *was* a fight through but the speed that the soldiers moved from one objective to another, from one trench to another, from one tree to another, it was all over in what appeared to be seconds. Then we were through the position and the platoons had regrouped in their specific arcs.

Astonishingly, the two platoons suffered only one serious casualty in the assault, a Rifleman who was hit by a burst of machine gun fire. 'I felt the machine gun fire go diagonally across the front of us,' Jackman remembers. 'It sprayed the ground several yards in front of me but then I saw it hit the section sideways and it got Shem Bahadur in the stomach. He went down still alive but was subsequently hit by one of the enemy's mortar bombs, which killed him.'

The hill behind them on which the mortars and heavy machine gun were sited remained enveloped in mist, but when Jackman called for support fire down it came: 'One of the sights I will always remember was when I called for the machine gun fire because, remember, they had their sights set on the bearings we had measured before on one of the earlier recces. Normally, a tracer bullet is one in five, but we had one for one tracer and when I called for the machine gun fire I saw two jets of red spray almost come out of the cloud and then just go straight down the riverbed exactly where I needed it, wonderfully reassuring.'

Satisfied that 9 Platoon was where it should be, Jackman, together with his radio operator, mortar fire controller (MFC) and orderly, ran across to see how 10 Platoon was doing on the other side. It was now becoming apparent that the Indonesians had been in the process of withdrawing to more secure positions on the far side of a river that bordered the back of the camp. From these new positions across the river they now began to bring down mortar fire, which caught Jackman and his party as they were crossing the open ground:

> I was faced with a sheet of flame and tremendous explosions, three simultaneously. I just felt as if I had run against not a brick wall but a train coming the other way, because I felt myself lifted off my feet and flung backwards. I had a terrible singing in my ears, I couldn't hear anything and all I could see was red. It cleared quite quickly and I found my orderly pulling my foot saying, 'Sahib, you're all right.' I was covered in mud from head to foot and what had happened was that three Indonesian 60mm mortar rounds had landed almost simultaneously, the first about seven paces in front of me and two either side of us. We were straddled, the four of us, and we were lucky in that we were running across a newly-dug cultivated patch. The mortars had dug into this patch and the earth had absorbed most of the impact of the mortar rounds, which had blown upwards as opposed to outwards. So we were very lucky.
>
> Anyway, that was a shock and it galvanised my MFC into action, Corporal Birbahadur Gurung, who without needing any instructions darted forward to a place where he could see more clearly. He could hear a mortar firing going, he spotted the source and then started to direct our mortar fire in a counter-bombardment. And it was quite extraordinary because the first ranging round he put down was about a hundred and fifty metres off. He made a quick correction using the knuckles on his hand and the second round actually hit the mortar pit. We saw the mortar go in the air and three bodies fly out. 9 Platoon were facing that and it was rather like a goal had been scored at Wembley, because a great cheer went up from the soldiers.
>
> At this point the enemy opened up with a 12.7 anti-aircraft gun, which fires a huge slug at about bomb-bomb-bomb-bomb speed as opposed to the rattle of a machine gun. So then we reckoned we had about three Browning machine guns against us plus this 12.7 from a position just over the other side of the river, about four hundred yards away, and all our concentration went now on

quelling this fire. I redirected the support group with their machine guns to a position where Sukhdeo could bring his four machine guns to bear on that site. The hill was now clearing of mist, so we got the machine guns to switch and they eventually ranged in on to the position. At the same time the MFC started to bring down tremendously effective mortar fire. He was sitting on an ant hill, totally exposed I remember, and the enemy machine gun fire was all round him.

By now it was broad daylight, making it easier for Jackman's mortars to locate and silence the Indonesian machine guns. However, their most lethal weapon, the 12.7 anti-aircraft gun, could not be sighted. 'It was still bomb-bomb-bomb-bombing away,' remembers Jackman. 'These shells were coming right across the ground and bouncing off; you could see the tracer coming towards you almost as if you had time to duck, you know, and lifting off and disappearing.' Finally, he collected together a rocket-launching team, led by Corporal Lok Bahadur, gave them four shells and sent them out into the surrounding paddy fields with orders to find the 12.7 and knock it out:

> About ten minutes later there was a terrific boomph from this river bank and an explosion in among the trees and the 12.7 stopped. It was in a bunker with overhead protection and Lok Bahadur had put his first rocket straight through the slit. So it was all over. Suddenly there was a deathly hush and I use the word deathly because it was. Not a bird singing, it was complete and utter quiet and I shall never forget it because the quiet was only punctuated by the screams of the wounded from the other side of the river and from in among the paddy. Against the background of total stillness it was very, very eerie.

As in the case of the cross-border raid from Sabah, the Indonesians never reoccupied their camp and never again crossed the border in that sector, allowing the local Murut community to return to its traditional pattern of life.

Chapter Seven

BORNEO:
A Model Operation

Confrontation in Borneo was perhaps the most satisfactory of all the post-war operations by the British Army in the sense that it was contained with the minimum of force, it was settled decisively and with relatively very low casualties and with almost no disturbance or loss of life to the civil indigenous population.

By January 1965 the question of a local insurgency along Malayan lines had ceased to be the major issue. Two thousand CCO members were known to be lying low in Sarawak and armed terrorists still infiltrated across the border, but the conflict had hardened into a straightforward fight between two professional armies. Over twenty-two thousand Indonesian regulars were now encamped on the Kalimantan side of the border, well-armed and well-trained but with poor lines of communication and supply. Opposing them were thirteen infantry battalions, adding up to no more than twelve thousand infantrymen and Marines, but so well served by the gunners, engineers, aircrews and other units in support that they rarely lost the upper hand. To Jeremy Moore, returning to Borneo to serve on the headquarters staff after eighteen months at Staff College, the campaign seemed rather like the Peninsular War in that 'there was a great feel that you knew people. I knew a lot of the company commanders who were involved and it was very much conducted at company level.'

Knowledge of those involved was not confined to the one side, since many of the best Indonesian commanders had trained alongside their British counterparts at Kota Tingi and elsewhere. Two Indonesian students had been on the same staff course with Jeremy Moore, one of whom went back to command the opposing parachute commando regiment: 'Having known him well and argued with him it was quite interesting to see how he would behave. I remember discussing this with my General, saying, "I know this guy and I can predict for you just how he's going to behave." His security when he mounted an operation was extremely good and until it took place he managed very well to cover what he was at. Nevertheless, the attack when it happened was entirely true to form.'

The unusual nature of the unspoken understanding between the two sides saw to it that no massed push across the frontier was ever attempted. 'We conducted the campaign so that we leant on the enemy militarily but didn't carry out crazy operations,' is how Jeremy Moore saw this final stage of Confrontation. 'But some of our operations were very offensive and very effective and as the enemy built up his camps near the border from which he wanted to raid into us those camps one after another got taken out or the communications between them were ambushed. He suffered very severe reverses in this and was slowly having to spend more and more of his time just guarding himself and pulling back, whereas we were expanding.'

'Claret' raids were extended by stages from five thousand to twenty thousand yards, although this was not a demarcation line that meant much to those on the ground. 'Obviously no chap sitting in a great office somewhere in Singapore or wherever knew exactly where you were,' explains Johnny Watts, commanding 'D' Squadron 22 SAS, who admits to a certain 'bending of the rules. I think people expected that, particularly from the SAS, who never do anything illegal but who exploit things as far as they can. You made sure that it appeared on the maps that you weren't going over 5,000 yards or something but if the difference between success or failure was going on for another day or two until you got to a river junction where you could watch and observe a lot more than you could by sitting somewhere on an artificial boundary, then you did it.'

The Indonesian response to the 'Claret' raids was to pull back in some areas but to concentrate more troops in the border areas opposite the First and Second Divisions in Western Sarawak. To meet this new threat 'B' Squadron was brought down to Kuching so that more passive cross-border intelligence-gathering could be carried out. Here they found themselves 'really up against it', with much less jungle to hide in on the Indonesian side and many more civilians and enemy troops about:

> The squadron by this time was becoming somewhat debilitated in that on a cross-border operation no man was allowed to take more than thirty-five pounds in weight for two weeks. But it could be longer if he had trouble getting back because of too many troops in the area. Then he had to cut down and go on quarter rations. So many of them used to come back after, say, three weeks very, very tired having lost a lot of weight and with boils and sores after living

this animal-like existence. You couldn't smoke, couldn't eat, couldn't whisper, couldn't do anything. You just sat there all day and then at night you found the nastiest, thorniest jungle you could, had a cold meal, stretched out on the ground and slept. So you can imagine the troopers suffered very severely over a time.

Having to worry over the fate of his men also put a severe strain on the squadron commander, who might have as many as twelve patrols out at the same time. 'It was one of the penalties of higher command,' explains Watts. 'I remember occasions when chaps would catch a fever six days' march inside Indonesia, with a very high temperature of 104° or 105°F, and there would be the nightly contact with the old morse, "Stokes is dying – or very ill". There was nothing his three companions could do except nurse him and hope he was going to get better. You wanted to be there, you know, but of course you had to sit there and worry about him.'

The purpose of these patrols was to provide early warning and intelligence and contacts were avoided – but inevitably clashes did occur. In February 1965 Sergeant 'Geordie' Lillico was taking his patrol into Indonesian territory opposite Sarawak's First Division when they ran into an enemy patrol coming the other way. In the first exchange of fire the lead scout, Trooper 'Jock' Thompson, received a wound that shattered his left thigh. Lillico was immediately behind him:

> I immediately suspected a head-on contact so I dived to the right-hand side of the bamboo to bring fire to support him, but I must have put myself into the line of the opposition lead scout and he shot me through my left hip. I knew I'd been hit because it felt like somebody had just given me a severe kick. I went down and looked across to where 'Jock' was lying, although at the time I didn't know he'd lost an inch and a half of his left femur. He had the presence of mind to swing his Armalite across and stitch this bloke up who'd just shot me. So that removed the immediate threat to our flank and left the pair of us in a prone position able to return fire to the other characters further down the track. Two went down under our fire and after that things went quiet, just sporadic shots. At the same time my third and fourth men, both being brand new, bugged out to the emergency RV. When I realised the other two lads weren't going to come forward I asked 'Jock' if he could move. I thought he just had a thigh wound, so I said, 'Do you think you can make it back to the RV?' He said he could, so I sent him on his way.

Assuming that the two unwounded members of his patrol would eventually return for him Lillico tucked himself under cover of the bamboo, exhanging fire with the Indonesians until he heard them withdraw. He was not in a great deal of pain and watched with interest as large bluebottles descended on his wound and laid their eggs – 'right under your eyes they just hatch out and start eating up all the tissue'. When the light began to fade he gave himself a jab of morphine and soon began to feel 'without a care in the world'. Meanwhile, Trooper 'Jock' Thompson was slowly dragging himself by his hands up on to a ridge towards the rendezvous, believing that the rest of the patrol would be waiting for him there. In fact, they had gone back over the border to bring help.

The next morning Lillico decided that he would have to move to a safer area and dragged himself into an overgrown *ladang*, where the trees had been felled and crops cultivated. Here he found himself a hiding place by wriggling under the roots of a tree that had been chopped down:

> It was about then that I was conscious of these characters coming looking for us. I could distinctly smell coffee, then the chatter of Indo voices. One or two jackfruit trees had been left standing and this guy managed to climb up one and although I was lying under this log in this water and I'd covered my face with mud it seemed to me that he was looking at me. There was a big cloud of these bloody bluebottles flying around me and I thought he must be able to spot me. Then the rest of them came up but they weren't doing a really careful search. They were spread too far apart and they passed on their way. Shortly after that I first heard the chopper. I got the SARB [Search and Rescue Beacon] out, which is issued one per patrol. I think I switched it on and then I decided, 'No, to hell with it. If that chopper comes in here the Indos will shoot the bloody thing down.' So I switched it off.

Thirty-six hours passed before 'Geordie' Lillico was finally rescued. His main concern was to satisfy his raging thirst. 'I was drinking all this soup out of this pig water I was lying in,' he recalls. 'There was also these bamboo husks that catch rainwater, with all the little mosquito larvae wriggling about in them, but it all went down to slake my thirst.' When the helicopter returned in the evening on a second search Lillico felt it was safe enough to signal his presence:

> I judged that these buggers would be far enough away for me to risk switching on the SARB and surprisingly he came straight over

my location. He had a bit of a job getting his helicopter into a position where the winch-man could drop the strap so that I could get to it and from the point of view of my professional pride the thing that annoyed me was that I was so weak. I managed to get to the collar and put my arms through it and signalled to them and they started to winch me up. I had my rifle in my hand but I was so weak I could hardly hold it with both hands and then when I was level with the door and these blokes reached out and pulled me to the door it was then that I dropped the bloody rifle. And that to me was a cardinal sin, you know. From the regiment's point of view you didn't come out without your rifle. That was one of the biggest sore points about the whole operation.

Lillico was flown to Kuching hospital and within hours was recovering from his ordeal in the next bed to 'Jock' Thompson, where he heard how Thompson had dragged himself for almost a thousand yards before being found by the Gurkha patrol sent out to rescue him. For Thompson it was the end of his soldiering days but Lillico was luckier and in due course returned to fight alongside his comrades in 'D' Squadron once more – but in a very different theatre of war.

Once the Gurkhas and the SAS had demonstrated the value of cross-border raids, other units that displayed the right kind of dash in jungle operations were also brought in on the secret, mounting their own 'Claret' raids with equal thoroughness. Among them was 40 Commando, to which the seventeen-year-old David Chisnall was drafted in 1965 on the Royal Marines system of 'trickle-drafting', which meant that he joined an operational patrol on the border within days of completing a mere week's training in jungle warfare. Not surprisingly, Chisnall felt 'very much the new recruit in those first long patrols, coming back in for five days doing guard duties in camp, doing the clearance patrols around the wire every morning and then going back out again for a ten-day patrol.' For him, as for every other newcomer, there was the first eerie experience of being on guard at night and seeing 'little lights flickering away in the jungle that you believe quite clearly are torches or people approaching' or hearing 'monkeys, baboons and wild boar moving around'. Then there was the 'awe-inspiring' tension of the first ambush, when long periods of discomfort and boredom had to be overcome by a strict self-discipline that was to prove invaluable a decade later.

On his first 'Claret' raid Chisnall was Number Two on the Army's new GPMG (General Purpose Machine Gun) but also had a number of other duties to perform: 'Part of my task was to fire the 94 Energa grenade from the end of my SLR [Self-Loading Rifle], help the machine gunner and then throw an 80 white phosphorus grenade on very co-ordinated timings. And with the excitement of all of that, knowing that I had three different duties to perform, I think that perhaps is why there wasn't that initial fear.' The raid itself went according to plan but in the rush to withdraw Chisnall made two mistakes. 'I leaned over and grabbed the GPMG by its barrel, burning both hands,' he remembers. 'I then lifted all the belt ammunition and wrapped it round me. The troop commander had laid some marker balloon cord to lead us into position in the early hours of the morning and we had also used "wait-a-whiles", very sharp-pointed ivy-type growths that you used to wrap around trees, as a localised defence. Having grabbed all this ammunition I turned around and got tangled up in an unholy mess of balloon cord and wait-a-while. The troop sergeant and the troop commander both had to cut me free with their commando daggers.'

Another youngster, Alec Grant, a signaller in the 1st Argyll and Sutherland Highlanders, remembers how scared he and his comrades were on their first ambush, set up to intercept an enemy group that had already made an attack and was being chased back to the border:

> I remember sitting at the rear of the ambush, being the signaller, with the tracker dog – a very nice labrador – and his handler, and it was amazing to see the reaction of his dog. You could tell immediately when they were coming because the dog stood up and pointed – and that gave us at least two or three minutes' warning before they actually arrived at the ambush itself. That was quite comforting because we were terrified at the time, but that was my one and only contact message that I sent in Borneo. Trying to get through on voice was just impossible so I switched to morse code and I remember sending, 'Contact, contact, contact.'

With follow-up troops close on the heels of the raiders there was always the risk of a 'blue-on-blue' contact: 'We cleared the ambush site and took the bodies with us but the follow-up troops were still coming up fairly fast and although we wore orange bands on our tropical hats we were actually shot at by our own soldiers, which was quite frightening.' This was followed by an unpleasant night in the jungle: 'We couldn't leave dead bodies just lying on the ground so we had to hang them from the trees to make sure that the wild pigs and things didn't get them. I don't think many people in our *basha* area slept that night!'

Like many other battalions, the Argylls returned to Borneo for a second and a third tour, with the fighting becoming more serious each time. 'It's always the enemy being hurt, never our own side,' Grant reflects; 'but we did take casualties, and to see it is your own comrades who have been killed and badly wounded, it certainly takes you a pace back. You have a completely different attitude the next time you go out on patrol.'

Not every death was as a result of enemy action. As in Malaya, accidents could – and did – happen. David Greenhough of 42 Commando remembers the evening when the alarm went off in his forward troop base:

> The sentry heard one of our alarms go off and we all stood to, lights out, standard practice. This had happened quite often before – it could be wild hogs or roaming dogs – and we thought it was nothing untoward. Somebody thought they saw something at the entrance to the camp itself on the track and the troop commander said he was going to investigate it. The troop sergeant was placed on the automatic weapon which was our main firepower, covering both exit and entrance to the camp. I wasn't personally involved, I was lying in a defensive position with my section when I heard the automatic weapon fire a burst – and upon investigation it was the troop commander we had shot, a young lad who had just joined us to begin his service career. He had explained to the sentry and to the troop sergeant that he was going to a certain point to investigate and remain there. But he ventured further and the sentry and the troop sergeant, seeing something moving where there shouldn't have been, opened fire. There was no blame placed on the firer of the weapon, and rightly so.

Life in these forward bases could be tedious in the extreme, with few creature comforts on offer. 'Discipline was tight in camp, let's make no bones about it,' declares Ron Cassidy, in 1965 a company sergeant-major in the 3rd Battalion of the Royal Green Jackets. 'You couldn't expect to run discipline as you would on a parade ground but nobody took liberties. You didn't abuse the system. In the six months that my battalion was manning those forward bases the men had four days off. Even when they were in base camp they were on duty. When you got up in the morning you either went out on patrol or you manned the defences. There was no relief, no relief at all.' With the company commander and his officers often out with the patrols the day-to-day running of the camp devolved upon the company sergeant-major. Ron Cassidy likens his role to that of a *gauleiter* or local mayor. 'I ran the base camp,' he declares:

> I had more men under my command than the company commander because we were constantly rebuilding our fences, our bunkers and all our slit trenches and the only way I could get this done was to hire the local natives. None of them had a name so I used to give them names. It was David One, David Two, Michael Three, Carl Four and so on and there were times when I had one hundred and fifty to two hundred doing this. I trained them smartly so they could stand to attention and salute me and call out 'Yes, sir' at my roll call every morning. So I spent most of my time during the day looking after the defences and making sure that I got them all off camp before last light, because the natives had a terrible fear of being caught in the dark.

As well as running his labour corps Cassidy did what he could to improve the comforts for the men: 'I designed showers for the company base, which became the first one along the Borneo front to have hot showers. It operated on two large forty-gallon oil drums and the idea was that you heated up the water in the bottom tank which rose to the top tank and then you turned on the tap and out came hot water. It was all right so long as you could get water up from the local river, but sometimes the river flooded and the pump sank into the riverbed and then everything used to come to a spluttering halt.' The CSM also saw to it that they made the best of the supplies that were parachuted in:

> The helicopter used to land every day to pick up our post and deliver stuff from battalion headquarters but resupply of food and stores used to come in by aeroplane. The Royal Corps of Transport were the loaders at the time and they used to pack the Hercules up with stores for us. It always used to come down in one-ton containers on parachutes and, because we were on a war footing, anything that got damaged you could always write off and get resupplied. Of all the stores that used to come down in cases, including fresh eggs packed in sawdust, the only ones I ever had to write off were the old NAAFI packs. Lo and behold, every time the parachute seemed to fail on them, so we wrote off all the NAAFI stores. The amount of chaps who used to walk around with Meerschaum pipes and packets of cigarettes and rolls of film and everything as they came back from patrol! It was almost Christmas every time they came in off patrol and it just added a bit of spice to life. We also used to have a canteen, self-made, a tin hut nailed on to a giant tree that used to sell beer. Our ration for everybody was

two cans a day total. That's if you weren't on duty. If you were in the defence platoon you never drank at all – and woe betide the man who had more than two cans of beer.

The ruse of ordering resupplies was one that most bases supplied by air quickly stumbled upon, just as the occupants came to realise the value of parachute silk, which could be used for hammocks if not already filched by the locals. Medical supplies, too, had other uses. It was 40 Commando who discovered that the green ointment carried by the Medical Attendants for treating blisters was an improvement on their own camouflage cream and was more permanent: 'We used to mix iodine and this green material to make brown, so that we had brown and green all over our equipment and all over our hands and faces for some days after our patrols.' Making the best of the rations available always challenged the ingenuity of the catering staff. The newly-introduced twenty-four-hour 'compo' pack with its blocks of dried food was acknowledged to be a great improvement 'but not for three months at a time'. Those who nibbled at their dehydrated meat seasoned with tomato or brown sauce tended to suffer from a raging thirst, always a problem in the hot and humid climate of Borneo where everyone sweated a great deal and required liberal appli-cations of 'fou-fou' powder to groin, armpits and feet.

On the other hand, it was a fact that every soldier had money to spend when he went on leave, as David Chisnall recalls: 'For the first time in my life I managed to save a hundred pounds – a thousand dollars it was in those days. I was determined to go off to the Cameron Highlands and Penang to spend it, which was one of the things to look forward to.' Many others preferred to head to the less elevated flesh-pots of Singapore.

Despite the protestations of General Walker and his Commander-in-Chief, Admiral Sir Varyl Begg, improvements in weaponry were slow in coming. However, Borneo proved a useful testing ground for the new semi-automatic Armalite, infinitely preferable to the cum-bersome and weighty NATO-issue FN rifle. American seismic detectors were tried with inconclusive results as were the Claymore mines that could be fired at the press of a button to release a hail of small pellets over a wide arc. Electronic listening devices were employed with some success to pick up radio traffic across the border, but never matched the reliability of the human 'eyes and ears'. Another remarkable innovation that made its début in Borneo was the infra-red night-sight, known colloquially as the 'black box'. David Greenhough remembers how vulnerable was his forward troop base to sniper fire:

We were used every night as targets for the terrorists. They would come down and just sit and try and pick us off or at least try to keep us awake. With the arrival of the black box there was a desperate change in their activities. They always recovered their dead so, having dropped the first guy, his number two man would attempt to pick him up and you killed him also. After a couple of nights of this their activities suddenly ceased and it was known as local magic. We used a little bit of propaganda on the locals through our interpreters saying that since we now had this black box magic all would be finished very quickly – and it seemed to work.

As a consequence of his robust campaigning both on behalf of his forces in general and the Gurkhas in particular, General Walker had not made himself popular in Ministry of Defence circles. There were Army commanders who felt that Walker had overplayed his hand in exaggerating the threat posed by the Indonesians, just as there were commanders who believed that he and other senior officers with Gurkha links had seen Confrontation as 'a God-sent opportunity to ram home to the Ministry of Defence the indispensability of the Gurkhas and their brilliance in conducting operations in south-east Asia'. Walker himself remains unrepentant: 'When it was decided that the Brigade of Gurkhas was to be cut – in the middle of a campaign, let me remind you – I resisted. The Gurkhas had no MP to represent them in Parliament and I, therefore, as Major-General of the Brigade of Gurkhas, regarded myself as their MP and it was up to me to fight their battles. And so I fought hard and for fighting hard I was hauled over the coals to such an extent that I was withdrawn from the middle of an important operation in Borneo and flown home and threatened with a court martial.'

When the time came in 1965 for Walker to hand over as Director of Operations, Borneo, to General George Lea he was denied the customary knighthood:

It was very funny because Lord Mountbatten [Chairman of the Chiefs of Staff Committee] came to visit Borneo. He came down the steps of the aeroplane and Admiral Begg was next to him. I was on the right of the line and he said, 'I'm very sorry indeed about your "K".' He saw that I was absolutely astonished so he turned to Admiral Begg and said, 'Doesn't he know about the "K"?' Then in the hearing of the rest of the line Lord Mountbatten said, 'You were put in for a knighthood and it was turned down by the Chief of the General Staff because of your resistance to the proposed cuts of the Brigade of Gurkhas. We then put you in for a CMG and that was turned down and you are now going to get a DSO.' I said, 'But a DSO – I have two already – and a DSO is for gallantry under fire.' So when the citation was written it was done in such a way that it appeared that I was flying over the jungle close to the frontier and continually under fire. It didn't aggravate me but it aggravated my soldiers and I got scores of letters saying, 'This is quite disgraceful.'

General Lea took over command as Confrontation was coming to its climax, with both sides manoeuvring to drive the other back from the border area. By degrees, the Indonesians were being forced to abandon their forward positions and at least one Indonesian local commander sent a runner across the border to his opposite number informing him that he was withdrawing some fifteen kilometres back: 'We got a message saying, "I will not disturb you. I've withdrawn back to this village. I'm carrying out no more offensive operations against you. Please leave me alone.' However, with *Konfrontasi* helping to fuel Indonesia's economic problems it became increasingly vital to President Sukarno's political future that his forces should secure a decisive military victory. This was the background to the battle of Plaman Mapu, where a battalion of the Indonesian Parachute Regiment came within an ace of wiping out the company base of 'B' Company the 2nd Parachute Regiment.

Plaman Mapu was a very typical forward company base, sited on a hill-top a thousand yards back from the border. It had the usual rabbit warren of underground bunkers with a command post at the centre and linked by slit trenches to three strong points defended by GPMGs. 'B' Company of 2 Para had taken it over in February 1965 and over the next few months had followed the commanding officer's policy of getting as many men out on patrol in the jungle as possible, leaving only the bare minimum of defenders in camp. Throughout the two months preceding the attack, evidence began to mount up of Indonesian preparations for an assault, but warnings of troop movements were misconstrued and a number of newly-cleared positions discovered in the jungle around the base were mistaken for ambush sites. Nevertheless, 'we thought one of the company bases was going to be attacked because the tension was building all the time.' So states John Williams, Company Sergeant-Major of 'B' Company, who was to play a pivotal role in what followed.

On the night of the Indonesian attack he was one of the twenty-seven defenders: 'We had a company commander, John Fleming, we had an artillery control officer, a young platoon commander, a mortar section of seven soldiers, myself, Corporal Bourne and a

weak platoon of fifteen soldiers made up of young eighteen- and
nineteen-year-olds who had just done their jungle warfare training in
Malaya' – who were subjected to what was later described as 'a
fanatical assault by soldiers equally as good as the Japanese'.

The first that Williams knew that an attack was under way was
when he was woken by gunfire in the early hours of a 'pitch-black
night with the monsoon rain falling in buckets'. A carefully co-
ordinated barrage of artillery, mortar and rocket fire began to fall on
the three machine gun posts:

> The first intimation that I had was leaping out of my hole in the
> ground with my boots, slacks and belt order on and rushing outside
> to bump into one of the machine gunners, who had taken two
> rounds in the head and had his pistol in his hand, firing it all round
> him. The bullets had creased his skull and had sent him a little bit
> crazy and he was yelling, 'They're in the position! They're in the
> position!' In fact, he stuck the revolver in my stomach, saying,
> 'You're one of them' – and was going to press the trigger before I
> managed to take the pistol from him. It was unbelievable because
> what the machine gunner had said was true. In that first barrage of
> fire one of our two mortar positions was destroyed, along with half
> the people who were manning the mortar. They had killed two
> soldiers and wounded several others which brought our numbers
> down to eighteen who were on their feet and able to fight.

Reporting to the command post, Williams asked the artillery
control officer to bring fire down on the half of their position that the
enemy had taken in their initial assault. He then ran round to the
other side of the hill-top to find the platoon commander and organise
a counter-attack:

> The position was laced with fire, it was still pouring with rain and
> very, very muddy. Visibility was down to about five or ten yards and
> the only illumination was coming from the incoming tracer rounds
> and the shell fire and mortar rounds coming into the position. All
> the soldiers facing the assault had either been killed or wounded so
> all the fire was incoming because there was no enemy coming at the
> other positions and, very professionally, the soldiers in the other
> sections were not wildly firing their guns. I ran across the open
> ground under fire to the slit trench where I knew the platoon
> commander to be and told him he had to bring his soldiers with him
> and we would mount an immediate counter-attack against the
> Indonesians who were in the position. As I was leading the officer
> and his men back across the position a mortar bomb exploded in

the middle of the section, badly injuring the officer and half his
section, so we were left with five men with which to counter-attack
the Indonesians – there must have been about thirty or more in the
position. I shouted across to one of the other section commanders,
Corporal Bourne, and he was able to give me supporting fire as we
put in the attack. The situation was very confused, but I shouted to
the men around me that anything that came in front of them was
enemy. There then followed a savage close-quarter battle with these
Indonesians. One shot when one was able to but in nine cases out
of ten it was hand-to-hand stuff, actually one-to-one combat. It was
very frightening but it became a survival experience because one
knew that if one didn't manage to push them out of the position or
kill them, then they would kill you and overrun the position.

Having successfully pushed the Indonesians out, Williams tried to
secure the perimeter but realised that the enemy was massing for a
second attack on the same sector. This was where the machine
gunner had been injured in the first barrage, so the GPMG was still
unmanned:

I then had to run across open ground to the machine gun and I
remember thinking to myself, 'I've got to get more ammunition on
to that gun because that's the only weapon that's going to keep
those Indonesians out.' How I got there I don't know but I did and
I managed to lace on to the gun several belts of ammunition. At
this stage I was covered in mud from head to foot, my hands were
slippery and muddy, it was pitch black but I knew where the belts
were and I knew what I had to do. One would imagine that you
couldn't do it in those circumstances but it was as though you were
doing it in a barrack-room and you just latched them on. I then
lifted the machine gun off its pivot and directed it against the
Indonesians as they came across the position. When they discovered
that the machine gun was working again they diverted the attack
and about thirty of them, a platoon strength I would imagine,
assaulted the bunker. What demonstrated to me the professionalism
of the men assaulting us was the person who got closest to me. I
killed him when he was three yards away from me and, next
morning when we were removing his body for burial, we found that
he had obviously taken part in the first assault, because his left
thigh had received two bullets and had been tourniqueted. It must
have been very, very difficult for him to stand, never mind run up a
hill, which to me epitomises the professionalism of the TNI, the
best trained of the TNKU's special forces.

Sergeant-Major Williams was himself displaying quite exceptional professionalism. His machine gun was hit three times and the radio beside his head was blown up before he himself received a severe wound to the head. 'Although I didn't realise it at the time, I was then blind in one eye,' he recalls. 'That side of the head had gone.' Even so, he kept firing until all those in front of him were dead or disabled. In the meantime, Corporal Bourne had brought his men round along the slit trenches and was able to direct fire from a second direction with a section attack, which was enough to again drive the Indonesians back. Other defensive fire was also coming in; supporting artillery fire from the howitzer sited in the company base behind them and mortar fire from their own undamaged 3-inch mortar: 'The mortar platoon sergeant had got his one remaining mortar operating and he was firing it perpendicular, straight up in the air, so that the rounds were falling approximately thirty-five yards away.' It was enough of a deterrent to give them a short breathing space that lasted about twenty minutes before the next attack.

Despite his appalling injury – 'one knew the pain and one knew the bleeding but something kept one going. It's the survival both of yourself and of your soldiers and you knew that if you didn't keep going then all was lost' – John Williams was able to collect a number of wounded men and bring them into the shelter of the command post: 'I found the young McKellar. He had half his head severed by a piece of shrapnel and all I did was close the two halves of his head up and tie it with a bandage and tell the cook, Lance-Corporal Collientle, who had been wounded sending up the mortar illuminating rounds, to hold him because somebody should be with him when he died.' Hearing 'yells and screams and commands' from the perimeter Williams knew that a third attack was imminent. Going round the position, he established that there were now only fourteen men able to fight:

> I knew that should a further determined assault be made our chances of surviving it were very, very slim. We'd been fighting for about an hour and a half – although it went in a flash – and dawn was not far away. Our only hope lay in surviving till first light and waiting for the helicopters to come in and relieve the position. So we were masters of our own destiny at this time and *we* had to repel any further attack, so I got Corporal Bourne and his section with a couple of boxes of thirty-six grenades and we started throwing the grenades into the dead ground where I thought they were forming up, about forty yards downhill from where we were. We could hear screams and shouts so the grenades or the mortar or the gun was

having its effect. I think it was the gun then that saved us from a
third attack. The light was gradually getting stronger and stronger
and then we heard the sounds of the withdrawal of the enemy,
although we were still under fire from their rockets and their
mortars from the base-plate positions, which they had hacked out in
the jungle.

Once the incoming fire had stopped Williams called for volunteers
to go out with him to clear the perimeter: 'It says a lot for those young
soldiers that every one of the fourteen stepped forward to come with
me.' Not long afterwards the first helicopter load of Gurkha
reinforcements arrived, followed by a doctor and medical team.
After a brief game of hide and seek with the doctor Williams was
found and his injuries looked at:

> All I knew was that I couldn't hear and I couldn't see. All I could
> see was the look of horror on everyone's faces as they looked at
> me, thinking, 'How's this guy walking?' So we were just flung into
> this helicopter, seven of us, some wounded worse than others, and I
> can remember looking round the helicopter at that stage. We were
> all in various stages of dress or undress. I was still only wearing my
> trousers, my belt order with my ammunition and waterbottle on
> and my boots and the others were similarly dressed. They looked a
> very sorry bunch, with blood coming from their wounds and field
> dressings, but the other thing that they all had is that everyone had
> their guns in their hands. And it was at that stage that I said,
> 'We've come through,' and it suddenly washed over one. And the
> people who had done it were eighteen- and nineteen-year-old
> soldiers, not battle-hardened veterans but eighteen- and nineteen-
> year-old boys who nine months before had been long-haired
> 'hippies' on the streets of our cities and towns.

Six months and many operations and medical boards later John
'Patch' Williams – less one eye and part of his head – was back on
parade with other Borneo veterans at a medal ceremony where he
received a Distinguished Conduct Medal for one of the most
outstanding acts of bravery and leadership witnessed during Confrontation. By then it had become clear that Plaman Mapu had been
a turning point for the Indonesian forces. No other concentrated
attack across the border was ever again attempted, while growing
discontent in Indonesian military and air force circles at the folly of
President Sukarno's pursuit of Confrontation finally came to a head
in September 1965 when an attempted coup by Communist elements
in the Indonesian armed forces was followed by mass round-ups and
killings. As Sukarno's power dwindled, secret talks with Malaysia led

to a steady de-escalation of the conflict, culminating in the downfall of Sukarno and the signing of a peace treaty in August 1966.

From the Commonwealth point of view the outcome provided much cause for satisfaction. The stability of the region had been secured, as had Malaysia's right to determine its own future. One hundred and fourteen soldiers from Commonwealth forces had died over a period of five years – and only thirty-six civilian non-combatants; figures that remained in stark and startling contrast to those emerging from that contemporaneous conflict in south-east Asia, where fifty thousand American soldiers alone perished. 'Borneo could so easily have become another Vietnam,' remarks Brigadier 'Birdie' Smith, now a well-established military historian. 'It is against this background that its success must be measured. Only leadership of a very high quality and troops of a very high standard of training and versatility prevented the conflict from escalation into a full-scale war.' 'Geordie' Lillico of the SAS Regiment takes a more soldierly view. 'Everything worked a treat,' is how he sums up Confrontation. 'It was the first time to my knowledge and to my experience where we managed to bring into play just about the full scenario of all three services. Everybody was in theatre, we were all on the same little operation.'

Pulling out of Borneo aroused different feelings in different people, but for many it was a mixture of emotions. Ron Cassidy admits to being both sad and relieved to be leaving Neebong, where he and his company had spent six months of their lives in 1966:

> There was sadness because we knew we were leaving people like David, the village headman, and his longhouse and all his natives. We had made them almost dependent on us, which was a great shame. The cultivation of the land had degenerated because we had made life too easy for them. But when it was time to leave, David organised a party for us. He selected two of us to attend – Mike Carlton-Smith, the company commander, and myself, the company sergeant-major. He selected the two most bosomy and attractive girls in the village to come and sit beside us at the feast, which was chicken and rice and some other stuff that was a glutinous mess. Those parts of the chicken that you and I would throw away were looked at as delicacies and each girl vied with the other to feed the one or the other of us with the best delicacies, and how we got through the evening I'm not sure. At the end David made a speech and all the villagers applauded us and they gave us some gifts, one of which is a bead necklace which my wife wears to this day, not of any value except to us and obviously to David.

But there was relief that at last we were getting away from – let's make no bones about it – a pretty dangerous situation at times. All my recollections of Borneo are of the hard work, the living in the trenches, which was the making of our Riflemen. Tremendous. But sheer happiness, too, having been away from one's family for one year; relief and sadness and happiness, all rolled into one, stepping into that aircraft and leaving it all behind us and coming home.

II. WAR IN THE DESERT, BUSH AND OLIVE GROVE

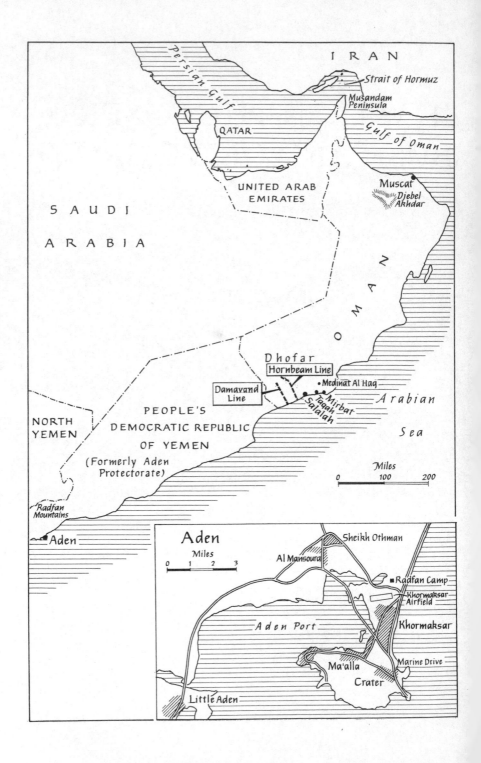

Chapter Eight

KENYA:
Fighting the Mau Mau

I think it's true to say that really I never ever feared the Mau Mau. The Mau Mau almost seemed to be fighting a tribal war and it was the innocents that got hurt all the time, the natives and the unprotected settlers. A lot of our role was food denial and protection of native villages but I can't say that I felt I was in danger of my life when fighting the Mau Mau.

As an armed insurgency the Mau Mau Emergency 'didn't rate very highly in most Army officers' points of view'. Compared to Malaya the little war against the Mau Mau in Kenya was a sideshow as far as many people in the British Army were concerned, limited in both scope and duration. Whereas the insurgency in Malaya affected the entire six thousand square miles of the Malayan peninsula and all its inhabitants, the Mau Mau troubles were confined to one area of less than two thousand square miles, about twice the size of Wales. And while a State of Emergency was indeed maintained in Kenya for more than seven years (1952-60) the fighting itself was essentially a three-year affair followed by a fourth year of mopping-up.

However, the violence perpetrated by the Mau Mau gangs in the first year of the Emergency, which climaxed on the night of 26 March 1953 when eighty-four Kikuyu civilians were hacked to death with *pangas* and Nàivasha Police Station was overrun, far exceeded the horrors inflicted by the CTs in Malaya. In four years the Mau Mau killed over eighteen hundred 'loyal' civilians, as well as six hundred members of the security forces. Of the latter only sixty-three were European, for the real brunt of the fighting was borne not by the visiting British battalions, important as they were, but by local forces: the King's African Rifles, the Kenya Police, the part-time Kenya Police Reserve and Kenya Regiment territorials and, above all, the tribal loyal civilians who made up the Kikuyu Home Guard and the Tribal Police. These last two groups of militiamen accounted for over four and a half thousand of the ten and a half thousand Mau

Mau terrorists killed over that four-year period. For these local forces and for the seconded British Army officers and NCOs who trained and led them Mau Mau was anything but a sideshow. It was a very serious and, sometimes, a very frightening business.

Mau Mau has been represented variously as an anti-colonial freedom-struggle, as a tribal war in which gangs bound together by blood-oaths turned on their own people, and as a revolt against the British colonial government in Kenya by its largest, most politicised tribal grouping, inspired initially by grievances over stolen lands. Confusion over the exact nature of the Mau Mau rebellion was reflected in very mixed British attitudes, as Ron Cassidy remembers from the time when the Rifle Brigade was trooped out to Mombasa in 1953. 'You could walk into a pub in London and find collection boxes for widows of Mau Mau,' he recalls. 'And when the Buffs [Royal East Kent Regiment], who got on the *Georgia* as we got off, got home to Liverpool some of them were stoned.' The battalion itself had been given no clear idea of what to expect: 'We weren't sure really what we were going to meet and it took a long time to understand what the Mau Mau were doing which, basically, was terrorism all over – although that word wasn't used in those days. Some of the things they got up to were quite horrific and it was mostly the innocent they killed and so our role was to protect people and hunt out the Mau Mau and bring them to justice.'

Pleased not to be going to Korea – 'we'd already been issued with all our Arctic clothing and the advance party had got as far as Singapore when the armistice was signed [July 1953]' – the men in Cassidy's battalion embarked for Mombasa in the trooper SS *Georgia* in a holiday mood, 'with the Riflemen and junior NCOs on the troopdecks, the senior NCOs sharing cabins and the officers with their own cabins.' RAF personnel looked after the passengers – 'for some reason troopships were always run by the RAF in those days' – and organised a daily routine that always began with PT on deck. After disembarkation the whole battalion formed up to do 'the traditional march through the town of Mombasa, which to most of us was a nightmare because of the heat and our regimental pace of a hundred and forty to the minute.' After moving up-country by train to Thika, on the edge of the high country north of Nairobi, the troops began operational training.

In the nine months since the State of Emergency had been declared in October 1952 some fifteen thousand Mau Mau adherents were believed to have consolidated themselves into two main fighting organisations linked to a third support group that provided supplies and recruits. This support organisation was based in Nairobi and the nearby Tribal Reserve while the two fighting groups, styled the Kenya Land and Freedom Armies, established themselves in the two forest upland areas of Mount Kenya and the Aberdares. Each group was composed of a number of gangs several hundred strong, poorly-armed and ill-organised but powerful enough in the early stages to raid and massacre with devastating effect. Like the authorities in Malaya, the civil administration in Kenya was slow both to accept the seriousness of the situation and to get the necessary combined act together. However, just as Malaya had the right supremo in the person of Sir Gerald Templer so Kenya was fortunate in having as its military GOC General Sir George Erskine, who took over as Commander-in-Chief East Africa in June 1953. 'Greatly underrated,' is one officer's verdict on Erskine, 'but as far as his understanding of counter-insurgency methods go, probably the most advanced commander we have ever produced.'

In the face of considerable criticism, General Erskine pushed through a package of drastic emergency measures – curfews, round-ups and resettlements, death penalties for convicted Mau Mau adherents, shoot-on-sight policies in Prohibited Areas – that were aimed at breaking up the gangs and cutting them off from their supplies. All these measures took time to come into effect and, until they began to bite, the lack of detailed information about the Mau Mau gangs in the forest and their supporters in the towns and Reserves meant that most military operations were hit-and-miss affairs.

Like other British battalions posted to Kenya, Cassidy's unit was given a large area of forest to look after and charged with eliminating the Mau Mau presence within it. The area was divided into sectors that became the responsibility of individual companies, who sent out patrols in platoon or section strength. Inevitably, they began by making mistakes. 'You tended to be a bit clumsy,' Cassidy admits; 'you tended to light bonfires at night to keep the animals away and, of course, what you were doing was sending up smoke signals to the Mau Mau saying, "Look, boys, here we are." ' Just as inevitable were the jitters that came with inexperience:

> We had trip wires with fixed Bren guns and the idea was that if anyone disturbed the trip wires you'd all open fire. But the Mau Mau were very astute and as soon as they triggered off something they were away like gazelles. This particular night we fired off all our Bren guns and 2-inch mortar illuminating flares, which had short parachutes on to bring the flares down, when lo and behold, twenty minutes after this incident something disturbed the trip flare again and we blasted everything off. Then, as you inevitably do

when you're blasting away, you get a lull and all we could hear was 'Stop firing! Stop firing!' And it was this bloody platoon commander who'd gone forward because he wanted the parachute silks for his handkerchiefs.

Patrolling dominated the lives of Cassidy and his fellow Riflemen. 'We used to spend many, many long hours in the forest, patrolling miles upon miles. It was hard work and we operated sometimes in terrible conditions, conditions where we used to have to give mules rum to keep them warm at night, while the poor old British soldier got nothing.' Even if contacts with the Mau Mau gangs were few there were always other diversions to keep you on your toes and provide a challenge: 'For one thing, if you didn't meet the Mau Mau – and in truth we didn't often – you were guaranteed to meet animals, and the animals you always had the misfortune to bump into were those that you couldn't really handle.' Accidentally walking into the middle of a herd of browsing elephants happened often enough to be regarded as commonplace: 'They can stand in the bamboo and not make any noise when they're eating and then they pick the scent up and you'll get that awful elephant roar that frightens the life out of you.' Being charged by rhinos was another hazard:

> Each patrol had a tracker and he became part of your set-up. This tracker advised us that when we got charged by a rhinoceros all you had to do was to step out of the way and they carry straight on because their weight takes them all the way through. The platoon also had attached to it a chap from the Kenya Regiment who came really to teach us the ways of life within the forests. Well, one day we did get charged and the platoon reformed and the only man missing was the Kenya Regiment sergeant. We found him about two and a half hours later up a tree and after that we realised that possibly we knew more about the forest life than he did.

Where contact with the enemy was made the chances were that it was by accident rather than intent, as Ron Cassidy himself experienced:

> I was stood in a glade with my patrol and two Mau Mau suddenly appeared on the opposite side of the glade ten yards away, and by the time we got our rifles up and fired they had disappeared. There's a thing about the British soldier; it's a terrible job to get him to open fire but when he does, my goodness, it's difficult to make him stop and he will repeatedly keep firing. There was bamboo cut down, trees cut down and no sign of the Mau Mau. And yet four months later we captured one who had obviously had

a bullet gone through his tummy and out the back, and after a
lengthy discussion with him it transpired that he was one of these
characters we had shot at. So he'd been shot through his tummy
and had kept going and I think they had this feeling that they
wouldn't die.

For all the setbacks, the experience of combating the Mau Mau in
Kenya proved an extremely useful one for young soldiers like Ron
Cassidy. Kenya was where he 'learned the art of growing up and
becoming a section corporal, with the responsibility of your own
patrol and the responsibility of their lives, albeit, I don't think we
were in much danger.' The mistakes made and skills learned gave the
Rifle Brigade a head-start when it moved on to Malaya: 'All the bad
lessons were never repeated in Malaya and I'm glad of that because I
have a feeling that if we had taken some of the bad things that we did
in our early days in Kenya it would probably have cost us a lot of
lives.'

One battalion that reversed this process by coming to Kenya in
April 1953 after an earlier tour in Malaya was the Devonshire
Regiment, with results that proved that jungle warfare learned the
hard way also had its advantages. 'We did have the benefit of
Malayan experience and it was to help a lot,' declares Peter Burdick.
'For that reason we probably had the edge on other battalions that
hadn't had that experience.' He himself was a 'green young platoon
commander' who was able to learn a great deal from the old Malayan
hands and, in particular, from his platoon sergeant. 'Sergeant Sellick
was a most excellent, experienced man,' Burdick recalls. 'A most
likeable man who virtually brought me up and taught me all I knew
about soldiering. He taught me how to handle soldiers and taught me
in a few months more than I'd learned in eighteen months at
Sandhurst. Sergeant Sellick commanded half the platoon and I
commanded the other half, and we worked out a sort of system
between us of how we would do our patrolling.'

Careful preparations always played an important part in their
patrolling routines, as did security at the start of the patrol: 'You
couldn't just go out of your patrol base back in the Kikuyu Reserve
and into the forest because there was every possibility that the wrong
people would see you do it. So we used to creep out in the pitch dark
and often we used to deliberately make a little hole in the barbed
wire round our camp and creep through that.' Hard information in
these early days was rarely forthcoming, but: 'We knew the Mau
Mau wouldn't be far from water. We knew they wouldn't be far from
trails so it was a cat and mouse situation in the forest. The Mau Mau

knew we were hunting them and they were fairly fly. They had very good systems of sentries around their camps so you would be very lucky if you ever managed to get anywhere near one of their hides, because usually the sentries would hear you coming. It all boiled down to stealth and if, as a platoon commander, you kept your patrol moving really slowly and really carefully and never made any noise you could strike lucky.'

In the eighteen months in which he served as a platoon commander in Kenya Peter Burdick had four successful contacts, three of them while on patrol:

> I would go in front, behind me I had my Bren gunner – the Bren was the main weapon of the patrol – and behind him I used to have my best shot. We had a drill worked out that if we met a Mau Mau gang coming the other way – and this was one's prayer, I suppose – and if we saw them first I stepped just to the left of the trail, which was only about a foot wide with very thick undergrowth either side, and my Bren gunner came up on my right so that we immediately doubled the firepower. We worked out this drill and we put it into practice once or twice. The first time this happened we'd started a patrol off in daylight, rather against our own rules, and we were going along – mercifully very slowly – when I saw two or three Africans, about fifty yards away, coming down the trail towards me. There was no doubt whatsoever that they were Mau Mau because the forest was prohibited to Africans and any African who was there knew he would be shot on sight. I just looked out of the corner of my eye and saw that Lance-Corporal Padden, my Bren gunner behind me, had seen them. I went to the left and, as we'd agreed, he immediately came up on my right and I raised my little 9mm Sterling sub-machine gun to my shoulder – it wasn't much good if you didn't aim it. He carried his Bren gun always, as most Bren gunners did, with the sling over his shoulder and he fired one or two very long bursts from the hip and I fired two or three bursts from the shoulder, aiming as quickly as I could in the time that I had. The moment I took my eye away from the sights I looked up the trail and there was nothing there – and my heart sank because I thought, 'Here we are, we've had an opportunity, we've seen three Mau Mau, possibly more behind them, and we've failed.' Then we got to the spot and there – I must confess to my joy – was one very dead Mau Mau.

A second contact by the same platoon produced a more valuable kill: a courier with a bag full of papers and messages that provided valuable information for the intelligence organisations to work on.

ABOVE Mau Mau atrocity: a British soldier surveys the scene of a massacre, with the bodies of Kikuyu loyalists literally hacked to pieces by *pangas*, Kenya, 1953.
BELOW Brew-up: British troops in a prohibited area in the upland forest display a careless disregard for their enemy. The photograph was probably taken during the latter stages of the Mau Mau Emergency.

Greek Cypriot terrorism: ABOVE EOKA terrorists strike a pose for the camera; BELOW Two sergeants of 3 Para escort a Greek Orthodox priest to detention.

ABOVE Aiding the civil power: Marines of 45 Commando escort Cyprus police and an informer in the Troodos Mountains, 1956. BELOW Men of the Royal Northumberland Fusiliers, with their distinctive hackles worn over their cap badges, on stand-by. This was during the street disturbances in Aden in 1967. A decade earlier they had served with distinction in Korea and in Kenya during the Mau Mau Emergency.

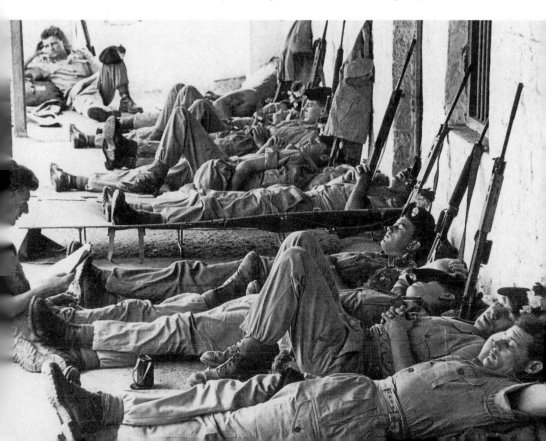

Incidents in the Crater, Aden. Four of a series of photographs taken by the brilliant Terry Fincher of the *Daily Express*: ABOVE A grenade has been thrown at a patrol of the Northumberland Fusiliers, wounding a soldier, and the grenade thrower has himself been shot; BELOW The wounded Fusilier is attended to; OPPOSITE PAGE Following another grenade-throwing incident and wounding, Fusiliers go in hard, arresting and questioning suspects.

Farewell to comrades: last post and salute at the Happy Valley Cemetery, Aden, at the burial of the Royal Northumberland Fusiliers killed in the Armed Police Barrack ambush in June 1967.

ABOVE 'A very unusual man': Major Johnny Watts, Commander of 'D' Squadron 22 SAS, after capturing the heights of Djebel Akhdar, Oman, January 1959. BELOW Troopers of 'A' Squadron 22 SAS check their weapons after being landed by helicopter on high ground in the Radfan, Aden Protectorate, 1964.

The secret war in Dhofar: ABOVE Captain Shaun Brogan of 'A' Squadron 22 SAS negotiates with *firqats* before the launch of Operation 'Jaguar' in October 1971; BELOW Troopers of 'A' Squadron firing a GPMG from a sangar near 'White City' after going back on to the *djebel*, Dhofar, Oman.

In addition to patrolling in the forest the British battalions also took part in two other types of operations: large-scale sweeps in the reserves, where there was more open country, and cordon-and-search operations in the African townships. None of the sweeps that Peter Burdick took part in produced results but, frustrating as they were, they did provide a change of scene for a day or two. Huge numbers of troops were usually assembled and spread out in extended line, moving forward 'like a brush sweeping up dust' with stops on either flank and at the far end of the drive so that the whole thing was 'rather like a pheasant shoot'. Ron Cassidy participated in one particularly unpleasant sweep through a swamp that produced unusually heavy casualties in the form of several Riflemen badly stung by wild bees.

Much more appealing from the troops' point of view were the cordon-and-search operations: 'We used to tear down the road in the three-tonner, brakes slammed on and scream to a halt, tail-board down, dash out and put a cordon round, night or day, anytime. Then it was just a matter of waiting, standing around while they kept everybody in and chasing back the Africans trying to come out so they were interrogated by the police.' This was the private soldier's point of view, as recalled by Tommy Hewitson, who came out to Kenya in September 1953 as a National Serviceman in the 1st Royal Northumberland Fusiliers. 'The privates knew nothing about it. They just woke up in the morning and were sent out on a cordon,' he explains:

> You live in your little platoon or your section and that is as much as you know. Sometimes you have a good platoon commander who will explain to you what is happening and sometimes you will get a guy who will just say, 'You're going here.' You don't know why you're going here but you just finish up in this spot. Somebody just says to you, 'Stop there,' and you stop there and you just stay there until somebody comes and tells you, 'OK. We're going back now.' We used to sit there for hours and hours and hours. The officers were very superior guys and they never condescended to speak to the men. It was purely, 'Do this' and 'Do that'. The old class system was always very, very rigid, very strong but the reason the system worked – and I've thought about it often – was because all a National Serviceman wanted was to do his two years. He wanted to get out and he didn't want any sort of hassle, because any time that he spent in detention was added on to his time.

When not on operations, life for Hewitson and his fellow Fusiliers in their camp at Moyengo Gate was very restrictive:

It was really boring because we weren't allowed out of the camp after six o'clock at night. Everybody was confined to camp and everywhere you went you carried your rifle and fifty rounds of ammunition, even if you went to the camp cinema – if you can call a screen up in a field a cinema. We used to call it the Billodeon because the Quartermaster, Major Bill, very nice guy, used to run this cinema. You used to take your box and your blanket and they used to charge a shilling. They used to bring a few leather armchairs from the officers' mess for the officers and we'd be sitting behind them. If you hadn't a shilling you used to lie around behind the screen and watch it from outside while the guys on stag [sentry duty] used to be wandering about and watching, too. There was a little place organised by the Padre probably and some of the ladies of the town, the Townswomens' Guild or something, which we used to call the Asher Arms where you could go in the afternoon and get bacon, egg and tomatoes and a cup of tea and a look at the English papers. And the NAAFI was there, the beer was cheap and cigarettes were cheap, but we really hadn't very much money as National Servicemen. We got about thirteen shillings a week overseas allowance but we had only four shillings a day as National Servicemen and three shillings of that was kept for National Insurance stamp and stoppages.

What made the discomforts and privations bearable was the strong sense of comradeship and regimental loyalty in old county regiments like the Northumberlands. 'I'm not saying we were better soldiers than anyone else but we thought we were,' explains Hewitson. There was a genuine bond of shared community in the battalion:

The Northumberland Fusiliers was a family regiment in lots of ways. As I read back through the gazettes and the regimental history the family names are repeated and repeated and repeated. Every family in Ashington where I live must have had someone who served in the Northumberland Fusiliers. It was mining and soldiering. I used to look out of my living room window into a living room window just across the road where a guy called Cunningham lived and he was in the 1st Battalion. Out the back there was a guy called Jimmy Charlton who was a clerk in the MT in the 1st Battalion. In the next street was a lad called Eddie Boyd who was in the Rifle Company and a man called Ian Hamilton, who was the commanding officer's bugler. Ian and I used to stand in the queue in the cook house and it was just as if you were at home with the guys talking. There you had the Newcastle guys, the Morpeth, Gadgies, Newbiggin, Bedlington, and everybody spoke a different language. Newcastle spoke an entirely different sort of accent or twang. Morpeth had a burr and would use words that nobody in Ashington would use and it's only six miles away. Newbiggin and Ashington were three miles away and there still was that difference of speech.

In April 1954 the whole battalion was brought into Nairobi to join with other units in a major operation aimed at destroying the Mau Mau support organisation in the city. As well as the Northumberlands there were 'the Buffs and the Devons and the Black Watch, then we had the KOYLIs and the Gloucesters, the Shropshires and the Royal Irish Fusiliers – they were crackers.' Operation 'Anvil' lasted a month and resulted in the rounding-up of over sixteen thousand Mau Mau suspects.

> We travelled overnight to Nairobi in convoy and arrived in the early hours of the morning. The companies went straight out to the African locations and put cordons round. The police came and erected barbed wire compounds and then they brought in hooded men who were Mau Mau who had been captured and had turned coat and said they would become informers. They brought everyone past these guys and they were just pointing the finger at them, guys they knew from the different gangs, carriers, staff officers and what have you. Then they took these guys and locked them up in a place called Langora, a prison camp just outside Nairobi.

'Anvil' effectively destroyed the Mau Mau movement in Nairobi, cutting off the major supply lines to the insurgent groups in the forests. The security forces then applied the same policy of mass internment of suspects in neighbouring Kikuyu areas, while at the same time providing protection to cleared villages by setting up local home guard units in the shape of the Kikuyu Guard. Tommy Hewitson was among those detailed to provide an escort to move detainees from Langora to a second prison camp, in the process witnessing much 'needless brutality' that made him wonder if the British 'for all their years of colonial rule' hadn't made 'a hash of a lot of things'. At Langora he watched the Askari policemen drive the prisoners into buses 'leaning over the wire whacking them, beating them with sticks and whips'. When he tried to intervene Hewitson very nearly found himself in serious trouble:

> This Askari was literally beating up this poor old guy who could hardly walk. I threatened to shoot this Askari corporal. I jumped up and I'm not telling you what words I used but I told him to get

out of the road. Then this police inspector came, demanding to
know why I was interfering with his Askaris and I told him what to
do as well and things started to get heated. In fact, it was the
adjutant who told me to get out of the bloody road and he sorted it
out from there.

The British troops themselves did not always act in ways that
brought credit to their regiments. While escorting these same
detainees to their new detention centre by train a number of soldiers
searched their prisoners at gunpoint and robbed them of their few
remaining possessions – 'then the SIB [Special Investigation Branch
of the Military Police] got on board and they started searching the
guys. They found one corporal who had a water bottle full of watches
and another who was folding pound notes and stuffing them in the
cracks round the door of the carriage and they found a few more.
Some of them were court-martialled, some of them were busted,
some of them got jailed, some of them I think got away with it and
after that this battalion was known as the Nairobi Bandits. But, of
course, they claimed that every other battalion was doing it as well.'

As more and more Mau Mau were captured or interned so the
intelligence began to build up, allowing the security forces to act on
the basis of solid information rather than on chance. Here a major
contribution was provided both to the campaign itself and to the
development of Army intelligence-gathering as a whole by the
activities of a small group of Army officers who were transferred to
special duties with the Kenya Police Special Branch in mid-1953.
One of these officers was Frank Kitson, a Major in the Rifle Brigade
who was to play a decisive role in this group's activities. 'The idea of
putting Army officers into a police intelligence organisation was a
perfectly logical one,' Kitson explains. Army commanders needed
intelligence and background information on a scale that far out-
stripped the resources and manpower of the Kenya Police Special
Branch, 'so they used Army officers who knew exactly what the
requirement would be for the troops, who could get into Special
Branch and expand the thing, getting their own contacts and bringing
in a lot of their own sort of information.'

Taking their orders from the head of the Police Special Branch but
with little support in terms of funds or facilities these officers were
sent out to different Districts within the Mau Mau areas where each
built up his own intelligence network. Their prime role was to gather
information to give to the security forces 'to enable them to develop
their operations in a sensible way'. One means of doing this was to
'try and have our people around where any action was going on to get

our hands on the prisoners and then we tried to get from them by talking to them information that was of immediate value'.

It was just such immediate information that enabled Peter Burdick to 'go to war in a mobile laundry unit' near the end of the Devons' tour in Kenya in late 1954. He was then acting as a company second in command on administrative duties with almost the entire company out of camp when word came in on the radio of a hot tip: 'A sweep was going on at the Tana River and on one flank of the sweep there was a large gang of Mau Mau, which could be trapped on one side of the river if someone could get to it within a few hours. We were the only people who could do anything about it because everybody else was too far away.' It then turned out that the only vehicle in camp was a 'three-tonner that carried a mobile bath unit, which had arrived about half an hour before.' Burdick commandeered both the vehicle and its RAOC driver: 'I said, "How about taking us out on an operation?" He said that providing I gave him a direct order he was bound to do that, adding privately that it was the opportunity he had been waiting for for a long time.'

Collecting his sergeant-major and half-a-dozen of the camp sentries Burdick piled them all into the back of the mobile bath unit and then directed the driver to head into the bush at top speed:

> After about fifteen minutes' driving we realised we were getting into the right area because we heard a lot of warlike noises. We could see one or two of the Piper Pacer aircraft that were used by the Kenya Police Reserve to support our operations. We went past a police post and there was pandemonium going on. I managed to get hold of the officer in charge and said to him that perhaps we could tie operations up a bit between us but half his people had already had their instructions and gone off so it was evident to me that we had just got to work on our own. So on we went and parked our truck perhaps a few hundred yards from the Tana River. We got into extended line and then moved in the direction of the river. To my astonishment I saw a considerable number of African heads and hats bobbing about in the trees and realised that we had struck gold and that almost for the first time in my tour in Kenya we had got hold of a really good bit of information.

Burdick and his men closed on the Mau Mau, each man firing individually as 'opportunity targets' presented themselves 'like some sort of grotesque fairground booth'. Those Mau Mau who survived took to the river where they were chased and dispersed by further rifle fire. 'It sounds awfully merciless now but it was the only way,' Burdick maintains. 'The water was flowing fast and to this day we've no idea what damage we caused but I have a feeling we probably got most of them. It was a good action for our company and a reflection of the provision of good information at last.'

However, to some of the Army officers involved in Special Branch intelligence-gathering it was becoming apparent that the information they were collecting could be used far more effectively if it could be built upon rather than used at once: 'The Army didn't seem at that time to understand that you could get information and then develop it by getting more information. It reckoned that intelligence had to be something on which it could act, but if you used the information you got as a base for operations to get more and then put the two lots together you got more and more information – until finally you got the pin-point information that enabled you to go at once and ambush or arrest or kill or do whatever you wanted to do to the terrorist.'

Working on this principle of always developing information, Frank Kitson and his team of Field Intelligence Assistants – young Europeans from the white settler community who had joined the Kenya Regiment or the Kenya Police Reserve – then went a stage further: 'We used our own men to act on our information and didn't give it to the security forces at all. Let us say that there might not be time for them to get it before the target had shifted, so then it was worth actually taking the action yourselves.' What emerged from this were the highly-effective covert operations in which counter- or pseudo-gangs went into the bush disguised as Mau Mau adherents themselves. Their effectiveness stemmed from the fact that many of the members of these counter-gangs were indeed Mau Mau – or, rather, former Mau Mau members who had been 'turned'. 'A member of an enemy gang would almost certainly end up being condemned to death because it was an offence punishable by death to be a member of the Mau Mau,' Kitson explains:

> So that is what would normally happen to a prisoner ultimately if he was a member of an enemy gang. Now when you've got a framework that consists of a sufficiently strong deterrent like the threat of being hanged, on the one hand, and a sufficiently strong incentive in the form of a reward on the other, then you've got something in which to work. Then you have to see what it is that made him an insurgent in the first place and try to persuade him that that was the wrong judgement in his case. After a few months we were also looking very much for the fellow who, although he might not have any immediate information of value, would have an immense amount of information with regard to his gang. So we seldom bothered to put much pressure on him to get immediate

information. We were really assessing whether he would come
to us. Was he going to be someone we could keep as a member
of our team, almost as a friend?

Once a Mau Mau gang-member had been turned he could be sent
out to build up informers – or he could be used as a member of a
pseudo-gang:

> We would make a gang up consisting of three or four of these
> people and one of our white Field Intelligence Assistants, and they
> would move around rather like a small group from a gang coming
> out of the forest and moving around in the reserve to collect
> supplies, talking to the local people who they thought were Mau
> Mau supporters, and by doing that we would get a lot more
> information about who the supporters were. We could probably get
> back to the gangs themselves, because quite often a much bigger
> gang would come out of the forest. Then you could probably
> surround a group of high-ranking members of the Mau Mau in a
> hut, possibly, and capture them all as they were. One of the ex-
> Mau Mau would act as the leader because he'd have to do the real
> talking to the supporters or the real gangsters, because however
> well you disguised your Field Intelligence Officer, he wouldn't be
> able to talk Kikuyu convincingly enough to fool them. The white
> man who went with them – if one did, and they didn't always –
> would be there to control what was going on, to decide whether to
> take action or to break off and go and report it. There wasn't that
> much difficulty in disguising our people well enough for that. If
> you're not expecting something you don't see it. That, really, is
> what it amounts to and, with a bit of care, we did it umpteen times.
> I mean, I even did it once or twice – not very often because I was
> running a large area and it wasn't my business to go and do the
> minor patrolling, but I did do it once or twice just to get the feel of
> what the chances were of one's cover being blown – and, after all, if
> I could do it just about anyone could.

Although carried out on a comparatively small scale these covert
operations were extremely successful, if hazardous, and were a
major contribution in the break-up of the gangs in the districts in
which they worked. By the end of 1954 the effect of General
Erskine's military measures combined with political and agricultural
reforms had cut away Mau Mau's popular support among the
Kikuyu. The gangs became more and more fragmented, seeking
refuge ever deeper in the forests as the hunt continued. When
Lieutenant Christopher Dunphie came out to join the 1st Battalion

the Rifle Brigade in January 1956 shortly before its departure for Malaya the Emergency had already been greatly scaled down. The operations continued but the crisis was over and from a twenty-year-old subaltern's point of view 'life was marvellous. To join a platoon, to get to know one's Riflemen and to be immersed in battalion life, which was demanding but essentially fun, was really terrific. On the occasions when one wasn't on operations one could get away and shoot duck on Lake Naivasha or go and shoot bush-buck or water-buck somewhere. There was so much to do.'

But not every soldier saw it that way. As far as National Serviceman Tommy Hewitson was concerned, 'the whole campaign was a complete and utter waste of time. I could never see any point in what we were doing, really. It seemed to me I spent most of my time chasing after will-o'-the-wisps, shadows, and I spent some very uncomfortable hours. It was so bloody stupid. Kenyatta [gaoled in 1952 as the suspected leader of Mau Mau] eventually became the head of the country, after so much loss of life and misery and misfortune – not just on the British side but on the other side as well.' Perhaps the bitterest memory was the loss of comrades and the circumstances of their deaths:

> There was a lad from Ashington, a lad called Sobie. He had been with this patrol of four or five men and the corporal had put Sobie on stag [guard]. Everybody was frightened, trigger-happy. They hadn't been there very long, you see. Everybody was a bit nervous and they didn't know what the score was. Well, unfortunately, Sobie must have been a bit cheesed off sitting where he was and he started to wander about. He came back into the patrol from behind and the corporal in charge of the patrol opened fire and that was it. Sobie was dead and it was as simple as that. We also had a guy called Munster who was shot accidentally while mucking about with another guy with a revolver, and we had a guy called Napper, in the motor platoon, who was killed during a sweep. He leaned over the barrel when the mortar bomb came out and that was the end of him. This wasn't dying gloriously for Queen and Country. This was pure stupidity and negligence and a lot of inexperience and fear. I think it often happens. If they had been killed by a Mau, well, then there may have been some point to it all, but absolutely no. It was a sheer waste, sheer waste of young men's lives.

Chapter Nine

CYPRUS AND SUEZ:
A Bit of a Backwater

It soon became a frustrating exercise because we were chasing the terrorists, small groups of them or individuals on occasion, making grand exercises, toiling up the mountains, looking for the 'pimpernel' who was the EOKA terrorist, who had the advantage of his own ground, of being shielded by the villagers, sometimes out of patriotism and sometimes out of fear. And there were very few occasions when one was physically able to pin the enemy down or corner him. There were successful operations but for every one that culminated in capturing or killing a group of terrorists, there were many, many scores of operations that produced absolutely nothing but thin air and an exhausted group of soldiers.

When John Stevenson first came to Cyprus in 1951 with 'the good old 43rd and 52nd' the island was seen as a 'wonderful station with no civilian troubles at all'. His memories are of 'very good weather, lots of sport and a little bit of military training. Both the Turks and the Greeks were very friendly towards us. It was great fun going into the Troodos Mountains and into Nicosia in the evening. In fact, everyone was very pleased to see us – especially our money!' Within months the regiment was on the move again, back into another Middle Eastern hotspot – the Canal Zone – and when it next returned to Cyprus five years later the old 'languid' atmosphere had gone. The island was still 'a bit of a backwater' but one on which the British authorities had 'lived for so many years that they hadn't really appreciated that they now had in their midst a terrorist organisation, which was going to cause a lot of trouble.' That organisation was EOKA, the National Organisation of Cypriot Fighters.

Britain had administered the island since 1878, initially on behalf of the Turkish government, but from 1923 onwards as a British Crown Colony. Despite the historical overlordship of the Ottoman Turks, four-fifths of the population were Greeks who had long sought unification of the island with Greece, under the slogan of

Enosis, or 'union'. These aspirations had been resisted both by the minority Turkish population and by the British authorities. In 1954 matters came to a head when large numbers of British troops were transferred to Cyprus as part of an agreed withdrawal from Egypt. The importance of Cyprus as a strategic base suddenly assumed new significance. 'I don't think the authorities had really come to terms with the fact that the Greek Cypriots no longer wanted to serve and live under a British colonial rule,' is how Henry 'Todd' Sweeney interprets the Greek Cypriot response. 'One of the spurs was when one of our colonial ministers said, "Oh well, Cyprus. We shall never hand Cyprus over. It will remain a colony." This was at a time when we'd handed over India and were thinking of handing over other places in different parts of the world, but the statement that Cyprus would remain a colony was one of the spurs that led the Greek Cypriots to importing Grivas from Greece and setting up a terrorist organisation to try and push the British out.'

Unknown to the British, the head of the Greek Orthodox Church in Cyprus, Archbishop Makarios – an 'evil man' in the eyes of many British soldiers – invited a retired Greek Army Colonel named George Grivas to organise and lead a military resistance movement. With less than a hundred guerrillas under his command, Grivas orchestrated a classic terrorist insurgency, beginning in April 1955 with a bombing campaign. Riots, strikes and civil disobedience protests were combined with murders of civilians and other soft targets, often off-duty policemen or soldiers out shopping with their wives. Since Grivas and most of his bands of guerrillas were believed to be operating out of the mountains – either in the Troodos that dominate the western half of the island or in the lesser Kyrenia range north of Nicosia – it was in these two areas that Field Marshal Sir John Harding, recalled (in September 1955) from retirement to become Governor of Cyprus and Director of Operations on the Templer model, concentrated his military efforts:

> He and the Brigadier, 'Tubby' Butler, were good friends and they
> hatched all sorts of schemes and we set about mounting various
> operations either up in the mountains of Troodos or up on the
> north ridge of Cyprus from Kyrenia. We carried out some very
> successful operations, but you didn't know where Grivas was,
> although you had an idea he might be in a certain area, and you
> had to work to a very largely orchestrated pattern which was above
> the battalion, it was brigade and larger. But our intelligence was
> not good – and if you haven't got intelligence you just founder.

That was how Mike Gray remembers Operation 'Pepperpot' in which the Parachute Brigade eliminated two important EOKA cells, but failed to catch Grivas or the bulk of his forces. Another young parachute officer, Johnny Watts, regarded such large-scale operations as a waste of time and effort:

> A big, fat white hand coming down on a map and the order 'Circle that area with ten thousand chaps' was totally counter-productive, because you were working in the local environment among people who looked at the terrorist guerrillas as freedom fighters. They were the Robin Hoods against us, the Sheriffs of Nottingham, and the more the big numbers ploughed around and got nowhere, and the story spread that, in fact, Alphonso was hiding under a hole in the tree and this soldier came and sat down and read the *Daily Mirror* over his head but didn't know he was there, the more it added to the legend, and it just demeaned your own military prestige and effectiveness.

What made their relative lack of success all the more difficult to accept was that the Parachute battalions had come to Cyprus in peak condition. 'We were exceptionally well-trained,' declares John Williams, then a young private soldier. 'We were very, very fit and we were led by some very good soldiers. We had rehearsed and trained until we were a well-oiled machine.' He and most of his comrades knew and loved the island. They had spent leaves there while serving in the Canal Zone, staying at the Golden Sands Leave Camp at Famagusta and meeting 'nothing but kindness and hospitality from everybody' when they had toured the island on bicycles. Though saddened to see Cyprus gradually being 'split asunder for political ends', Williams had been looking forward to his first taste of operations with a great sense of 'excitement and adventure. I was excited at the prospect of actually achieving something, some purpose to one's training and to sorting out some of the problems that were facing this lovely island.' He was soon disillusioned:

> We spent nearly all our time in the Troodos Mountains chasing the shadows that were the EOKA. One became more and more frustrated because whilst one was doing these massive sweeps in the mountains where we thought the terrorists were, back in the villages and towns the terrorist was sneaking in and planting his bomb, shooting policemen in the back and making life thoroughly miserable, not caring who his victims were – man, woman or child, policeman or soldier – so long as he got a victim and captured the headlines and gained some publicity for the EOKA cause. I remember feeling so frustrated about it all.

While the Parachute Brigade and the Royal Marine Commandos slogged over the mountains, other units concentrated on combating EOKA in the villages and towns. Here, too, there were many frustrations. 'We would get some information that a terrorist was in the village of Zupi, say,' explains 'Todd' Sweeney, whose company of Riflemen found themselves repeating old drills that they had first put into practice in Palestine. 'We would sneak off in the middle of the night, drive part of the way, put our lights out, drive another part of the way and de-bus. Then we would go very quietly, surround the village, go in with the police and search the various houses. It was fairly ham-fisted because we didn't have the exact information. We just knew that somebody was hiding in a village. The intelligence was being built up, photographs of the leaders were taken, some of their hide-outs were discovered but we never really got any hot intelligence which we could follow up.'

Operation 'Pepperpot' had, in fact, driven Grivas out of the mountains and it had also uncovered valuable information about his organisation, including documents implicating Archbishop Makarios. The Archbishop's residence was surrounded and he was arrested. This action not only caused much satisfaction among the troops but also produced the best joke of the campaign. The Argyll and Sutherland Highlanders had supplied the cordon round the Archbishop's palace and on hearing that Makarios had been arrested one of the Jocks was said to have replied, 'Makarios? Makarios? Which company is *he* in?'

As well as documents, large numbers of photographs were uncovered, as Mike Gray explains:

> They are very flamboyant people, the Greeks, and they loved taking macho photographs of each other, and stupidly they left their film behind, so we had some most wonderful photographs, really clear, of all these groups, together with their weapons and things in profusion. I had a stack of these blown up to about a foot square showing all the terrorists, all of them numbered with their code names on the back so we knew precisely who it was we were looking for and all their life stories. In addition, Special Branch had produced a massive sheet, about three feet by two, of little passport photographs of all the wanted men that used to appear on walls, with big crosses on it when some of them were caught and put in prison or killed.

But while the identity of the hard-core terrorists was known, information about their movements and intentions was much harder to come by. In the big towns the support or acquiescence of the

Greek population made them very hard to pursue and, at the same time, very dangerous. In Nicosia terrorists of the calibre of the notorious Nicos Sampson operated with impunity, especially in what was dubbed the 'Murder Mile': 'This infamous terrorist Nicos Sampson was a photographer whose shot of a girl kneeling by the side of her dead fiancé went round the world as one of the most brilliant Press pictures of all time. What we didn't know was that Nicos Sampson had shot the chap, got rid of his revolver, picked up his camera and taken the photograph of him. He carried out most of his murders in Ledra Street, a place you just didn't walk down. It was a narrow, twisting street and it was highly dangerous, so you just kept out of the place altogether.'

Few units came through without one or more of their personnel being attacked in what they regarded as thoroughly vile circumstances. In the Royal Horse Guards two officers were shot at point blank range within the space of a few days: 'One was our beloved doctor, Gordon Wilson, shot in his Mercedes going to look at a Greek family, and the other was Stephen Fox-Strangways, who was doing the shopping in Limassol where he'd done it for a year in a little grocer's shop. He and the mess waiter were shot in the back.' The commander of the squadron concerned was Roy Redgrave. 'I had quite a problem telling people to calm down and let justice take its course,' he recalls. Some slight satisfaction was obtained when explosives were found in a building opposite the grocer's shop – and were judged to be in too delicate a condition to be moved: 'So we put sandbags round them and the explosives were themselves detonated in a controlled manner using more explosive – and that was the end of the local cinema.' There was satisfaction, too, when the terrorist Nicos Sampson was finally unmasked as the result of a tip-off – and regret that the Royal Horse Guards trooper who shot him in the leg when he went for his gun hadn't finished him off. Although sentenced to death, Sampson was reprieved as part of a political deal and later released, going on to lead a revived EOKA death squad in Nicosia in 1963: 'If he'd been killed it would have avoided all the bloodshed when he announced that he was President [in 1974] and virtually forced the Turks to invade and create the situation which exists in Cyprus today.'

Another terrorist hot spot was Limassol. There had been nineteen murders in the streets in the three weeks before Sweeney's battalion, the Ox and Bucks, took over from the Norfolks in November 1956, a clear indication that they were 'coming into a very difficult area'. Yet much to the regiment's surprise and satisfaction there were no more murders in the town itself for the rest of their tour. 'We rather prided ourselves as a regiment that we kept Limassol quiet for a couple of years,' states Sweeney. 'The way we operated was that the police and the Army worked very closely together and with a paramilitary force largely composed of Turks who acted as part-soldiers and part-police. We would do most of the patrolling of the towns and they would do most of the patrolling of the countryside while we guarded all the police stations. After the nineteen murders the tension seemed to slip away from Limassol and boiled up in Nicosia.' Only many years later did the full reason become known. 'I was working at the United Nations when I met a man named Demos Hadjimiltis,' Sweeney recounts. The name was known to Sweeney as one of those that had been on his wanted list. Hadjimiltis had been the EOKA district commander in Limassol but had never been captured. They talked and became friends and the truth emerged:

> He told me that far from it being the Oxfordshire and
> Buckinghamshire Light Infantry that had kept Limassol quiet from
> late 1956, *he* had been keeping Limassol quiet, because at that time
> Grivas had been transported from Nicosia to Limassol and had
> been hiding in Limassol for most of the time we were there.
> Hadjimiltis had a very charming wife called Nina and she had been
> the messenger between Grivas and himself. Nina was constantly
> picked up by the police and questioned but she never gave away
> where Grivas was. On one occasion Demos Hadjimiltis had been in
> a garage of a house when the soldiers of my regiment turned up,
> blocked either end of the road and began searching all the houses
> with the police. He had a gun and was determined to die but before
> he died he would shoot a couple of soldiers when they burst in at
> the door, because he knew there was no way out. The way you
> made sure that houses were properly searched was that the soldiers
> were given a piece of chalk and they put a white cross on the door
> and that showed the next team – because they were leap-frogging
> one another – that the house had been searched. The soldiers had
> reached his garage and were about to open the door when he heard
> a shout of 'Tea up!' from the end of the street and one soldier
> turned to the other and said, 'Come on, let's go and get some char
> and a wad [bun].' They put a cross on the door and went to the end
> of the street and he got away.

Searches were not popular among the troops so it was not surprising that they were sometimes conducted without much enthusiasm. 'It was a thoroughly unpleasant job that soldiers shouldn't really get caught for,' is the opinion of Roy Redgrave, who commanded one of the three Royal Horse Guards armoured car squadrons sent to Cyprus in the latter half of the EOKA Emergency. 'I disliked going through some person's miserable possessions but you still had to rootle through them. If it was summer there'd be complete families asleep on the rooftops, so you'd have to gain access to the rooftops and prod them, make them turn over, see if the guy you wanted was there.' Another role that he found equally distasteful was having to escort an informer as he went about the business of identifying suspects: 'We'd turn up with an armoured car or Saracen and put him in the driver's seat with a mask over his head and then parade in front of him all the suspects, like a police identity parade, and he would nudge the policeman behind him to indicate who the baddies were.' Bringing a hostile village to order could also be unpleasant – although it did sometimes present a challenge:

> I was told to go to a village with a name like 'Palitechno' to remove all the signs on the walls. This was a very big, pro-EOKA village with two churches and I wondered how I was going to do it as I barely had a hundred men. I went and had a look at it in daylight with the police sergeant who showed me the offending signs, which didn't mean much to me as they were written in Greek anyway. I spotted they were only in six places and I said the only way to do this is to get in, get it done and get out again in ten minutes, before the hornet's nest is stirred. We got great buckets of a tar-like substance with brooms and brushes and split the men up into groups. Then we roared into the village at ten o'clock on a Saturday night when we knew there was a cinema on. We dragged them out of the cinema, took away the barber from his shop where he was busy shaving a fellow, and each of the men were given the brooms and brushes and told to obliterate the mess. We did it and got out as quick as we could, just as the church bells began to ring and people began to pour out. Afterwards, of course, we were accused of the most appalling atrocities, of pouring the tar down the sleeves of the poor people rather than waste any. But it was not a job that soldiers should have been given to do.

What soldiers were quite happy to do were duties and drills that they had been trained to perform. Even riots could be 'tremendous fun' if they involved Turks rather than Greek Cypriots, because the former stuck to throwing stones and bottles 'unlike the Greeks who would shoot you in the back' – and because the Turks rarely involved their womenfolk. Having to deal with Greek Cypriot women in various forms of confrontation was a feature of the EOKA Emergency that every soldier disliked intensely. They played a major role in the *Enosis* campaign and only rarely were the security services able to get the better of them. 'It was much more difficult when you came across a disturbance that was entirely orchestrated by women,' Redgrave declares, but he remembers one instance where his unit did score a point over them. This was after the womenfolk of a Greek Cypriot village had stoned a passing military convoy and he was ordered to go and teach them a lesson:

> I surrounded it with my cars and I sent my second-in-command into the village. He was a tall hunting gentleman from Leicestershire, very casual, very calm, and he said, 'Let me do it my way.' The Land Rover dropped him in the village square and there was not a soul to be seen. They'd all gone to ground, except for the EOKA flags, but he knew everyone was watching him. He sat down outside the café and he ordered a coffee and a glass of brandy and he said, 'I want to see the mayor, the schoolteacher and the priest.' They all turned up, he ordered them each a coffee and a brandy and then, using the schoolteacher – who usually spoke English – as an interpreter, he said, 'You know, it is a bit much if you chaps can't control your women. I mean, is this really how you fellows work out here? Do the women wear the pants?' After a couple more drinks he absolutely shamed them and we never had any more trouble.

The troops based outside the big towns and villages rarely had to face the Greek Cypriot women, but when they did it could be quite a revelation – as Royal Marine Commando David Storrie discovered when he came down to Limassol on convoy protection and saw for himself 'these schoolgirls in their blue tunics and their white shirts, nasty little bitches who were extremely wise with regard to civil disobedience. One looked with horror at these sixteen- and seventeen-year-old girls who mouthed their obscenities in Greek and obviously hated you for being there. One had anticipated the hostility but nevertheless it was an extremely difficult problem.' Paratrooper John Williams, too, found the schoolgirls very hard to take:

> The worst experience that I felt as a soldier was the use made by the terrorists of the young innocents, the young schoolgirls and schoolboys who used to have to pass through a search area to ensure that they weren't trying to smuggle any weapons or arms. The young girls were used extensively to do just that. Many grenades and bombs and parts of weapons were smuggled through the cordons by the young girls, strapped to their upper thighs and underneath their dresses because they thought the British soldier –

and they were quite right in thinking it – shied away from searching the young schoolgirls. On some occasions one did have either a policewoman or a member of the WRAC with you who were then able to search intimately but there were many, many occasions where there weren't the servicewomen available for this to happen.

One unit – reputedly, it was a well-known Irish regiment – got over the problem of shortage of womanpower by dressing up one of their younger officers as a policewoman to search a bus in which the women passengers were suspected of hiding arms: 'Thank God, he found a large amount of weapons and the women were arrested but, of course, there was a God Almighty row afterwards and everybody was frightfully upset, claiming that this was a foul!'

At the heart of the security forces' problems in Cyprus was the failure to convince the Greek Cypriot population that EOKA's twin goals of a free Cyprus and union with Greece were impossible to achieve – and that their best interests lay in supporting the authorities. What had worked in Malaya and in Kenya was not going to work in Cyprus. Confusion over the political intentions of the British Government, which negotiated with the rebels at one moment and then took military action against them the next, was to prove fatal in the struggle for Cypriot hearts and minds. The deep split between the two communities impaired organisations like the Cypriot Police, whose seventeen hundred members had divided loyalties. In Malaya the Special Branch had entered the Emergency with thirty policemen. In Cyprus there were three, two of whom were promptly murdered. The drafting in of some two hundred volunteer police sergeants from Britain was no substitute for local knowledge. A lack of co-ordination between police and Army and a failure to build up an effective intelligence-gathering machine on the Malayan and Kenyan models was to dog the security forces to the very end.

In such circumstances there was a real temptation to cut corners to get results – and to take sides. 'We had to find our intelligence locally,' explains Mike Gray, who came to Cyprus in 1955 with the 2nd Battalion the Parachute Regiment. 'Every campaign we go into we seem to start off with a blank sheet and then we build up intelligence. You might have thought, after all the experience we have had, that we would have gone in a bit better prepared, but we never have.' This intelligence had to come in the first instance from the police. 'You have to establish a very close link with the police and you've got to be frank and honest because if you don't work with the police, the civil authority, you will get nothing.'

But what this boiled down to in Cyprus was taking sides: 'The

Greeks quite clearly did not like us. We had really let ourselves down historically over the years and EOKA, in assisting the links with Greece, were all very important to them. So there was a tendency for soldiers to lean towards the Turk, who was robust, tough, hard-hitting and a good friend, although at the same time you realised that by doing so you were only antagonising the Greek Cypriots and creating a divide.' In the Cyprus Police there were many more Greeks than Turks but the loyalty of the former could not be guaranteed, whereas 'you could always trust the Turkish sergeant. You knew he was on your side but, that said, he was a ruthless bastard at times, much more robust than you wanted him to be. If you were not careful your soldiers would emulate his tactics and that would cut across all the ethics that you had been trying to preserve to make sure things were done as cleanly and within the law as possible.'

It was while working with one of these Turkish police sergeants that Roy Redgrave witnessed a demonstration of 'robustness' that gave him considerable food for thought. This involved a Greek Cypriot informer who had apparently agreed to reveal the where-abouts of a large cache of arms:

> The Land Rover pulled up, a smartly-dressed Greek got out and he was taken to the top of a hill in an orange grove. Then the police sergeant said, 'Tell us where the stuff's buried.' The fellow refused. The policeman gave him an enormous belt with his rifle a couple of times and the chap said, 'All right, all right, all right!' He took him to a corner of the orchard and what we dug up was five hundred pounds of explosives and I don't know how many rounds of ammunition. We loaded a lorry and a half with the stuff – and one was left wondering, OK, this isn't Queensberry rules but if we hadn't dug it up somebody else would have and more people would have been shot and killed.

Allegations of bias and of ill-treatment of Greek Cypriot detainees were a constant feature of the Cyprus campaign, testifying both to the effectiveness of EOKA's propaganda machinery and to the readiness of the British Press to make the most of a good story in what had become the most accessible conflict that Fleet Street's editors had ever known. With their popular image as hard men preceding them it was almost inevitable that units like the Argylls and the Paras would be among the first to be called to account. One of the Parachute battalions had its reputation severely dented when its intelligence officer was court-martialled. 'He was a young officer who was commissioned with me,' remembers Johnny Watts:

He got caught up in the interrogation of suspects, waiting for somebody to come out with information. Then he got involved and was so keen to get results that the next minute he probably punched the fellow himself. Very sadly, though quite rightly, he was court-martialled for it and cashiered. That was a very isolated incident but there was a lot of propaganda put out by EOKA of mal-treatment on a massive scale of civilians. I remember a United Nations team and Mrs Barbara Castle coming out. I was one of the people accused of burying Cypriots up to their necks in sand on Famagusta beach and putting jam on their heads to attract the ants – something straight out of the *Boy's Own Paper*. Goddammit, I've never done anything like that, but all these things were very often repeated in the media and, you know, if you throw enough mud it sticks.

Roy Redgrave, too, commanding his armoured car squadron in the north of the island, found the mud-slinging hard to take. This was in the latter stages of the EOKA Emergency when the authoritarian Field Marshal Sir John Harding had been replaced (in November 1957) as Governor by the more conciliatory figure of Sir Hugh Foot. For all the new Governor's charm there was always a feeling in Redgrave's mess that he was 'leaning over backwards to try and help the Greeks'. His interventions were not always well received, as on the occasion when a terrorist group was captured and then subjected to a prolonged period of interrogation by the Cyprus Police:

Every so often someone would talk and we'd have to send an armoured car to collect him and an armoured personnel vehicle and go into some field and, lo and behold, there were the weapons. They were singing like canaries, as they say. And in the middle of this operation – I was at the bottom of the hill with my head-quarters and I think we were cooking a chicken on a radio aerial over an open fire – we saw this column of cars coming and it was the Governor who had heard that there was torture and, in particular, ice torture. So he charged into the military intelligence and police officers, who were running that side of it, and said, 'I understand there's torture here. I understand you're using ice.' And the little man in charge there said, 'No ice, sir!' The Governor insisted on seeing every single Greek who was up there. They were all brought in and he made them strip off and there wasn't a single mark on any of them. He asked them if they had any complaints and there weren't – but the police and the interrogators said, 'My God, if this is the support we get, to hell with it.'

When Mike Gray's 2nd Battalion joined the rest of the Parachute Brigade in Cyprus in 1956 the furore over the treatment of suspects was at its height: 'Whenever we picked up people they would then try to damage themselves to pretend that you had damaged them. You then had to be very careful that you did a full report on what had happened to them from the time that they had been picked up, because you realised it was a very dirty business once the Press got hold of it.' It was here that Gray came to realise the vital importance of working within the law in anti-terrorist activities – 'you've got to be meticulous in producing evidence, like any criminal activity' – as well as the need to maintain good relations with the Press – 'we were not good at it in the Army nor, indeed, politically at that time in Cyprus.'

Gray first became aware of the power of the Press at the time of the Suez Crisis in November 1956. In March of that year the last British troops had been withdrawn from Egypt's Canal Zone. In July President Nasser of Egypt nationalised the Suez Canal, which was seen by the British and French powers as a threat to their regional interests. Plans for a joint invasion were drawn up and in Britain large numbers of British Army 'Z' Reservists were called up. In Cyprus operations against Grivas and his men were all but suspended as the Paras and Commandos began preparing to mount a combined air and sea assault on Port Said, in which Cyprus was to be the launching platform. Whatever the rights and wrongs of this armed intervention – 'generally speaking people were more in favour than against for the simple reason that it was professionally stimulating' – those involved trained with enthusiasm. Whenever they could get away the officers made for the Ledra Palace Hotel in Nicosia for a bath and a drink 'because all you had in your camps was a dusty old shower out of a tin can' – and it was here that they met all the Press correspondents. Gray remembers how he was first approached at the bar by Donald Seaman of the *Daily Express*:

> Somebody came up to me and said, 'I gather you're in the Para-chute Battalion. Have a drink with me.' I thought, Oh bloody no, this chap wants some information from me and I mustn't talk to a Press man. But he said, 'Look, whether you like it or not I shall get a story, so you might as well tell me what the hell is going on. I've just come back from Port Said and perhaps I can tell you one or two things. There are a couple of you here; both of you come up and have a bath in my room, I'll give you a drink and we'll have a natter.' We did. We sat and talked and he said, 'You've told me no more than I know already but just remember when you are dealing

with the Press that it will always get its story. If you tell me the truth I can then make a sensible judgement about whether or not to print it. I'm not going to cart you because we'll meet again, lots of times.' Donald Seaman and I became very good friends later on as a result of that meeting and from then onwards I've always been absolutely honest – as far as I was able to be – with all Press men.

An account of the Suez Invasion has no place in this narrative, except in so far as it provided a violent two-week interlude in the Cyprus campaign. Its sudden termination in the form of a ceasefire imposed by the United Nations was a devastating psychological blow to those who took part in the assault and the race to seize the Canal, coming as it did just when complete victory had seemed within their grasp. 'We had screwed ourselves up for this operation of war and then suddenly, just like that, were told to stop,' Peter Field remembers. 'It really was the most extraordinary feeling to be told, "Stop! Stay where you are. It's all over." The reaction was one of stunned silence. What the hell have we been doing this for if it can be stopped just like that? Why did we come in the first place? I saw the Parachute soldier for the first time question authority. His morale you could see beginning to slip. I think it may have been even harder in the 3rd Battalion where they took casualties. Why were those men's lives not cared for more thoughtfully? I regret that decision, suddenly being told to stop.'

While the 1st and 3rd Battalions of the Parachute Regiment returned to Britain the 2nd went back to Cyprus, where at last the military campaign began to turn in their favour. They moved up to a village named Platres high in the Troodos Mountains and from here set up a number of platoon posts in the surrounding hills. About fifty EOKA terrorists were known to be still operating in the area:

> The approach to the operations was very typical of our
> commanding officer. We again broke up into small group patrols,
> we were out for long periods and we'd go out and stay out.
> Frequently there would be a large-scale sweep of the area but
> instead of just flying in with the helicopters or going in by all the
> roads, small parties of us would go in well ahead, maybe a day or
> two in advance, and hide up and lie low – and it was these parties
> that, when the big sweep was on with all the noise and bustle of the
> helicopters flying in and trucks on the road and so on, invariably
> were the most successful, that picked off the EOKA as they were
> getting out of the area as fast as possible. Nothing was conventional
> at all. We were operating in small patrols, going out at night,
> making great use of radios, working in co-operation with each

other, individual initiative, suddenly an opportunity coming, not
waiting and reporting back, 'Can I go and do this?' but seizing the
initiative and getting in there.

As a subaltern in the Queen's Royal Regiment in Malaya, Peter
Field had seen how the services and the civil authorities had worked
together and now he saw it starting to work in Cyprus:

> With the co-operation of the RAF flying Sycamore helicopters and
> the co-operation of the police and the intelligence services we
> began to get information and success beyond anyone's expectations.
> There was an element of luck, certainly. We had a lucky catch in
> the early days and everything snowballed from that, but behind it
> all was an outstanding intelligence-gathering organisation headed by
> a military intelligence officer attached to us. Once we'd had a little
> nibble of success from the interrogation of these prisoners and of
> people in the villages one piece of information led to another –
> which led to another. So it grew and I think the final catch was
> somewhere in the region of forty, maybe even fifty, and the EOKA
> campaign in the mountains actually ceased from our operations
> there.

As in Malaya and Kenya, it was the carrot and stick of financial
rewards offered and dire penalties threatened that won over prisoners and informers. The operation that Peter Field remembers
best – and with good reason – involved one such informer who had
been offered a very large sum of money to reveal two underground
hides:

> We set off during the night with this fellow and two or three of the
> policemen, who were all Turks. We eventually found the first cave,
> an underground man-made cave, and it was full of a tremendous
> range of supplies – food, ammunition, a lot of explosives but no
> EOKA terrorists there. Then we set off for the next place, which
> was some distance away. The dawn was coming up now and,
> because you have tremendous fields of visibility in the mountains, I
> was very conscious that we'd be spotted. We began to get close to
> the area and I saw tracks of a particular studded boot that they
> used to wear, so I branched off ahead of the party to have a look
> for myself.
>   I found these tracks led to a trap door in the ground. The others
> were coming up behind me so I lifted the trap door and saw this
> shaft going straight into the ground with a ladder alongside it.
> Stupidly, without thinking, down I went and found at the bottom of
> the shaft was a tunnel going off to one side. I started going off along

that – they often booby-trapped them so I was feeling around for a cable or anything like that to give it away – and I went round a small bend. There was a dim light ahead of me and there were three guys sitting in a room. On my hands and knees I couldn't get at my pistol, I had nothing in my hands, I was just in this single little tunnel and there they were with their weapons at the ready, and it was an act of God that they didn't start firing. I have never backed out of a tunnel so fast in my life. I got back up to the top and the policemen, speaking Greek, called on them to surrender. The three of them came out and in there we found a lot of weapons and a lot of supplies. But that was a very lucky escape for me.

For Roy Redgrave, too, trying to cover a rural area of twelve hundred square miles between the Troodos Mountains and the Kyrenia range with a squadron of a hundred and ten men, sixteen armoured cars and four Saracen armoured personnel carriers, there was the occasional lucky break:

There was a company of Irish Guards staking out a possible hideout and they radioed through during the night that they'd been attacked. Our commanding officer, Julian Berry, happened to be at dinner with the commanding officer of the Irish Guards and over the port they worked out an operational plan, and in the middle of the night we were winging through these Cypriot villages so that come the dawn we were cutting off all the roads where this Irish company had been. Then at dawn these two commanding officers arrived in their dinner jackets to see that all was going well. It was a surprise to us but an even bigger surprise to EOKA and on two of our road blocks we picked up a number of wanted chaps.

Redgrave had set up his mobile headquarters in the car park of a local monastery and as he drove along a forest track the feather of a hoopoe lying under a stone happened to catch his eye:

There was no way a feather could get under a stone like that so I stopped and saw that it pointed to a crest on a hill. With a corporal I started up in that direction and then I saw – I half expected it – the marks of the boots which these EOKA people used to wear. I got to this crest and there was a little circle of stones and what looked like rabbit droppings, which I realised were olive stones. Then I looked over the crest and there was the monastery on the other side of the valley – and hanging out of one of the windows was a large blue and white towel. With my binoculars I could see the aerials of my armoured cars, which were parked on the other side of the monastery. So I said to the corporal to go down to

the radio car and tell headquarters to move two miles away. I sat
and watched them drive away and then when I looked back to the
window again the towel had gone – and that proved that the
monastery was linked to the terrorists. So we put an ambush in and
two or three days later caught the men we were looking for. But it
was pure luck that I'd seen that hoopoe feather.

Such successes were few and far between. Instead of growing
weaker for lack of support, as the terrorist groups in Malaya and
Kenya had become, EOKA grew in strength as new recruits joined
its ranks or took the places of those who had been captured or killed.
The British Government's response was the appointment of Sir
Hugh Foot, who looked for diplomatic and political solutions rather
than military ones. As the military pressure on his men eased, Grivas
turned his attention on the Turkish civil population and began a new
phase in EOKA's campaign: 'The Greeks began mopping up these
tiny little Turkish *chifliks*, hamlets of about six houses. At night the
Greeks would arrive in busloads and attack these places, burning
them to the ground. We'd be rushing from one place to another,
catching buses and sending them back to the villages and so on, but in
fact we were losing because the Greeks were systematically carving
up these Turkish villages.'

By the summer of 1958 the British forces on the island were doing
no more than trying to contain the situation while political negotiations involving Greece and Turkey as well as the two Cypriot
communities proceeded. All the while the Greek and Turkish
Cypriots struggled to gain ground in sporadic inter-communal riots
and attacks. As far as Redgrave and his men were concerned, the
nastiest incident took place in early June outside a Turkish village
called Gunyeli:

It had been building up, with busloads of these Greeks descending
on Turkish villages, when a young RAF officer driving through a
village suddenly spotted thirty-five Greeks in a bus about to duff up
the Turkish community. He alerted the nearest armoured car troop
that he saw and we arrested these people and took them to the
police station eight miles away in Nicosia. But as we approached
the ramparts of Nicosia a frantic message came over the radio from
the police station saying, 'For God's sake, don't bring those people
here. We have a Turkish riot going on at the moment and if those
Greeks come here they'll eat them!' We wondered what the hell to
do, so I said to the convoy, 'Take the next turning off and get away
from Nicosia.' We drove through two Turkish villages – the Greeks
hung their blue and white flags up and the Turks their red flags, so

you knew which was a Greek and which was a Turkish village as you drove through – and when we were clear of the village of Gunyeli the Greeks could see their little village in the Kyrenia range. I said, 'Stop the bus, make them get out and as a punishment make them walk back to their village across the fields.' There was a platoon of Grenadiers on duty in the area and they escorted this group of Greeks across about five hundred to eight hundred yards. Then it looked okay and they let them go. But they'd hardly disappeared out of sight when suddenly the sky was filled with black smoke. A cornfield had been set on fire either by the Greeks or by the Turks to produce an incident. By the time our armoured cars had got back – and it was a bumpy ride – to where these Greeks were, four of them were dead. Gunyeli is a village of professional butchers and the Turks had really got stuck into them. Then we had the most tremendous cops-and-robbers' afternoon with Turks on motorbikes gripping knives in their teeth being chased by scout cars or by light Auster planes.

Redgrave and his troop commander were subsequently accused of having tipped off the Turks and provoked the massacre: 'So then we had the most appalling Court of Enquiry run by the Chief Justice in which all my troops were involved. Although we were completely exonerated it was incredibly unfair and very hard because, while we were being called in, most of the day and night we were still keeping the Greeks away from the Turks. We were being quizzed and getting awful stick in the papers and all the time the Greeks and Turks were relying on you to stop them killing each other.'

In December 1958 the foreign ministers of Britain, Greece and Turkey met in Paris to reach a settlement that would give Cyprus its independence – but without *Enosis*. Archbishop Makarios was forced to comply and in February 1959 an agreement was signed. It was a bitter moment for Grivas and his EOKA die-hards – as it was, to a lesser extent, to British soldiers who had seen at least one of their own comrades die for every terrorist that they had killed. John Williams, for one, finds it hard to forgive Grivas and his band of terrorists for what they did to their country:

That Makarios was the mastermind behind Grivas and his band and that the Church was sheltering and shielding them at all stages of the campaign was brought home to me when peace was declared and the terrorists – Grivas and all his men – were feted by Makarios in Metaxas Square in Nicosia. So the EOKA terrorists came home and were treated as heroes, and according to the history books there should have been a happy ending. But I've returned to

Cyprus over many years and I've seen the island just torn apart,
culminating in the invasion of the island by the Turks and the
splitting of it between Greeks and Turks. Homeland Greece and
Homeland Turkey have just torn the island apart for their own
benefit and it's very, very sad to see. I actually lived in the
community for three years and have got many, many good friends,
both Greeks and Turks. They still bear the grudges of those EOKA
days. They put it down to Grivas and Makarios because they say
that is where it started.

From a military point of view the unsatisfactory resolution of the
Cyprus conflict posed as many questions as it answered: how to
combat terrorism without a clear political agenda; how to remain
impartial in a divided community where one side lends tacit support
to terrorism; how far to curtail civil liberties in a western-style
democracy when terrorism threatens that democracy – all questions
that would again resurface to trouble the armed forces a generation
later. Few soldiers, however, indulge in post-mortems. For them it
was a question of learning by experience – and moving on. 'Before
we left Cyprus we put on a pantomime,' Roy Redgrave recalls. 'We
made fun of almost everything that had irked us while we were there
and it all went down very well in the cookhouse and the regiment.
But I was suddenly summoned to bring my show to Government
House to produce this somewhat dubious performance in front of the
Governor who, to give him credit, sat in the front row and laughed as
loud as everybody else.' After handing over to the 12th Lancers the
Royal Horse Guards sailed in a troopship back to Southampton:

> There were hundreds of little boats to greet us on the Solent and
> everybody was honking their hooters and sirens. It was an amazing
> experience. Then when we got to Windsor our old friends the Irish
> Guards met us with their band and we marched through the town to
> our barracks with the place absolutely packed. We really felt great
> heroes and terribly pleased with ourselves. My next posting was to
> go back to Cyprus. I refused and was sent to Paris instead.

Chapter Ten

SOUTHERN ARABIA:
The Green Mountain and the
Barren Rocks

*They knew you wouldn't go and blow their houses up and you
wouldn't shoot indiscriminately, that you were trained and that you
had to follow certain rules of engagement, and that you weren't going
to fire at anybody unless you were fired upon, which was part of our
discipline. The terrorist, both in Aden and in other parts of the
world, used that against us time and time and time again, knowing
that our basic humanity stopped us from being as ruthless against the
civilian population as the terrorist was to his own people. So we were
in a 'no win' situation. We were in the situation again of trying to
force a military solution on to a political problem that our politicians
couldn't sort out.*

In 1957, while British forces were still embroiled in counter-
insurgency wars in Malaya, Kenya and Cyprus, a rebellion broke out
in the South Arabian Sultanate of Muscat and Oman. Drawing
support from Egypt and Saudi Arabia, a group of tribal leaders
declared against the Sultan and established themselves on the great
mountain massif known as the Djebel Akhdar or 'Green Mountain'.
Oman was a country with which Britain had treaty obligations going
back to the days when its Sultans were also rulers of Zanzibar, but
when the Sultan asked for military assistance the British Government found itself in a very awkward position. In the aftermath of the
Suez debacle and with major cut-backs heralded in its 1957 Defence
White Paper, the Government would not countenance any sort of
public involvement in the Middle East. On the other hand, there
were a string of colonies and protectorates in the area, from Aden on
Oman's western border to Kuwait, Bahrein, Qatar and the Trucial
States north of Oman, that would interpret Britain's failure to assist
Oman as evidence of Britain's further decline as a world power. So a
compromise was arrived at whereby a number of British Army

officers and NCOs were seconded to the Sultan's Armed Forces and RAF planes bombed rebel positions on the Djebel Akhdar.

It had been estimated that to dislodge the rebels from their mountain stronghold would require at least a full infantry brigade. However, an alternative plan was devised that had its genesis in the Mau Mau counter-gangs developed in Kenya. The originator of this plan, Frank Kitson, flew out to Oman where he met the Colonel of 22 SAS, who had his own ideas on how to tackle the problem. Together they worked out a revised plan for a covert, low intensity operation that they believed would stop the revolt in its tracks without causing many casualties and without drawing attention to itself from the outside world. Their scheme was approved and in October 1958 'D' Squadron 22 SAS was pulled out of the Malayan jungle and flown secretly to a hastily-built campsite in the desert north of Muscat. So understrength was the squadron at this time that its four troops were barely able to muster forty fighting men between them. The prospect of seizing the vast mountain fortress that dominated their western skyline was extremely daunting.

'My brief,' explains 'D' Squadron Commander Johnny Watts, 'was either to kill the leaders of the rebellion in a *coup de main* type operation if intelligence could show us where they actually lived, or somehow to get myself on to the mountain with my squadron to make room for the Sultan's Army to re-establish his authority over this mountain massif.' To succeed the operation had to have good intelligence and in this instance 'there was no intelligence at all, because no one knew anything about the mountain, which had never properly been mapped, or how many people were up there. Legend had it that they could call upon five thousand tribesmen plus a trained military hard-core who had all the specialist weapons. So one was entering a total fog.'

The first problem was the Djebel Akhdar itself, which 'Geordie' Lillico, then a trooper with 17 Troop, likens to 'a large plate which had been thrust roughly about six thousand feet above sea level, though parts of the rim of this plate went even higher to about eight thousand feet, so that you had to climb up to eight thousand feet and then drop back on the inside to six thousand feet. It was cracked all round like cracks on a plate with fissures and *wadis* [dry valleys with steep sides], and up one or two of the bigger ones the ancient Persians had built these *falages* [channels] for collecting water and the Arabs had built small tracks just wide enough to take a loaded donkey.'

Over the centuries the Green Mountain had acquired an 'aura of impregnability':

They grew flowers up there, roses to make rosewater, apricots, pomegranates, grapes particularly, so that compared to the rest of Oman which was very barren and arid it was a sort of Shangri-La. But the tribe called the Bani Riyam, who lived up there, also owned many of the big villages at the foot of the mountain; they were a very powerful tribe and nobody else, Arab or Omani, was ever permitted to go up there on pain of death. There were, in fact, four traditional ways of climbing the mountain and they all involved going through great *wadis*, huge ravines with towering cliffs on either side where one man could hold off an army. So, of course, it was suicide to poke your nose into these ravines, which we did occasionally just to test the opposition and were met by a fusillade of mortar bombs and machine gun fire.

The four troops divided into two groups, one probing the north side of the Djebel, the other the south. It soon became clear that all movement had to be confined to the hours of darkness: 'They had a series of outposts, observation posts, scouts and so on as well as local informants in the villages at the foot of the mountain, and on a huge mountain like that you could see for thirty miles. So all operations had to be conducted at night, which was very similar to working in the jungle because you got the whispering and the hand signals and the small numbers of men.' The danger of underestimating the enemy was soon brought home to them when 'a well-known character called "Duke" Swindles, who'd just won a Military Medal in Malaya, committed the cardinal sin of silhouetting himself on a skyline and got shot right through the heart. It was a bit of a morale blow to us being that "Duke" was a real old soldier, well-liked by the whole squadron.'

Despite this set-back both groups continued to probe the rebels' defences, with 16 and 17 Troops managing to establish a toehold on the mountain's northern rim, on a high point that they named Cassino. From here they made a devastatingly effective raid on the enemy's main strongpoint in that quarter on Christmas Eve, returning unscathed to celebrate Christmas Day 'with a few bottles of whisky and one of the donkeys, which we had to shoot because it went lame'. On the south side, too, 18 and 19 Troops were kept very busy:

We started launching a series of probing patrols on various parts of the mountain, working by night, hiding by day and moving again the following night, trying to establish some sort of dominance over the enemy by a series of short-range contacts – and trying to find a hidden route up this great mountain. So over the next couple of months 'D' Squadron had a series of patrol actions all the way round the mountain, until I finally identified an area that we might be able to get up at night, that wasn't opposed by large numbers of the enemy and where we might take them by surprise.

Working largely from air reconnaissance photos, the Squadron Commander plotted out a route that might just get them up on to the Djebel in one hard climb and still give them time to take the enemy's main picket by surprise before dawn. To make the enemy believe that this final assault would be coming from the north, 'A' Squadron was also flown in from Malaya at the start of the New Year to put in a feint from their Cassino position on the northern rim of the Djebel. Then after dark on 25 January 1959, the main assault party set off to take the Djebel, each man in the party weighed down by well over one hundred pounds of ammunition and equipment. 'It was a long, hard march,' remembers Lillico:

> After the plans had been laid and disinformation spread to the Arab donkey handlers to concentrate the opposition on the opposite side of the Djebel, the great night arrived and about six troops of us, followed by a few engineer lads, marched the equivalent of about twenty-odd miles in distance plus an altitude of about six to seven thousand feet. We were still short of the rim of the Djebel just after first light and I'll always remember the Major turning round to me and saying, 'Do you think we've cracked it?' and I said, 'Well, I reckon we're there.' But we had to dump packs, two troops of us, after staggering up that altitude with full kit, and sprint on to the rim at first light.'

Below the final lip of the plateau was a lower rim with a cliff face that had to be descended without anyone having any idea of its height. 'Even in the moonlight it looked like a precipice,' recalls Watts:

> I said, 'Right, we need a fellow to go down,' and some brave fellow was elected. There was a lot of slithering and a bump at the bottom and a whisper came up, 'Okay but, Jesus, I wouldn't wish it on my mother-in-law.' So another guy went and finally we got about twenty-two fellows down and I left a strong troop at this machine gun nest to sort out the enemy, who hadn't actually woken up and were still asleep in their caves. The twenty-two of us started off in single file following a sort of *wadi* till we came to a climb of about six to eight hundred feet. The men were getting very, very exhausted because they'd been climbing rapidly but I remember a certain hysteria hitting us as we approached this shallow crest.

After weeks of what we used to call 'Djebelitis', of being under the eye of this mountain where you felt that whatever you were doing a pair of eyes were watching you with this huge mountain dominating you, suddenly you were going to reach a point where no one was going to look down on you any more. So the first eight or ten of us started to break into a run to try to be the first British chap ever on the mountain, as we believed. I remember looking back and seeing fires in these caves where the machine gun crews were cooking their breakfasts and I thought, 'That's all right, we're behind them. The fellows we left behind will knock them off.' And the next thing we heard were grenades, explosions and machine gun fire going off as they dealt with the fellows in the caves, who had been secure in their belief that the Djebel was invincible.

Promptly at dawn RAF Valettas made a supply drop of water and ammunition in canisters, which was taken by the defenders massed on the other side of the plateau to be paratroopers landing: 'They'd never heard of resupply by parachute and they thought they must be men, so they started arguing among themselves with the usual argy-bargy of whether they should attack us or not. If they had I think they probably would have overrun us. So, as much due to their caution as to our bravado, there was a stalemate. They didn't attack us and that gave us the opportunity to build up.' Once 'D' Squadron was firmly established on the Djebel Akhdar resistance crumbled, as Lillico describes:

We then started to move forward on to the Djebel plains looking for trouble and the rebellion at this stage folded. All the notorious characters made themselves scarce, the ordinary tribespeople, fearful through their propaganda of what we were going to do to them, all hid up in *wadis* and fissures with their families, while the troops were allocated the various main villages with large caves behind them that were being used as storage for all the ammunition and supplies. Then it just became a question of doing house-to-house searches and rounding people up. We confiscated all their weapons, nearly all Martini Henry rifles from the tribesmen, and we captured a number of .5 Browning machine guns and a few American-made mortars as well. After that the politics took over, various dignitaries arrived from down below. We were ordered to give them back their weapons and immediately start practising hearts and minds on them.

As far as the SAS were concerned that was the end of the Djebel Akhdar campaign. 'It was all over and we were very happy,' declares

Johnny Watts. 'The whole campaign had been conducted with economy of force, very little bloodshed. We held them in great honour for fighting so well and I think they admired us for the compassion we showed to their wounded and for our help in getting rid of this very despotic, paramount sheik whose ambitions they had had to support. It was the last of the old-fashioned little skirmishes.'

Skirmish or not, this demonstration of the SAS's strike capacity made a considerable impact in defence circles, as Frank Kitson points out: 'It was the result of the SAS's intervention in Oman in 1958 that enabled the people who wanted to keep the SAS going to do so in the face of a lot of opposition from people who would rather have used the resources in having more conventional forces. It was an immensely important thing for everything that happened to the British Army afterwards that the SAS so proved their value there that they were kept in the order of battle.'

The SAS Regiment's next major engagement was Confrontation in Borneo where it further underlined its value and its versatility as a special forces unit. In the meantime the second round in the South Arabian power struggle commenced as Britain stepped up the pace of its withdrawal from Empire. In 1962 Egyptian-backed revolutionaries established a People's Democratic Republic in Yemen. A year later they began to export their revolution across the border into Aden, where the National Liberation Front (NLF) signalled its intention of driving out the British imperialists by throwing a grenade at the British High Commissioner. The British Government's response was to give notice that Aden Colony and the British Protectorates in the region would be given their independence in 1968 – but that a British military presence would be permanently maintained in Aden. As far as the NLF and its backers in Yemen and Egypt were concerned this was too little too late. In 1964 nationalist guerrillas moved into the mountainous Radfan country adjoining the Yemeni border, an area renowned for the inveterate hostility of the local tribes. A brigade of the newly-formed Federal Regular Army, commanded by British officers on secondment and spearheaded by Royal Marine Commandos and a company of the 3rd Battalion of the Parachute Regiment, fought its way into the interior and succeeded in scattering the dissidents in a campaign reminiscent of the North-West Frontier wars of the old British Raj.

Successful though it was in military terms, the Radfan Campaign could do nothing to stem the new mood of Arab militancy that was sweeping across Arabia. Trained insurgents continued to come over the border from Yemen, finding support among the Adenis to an extent that belated hearts and minds programmes by the authorities could not counter. An effort to get an effective Special Branch network going had been made at the time of the Djebel Akhdar rebellion in neighbouring Oman, but the seeds had fallen on stony ground. There was, in one officer's opinion, a lack of commitment on the part of the local authorities. This was brought home to Major Johnny Watts when 22 SAS returned to South Arabia to support the troops operating in the mountains. 'D' Squadron was sent up-country to a remote mountain region called Mishwara – 'if the Radfan was bad Mishwara was out of sight' – through which passed bands of guerrillas from Yemen on their way to attack the British airfield at Habilayn:

> Because there were no maps of the Mishwara and because no one knew anything or how many people were there I asked a British District Officer for some help. I remember this conversation in his *dak* bungalow. I said, 'Have you got one or two local Arab tribesmen who could act as guides or to whom I could talk about this huge area, which *wadi* is which, where they lead to and so on?' He said, 'No, I haven't.' I said, 'What? Do you mean to tell me that in this district you cannot produce one or two Arab tribesmen who know the area, whom I could trust and you could trust?' And he said, 'No, I cannot produce anybody.' I said, 'What the hell have we been doing here for a hundred and thirty years if there isn't anybody prepared to help us when we need help? Do you blame them for wanting to throw us out?' He couldn't say anything and so I said, 'So we deserve to be thrown out.'

Working without local support and, indeed, without the knowledge of the locals, 'D' squadron moved into the mountains by night marches, hiding up in high ground by day. 'I've never been so thirsty in my life,' Watts remembers. 'We used to carry a two-hundred-foot line of rope and a canvas bucket between a half troop of eight men and at night we would creep into an Arab village, which were very poverty-stricken places in this benighted country, and get to a well without the dogs cottoning on to you. You would lower this canvas bucket on two hundred feet of rope, because some of the wells were very, very deep, and haul the water up quietly. Of course, when it came up it was full of snails, which can give you bilharzia, but you had to drink it. Then you filled your water bottles and plastic containers and scooted up the side of the mountain again so you weren't caught on low ground during the day.'

When the squadron did finally meet up with the enemy luck was not on its side. 'It was one of the big mistakes of my life,' admits Watts, 'which my NCOs who were with me still abuse me about when we meet from time to time.' He had split the squadron into two, leading one group while the other followed about two hours behind:

> At one stage we passed through a very narrow little *wadi* where we had to squeeze between boulders and I remember noticing a big space of maybe ten yards by fifteen of flat sand in this very bouldery *wadi*. Then we pushed on until we entered a major *wadi* system where we were hugging one side of the *wadi* wall because that was the only way to keep your direction in the pitch black. We and the gang must have passed each other about fifty yards apart, both going very quietly. They were on the left side of the *wadi* coming south and I was sticking to the west side and going north. Anyway, these enemy chaps arrived at the sandy area that I'd noticed earlier. It was a lovely place to have a kip so they dossed down and they took their shoes off. This is why we know how many there were because we found twenty-two pairs of sandals.

As Watts and his group were climbing out of the *wadi* to reach high ground before dawn they heard firing from behind them. The second SAS party had been fired upon by an alert enemy sentry as they emerged on to the sandy area of the *wadi*. After a brief firefight the enemy began to withdraw back up the *wadi*. Urged to go back down and ambush them as they came past, Watts decided that the risk of firing on his own men in the dark was too great: 'It's happened lots of times when people at night have shot down their own people, so I took my men well up on the side of the mountain. But my fellows are still upset to this day, because we could have got the lot of them. Anyway, we got our revenge. We killed and wounded a lot of them and our two badly-wounded guys survived. A helicopter pilot came down at dawn into this ravine with sheer walls of hundreds of feet guided by a couple of SAS guys on the ground. He made it and I think we put him in for a medal.'

This was one of the more memorable episodes in a series of comparatively minor, often frustrating operations that 'A' and 'D' Squadrons carried out in Aden from 1964 onwards, operating by turns in short three-month tours. John Woodhouse had built up a cadre of NCOs and troopers of outstanding quality, yet in Aden they never found the decisive roles that they had filled so well in Borneo. The SAS mystique, so painstakingly and unobtrusively built up over the previous decade, took a particularly heavy – and public – knock when a troop commander was killed after being caught with his patrol in open ground in daylight and his head was displayed on a pole in the streets of North Yemen.

After their reverse in the Radfan the NLF had begun to direct their main energies towards the city of Aden itself. In November 1964 they embarked on an all too familiar insurgency campaign designed to weaken the Government by attacking its supporters and by intimidating the civil populace into compliance. For the infantry battalions flown in to police the backstreets and shantytowns of Sheikh Othman, Tawahi, Ma'alla and, above all, the notorious Crater District, it was a case of Cyprus repeating itself, of 'the terrorist situation once again, living in one's fortified barracks and patrolling, trying to catch the elusive terrorist who never committed himself to meeting you face to face but used the weapon of the terrorist of all times, the stealthy bomb.' In Aden that meant chiefly the fragmentation grenade, thrown at mobile or foot patrols in 'Grenade Alley' or (as in Cyprus) 'Murder Mile' as they ran the gauntlet of the NLF's 'Cairo Grenadiers'. The casualty figures for the first three years of the Aden Emergency – thirteen dead and three hundred and twenty-five injured – reflect the high level of non-lethal injuries caused by grenade fragments.

An 'unreal campaign', is how one Parachute officer describes his time in Aden, 'the most pointless I've ever been involved in'. The barren rocks of Aden had never endeared themselves to British soldiers, who saw it as no more than a sea-port where 'the steamships used to stop for coal' in days gone by – so the news, publicly announced in February 1966, that the British Government was going to break the pledge made to its local allies in 1962 and to pull all its troops out after 1968 was greeted with much satisfaction. Only gradually did the full implication of this decision become apparent as Adenis who had hitherto supported the British switched their loyalties, as intelligence all but dried up and as the terrorists themselves gained in strength. Worst of all, the NLF acquired a rival in the shape of the Front for the Liberation of South Yemen (FLOSY), forcing up the pressure as the two parties vied for public attention: 'FLOSY and their opponents, the NLF, were at each other's throats and we, unfortunately, were in the middle trying to keep them apart, so we never knew who our enemies were.'

It was into this deteriorating situation that the 1st Battalion of the Royal Northumberland Fusiliers were plunged when they flew into Khormaksar Airfield in September 1966 to take over responsibility for the Crater District of Aden from the East Yorkshire Regiment. 'We arrived in Aden about 3 o'clock in the morning,' recalls Bill Pringle, then company sergeant-major of 'X' Company. 'After a quick briefing I was taken in a helicopter to do an aerial recce of Crater, which was really an extinct crater that housed seven hundred thousand Arabs, give or take a thousand or two.' It was an area that could be easily contained as there were only two roads leading out of the town but, with its 'seething mass of people in a labyrinth of tiny streets', it was almost impossible to control. 'We had this aerial patrol,' continues Pringle, 'shook ourselves out, had an hour's kip and then at 6 o'clock that evening "X" Company moved into the Crater on internal security. At 7 o'clock, on the dot actually, two or three shots were fired, one Arab was wounded and another was killed. We had to bundle the body into the back of the Land Rover and drive to the Armed Police Barracks, which was where our headquarters was situated while we were in Crater. Blind panic, as my driver had never been involved in anything like this before and the first thing that happened as we drove there was that we ran into a herd of goats, killing one. Anyway, that was our first twenty-four hours in Crater.'

In fact, no grenade had been thrown. 'We had an empty sardine can thrown at a patrol and the patrol shot the man dead immediately, not knowing whether it was a grenade or not,' explains Dick Blenkinsop, the commanding officer of the battalion. 'It was the right action to take and I think we had one other occurrence like this which established us as not to be played with – "although gentle of nature, don't interfere with" – and we had a remarkably quiet time for nearly two months. There was the odd break-out here and there, the odd rioting and banner waving but we kept control of it, we weren't knocked about or worried.'

From November 1966 onwards, when FLOSY entered the fray, tension in the city began to grow and, inevitably, the Northumberlands took their first casualties. 'On November 11th, Armistice Day, we were driving into Crater along Marine Drive,' remembers Bill Pringle:

> At 7 o'clock, as we were turning slowly towards the Municipal Market, I noticed a crowd of Arab girls, about eleven years of age, all dressed in white and my attention was drawn to an Arab in the centre of that crowd of girls. The reason my attention was drawn to him was because he had a terrified expression on his face. I said to the guy riding shotgun on our Land Rover, a guy called Fusilier Reagan, 'Keep an eye on him, Reagan, I don't like the look of him.' Within two minutes of my saying that this guy threw a grenade. The first reaction in normal circumstances would have been for the driver to put his foot on the accelerator and move out of the killing range as quick as he could and then we would de-bus and fly back in the hope of catching the grenadier. Unfortunately, in this instance we couldn't because there was an Arab taxi in front

of us and an Arab taxi behind. So the grenade went off as we were jumping out of the Land Rover, throwing us over. A couple of Arabs were killed, one with the base plug of the grenade embedded in her brow, and another was quite seriously wounded.

We started running after the grenadier, who was disappearing up one of the bazaar roads. Now when a grenade went off in Aden all the Arabs converged on the area, hoping to see blood and hoping, especially, to see British blood spilt. They were coming down the bazaar road as this grenadier was making his way up, so he was fighting against the tide, as it were. Reagan, who was also battalion cross-country runner, got to this guy first and apprehended him the hard way with his rifle. Then I arrived and I noticed this stream of blood squirting up about a yard into the air from my right shoulder. I realised that I'd been wounded, but I didn't feel any pain, although my ears were ringing from what I thought was just the sound of the explosion. So we got this Arab back to our Land Rover where the driver had managed to control all the Arabs in the area by firing a few rounds, and they were all lying flat on their stomachs. Then I sort of sank to my knees and realised that I'd been really hurt.

While CSM Pringle was recovering from wounds to his neck and shoulder things began to hot up all over Aden: 'While I was in Kamatha Beach Hospital, lying there like a twisted sick report, a series of people were being admitted from the battalion suffering from all sorts of wounds. Someone had a great idea to invent a tie called the Aden Grenade tie, which was a black tie with a red dhow on it. I bought my tie in good faith, but you can imagine that by the end of the tour everybody in the battalion was entitled to wear a tie!'

In contrast to the secrecy that had prevailed during the Djebel Akhdar campaign and throughout much of the Borneo Confrontation, Press attention in the Aden troubles was widespread, with interest building up as the count-down to the British withdrawal proceeded. From a commanding officer's point of view it paid to have good relations with the Press and Dick Blenkinsop, for one, found the reporters sent out by the British Press and the BBC 'extremely helpful. I found it always enough to say, "Gentlemen, I don't want you to repeat what I'm saying but let me bring you into the picture, off the record," and I was never let down once.' Ordinary soldiers, however, took a more jaundiced view of the Press, even if they never doubted the courage of some of its more determined representatives. Bill Pringle recalls one incident when 'a lot of shots were flying over the place. I heard the jabber of a conversation and turned round and there was this guy sitting on the bonnet of a vehicle speaking into a machine, recording, while we couldn't have been any nearer the ground. He was either very brave or purely idiotic.'

Where the real difficulties arose was when Press photographers were present at violent incidents. 'They were very brave, some of these photographers,' comments Blenkinsop, 'but I can think of one photograph that got home with a Geordie's boot definitely disappearing up some foreign chump's axle and I think it created quite a lot of unhappiness at home.' What such photos failed to convey were the surrounding circumstances, as Bill Pringle explains:

> I can remember one incident quite clearly which concerned a chap from my company called Fusilier Davage, who was a Newcastle man, a tall, handsome guy. A grenade had been thrown at their section and he was wounded in the stomach with a grenade fragment. Very fortunately, another member of that section had noted the Arab who had thrown the grenade and he was shot as he was trying to escape. To put it bluntly, he was shot through the backside and lost his marriage gear. On that particular day this was just one of the incidents photographed. There were several more and there were pools of our blood around Crater and, as a result, another guy in my company called Donaldson must have been quite incensed because he raised his boot and booted one of the Arabs in the backside. That incident was photographed and went right across the world, which brought comments from far and near against it and about the brutality of the Geordie troops, which wasn't right.

Dick Blenkinsop also defends the behaviour of his men in what were very trying circumstances. 'The word I'm looking for is anger,' he declares. 'When you've just had a grenade thrown at you you do get damn cross. The soldier preferred not to shoot if he could capture and you get a certain amount of enthusiasm where the boot or the fist is used.' But that was only part of the picture: 'You also get very sad as well. I can remember walking along a back street and a grenade was thrown. There was a shop there with sewing machines going and two little children who were hurt by this grenade were lying out in front of the shop and still the sewers went on sewing. Nobody moved or did anything to help. Anybody would be angry in the same circumstances and I think my soldiers were remarkably self-controlled actually.'

This self-control was to be put to the test after a particularly tragic incident that occurred on 20 June 1967, just as the Northumberlands were completing their tour and were in the process of handing over to the Argyll and Sutherland Highlanders. 'The tragedy at the end in Crater is probably one of the saddest days in the whole of my life,' admits Blenkinsop. 'Our tour was virtually completed. The arms had been handed in to the armoury, the advance party had already been flown out and the next company was getting ready to go when the Armed Police, who had been our good friends for a very long time, suddenly mutinied. Their children, their wives, had been looked after by my doctor who spent a great deal of time there. We gave them a lot of help and many of them we knew well so it was really rather like your friend of many years suddenly stabbing you in the back.'

The background to the Armed Police revolt lay in the increased political pressures to which members of the local military and police forces were being subjected. The appointment of an Arab officer to take over command of the South Arabian Army from their British commander led to protests from his rivals, developing into scattered acts of mutiny. Police recruits in barracks near Khormaksar Airfield then opened fire on a passing Army truck, killing eight British soldiers and wounding another eight. Hearing reports of fighting, the Armed Police at their headquarters in Crater prepared to defend themselves. At this point a joint patrol of Northumberlands and Argylls drove into Crater. Alec Grant, then the commanding officer's driver and signaller, was a member of the Argylls' advance party who had flown into Aden only a day or two earlier:

> The normal practice is that the outgoing battalion takes the incoming battalion round the various sites and shows them the points where problems are likely to occur and this was a normal day as far as we were concerned. I mean, we were carrying out our normal daily duties and the commanding officer was in his office and we didn't hear anything about this incident until well after it had occurred. The patrol had been coming up Queen Arbour Road from the Courts' end and the Police Barracks were adjacent to Queen Arbour Road and they had apparently opened up on the two Land Rovers and had caused absolute havoc. Only one soldier, who had hidden himself in the flats on the other side of the road, eventually got out.

A second patrol followed and the leading vehicle was also ambushed, resulting in four more deaths. Confusion followed. 'There was no immediate follow-up at all,' declares Grant. 'We actually were extremely frustrated. We wanted to go in and get our boys back and the thought of these soldiers – some of them could still have been alive – being left there, we felt that they had been sacrificed. There was a lot of anger around at the time and both regiments would quite happily have gone in and sorted it out there and then.' Among the Northumberlands, too, the 'natural instinct of everybody was to pick up their weapons and their equipment and fly down to Crater and extricate these guys but, unfortunately, politics didn't allow that.'

Both Colonel Blenkinsop and his opposite number in the Argylls, Colonel Colin Mitchell, went in person to Brigade headquarters to beg permission to re-enter Crater and recover their men – and both were refused. 'A great pity,' reflects Blenkinsop, while accepting with hindsight that there were good reasons why no action was taken in Crater. Colonel Mitchell's frustration was more publicly expressed, giving rise to the rumour that both he and Colonel Blenkinsop had been temporarily relieved of their commands. In fact, both men had been forced to obey orders that neither approved of. 'Colonel Mitchell was extremely angry,' Alec Grant remembers:

> If you look back now at some of the photographs that appeared in the Press at the time you can tell by his face that he was not pleased and we knew, as his closest crew, that he wasn't. He was a very good commanding officer and if he had said, 'Pack up your kit, chaps, we're going here', we'd have gone quite happily, because he was that sort of commander. He had that sort of charisma, a one in a million type individual, the right man at the right time in the right job. Unfortunately, some of the other people weren't the right people in the right jobs at the right time, but that is my opinion.

What those closely involved in the Crater incident could not appreciate was that unless the situation was defused there was a real risk of other local forces being drawn in. 'Telephones were buzzing not only in the area of Crater in Aden but also up-country where there were several battalions of the South Arabian Army,' explains an officer who was drafted in during this period to take over as Brigade Major. 'The situation was not only very volatile but also extremely dangerous in that what were described as "the white faces up-country" were in danger of being murdered. So I think it was judged that the best thing to do, in all the circumstances, was to seal Crater – and that situation prevailed for a very long time.'

After negotiations with the Armed Police the ten dead were recovered and buried with full honours in the military cemetery. 'A very sad occasion,' remembers Dick Blenkinsop. 'I remember clearly going round to Silent Valley, the cemetery towards Little Aden, and the coffins with the Union Jacks that were there and the band playing the Last Post. It was a very emotional occasion.'

With the hand-over completed there was nothing more the Northumberland Fusiliers could do. Bill Pringle's 'X' Company was the last to leave Aden: 'On the day I was due to hand over our positions on the hillsides looking down on Crater to 'A' Company of the Argyll and Sutherland Highlanders their CSM arrived at twelve o'clock and at that stage I had enough ammunition to hand over to him so I told him not to bother bringing any when they took over.' To the company's great satisfaction an incident occurred in the afternoon and they were able to return fire: 'I think it was about eighteen thousand rounds expended and I had to get on the wireless net to the sergeant-major of the Argylls and tell him to bring some more ammunition down when he came.'

It was left to the Argylls to salvage something from the situation, which Colonel Mitchell set about doing with characteristic élan, as Alec Grant recalls:

> It was fairly obvious that we were going to have to go back into Crater at some stage to sort it out and I remember doing various recces with Colonel Mitchell and the rest of the crew. We set off towards Crater one day and we were just bumbling along to see how far we could get. In Aden they used to have these great long trailers pulled by hand and on this occasion one of these trailers was loaded up with Coca Cola bottles. The Colonel was driving at the time and for some reason, whether it was done in an attempt to block the vehicle or whether the chap panicked, he pulled this massive long trailer across the road behind us. Of course, the Colonel decided this was not to be, so then we reversed at high speed through the centre of this trailer, ending up with four flat tyres and all covered in Coca Cola, which in the heat and the sweat really was a bit of a mess. As the Corporal in charge of the vehicle this didn't please me too much.

In the absence of the Aden Brigade commander, who had been invalided out, Colonel Mitchell applied the Nelson touch, putting his own interpretation on the GOC's instruction not to disturb the situation. The Argylls' famous re-entry into Crater took everybody by surprise – including most of the Argylls themselves:

> I must be very honest here and say that when we set off in the Land Rover we did not know as a crew that we were actually going back into Crater. I remember sitting in the Land Rover with all the rest of the companies formed up ready to roll and thinking, well, this is going to be interesting, although in some ways it turned out to be a bit of an anti-climax because the enemy didn't really react to any

great extent. We went in and the Chartered Bank, which was
destined to become battalion headquarters for the rest of our time
in Aden, had these massive great wooden doors. It was a high
building and we wanted to have the height for good military reasons
so we were going to blow open the door with a Karl Gustav anti-
tank weapon, which would have taken the doors open quite nicely.
Then somebody said there's no requirement to do that sort of thing,
so we pressed the bell and the caretaker opened the doors for us.
Then the Brigade Major came down and drove through the
remainder of Crater in his Land Rover up through Queen Arbour
Road and out the other end and he then gave permission for the
remainder of Crater to be taken over and, indeed, it was taken over
with the minimum of fuss.

In the opinion of the Brigade Major the re-entry was 'a pretty good
non-event' that was seized upon and greatly dramatised by the
British media avid for good news – which Colonel Mitchell had very
good reason for wishing to exploit to the full since the Argylls were
due to be disbanded in 1968 as part of the round of defence cuts set
out in the Defence White Paper of 1966:

> Colonel Mitchell's regiment at that time was threatened with going
> to the wall, so he was determined to keep the Argylls in the
> forefront of everyone's mind and he had the re-entry into Crater as
> something to hang his hat on. There are those who thought that the
> way he 'glamorised' that was very much overdone, and I have to
> say that what I saw of the situation on arrival – while accepting the
> difficulties, the emotion, the stress of what had gone before – I have
> to say that the re-entry was, as I think one of the company
> commanders described it to me, a very straightforward walk in. But
> the re-entry was one thing, taking control of the place was another
> – and that was the next phase.

It was here, in dominating the Armed Police and the civil
population, that the Argylls showed themselves at their best:

> We were constantly on the streets and you never knew where the
> commanding officer was going to pop up next. We would just stop
> and pick on any car and carry out our searches and that was more
> or less the level that the whole battalion worked. I remember going
> to visit 'A' Company and as we were driving past the police
> barracks there was this thud, which didn't really click to any great
> extent with us until there was this massive scream from the second
> vehicle, 'Grenade!' We just drove straight on and they caught the
> blast of it, nothing serious apart from cut hands and things like that

but again we had been attacked by the police who were meant to be on our side.

Colonel Mitchell's response was to surround the Armed Police barracks and then to drive in without an escort to confront the police commander – a 'very high tension situation', as Grant recalls: 'We could have had big problems if they had wanted to turn nasty. Of course, we had "A" Company and various other people looking over our shoulders and if the police had started something then they'd have come off worse – but that wouldn't have helped us. I don't think we'd have survived very well, but the police backed down.'

All this robust activity by 'Mad Mitch', as the Press had now styled Colonel Mitchell, and his men resulted in a sharp decline in terrorist incidents in Crater but the Press, radio and television coverage that accompanied these doings did not go down well with the rest of Aden Brigade, as the Brigade Major recalls:

> Colonel Mitchell had a very good young captain appointed as his public relations officer and he made a point of picking up the Press at the Crescent Hotel, where they were all collected together, all looking for their copy. They were taken down to his Officers' Mess where they were given the picture and 'Mad Mitch' became the cry. Editors at home said, 'Tell us about Mad Mitch and keep telling us, because it has caught the public's imagination.' Now this was something that was very frustrating for the other commanding officers who were having pitched battles, firefights, casualties etc while the Argylls were getting all the publicity. Al Mansoura was the area that the Lancashire Regiment had to handle and there was frequent shooting in that area. The 1st Battalion of the Parachute Regiment had re-established themselves in Sheikh Othman and they used to have regular shooting matches. 45 Commando were in Ma'alla and Little Aden and the South Wales Borderers were in a different part of Aden. So there was an effort made to spread the jam a bit but, frankly, the journalists weren't going to have much of that because their editors were pressing at the other end.
>
> What we didn't know was the impact that Colonel Mitchell was having on television, because we never saw it. That I learned when I returned to this country after the whole thing was finished. For example, I went to my barber to have my hair cut and he said to me, 'You are looking very brown, sir,' and I said, 'Oh yes, I have just got back from Aden.' He said, 'Aden! My goodness, you must know Colonel Mitchell. What a man!' My friends and my family were all saying , 'What a man! If you had seen him on television when he came home. We felt like getting a Union Jack and waving

it!' Colonel Mitchell made a tremendous impact and he recognised the strength of that. From his own standpoint and from his regimental standpoint he got the public relations bit absolutely right, and I learned a lot of lessons about that which I was able subsequently to apply myself as a commanding officer in Northern Ireland.

As a corporal and section-commander in 45 Commando during this period David Chisnall followed the exploits of the Argylls with mixed feelings. 'We picketed all the heights of Crater to allow the Argylls to go in there,' he asserts. '45 Commando had spent a week or so getting into positions, using ladders to climb rocks, picketing the heights for a long period of time, watching what was going on in Crater itself, using our own snipers to keep the locals down, so as to make it relatively safe – and I use those words carefully – for "infamous Mad Mitch" to walk straight into Crater and do his thing.'

However, 45 Commando was kept far too busy to be concerned about the doings of others. 'Aden was very much considered as the junior NCO's war, a forerunner of our experiences in Northern Ireland,' Chisnall observes:

> A section was nine-man strong and you would patrol down the streets of Ma'alla or in the back of the Kuchi huts or you would have a mobile patrol of two Land Rovers and you had the command of that small element. A section commander was allowed to use his initiative but on very strict orders and guidelines. You had to wait until somebody opened fire on you. The rules of engagement were very specific and I suppose a parallel can be drawn with Northern Ireland in that it was a close city environment where they could choose their own killing ground, throw a blast grenade or have a weapon placed that could be used to fire and kill before moving on just like an ordinary civilian. You were playing on their home ground, as it were. They were batting on a pitch that they knew, so to put snap ambushes or snatch squads to stop somebody meant that the section commander had to make those instant decisions.

Inevitably, there were occasions when an immediate decision taken turned out to be the wrong one, as Chisnall himself experienced:

> We were involved in VCP [Vehicle Check Point] work where the young section commander had to take it on his own initiative once some shooting had started to set up a control point and stop people coming through. I do remember very clearly one particular incident

when rounds were fired on the headquarters fairly close to us. My section cut off the escape route, the back road out of Ma'alla, and we stood in full view to stop this vehicle coming towards us in the dark. I remember it very clearly. He switched off his headlights, approached very slowly and it appeared that he was going to stop. At that stage he accelerated, put his headlights back on and tried to get past. In the heat of the moment, when the adrenalin was flowing, we instantly fired. The occupant was killed and he crashed into the wall of the place we were guarding. My first rounds in the magazine were tracer rounds and they ricocheted up towards the headquarters. They thought they were under attack and fired back at the headlights with a great velocity of GPMG and automatic rounds. I took cover underneath this car which unfortunately continued to attract attention from headquarters because the headlights were still on and they went on firing quite dramatically through this car.

Initial elation at having shot what the section believed to be a terrorist trying to break their cordon turned to dismay when the dead driver was discovered to be a doctor: 'He was probably on his way home and was frightened by what was happening in Ma'alla. Tragically, that's the way it occurred. It was a traumatic incident at the time, probably more so when you had time to reflect on it, but the pace of life was such that you were then on mobile patrols or guarding fuel dumps and other incidents would happen. Aden was very much like that, several small incidents which had their own significance in building your experiences. But over the years you have time to reflect and you reflect on how perhaps you would react differently to it if you could go back in time.'

A timetable for the final British withdrawal from Aden in November 1967 had been agreed well in advance, but there was every chance that things would go wrong, that one or other of the rival parties would try to stage one final assault on British troops in order to claim a military victory. 'It was a tense situation because what was happening in the political context was a power struggle,' explains the Brigade Major. 'If someone like a colonial power is pulling out, you have a power struggle over who is going to take over. There were factions whom we knew would be ready to step in, with all the difficulties involved, so from our standpoint the political guidance was clear. We were not looking for other than a calming down of the situation, an orderly withdrawal – and we achieved that. It was very successful.'

A Royal Navy Task Force complete with a commando carrier and helicopters assembled off Aden, ready to act should an emergency evacuation by sea prove necessary, and then the troops were brought down under cover of night to Khormaksar Airfield to be flown home. Sector by sector, Aden was handed over to the Armed Police and the South Arabian Army, with the Argylls lowering their regimental flag in the early hours of 26 November in Crater to the piped strains of *The Barren Rocks of Aden*. 'I wasn't sorry to leave,' declares Alec Grant. 'We'd have liked to have been harder in some ways than we were. Indeed, we'd have liked to have seen those who had committed the murders of our soldiers brought to trial and dealt with which, of course, was never to be. So it was in some ways a sad occasion because you were leaving behind people in the cemetery, but it was probably one of the few places we were quite happy to see the back of.'

Gradually, the perimeter was reduced until on 29 November only Khormaksar Airfield remained in British hands, defended by 45 Commando from a command post which they named 'Fort Alamo'. The Brigade Major was on the last plane out:

> As we were about to leave I lowered the flag of Aden Brigade, took it off the lanyard and put it in my shirt front – and I still have it. That was the end of it. We took off and then the helicopters moved back on to the carrier and the Task Force moved away – and that was the end of the British presence.

Chapter Eleven

OMAN:
Last of the Old Colonial-style Wars

We had one man in our troop whose father had been involved in the campaigns on the North-west Frontier in India. He used to carry the machine gun and we'd jokingly say to him, 'This is the same sort of thing that your Dad was up to.' It did have overtones of those old-style colonial wars. In fact, it was described to me as just that, as the last of the old colonial-style wars.

It has been calculated that 1968 was the first year since 1830 in which no shot was fired in anger by any member of the British security forces anywhere in the world. This 'year of peace' also marked the ending of the old post-war Army and the formation of what has been called a 'second New Model Army' – fully-professional, reformed and slimmed-down. The slimming-down process had started back in the late 1950s as a result of reduced government spending on conventional forces in favour of nuclear weaponry. Those were the days when life for the conscript and the private soldier had been 'rough and tough', when 'you weren't expected to understand anything' and followed the traditional Army axiom of 'If it moves, salute it. If it doesn't, stand to attention.'

For those who witnessed the transition from the old Army to the new, as Ron Cassidy did, the contrast was remarkable:

My goodness, when I look back! What was it, forty-five to a room? Coal fire in the middle of that room, lucky to have enough coal to keep it alight, certainly not enough warmth to keep us all warm. We washed out in the open, behind the coal yard, in running cold water in troughs, and the sergeant used to keep a bath book to make sure we'd all had a bath once a week. And you look at the complex they work in now. Ten-man rooms divided into two compartments of five, lovely showers, lovely baths, nobody has to worry about bath books. And the food! My goodness, when I look back at the hundredweights of potatoes I used to have to peel when

I was on defaulters and that seemed to be the staple diet. When we
went out on the range with a haversack ration you could guarantee
it had one slice with cheese and onion on it and one of jam.
Nowadays the messing officer and the cook-sergeant would be
lynched for putting out a haversack ration like that.

Yet for all the discomforts, there had been a remarkable sense of
community in this old Army. 'One developed a sense of being part of
something,' remembers Cassidy. 'We were very proud of our
battalion. My battalion, the Rifle Brigade, had won twenty-seven
Victoria Crosses, the most of any infantry battalion in the British
Army. It was that sort of thing you built up on. Our young subalterns
and our senior officers had this tremendous tradition. It was all part
of their family. Their fathers had been in the regiment and *their*
fathers before them sometimes and, indeed, in most infantry
battalions it was the same. We were a large family, we all knew each
other and everybody cared for each other.'

For Cassidy's Rifle Brigade, as with so many other regiments with
histories stretching back to the seventeenth or eighteenth centuries,
the cut-backs had come by stages. In 1958 they had joined with the
Oxfordshire and Buckinghamshire Light Infantry (itself an amalga-
mation of the 43rd and 52nd Foot) and the King's Royal Rifle Corps
to form the Green Jackets Brigade. By the end of 1962 the last of the
National Servicemen had gone, leading to more cuts in 1966, when
the Green Jackets Brigade became the Royal Green Jackets. Two
traumatic years followed as many of the old British Army county
regiments went to the wall or merged. Something of the old esprit de
corps may have been lost, but the soldiers that this new Army
produced were undoubtedly of an improved model. 'There is no
difference between the youth when I was eighteen and the youth
we've got now, none at all,' argues Ron Cassidy. 'What I find quite
remarkable is the difference between the training of them today and
what it was when I was a youngster.' 'Todd' Sweeney has seen the
same changes:

The infantry soldier just used to have to be able to fire his rifle and
march on the parade ground, whereas nowadays your Rifleman will
have to fire his modern weapon which has replaced the rifle, he'll
have to fire the light machine gun, he'll have to fire the three-inch
mortar, he'll have to operate a wireless set, he'll have to drive an
armoured personnel carrier, he'll have to operate an anti-tank
weapon and he's got to be able to jump in and out of helicopters.
He's a much more sophisticated individual altogether – and he's
better led. The officers are much better trained than they ever used

to be. They're much more professional, the younger officers, particularly, who are much more dedicated and, I would say, much fitter.

Professionalism in the new Army came not only from improved training but also from selection procedures that made better use of the manpower available. In the Special Air Service Regiment the procedures for pulling out the most suitable from the many volunteers who applied to join its ranks had been developed into the most exhaustive – and exhausting – selection process ever devised. Shaun Brogan remembers reporting for the officers' selection course at the regiment's new headquarters in Hereford one afternoon in January 1969:

> By 8 o'clock that evening we were swimming in the River Wye. We'd been issued with our kit, shown all sorts of minefields on a map and told we had to meet an agent at point X, which meant going across this bloody river. I was scurrying around soaking wet in this clearing in the woods looking for the agent and there was only this woman in a car. I thought she'd be petrified if, with a blackened face and wet through, I knocked on the door of her car, but eventually I did it. I had to say something like 'The moon is blue' and she then gave me the grid reference for where I had to go to rescue a Russian scientist. I had to climb into a compound, stab two dummy guards and give the Russian scientist a pill. This was actually a water-sterilising pill which, of course, we had to protect very carefully when we swam the river. A number of officers were so put off by this apparently unsupervised solo swim that two or three of the thirteen on selection left that first night.

This was only the first of a series of programmes and tests that made up the SAS selection course, lasting three weeks for the troopers and a month for aspiring troop commanders. For the latter, the worst part of the business was the five-day escape and evasion course, with its notorious interrogation session at the end:

> You were very tired when you got to this interrogation centre because you'd been evading capture for about four days with only one Mars bar and drinking water from streams and you'd been marching long distances. So far as I can recall I was nailed to the ground with nails through my trousers and shirt and with a bag over my head for about nineteen hours. You started to hallucinate and you had to keep hanging on to the fact that it was only an exercise. One of the ways I did that was that every hour I made myself physically smile to convince myself inside my bag that I was human.

Then you were stripped and had a number painted on you with a felt-tip pen on your forehead and on your hands. You were chained into blocks of concrete and mud baths and there was this 'white' noise and you could hear people being beaten up next to you – in fact, they were hitting mattresses but you didn't know it at that stage. There was no torture but a lot of psychological pressure and I found the whole exercise one of the most traumatic things – if not *the* most – I've ever done in my life.

For the few who passed the selection course it was an initiation into one of the British Army's most exclusive clubs where, by contrast with the rest of the Army, the key-note seemed to be informality. 'Nobody wore badges of rank at all in the SAS then and that was one of the little details I was so chuffed to be part of when I joined,' declares Brogan: 'The officers tended to be called "Boss" by the soldiers and quite a few, out of earshot of the Colonel, were called by their Christian names. I was about twenty-four and most of the soldiers in my troop were about twenty-eight. A lot of them had seen service in Borneo and Aden and they also had a great number of soldiering skills which I did not have. Therefore I had a great deal of respect for them.' However, Brogan had to learn that this respect was by no means mutual: 'A lot of the soldiers in the SAS had less than complete respect for officers. A lot of them had gone to the SAS to get away from stupid young officers and were quite anti-officer in their attitudes. Indeed, there is quite an anti-officer feeling through the SAS which means that a young troop commander has to prove himself to be worthy of the men's respect. I think it probably took me at least two years, but I found that respect leapt enormously when we came on active service in Dhofar.'

The word 'Dhofar' has quite a ring to it in Army circles. The five-year war fought there in the 1970s remains one of the very few where Communist insurgency has been decisively defeated – yet it was also the least publicised of any war in which British forces have been involved. 'It was, if you like, a secret war,' explains John Akehurst, who was to play a key role in the closing chapters of the conflict as Commander of the Dhofar Brigade. 'British involvement was not advertised in any way outside the services. The British Government didn't want to draw attention to it for fear that they would be seen to be starting a campaign, which they would be unable to pursue, the thin end of a dangerous Middle Eastern wedge, and they were perhaps nervous that we were going to lose it. But how did we fight the war without media attention? The simple answer was that the Sultan of Oman had total control over entry into his country. He simply didn't allow the world's Press in. They could speculate as much as they liked outside but they had very little hard fact to go on. For all these reasons the war was fought in secret.'

Dhofar is the most westerly province of the Sultanate of Muscat and Oman, a mountain region about the size of Wales abutting on to the eastern border of South Yemen, formerly Aden Protectorate; an area 'rather like Salisbury Plain', according to one Dhofar veteran, 'with great rolling plains interspersed with huge *wadis*, the only part of South Arabia where the monsoon touched for three or four months of the year, so that in the summer it suddenly became a sort of green Shangri-La.' Another soldier remembers Dhofar as 'the most fearsome country in which to move and fight' but with a beauty of its own: 'It's hard to imagine somewhere in Arabia looking like a Scottish glen, but after the monsoon there is a thick sort of misty, bug-ridden damp in these deep valleys, with craggy limestone outcrops going up to four thousand feet or so. Then out comes the sun and the whole province is bright green.'

The inhabitants of these mountains were the Dhofaris. 'It was the most feudal, tribal society I've ever known,' declares Johnny Watts. 'There was a famous old Dhofari proverb that says, "Me against my brother, my brother and I against the family, the family against the tribe and the tribe against the world." I mean, you cross a guy twice and he'd cut your throat, then your brother would have to avenge you, and so there were tremendous blood feuds that had gone on for centuries.' The Dhofaris were extremely hostile to outsiders, including other Omanis. 'A very proud, arrogant people,' is how Shaun Brogan saw them. 'They were well-known in the Arab world for being so difficult and there is an Arab proverb which says that if you have a Dhofari and a snake in your bed throw the Dhofari out first!'

Despite the proximity to South Yemen with its newly-installed Marxist regime, Dhofar seemed an unlikely setting for a Communist-supported insurgency – but that is exactly what happened:

> The history of the Dhofar conflict is a classic example of an old
> repressive, despotic ruler treating a province as his own personal
> fiefdom. It was a local protest against misrule started by good,
> devout Muslim tribesmen. It didn't amount to much and at one
> stage it looked as if it might collapse, and then the Brits left South
> Yemen [Aden] and the new South Yemeni Government poured in
> help. The Communists started to move in and as usual they got a
> grip on this group like nobody's business, with their trained cadres
> and their heavy weapons. By 1968 the Communists were beginning
> to dominate the whole of the *djebel* [mountains] and snuffing out

the original rebellious people, executing a lot of the old-time leaders who didn't like being told by someone that there isn't such a thing as God and you aren't allowed to pray. They made examples of them, standing them on the cliffs, cutting their throats and pushing them off. So by 1970 the Communists were dominating the guerrilla movement. They controlled the mountains and the Sultan's Armed Forces were virtually restricted to the Salalah plain where their firepower and artillery prevented the rebels from rushing the Sultan's palace. The rebels had cut the only main road so it was just a matter of gradually squeezing and starving the Sultan out. It was only a question of time before their first long-range rockets would start hitting the airport at Salalah.

It was at this very late stage in the day that the British Government felt impelled to become involved but, as in 1958, only insofar as offering 'discreet help' to Sultan Sa'id bin Taimur. A 'Mr Smith' was sent out to do a study of the war and to report back. This was Johnny Watts, the new Commanding Officer of 22 SAS Regiment. In Dhofar, as one of those who served alongside him explains, Watts seized the chance to apply all the lessons in low intensity counter-insurgency that he had been taught in earlier campaigns: 'He was an apprentice in Malaya, in the Djebel Akhdar he was coming into his own and by the time he was in Borneo he knew what the score was. So Dhofar was where the parting of the ways came, because that's when the politics came into play.' Out of Watts's trip to Dhofar emerged the 'War on Five Fronts' strategy, in which Watts and his SAS teams were to play the key role:

What I found was that everyone was giving up too quickly. The initiative had always been with the opposition but there were a number of things we could do to reverse the disaster that appeared to be about to encompass everybody. My first point was that a national aim must be produced, a co-ordinated national aim, not to kill Dhofaris or cap their wells and drive them off their land, not repressive measures which just made people more angry, but a national aim that would remove the roots of dissatisfaction with better government. Secondly, we had to produce an intelligence front, because no one knew anything about the enemy – their personalities, how many there were, what their equipment was, the lines of communication – it was all hearsay. The third and fourth fronts were straightforward hearts and minds, to set up, for example, a couple of civil action teams in the coastal villages of Taqa and Mirbat as a focal point for some sort of basic administration with an SAS medic and a dentist and a guy who knew something about hygiene. Then my last front was that I sensed that wherever you get a revolution you also get a counter-revolution. There was enough evidence to show that many of the original Muslim rebels on the *djebel* didn't like Communist intimidation and repression. I mean, you wouldn't believe the *wadis* full of bodies with their throats cut. So there was a backlash to this and the original rebels wanted to defect and come to terms with the Sultan – only there was no outlet for them. So what I wanted to do was to take these revolutionaries who wanted to come in, arm them and train them and then send them back against their fellow revolutionaries – but this time as soldiers of God and the government. Why use British or Baluch or even Arab North Oman troops who were total strangers? Why not fight fire with fire?

Using Djebalis to fight Djebalis was crucial to Watts's plan but he still had his doubts: 'What it did mean was, in fact, starting a civil war, of pitting brother against brother and family against family – and that is what it turned out to be. The Dhofari tribesmen now when they talk of the Dhofar War refer to it as "the war of the families". We've been in actions when you found some enemy dead and a guy would say, "Oh, God, Salim!" It could be his cousin or his brother fighting on the other side. Civil wars are the nastiest of all wars because of the dreadful emotions that they arouse. I've known cases where a man's killed his father, not deliberately, but he just happened to shoot a chap who turned out to be his father. So I had my reservations – but it was the only solution.'

The 'Five Fronts' plan was put to the then Labour Government in Britain – 'who didn't like it too much. You know, "Britain's Vietnam, why should we get involved in Arab affairs any more?"' – and to Sultan Sa'id bin Taimur – 'who said, "No, I'm not having armed Dhofaris" and wanted to pursue his repressive line.' So the plan was shelved – until several months later when the old Sultan was deposed in a palace coup and replaced by his son, Sultan Qaboos, 'a super young man who wanted to take his country out of the biblical days, introduce roads, schools, hospitals and decent living standards for all, unify his nation and set it back on the historic path that Oman had once been on when it was a very powerful country.'

This change of regime in Oman more or less coincided with a change of government in Britain in June 1970 – with the result that within hours of the palace coup an SAS team was on its way to Salalah. One of the new Sultan's first acts was to make it known that pardons would be offered to rebels who defected and came over to the government side: 'The word spread on the *djebel*, "Hey, if you're

fed up with the Communists you can sneak away and there are
fellows waiting to receive you." Well, thank God, we had some SAS
by then, September 1970, waiting for them, twelve fellows in the
whole of the country. These fellows would wake up one morning and
outside their little houses in Taqa or Mirbat there would be fifteen
heavily-armed, fierce-looking, bearded guys in rags with Kalashni-
kov automatic rifles and Chinese mortars who'd say, "Look, we've
come to surrender and we want to fight for the government now
against our Communist masters." So during the autumn we began to
pick up something in the region of two or three hundred of these
surrendered *adoo* [enemy of the government].'

Working in training teams of three or four known as BATTs
(British Army Training Teams) each with a team leader, an Arabic-
speaker and a medic, the SAS began to organise the surrendered
Djebalis into irregular counter-guerrilla companies known as *firqat*:

> *Firqat* is an Arabic word for unit, really, and they all were given
> names. They chose their own and the first was called after the great
> Arab hero Salahadin, the holy warrior, which was a pretty dramatic
> sort of word and that was a multi-tribal *firqat*, which was pretty
> unusual. Then we started tribal *firqat* and they used to choose
> names like Firqat Al Assifat, which means 'lightning', though in
> fact they were the slowest-moving bloody *firqat* of the lot. Then I
> remember these guys coming up to me and saying, 'Sir, we've got
> the name of our *firqat*. It's Firqat Gamal Abdel Nasser.' So we had
> British soldiers fighting with this *firqat* under the banner of Gamal
> Abdel Nasser!

Each *firqat* became a fighting unit with its own tribal leader, but
run and administered by an SAS team. 'We could organise things,'
explains one such team leader. 'Our job was to provide them with
services, leadership, training and organisation. We could operate the
radios, we could operate the mortars and machine guns. We could
pay them. We could provide all that, so in some sense we led them
and in some sense we were led by them.'

It was some months before the first *firqat* was ready to be put to the
test in combat, so that initially the SAS role was non-offensive.
However, this changed when supposedly reliable information was
received by intelligence sources in the Gulf that a hostile guerrilla
training team had been infiltrated into the strategically sensitive
Musandam Peninsula overlooking the Strait of Hormuz in the far
north of the country. The threat to the West's oil supplies was
considered to be so serious that the British Government sought and
received permission from Sultan Qaboos to mount an immediate

strike to eliminate the intruders. A small force drawn from 'A' and 'G' Squadrons was flown with all speed to Sharjah and deployed for an operation that had all the makings of a classic SAS operation. Imaginatively conceived, it was marred by the absence of a tangible enemy – and by a single fatality.

In charge of the operation was 'G' Squadron's commander, Major A. . . . The assault consisted of two phases, as he explains: 'The first was a drop by parachute into the centre of the Musandam Peninsula at a place called Wadi Rauda, which was a gorge a mile across and a mile and a half long with mountains on all sides reaching up to four thousand feet. We dropped our free-fall troop into this *wadi* at night from ten thousand feet, which was the first operational drop of that sort that the British Army had ever done – although one of our people was killed in a parachute malfunction.' Meanwhile, the rest of the force had embarked on a Royal Navy minesweeper, to be put ashore in rubber assault craft manned by Royal Marines of the Special Boat Section: 'We clambered up the cliffs and put an ambush and stop round the village of Gumda – where we found nothing because it was apparently the wrong village. It was the normal sort of military cock-up in that the intelligence people had got the various landing spots wrong and there were no guerrillas in the area.'

Despite this failure of intelligence the dramatic appearance of the SAS in this remote peninsula left the local tribesmen in no doubt as to where their future loyalties should lie:

> We then spent the next six months carrying out a very extensive hearts and minds operation. We built air-strips, we set up clinics, we brought our medics in, we brought in supplies and we conducted a certain amount of psychological operations, telling the local people how much better off they were under the new Sultan's regime. This was all very good preparation for the operations in Dhofar because we got to know the Sultan's Armed Forces, we practised our Arabic and we practised extensively our hearts and minds.

Down in Dhofar the same strategy was being applied with the *firqat* drawn from the rebels. Shaun Brogan was one of the four troop commanders in 'A' Squadron that relieved 'D' Squadron in Dhofar in April 1971. Like his colleagues, he found the Dhofari tribesmen very difficult to work with:

> The enemy, the *adoo*, did not respect the British on the government side at all. As a consequence of Aden they thought most of them were weak, lily-livered individuals who if pushed

hard enough would withdraw, and this expressed itself when we
were working with the *firqat*. These men were almost all SEPs
[surrendered enemy personnel] and when we started working with
them they believed that sooner or later we would crack, that we
couldn't hack it. And they said to us after we had proved ourselves,
'We thought that you would give up but we now believe that you
can keep going.'

But proving themselves to be better soldiers did little to ease the
difficulties:

We had constant problems with them throughout the campaign and
the comedian Bob Newhart's famous line, 'Looking back on the
mutiny', from his nuclear submarine commander sketch, became
the sort of catch-phrase of the whole war. We were always having
mutinies or near-mutinies among the *firqat*. They wouldn't go on
patrol unless we bought them more blankets or more pay or more
helicopters or more something. They weren't untrustworthy in the
sense that they might shoot you in the back and then run off back
to their former comrades. That never occurred to my knowledge,
although there were incidents where they cocked rifles in anger.
But you could never say to your squadron commander, 'The
operation's definitely going to start tomorrow,' because you never
knew for sure until perhaps the morning it was supposed to start.
Even then I've seen situations where the helis have arrived and
you've had to say, 'No. Go away. We can't make it today.'

Yet for all the problems, working with the *firqat* gave Brogan
enormous satisfaction: 'Though they were extremely frustrating and
difficult to work with, the Dhofaris had a personal pride and a
soldierly ability – the good ones, at least – which made them a joy to
work with in some circumstances. There was a great deal of rapport
between us in the SAS and them in the *firqat*.' It was also possible for
the SAS to learn from the *firqat*:

The *firqat* always wanted to be nice to the people who surrendered
from the enemy. At the beginning of the war we used to think, we
ought to grab these guys, black bag over the head, start running
them round and frightening the life out of them, because one had
been trained to do that. But the *firqat* would say, 'No, no, no.
We've got to be nice to them.' And they'd kiss them on both
cheeks and say *'Salaam alleykum'*, sit them down, give them cups of
tea and discuss the news. They were right and we in our instinct
were wrong because in this war the kindness, consideration and

respect with which people on the government side surrounded the enemy was one of the crucial war-winning factors.

As the numbers of *firqat* increased so more responsibility devolved upon the shoulders of individual SAS NCOs and troopers. 'It was food and drink to them and they coped with it very well,' explains Watts. 'But living and working, eating and sleeping all the time constantly with these fellows at subsistence level was a very stressful job. This was one of the keys to the success of the war. We knew it would be but it was very hard sometimes for the individual. Many of our soldiers caught brucellosis and jaundice and whatnot and, of course, their values were very different from ours and that sometimes put the poor SAS corporal with a couple of his mates miles from anywhere in the most difficult moral dilemmas.'

By the end of the summer monsoon the *firqat* had been built up to a fighting strength of some six hundred fighting men and were ready to be committed to the battlefield. In October 1971 Operation 'Jaguar' was launched under Watts's command 'to get the government back on the *djebel* [mountains] and establish a permanent base there'. His main force consisted of five *firqat* led by teams from 'G' Squadron together with a battalion of the Sultan's Armed Forces – plus a spearhead of sixty men from a second SAS squadron. As a rule only one SAS squadron at a time operated in Dhofar but now 'B' Squadron were brought in to act as a special *force de frappe* – 'sixty individually magnificent soldiers, a very formidable prospect, led by a very capable, super commander called Richard "Duke" Pirie.' In the event this reinforcement proved to be crucial, for not only did the strength of the opposition turn out to be far greater than anticipated but 'G' Squadron had been so devastated by hepatitis from drinking contaminated water that to begin with it was only able to put forty men into the field.

The main force entered the mountains from the north while a diversionary attack was put in from the east by a smaller group. In the absence of his squadron commander, who was still recovering from hepatitis, Shaun Brogan found himself playing a leading role as this second group pressed forward to meet up with the main body:

> As we got into the area we were attacked very lightly with a few long-range attacks which you can tell are long-range because instead of the bullets cracking as they break the sound barrier going past you they were just whining, having lost their velocity. Then over the next few days the attacks became more and more sustained until one evening as we were moving towards a low group of hills, skirmishing forward under fire, we had a fairly sustained contact.

We attacked and took the hills and the following morning we came under very intense enemy fire at dawn. Most of us were on this knoll with *firqat* on each side of us in this line of knolls. I was about two or three metres from Steve Moores, a sergeant, when he was shot in the stomach. He was writhing about in agony, poor fellow, and I remember shouting to members of the troop, 'Steve's been hit!' and thinking as I said it, 'This sounds exactly like a film,' because one's only experience of this sort of thing in fact comes from movies.

However realistic the training you just don't know until it happens how you're going to behave. I know I didn't behave all that brilliantly. We were trying to get the helicopter to come and evacuate Steve and I was trying to control the mortars which were on the other side of the *wadi*. I wanted to direct the fire but I was frightened and I was scared and I just forgot what to do. But on the other end of the radio was an amazing individual called Kevin Walsh, known as the 'Airborne Wart' by all his friends in the SAS. He realised what I was doing and calmly sorted it out with me and I never made that mistake again. Anyway, Steve was picked up, taken back to RAF Salalah and operated on but died on the plane while being flown back to the UK. So that for me was when the war started to get serious.

Over the next few days the fighting intensified as the two groups joined up and fought to establish a stronghold on the *djebel*. At one point Brogan was in command of a defensive position on a hill-top:

The last two years had shown the *adoo* that if they fought back hard enough in the first few days whenever the government forces got on to the *djebel* they could knock them off and send them scuttling back to Salalah. So they tried it again and consequently there was a real humdinger of a battle that lasted about four days. During these four days on that hill feature, which we came to know as 'Porkchop Hill' after a battle in the Korean War, we had something like forty contacts, forty battles with the enemy during which, it has been said subsequently, we came under more enemy fire than any British soldiers since Korea – from Kalashnikovs and SKS semi-automatic rifles, from 7.62 light machine guns and from 12.7 heavy machine guns whose bullets came in like express trains, from mortars and so on. And of course we were firing thousands of rounds of machine gun and mortar ammunition ourselves, so it was very intense fire on both sides. It got pretty close at times. I can remember how a sergeant named Mick Seal had to lift the back legs of the tripod of his machine gun to get it to fire at the *adoo* below him. And in one particular day I called for air support seven times and had seven pairs of Strikemasters up over our position, directing them against targets on the ground. They went through everything on the racks. That's either thirty-two rockets or sixteen rockets and two bombs on every jet, a great deal of money's worth of ammunition.

Having got his force up on to the *djebel*, Watts then set out to establish a line of strong points that could be used to blockade supplies coming across from the west. Unusually, both he and his two squadron commanders were as closely involved in the fighting as any other member of the force. 'Indeed, we carried out a number of personal operations where we had a fairly high-powered patrol,' remembers Major A. . . ., 'with the CO, two squadron commanders and several officers taking part in little operations of our own.' Here again the Strikemasters of the Sultan's Air Force were able to play a crucial role in support:

I remember going out once where we were deployed in four groups and all four got pinned down by the enemy. We called in an air-strike and I was talking on my walkie-talkie to another officer about fifteen hundred metres behind who was talking to the aircraft. Normally the radio antenna was camouflaged with bits and pieces but mine had come off in the heat of battle and every time I raised my walkie-talkie all the *adoo* fired in my direction. I got the giggles and couldn't stop laughing but eventually through this officer I directed the aircraft on to the enemy and said, 'Don't come over until I throw a smoke [grenade],' and all my people were listening to this. But before I had thrown smoke to indicate our position there was an enormous explosion about fifty feet in front of us as one of the rockets from the aircraft came in. I think there were twelve SAS people there and twelve pots of different coloured smoke were immediately thrown through the air to give a most marvellous technicolor display to the pilot.

Humour played a key role in defusing fear and tension in moments of crisis, as Shaun Brogan remembers: 'We used to repeat the old Long John Silver phrase "Them that dies'll be the lucky ones" when we were under intense enemy fire or "There ain't many gonna get outa this one alive". We'd actually shout these remarks to one another when we were being mortared or machine gunned. The other great remark that we used to say to each other was "You shouldn't have joined if you can't take a joke", and what taking a joke meant was, in the worst circumstance, getting killed. But the same applied to the enemy. They, too, shouldn't have joined if they couldn't take a joke. The bottom line for them was getting killed and the bottom line for us was getting killed.'

In the weeks that followed the launch of Operation 'Jaguar' death or injury was never far away for the hundred or so SAS officers and men. They were daily – and nightly – in the front line and had often to put their own lives at risk to preserve their precarious alliance with the *firqat*. In consequence a 'tremendous feeling of camaraderie and esprit' developed that made the deaths and serious injuries hard to take. 'There was always a tremendous quiet after you'd brought in your dead or your wounded home. We always had numbers not names because of security and when someone came through on the wireless, "Numbers 34 and 72 killed and number 18's lost his legs", that was hard, because one of the things about SAS soldiering is that you're a very close family.' No one was more affected by the inevitable losses than the regiment's commanding officer, Johnny Watts. 'He was a very unusual man and he bore personally the casualties that we took very heavily on his own shoulders,' explains Major A. . .:

> There was one incident where one of our people had gone forward to try and protect one of the *firqat* with covering fire after they had got themselves into an unnecessarily exposed position. He got very badly wounded and eventually died of his wounds but the CO was personally involved in carrying him out of this very exposed position and typically had no regard for his own personal safety. Immediately after this had happened he came on to my position and he was in quite a bad state. And that was typical of the man and this was why we all loved him so much and would have followed him anywhere, because he was so personally involved in everything that happened.

It was also as a direct result of difficulties with the *firqat* that Shaun Brogan received his 'Blighty' wound. 'There had been chaos in the middle of the night with the *firqat*,' he recalls. 'So we weren't in position surrounding a village by dawn as we had hoped to be. We were still moving to get to the village when we were ambushed from our right from a distance of about a hundred to a hundred and fifty metres. The dawn light was rising to our left and, of course, we shouldn't have been caught silhouetted against the light like that.' Brogan was with a group of about twelve SAS leading the *firqat* in arrowhead formation when the firing started:

> We all dived to the ground and as we did so I felt something go through my thigh. I was saying to myself, God, I've been hit! and,

of course, I was very frightened as well, because there were bullets zipping off the dust all around me. I was lying on the ground trying to look at my leg without raising my head and I could see a hole in the trouser pocket of my left leg. I was expecting the pain to come washing up my body any minute and was thinking 'Where's my morphine?', because we had morphine on our identity disc strings round our necks. At the same time I was trying to sort out in my own mind where the enemy were, because there's always this stunned silence when you come under fire and I was shouting to the machine gunners to open fire. Then my squadron commander dived down beside me and said, 'We've gotta pull back! We've gotta pull back!'

Brogan felt impelled to disregard the order. He explains:

It was one of those moments of supreme clarity when I *knew* that the way to get out of this was not to pull back but to go forward and I said to my squadron commander 'We're . . . going *that* way!' pointing towards the enemy. I was brooking no argument and, fortunately, he didn't argue with me. He just let me take charge and get on with it. The machine gunner on my right was firing very accurately and I could see his bullets bouncing around the rocks but the machine gunner in front of me was a comparatively young guy who had only just joined and I shouted at his Number Two, who was holding his belts, to get a grip and bring the fire down. I shouted to the troop, 'Look, we're going to skirmish forward. Pete' – a man called Pete . . . . – 'and I will go first.' Everybody said, 'Yeah, boss. Okay', and I then said to myself, 'Either my leg's going to collapse when I stand up or it'll work.' Anyway, I got up and it didn't collapse but I was sort of hopping and favouring the other leg as we went to the first tree and when we got there Pete . . . . turned to me and said, 'You'll have to go . . . faster than that, boss,' because, of course, he didn't know I'd been hit. Two other guys skirmished forward and two others after them and then the thing was really motoring and I had this supreme feeling – here we were, some of the best soldiers in the world showing these guys what real soldiers were like.

So the incident went on as we skirmished in pairs towards the enemy. Every time one of the machine gunners moved I fired my Armalite rifle on automatic to simulate machine gun fire, stuffing the empty magazines down my combat smock. Then I saw a man in greenish uniform kneeling up and firing at me. I went to fire at him and my rifle clicked. I'd fired off all six magazines. Pete . . . . was firing at some other target with an M79 grenade launcher so I told

him to throw me his rifle, which was tied across his back with a
piece of parachute cord. He chucked it to me, I picked it up and
fired but because the rifle had been joggled around it broke in half
where the body-locking catch is. I pushed all the bits back together
but I was all fingers and thumbs so when I went to fire the rifle at
this guy – who was still firing at me – there was no round in there
and it just clicked. At this point I said to myself, 'This is like
"Carry on up the Djebel!"' Then I cocked the rifle and fired about
ten rounds at this fellow, but I'd been running with all this huge
weight of ammunition and water bottles round my waist and I was
not that steady and I don't think I hit him.

Having driven the *adoo* off, the troop regrouped and pulled back
to a defensive position where Brogan began to direct mortar fire on
to the retreating enemy: 'I pulled my map out of my pocket and there
was this little hole straight through it and blood all over it. I'd
forgotten about my leg at this point and then the signaller next to me
said, "You've been hit, boss." I said, "Oh, it's nothing," and the CO
who was right nearby said, "Come on, Shaun. Let's have a look." So
there I was dropping my trousers in the middle of the *djebel*, showing
them these two neat holes in my leg, and he said, "That's a bloody
Blighty one, if ever I saw one."'

After talking down his own Casevac helicopter on the radio
Brogan was flown back to Salalah, still in a state of euphoria. 'That
morning the *djebel* was beautiful,' he remembers. 'It was suffused
with this purple dawn light and it was so beautiful flying over it.'

While Brogan was recovering from his wound in hospital the
fighting continued up on the *djebel* against an enemy that 'fought
hard and well, fighting for what they believed in while we fought hard
for what we believed in'. There were major setbacks when *firqat* for
one reason or another would suddenly decide to quit the field. 'Then
it became a question of wills', Watts suggests, 'between the enemy
who were numerous and some of them really dedicated and ourselves with our tribesmen who were still very fickle. Some days
they'd fight very well, another day they'd all go away.' Increasingly,
Watts found himself having to commit 'poor old "B" Squadron' as
his main fighting arm – until a low point came 'when they had taken a
lot of casualties and were very tired, but when I also sensed that the
enemy, rather like ourselves, was running out of steam. One could
tell it in the way that in close-range contacts they didn't push it as
much as they had done in the early days. So although we were
obviously knackered, I knew it was real willpower now, not firepower, as to who was going to last out longest.'

At what he regarded as a critical juncture of the war the CO went to see the commander of 'B' Squadron, Richard 'Duke' Pirie:

> The 'Duke' and I were sitting in his sangar, a little stone wall for protection against small arms, drinking coffee at midday and I said, 'Right, Duke, I want the squadron out tonight with the *firqat* and I'll give you two hundred of them and so on to engage the enemy' – near a place called Shahait, I remember. He thought for a minute and said, 'No, I'm not going to.' So I said, 'Duke, I'm not asking you, I'm *telling* you. You get out there tonight. I'll come with you and we'll give them a hammering and we'll come back, but this is a battle of wills and we've got to keep at them.' He said, 'I've lost enough guys. Enough's enough.' I can see it to this day – I pointed a finger at Duke and I said, 'If you don't take your squadron out tonight you're fired – now.' From the expression on his face, Duke could have torn me to pieces. He had his personal concern for the squadron but there was also the disgrace of being dismissed in the heat of battle, so he said very reluctantly, 'Oh, all right.'
>
> Anyway, to cut a long story short, off we went and we had one bloody great battle, you know, and we won it in that in the end they finally pushed off. But we lost a couple more guys and when we finally got back to our base at dawn there were our fellows lying there in sheets – and there's nothing worse than seeing your dead friend with a sheet round him. I said, 'Sorry, Duke. It had to be,' and he looked at me and said, 'I told you so.' But that's what you're paid for. And I *knew* I was right in what I did. Notwithstanding the dead we had on that particular night action, I don't regret it because a few days later when we went out again, they weren't there – and we had won. They had gone down into the great ravines to hide and were only prepared in the future to take us on on their own terms.

As a result of these operations a permanent base – initially named White City but soon changed at the request of the *firqat* to Medinat Al Haq, the 'Place of Hope' – was established on the eastern end of the *djebel*, together with a series of defensive positions known as the Leopard Line. It was then possible to build on this advantage, using the *firqat* to win over the Dhofari tribesmen within that area. 'This was perceived very much as not being a war in which we were trying to bomb people back into the Stone Age,' insists Shaun Brogan, whose injury healed well enough for him to be able to resume command of his Troop within a couple of months. Hearts and minds once again became the key. 'It meant fighting the war in as humanitarian a way as possible. There was the carrot and the stick.

The gun was there, but so was the medical treatment, food for the Djebalis, the improving of the water holes, the building of mosques and so on. Religious freedom was an integral part of the war-winning effort. The Communists forbade people from practising Islam, whereas the government forces said, "Of course, you can practise your religion – God is our guide."'

By the summer of 1972 a significant shift in the war had begun to take place. The *adoo* no longer had the initiative. The coastal plain was back under government control and co-ordinated development policies were being put into effect. The leaders of the revolt realised that to regain the initiative they would have to 'strike back at the government in a very dramatic way, to dismay the government and remind everybody that they were going to win.' Accordingly, they prepared to mount a major military strike that would make full use of the low cloud cover of the monsoon. The target was to be the little seaside town of Mirbat, about twenty-five minutes' flying time in a helicopter up the coast from Salalah: 'Mirbat had raised a couple of *firqat* and so they made a plan to teach them a lesson by slaughtering their families while the men were out on patrol. They amassed four hundred fighters with mortars, machine guns and so on and they were going to descend on them like Sennacherib, approaching down the various ravines and be there at three o'clock in the morning when one of the *firqat* was out on patrol and when there were very few soldiers left in Mirbat. They were going to kill every supporter of the government and his family, collect all the weapons and sack the town.'

There was no reason why the attack should fail. The town was on a point guarded on two sides by the sea, while two ancient mud-brick forts and a barbed wire perimeter fence protected the other two sides. Inside the larger fort were twenty-five men of the Dhofar Gendarmerie whose main firepower lay in one light machine gun. Thirty Omani Askaris armed with ancient .303s occupied the second fort, while another eight gendarmes guarded a picket outside the wire on an outcrop known as Djebel Ali. These militiamen were not expected to put up much resistance. However, it was known to the *adoo* that a BATT team of eight SAS men occupied a building, the 'Batthouse', situated between the two forts. They were expected to resist fiercely but to succumb to the first wave of attackers over the wire. In the event these eight defenders, led by a young Captain named Mike Kealy, proved the *adoo* wrong.

The attack began in the early hours of 19 July, but fortunately for the defenders it began badly, as Johnny Watts was later able to establish: 'The enemy had some strong characters and there was one man who didn't like the plan and took off with his fellows. That left just under three hundred, very heavily armed. Then that particular night there was one of the heaviest thunderstorms of the year so they underestimated how long it was going to take them to get to Djebel Ali, where they had intended to surprise the little garrison and cut their throats by three a.m. They didn't make it until dawn and they didn't take Djebel Ali by surprise and there was some shooting before the picket was overrun.'

The firing roused the SAS team in the Batthouse, who emerged on to the roof of the building just as the first salvos of 82mm mortars and RPG7 rockets began to rain down on the town's defences. This was the preliminary to a massed infantry assault with the fort occupied by the Dhofar Gendarmerie as the enemy's main objective. At the base of this fort was an old 25-pounder gun intended to give support to *firqat* patrols as they came into the base. Fortunately, two members of the SAS team had been given a crash course on how to man the gun and they immediately ran over from the Batthouse and with the help of an Omani gunner began to fire the 25-pounder over open sights at the advancing enemy. The two SAS men were Fijians; two enormous, taciturn men who had established themselves as much-loved SAS characters: Sergeant Labalaba and Corporal Takavesi. Both had distinguished themselves in Borneo and Aden, where Labalaba had led an undercover anti-terrorist plain-clothes team. Within minutes of opening fire they became the main focus of the enemy attack, 'firing at point-blank range at twenty-five to thirty yards with masses of these chaps attacking them in their gun-pit.'

Meanwhile, from the flat roof of the Batthouse Mike Kealy and the other five troopers were firing the team's mortar, the GPMG and Browning machine gun to great effect. It was now obvious to Kealy, however, that this was no ordinary attack and he radioed to Salalah for an air strike and for helicopters to evacuate the wounded.

By chance, the *adoo* had chosen to attack Mirbat just as 'G' Squadron was about to relieve 'B' Squadron after its four-month tour in Oman. On this particular day the main body of 'G' Squadron was gathered in Salalah under Major A. . . . before being dispersed to various points around Dhofar. 'We were going to go out that morning to zero the weapons on the local range at Salalah,' explains A. . . . 'I wandered into the Ops Room and it was fairly obvious that something major had happened. No one really had a clue what was going on because the people in Mirbat were so busy fighting off the enemy that they had very little time to report, but it became obvious that the town was totally surrounded and that they were going to require assistance.'

The men of 'G' Squadron were now standing by with their weapons and ammunition ready to go out on the range: 'Instead we got into helicopters and flew out. It was only afterwards that I discovered that two of the newest members of the squadron, who hadn't been in Dhofar before, thought they were still going to the range. The first time they realised that they were not firing at targets but at real enemy was when they were actually deployed on the ground to the south of the town, which was certainly a failure of briefing as far as I was concerned.'

Landing on the seaward side of the town, the squadron commander and his force of thirty men skirmished forward in two groups, taking the *adoo* who had come in over that section of the perimeter wire by surprise: 'It was one of those peculiar quirks of good luck in battle that the place we had landed at had effectively cut off quite a large group of *adoo* between the wire of the town and the sea and so we left a group on a bit of high ground and they effectively closed the neck of the bottle as we deployed round in groups into the town.'

Up on the main front the situation had become desperate. On the roof of the Batthouse one of the mortar-team was having to hold the barrel of the mortar in his arms in order to elevate it sufficiently to be able to hit targets immediately below them. Minutes earlier a last message had come in from the gun-pit from Labalaba: 'Takavesi had been badly wounded, the Arab gunner badly wounded and suddenly there was this dramatic message from Labalaba, "I've been chinned. I've been wounded and we're finished now". Then there was silence and no more firing from the gun-pit. So Mike Kealy took himself and another trooper, a medical orderly named Tobin, and they ran over several hundred yards of open ground with all these guns firing at them at virtually point blank range. He got into the gun-pit where he found boxes of grenades and started to fight himself.' Regardless of appalling wounds both Fijians were still fighting. Takavesi was propped up against a wall but firing his rifle while Labalaba, with a shell dressing over his mouth and chin, was loading and firing the 25-pounder on his own. As Kealy radioed for an immediate air-strike Labalaba was shot dead and Trooper Tobin mortally wounded.

Despite the very low cloud cover two Strikemaster jets were able to strafe the *adoo* coming over the wire with devastating effect: 'The two pilots were very brave and were coming down as low as twenty feet, machine gunning the enemy and so on, being directed by Mike Kealy in this gun-pit, who was firing his rifle with one hand and holding his radio with the other. So the struggle see-sawed backwards and forwards, with these guys on the wire waving on their fellows, in full view of Mike Kealy and Takavesi, who were dropping them like flies.' When Takavesi was too weakened by loss of blood to go on firing, Kealy fought on alone: 'There was Mike chest-deep in the bodies of his friends and his enemies, surrounded by blood and gore, shrapnel and empty grenade boxes, fighting on his own in a gun-pit for twenty minutes to half an hour.'

As the men of 'G' Squadron reached the Batthouse and the gun-pit the *adoo* began to withdraw – taking with them as many of their casualties as they could but leaving behind twenty-nine bodies on the battlefield and twelve prisoners. 'I found Mike Kealy, this very young Captain, standing in what had evidently been the focal point of the attack,' remembers A. . . .:

> There was this 25-pounder, which had bullet holes through it, there were grenades that had been thrown but hadn't gone off and there were the bodies of the enemy within five to ten feet of the edge of the gun-pit. Labalaba had just been picked up, as had Trooper Tobin, who subsequently died of his wounds, and Takavesi, this enormous Fijian, who had what the surgeons in Salalah described as the worst chest wounds they'd seen. The whole scene was one of absolute chaos and I was dumbstruck by what had happened there, because it was obvious to me that a very heroic action had been fought. But it was the composure of Mike Kealy that struck me. He was totally in charge. He was very concerned about some of the *firqat* who had been out on patrol and so he asked if he could take a group out to Djebel Ali to find out what had happened to the picket there. I allowed him to do that but I have never in my life before or since seen quite such a demonstration of leadership and bravery as I saw on that day.

As the most senior officer present it fell to the commander of 'G' Squadron to put in commendations of bravery: 'I was very determined that the bravery of the defenders of Mirbat should be recognised but in those days, because the operations in Oman were covert, this did make us very circumspect about putting in people for awards. There were all sorts of actions that took place in Oman where outstanding gallantry was displayed which deserved the very highest awards and Mirbat was a good example.' In more public circumstances Captain Kealy and Sergeant Labalaba might have been expected to receive the Victoria Cross. Three years passed before it was announced that Captain Kealy had been awarded a DSO. Sergeant Labalaba received a posthumous Mention in Despatches.

As happened at Plaman Mapu in Sarawak, the repulsing of the

enemy at Mirbat had far-reaching consequences. Johnny Watts, who some years later was able to question some of the *adoo* commanders involved, is in no doubt as to its significance: 'I think we knew after Operation "Jaguar" that we were going to win but it was a question of convincing people, the doubters, that we were. After Mirbat there was no question. It was the beginning of the end. The *adoo* started fighting among themselves, someone blaming somebody else and factions fighting, but it was the last time they ever got together a large force to overrun an important government position.' Major A. . . . also regards the Battle of Mirbat as 'a crucial turning point. The fact that we showed we were prepared to stand and fight to protect the villagers and the *firqat* had a dramatic effect on the whole war. I took part in many operations after Mirbat, but they were very much operations of the whole side, with the Sultan's Armed Forces. It took another three years before the war was over but I think that the turning point was at Mirbat.'

When John Akehurst came out to Oman in August 1974 to take over command of the Dhofar Brigade the war was being fought on a totally different scale. Although he commanded some ten thousand troops it was not, he insists, a British war: 'This was the Sultan of Oman's campaign to secure his own country, in which we provided some three hundred loan service officers, senior warrant officers and NCOs. Then there was the SAS squadron, about eighty strong, whose value was out of all proportion to their numbers, though they weren't the sole British people involved, which is the perception of some people.' The Dhofar Province had now been cut in two by the Hornbeam Line, made up of barbed wire and mines, which was 'beginning to bite as I arrived, cutting off the people in the east from their supplies.' Akehurst's first task was to pacify this eastern sector:

> The way we decided to do this – and I was given this idea by an SAS sergeant, in fact – was to get the local *firqat* to move back into their tribal areas. The whole province is divided into tribal areas and within these tribal areas they bred and fed their cattle and brought up their families and they didn't stray into anybody else's area. These tribal areas were profoundly important to them, so if we could get the *firqat* to say, 'We will go back to our tribal area and this is where we'd like to set up the capital of our tribal area', then the brigade would mount an operation to capture that area. Our engineers would then bulldoze a track to the centre of that area and up the track would come a water drill. Water would be found and brought to the surface and suddenly there was a centre for cattle in the middle of their tribal area. At this stage we could

say, 'Now you must defend this tribal area and if there is any
enemy in it causing any trouble we will cut off the water. We will
help you maintain the pump, we will set up a mosque, a shop, a
school and a clinic for your community, but any trouble from the
enemy and you lose the lot.'

Akehurst's civil development strategy was so successful that 'once
established, none of these positions went sour, the policy worked
one hundred per cent and the eastern area was pacified'. Also
working in alliance with the Sultan's Armed Forces was an Iranian
battle group lent by the Shah of Iran – 'totally arrogant and very
unprepared to accept any advice or instructions from their British
commander'. This fifteen-hundred-strong force was now sent into
the *djebel* to establish a new defensive line, the Damavand, half-way
between the Hornbeam Line and the border with South Yemen.
'They had the most terrible trouble and took a lot of casualties,'
Akehurst explains. 'At this stage in about December 1974 I was
ordered to mount an operation to take some of the heat off the
Iranians. We had to mount the operation at very short notice and we
made a fundamental error.' The *firqat* were now several thousand
strong and Akehurst decided that a *firqat* contingent should lead the
attack. The result was near disaster: 'Every four hundred yards they
moved forward the *firqat* demanded to be shown air support, to be
shown artillery support, to be shown armoured car support, which,
of course, slowed up the whole thing and the enemy was ready for
them.' The *firqat* were replaced by an Omani battalion, which went
badly off course as it made its approach, eventually running into a
massive ambush. Akehurst had to watch these events from a scout
helicopter hovering above the battle. 'It was the worst single disaster
of the war,' he recalls. 'I could watch it going on and couldn't think of
any way in which to influence it. I don't think I've ever felt more
impotent in my life. However, over the next three weeks there was
some vigorous action and the heat was taken off the Iranians, who
were able to complete their advance and build the Damavand Line.'

By the end of the summer monsoon in 1975 the Dhofar Brigade
was poised to begin the last operation of the war. The main thrust
was to be a helicopter-borne assault across a deep *wadi* while a
diversionary attack was staged from an isolated mountain position
close to the border that had been seized at an earlier stage of the war.
Attempts to break out of this position had been tried but had always
failed: 'Here there was a battalion of the Muscat Regiment and their
job was to mount an operation out of this position towards the sea to
make the enemy think that this was where the final assault would

come.' The break-out proved astonishingly successful as the battalion commander, Lieutenant-Colonel Ian Christie, managed to get his entire force down a thousand-foot cliff and through a minefield without being observed:

> I went to see him the next morning and we sat on top of this cliff
> and looked down at the lower plateau, which had been virtually out
> of bounds to us for three years, and I said to Ian Christie, 'What
> would you need to go on to the sea? Do you think you could do it?'
> He said, 'I'd need two more companies but, yes, I could do it.'
> There was absolute silence down below. No contact or anything. So
> I metaphorically threw three months of planning out of the window
> and backed Ian Christie. That night and the next day he used the
> forces that we had assembled for the other operation, got down to
> the sea, sealed it and that cut off the enemy's lifeline to his base.
> We conducted further operations to mop up but that was the coup
> that really ended the war.

Just a few weeks later Akehurst was in Salalah attending a reception given by the Sultan of Oman for the diplomatic corps when he was summoned to attend the Sultan: 'I went forward and sat beside him on a bench and he said, in effect, "Well, how's the war going?" I said, "In my opinion, your majesty, you have just won it. My objective was to secure Dhofar for civil development and your civil developers can now go anywhere in the Province. There are still enemy around but they are a minor internal security problem." Ten days later the Sultan announced to the world that he had won the campaign.'

For the West there were obvious advantages in the outcome. 'I don't think anybody in the West who wasn't involved realises just how near Oman came to losing to Communist control,' Akehurst declares. 'If the Communists had got control of Oman the other Gulf states would have gone down like dominoes and it could have had a profound effect on the whole international situation. That sounds a bit grandiloquent, perhaps, but I believe it to be true.'

But was the suppression of the revolt in the best interests of the people of Oman? Shaun Brogan certainly had his doubts to begin with:

> Were we just propping up a despotic right-wing regime? I spent the
> first four months of my involvement in Oman asking myself if that
> was what we were doing. Part of me was really keen to be involved
> in any war, because I was a soldier and I wanted to prove myself.
> But another part of me – the more reflective part – was thinking

about this matter and I came to the conclusion that the Djebalis, the mountain people of Oman, really are far better off than they would have been if the Communists had won the war. It's good for the West that Oman didn't fall to the Communists and it's good for the people of Oman, who I think are materially and spiritually better off for the government forces having won.

As to the SAS's involvement in Oman, Brogan is adamant that they brought an important moral quality to bear on events:

> The war in Dhofar was a hearts and minds campaign in which the SAS provided one of the main thrusts in developing that idea and in constantly pushing that message throughout the war. Left to their own devices, the Sultan's Armed Forces had been involved in bombing *wadis*, blowing up and poisoning wells and killing innocent people. It was our involvement in the war that gave it a moral dimension which could have been missing without our participation. In that war in particular the SAS demonstrated its belief in applying massive force at a very small point, very quickly and very suddenly, so that you overwhelm the enemy and shock him into defeat. It isn't about licking your lips and killing people. It's about doing the job professionally.

While recovering from his leg wound in Salalah, Brogan had received a letter from his old regiment inviting him to return to command its mortar platoon: 'Now in a mortar platoon in peacetime you probably have something like two to three hundred rounds of live ammunition to fire in a year. In one week in Dhofar we were firing a thousand rounds or more per tube in the very intense periods of the war. At one stage I'd had something like sixty SAS under my command and two hundred *firqat* and helis and artillery and all the rest of it.' The war itself had been another powerful attraction: 'War is a very intense experience and the seductiveness of the war in Dhofar was that it was very exciting and not that many of us were killed. There are a number of names running into the teens of the people killed in Dhofar on the clock tower in Hereford but not that many for five years of war.' Another element that he knew he could never find elsewhere was the special comradeship that he had shared:

> We were very relaxed. I mean, some people wore shorts, some wore long trousers, some cut their long trousers down if they got ragged and wore them as shorts. Wearing sweatbands or *shemags*, which are squares of cloth that you fold up and wrap round your head, and wearing huge belts of GPMG ammunition, we looked like pirates. There were always a great number of characters with

funny nicknames in the SAS, people like 'Whispering Leaf' and
'Jock the Clog' and the 'Airborne Wart'. Some of the best moments
of the war were the moments when we used to sit around and tell
each other stories, often funny stories involving these characters in
the SAS.

After that, 'to go back to an infantry battalion and count soldiers'
socks was too boring to contemplate'. After Oman Brogan left the
Army and went to university to take a degree in Politics, Philosophy
and Economics. When the war was over he and his wife – herself a
doctor – returned to Oman: 'I went back to work in the department
of the government whose job, in essence, is honouring the promises
made during the war to the rebel tribesmen that there would be a
better life if they supported the government. My wife and I, among
others, are lucky enough to be doing exactly that, honouring those
promises.'

Johnny Watts was another soldier who in time went back to Oman,
where he ended a distinguished military career with a long spell as
Commander of the Sultan's Land Forces and Chief of the Defence
Staff. Major A. . . . also returned briefly – and spectacularly – to the
area in 1977 as he and another colleague in the SAS chased a
hijacked Lufthansa aircraft from Dubai to Aden and then finally to
Mogadishu Airport in Somalia, where the aircraft was successfully
stormed and three of the four hijackers shot dead. Major A. . . . also
provides the final postscript on the heroic stand at Mirbat, following
the death in February 1979 in the Brecon Beacons of Mike Kealy:

> When Mike came back as a squadron commander I was then
> second in command of the regiment and sadly I was with the group
> that found his body on the Brecon Beacons when he died of
> exposure on a training exercise. Because of what had happened at
> Mirbat, where we had assisted there, it was rather sad that I should
> be the one that actually closed his eyelids when he died.

III. WAR AT HOME

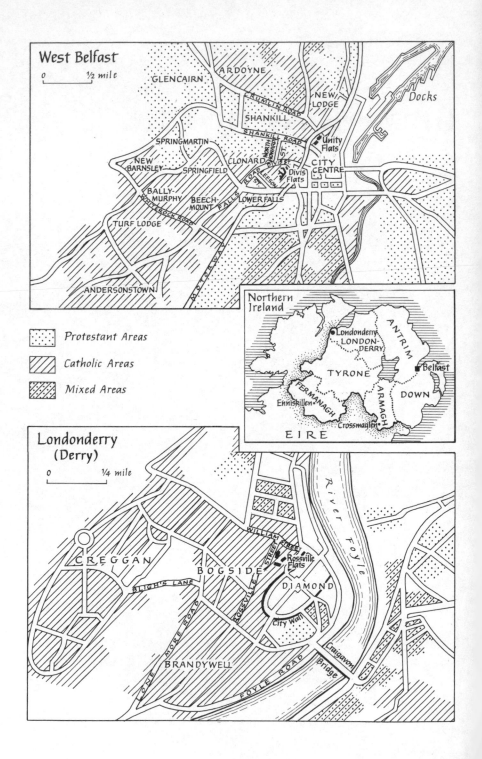

West Belfast

0   ½ mile

GLENCAIRN
ARDOYNE
CRUMLIN ROAD
NEW LODGE
Docks
SHANKILL
SHANKILL ROAD
SPRINGMARTIN
NORTH HOWARD ST.
Unity Flats
NEW BARNSLEY
CLONARD
CITY CENTRE
SPRINGFIELD
FALLS ROAD
LEESON ST.
Divis Flats
BALLY-MURPHY
WHITEROCK ROAD
BEECH-MOUNT
FALLS
LOWER FALLS
TURF LODGE
MOTORWAY
ANDERSONSTOWN

Protestant Areas

Catholic Areas

Mixed Areas

Northern Ireland

Londonderry
LONDON-DERRY
ANTRIM
TYRONE
Belfast
FERMANAGH
ARMAGH
DOWN
Enniskillen
Crossmaglen
EIRE

Londonderry
(Derry)

0   ¼ mile

CREGGAN
BOGSIDE
WILLIAM STREET
Rossville Flats
BLIGH'S LANE
ROSSVILLE STREET
DIAMOND
River Foyle
City Wall
LONE MORE ROAD
BRANDYWELL
FOYLE ROAD
Craigavon Bridge

Chapter Twelve

NORTHERN IRELAND:
The Honeymoon

In the area we were in – the Falls, Ballymurphy, a lot of those emotive names – we found ourselves, night after night after night, in major riot situations, facing the very daunting prospect of the ebb and flow of large sectarian mobs, Protestants confronting Catholics, which we had to separate out. Sometimes it was Catholics alone having at us, sometimes Protestants alone having at us, but with a pattern which tended to unfold in the same sort of way each day. With hindsight one can now see that this was the end of what the GOC, General Freeland, described as the 'honeymoon period'.

Stuart Pollitt was there 'actually at the kick-off'. For him 1968 had been a 'low point' in his life as a soldier as his own regiment went to the wall and he was shunted from one unit to another. He had been serving with the Lancashire Fusiliers in Hong Kong when that regiment was disbanded. Then he had spent nine months with the 4th Battalion of the Royal Anglian Regiment, previously the Royal Leicesters, before it, too, was broken up. Given the choice of opting for one of the other three Royal Anglian battalions, he had gone for the 1st Battalion, formed from the Norfolk and Suffolk Regiments. 'A lot of people decided not to soldier on at that stage,' he recalls. 'They felt there wasn't a place for them. It had been like a family, that's the best way to describe it; they were all local lads from Liverpool and Manchester etcetera and they just didn't want to go anywhere else. "Twelve VCs before breakfast" was the cry in the Lancashire Fusiliers and we all realised that once the battalion went all that would die with it. So for me a lot of the esprit de corps was lost with the county regiment and yet there was a sort of inter-marrying of regiments with the 1st Royal Anglians and a new esprit was born.'

A major factor in helping this new feeling to develop in the battalion was the quite unexpected advent of active service. Much to his surprise, Stuart Pollitt suddenly found himself in the autumn of 1969 'at the start of the Troubles in Northern Ireland'.

The British Army's operational involvement as an aid to the civil authorities in Northern Ireland in what was quickly – if euphemistically – dubbed the 'Troubles' began on the afternoon of 14 August 1969 when companies of the 1st Battalion the Prince of Wales Own Regiment of Yorkshire were committed to the Bogside in Londonderry. 'People have lost sight of why we went there,' remarks one of those involved in this first stage of Army intervention. 'We really went over to look after the Roman Catholics, who were getting a bloody nose off the Protestants.'

There had been serious unrest in the Province during the last months of 1968 as civil rights' marchers had sought to draw attention to the many injustices suffered by the minority Catholic community in the face of long-standing discrimination by the Unionist Government. Their marches had been banned by the Government and broken up by the Royal Ulster Constabulary supported by the Ulster Special Constabulary known as the 'B' Specials, an armed and exclusively Protestant force that had a reputation for sectarian thuggery. In March 1969 belated attempts to bring in Government reforms to improve the lot of the Catholic minority had provoked a bombing campaign aimed at electricity and water supplies – almost certainly the work of the Ulster Volunteer Force (UVF), one of a number of extremist Loyalist organisations that included the Ulster Protestant Volunteers, the Loyal Citizens of Ulster, the Orange Volunteers and the 'B' Specials Association. Then, in August 1969, there began the traditional 'marching season' whereby the Protestants celebrated their three-hundred-year ascendancy over the Catholics. Its most provocative manifestation had always been the Apprentice Boys' March through Londonderry.

A violent confrontation ensued as Catholics threw stones and petrol bombs at the Protestants and as the Protestants tried to tear down the barricades that the Catholics had erected round their district known as the Bogside – which was proclaimed 'Free Derry'. Similar confrontations between the two communities then followed in other towns in Northern Ireland, culminating in a night of horrific violence in Belfast on 14–15 August as marauding gangs of Protestants and Catholics firebombed each other's neighbourhoods. The RUC was no longer able to cope and, on the afternoon of 15 August, soldiers from the three garrison battalions in the Province moved on to the streets of Belfast and Londonderry. That same night the first reinforcements began arriving from the mainland and within a fortnight the Army presence in Ulster had risen to six thousand men.

In both Belfast and Londonderry the barricades had gone up and a series of 'no-go' enclaves had been created whose names were very soon to become familiar words in every mess and barrack room in the British Army. In Londonderry the population was predominantly Catholic, concentrated in the districts of Creggan, Brandywell and Bogside on the western side of the River Foyle. In Belfast, however, the Protestants were in the majority and the distribution was more complex. East of the River Lagan, which ran down to the docks and the shipbuilding yards, the population was almost entirely Protestant and middle class. On the other side of the river in West Belfast the Catholics were largely confined to the area east of the new M1 motorway but in two main sectors – Ardoyne, New Lodge and Unity in the north and the much larger enclave of Andersonstown, Turf Lodge, Ballymurphy, Springfield, Clonard and Lower Falls in the south – divided by the solid Protestant wedge of Glencairn, Spring-martin and Shankill.

As far as those in the Army were concerned they went into Belfast and Londonderry not just to keep the two warring communities apart but also to protect the minority community. 'We felt that we had gone out there to protect the Catholics,' remembers Stuart Pollitt. 'At that stage it was the Catholics who were giving us cups of tea and the first shots fired at the Army were fired by Protestants. We were there to keep the peace, that was the main role, but when one side is giving you cups of tea and the other side's shooting at you, you do tend to lean towards the faction that is giving you cups of tea.' In these early days his sympathies lay very much with the Catholics: 'I felt sorry for them because just about everybody had invaded them at some stage of the game, but it's interesting to note that in the time we were out there this changed. Within about six months it was the Catholics who were firing at us and the Protestants giving us cups of tea. This was what confused everybody. We never really knew how this change took place. It just happened.'

Someone who was better placed to observe the change and how it came about was the commanding officer of the 1st Battalion the Parachute Regiment, which came to West Belfast on 11 October. 'The night we arrived was the night after Constable Arbuckle was shot,' this officer recalls. 'In fact, his blood was still on the Shankill Road and the factories and streets were still burning.' A government report recommending the disbandment of the 'B' Specials had just come out. They were to be replaced by a part-time military force to be known as the Ulster Defence Regiment (UDR) that would come under the direction of the General Officer Commanding (GOC) Northern Ireland. These proposals had angered the Protestant die-hards in Belfast who marched on the Catholic Unity Flats with UVF gunmen in attendance: 'The commanding officer of the Light

Infantry Battalion had been wounded by ricochets when they had been shot at from the rooftops and he was in hospital. I was sent for in the middle of the night and told to take over the Shankill and a sizeable amount of the Falls Road and the city centre from the Light Infantry, which I did.'

Having always worked closely with the local police in other theatres overseas, 1 Para's commanding officer made it his business to call at the local police station as soon as he could: 'I went up to Tennant Street Police Station and checked in with the Chief Superintendent, who was a very, very sad man. He couldn't understand what was happening. He had been up and on duty and everything was going wrong. Some of his men had been quite badly hurt and he just couldn't understand the situation. He had relied to a large extent on the "B" Specials for his information and suddenly the "B" Specials didn't exist any more. They had gone and so had his intelligence. There was no military intelligence that I could get my hands on and so we really had to start from scratch.'

In fact, the Army's principal concern at this time was to restore normality. 'The mission I was given was to "reduce tension, to allay fears and to hasten by every means in our power a return to normal life and individual freedom", which is a most unusual military aim.' Often in the absence of the local authorities and without much 'voluntary contribution' from a large segment of the local population, units like the Paras found themselves acting in most unexpected roles: 'Street lights would go out and they would ring my headquarters up and ask me what I was going to do about it. Undertakers wouldn't turn up to take a body away and we would be rung up and asked if we would do something about it. The sewage system would get blocked and we were rung up. We began to appreciate that we had to get that civil community back to work, because as a military force you can't do it.' In his new role as a 'community relater' the commanding officer began by making his men relate at street level:

> I said to all my soldiers – and there were six hundred of them on the streets – talk to everybody, keep talking, keep a smile on your face, always laugh, it doesn't matter what the joke is. Grit your teeth if someone is being offensive to you but keep talking, because the Irish just love to talk – and it worked. We made lots of friends and we established a link with both communities on either side of what had now been called the 'peace line', which was a long barricade between the Shankill Road and the Falls Road. It had been constructed to stop the so-called 'marauding gangs' of hooligans coming up from the Catholic side and setting light to

more Protestant houses and equally to stop the marauding gangs
from the Protestant side. Then there were areas in parts of the
Shankill, which I was told were 'no-go' areas for British soldiers. I
said, 'This is stupid. A lot of my soldiers come from Belfast. We
will go into them. We will go into them armed and when we drink
tea, two people will drink tea, two people will watch them, but we
will talk.' And we did all we could to allay the fears of those dear
old ladies who used to stand on their doorsteps wondering whether
their houses were going to be burnt down.

What amazed those who knew nothing of the Ulster scene was the
remarkable friendliness of the local inhabitants, Protestant and
Catholic alike. 'I always thought,' continues the commanding officer
of 1 Para, 'in those early days of community relations that the
humour in Ireland, the warmth and the genuineness of those people
on the streets, where you could sit and drink tea and have lovely
warm cakes and scones with them, I thought that that warmth and
humour would eventually win through – but it hasn't been like that.'
Side by side with the warmth was an irrational animosity towards
each other that horrified outsiders: 'This was something we didn't
understand. It took a long time to adjust to this because the depth of
feeling that existed on both sides of this so-called peace line was
intense hatred for each other, and yet the people were genial when
you were among them. It was quite amazing how genial they were.'
This paradox was not only experienced by 1 Para. The men in the
Royal Marine Commandos who also went to Belfast during this first
period found the same attitudes. One officer remembers how, on
arrival, his unit was advised to give two separate cocktail parties, 'a
cocktail party for Protestants and a cocktail party for Catholics,
which we found very odd. At the Protestant cocktail party they said,
"Of course, we've got nothing against Catholics but you realise
they're the cause of all the problems," and at the Catholic cocktail
party they said, "Of course, we've nothing against Protestants but
you realise they're the cause of all the problems." It was quite a
strange experience for us to find people who were intelligent and
sensible on the one hand, and on the other were making such
irrational and totally ridiculous statements.'
A senior Royal Marine officer who was then a company commander recalls how his men would be offered 'tea and stickies' by the
women of both communities: 'If you didn't know where they lived
and what their surnames were, there was no difference between
them. That has always struck me. I have been over there five times in
all and I've never got over the point that they are so alike that they

cannot see it themselves. There are very nice people on both sides.' However, there were also nasty people on both: 'Each little street in West Belfast was a village and had very much a village mentality and what the other side couldn't see, because they didn't talk to each other, but which we in the middle could see was that they were exactly the same animal. The hard-nosed seventeen- to eighteen-year-old Protestant lout was exactly the same as the seventeen- to eighteen-year-old Catholic lout. They just chanted different tunes.'

But however much the two communities had in common they followed two quite separate traditions, as the commander of 1 Para soon discovered:

> I had a company in the Catholic area and another in the Protestant, and I went down to visit the company in the Catholic area – I think it was St Congell's School. There weren't very many places where you could sit and have a discussion and so I was sitting talking to my company commander in a classroom. As you do when you are sitting at a desk, you open the lid, and I opened the lid and took out a history book as we were talking. Then I began to read the history book and the history that I read astounded me. It didn't read like the history that I'd been given when I'd done my homework before coming to Ulster. So out of curiosity I took it and then went to visit my company at the top end of the Shankill Road in another school. I asked the company commander there for a history book and we compared the two histories. There must have been about eight hundred yards between the two schools, but the two histories were totally different. The two communities had been brought up with two separate versions of history.

The main threat to community relations throughout this period was perceived to be from the powerful Unionist extremist groups rather than from the Republicans. Indeed, the illegal organisation known as the Irish Republican Army (IRA), with its goal of the overthrow of the Ulster Union and the unification of the 'Six Counties' with the Irish Republic, lacked popular support. 'I think it was caught off-guard,' declares 1 Para's commander. 'People thought it was organised but it was not. We were not talking about the IRA then. We were told to avoid the use of the letters "IRA". We kept off it completely. We didn't blame them [for the violence] and indeed it didn't appear to me that they were in any way geared for a fight at that time. They were much more interested in having a boxing match with us. The split between the Officials [Official IRA] and the Provos [Provisional IRA or PIRA] hadn't really started.'

As part of the process of restoring community relations the CO set about making contacts with the local Republican elements:

> We had to look hard at how we could involve ourselves with the community, not just with the day-to-day activities in the street but in other ways. We had some very good football teams and a boxing team and I had some exceptionally good cross-country runners so I despatched my second-in-command around the area to find out where there was likely to be some competition. One invitation I got was to go into the Falls Road to meet some people who were the leaders in the community and discuss the possibility of a boxing match. After we did a little homework we discovered that about four of these people were in the old [Official] IRA. I had asked my Intelligence Officer to look into this much more closely because I didn't want to be lured into a trap, but at that time it wasn't like that. I went to this little garage and I sat with these three or four alleged members of the IRA and discussed whether or not we should box with the Immaculata Boxing Club or whatever it was and we did agree that we would. We had in those early days three or four boxing matches, which were amicable and fun and in which they didn't try to score points off us. I then invited these men to come to my mess, together with some leaders of the Protestant community. They came and, of course, they stayed on either side of the room but they actually came and drank with us. Looking back on it, it seems impossible that that could have happened, but I think when you look back in history at this particular period of history, those battalions that were there in 1969 and early 1970 established a close friendship with both the Catholic and the Protestant communities – and we held a ring for them to do something about the political situation.

But while the Army held the ring the politicians prevaricated and the extremist groups organised. In January 1970 a group of Republicans angered by the IRA Army Council's proposal to recognise the Northern Ireland Government at Stormont formed themselves into the breakaway group that became the Provisional IRA. Its first objective was to alienate the Catholic population from what it saw as a British Army of occupation and when a fresh round of Orange Marches began in April the Provisionals ensured that violent confrontations would ensue. The common Army view was that the Orange Parades should never have been allowed to take place. Another serious error was made when the battalions that had made such progress in restoring calm and building up good relations after the disorders in October 1969 were replaced: 'We were taken away after a four-month tour because that was what the Ministry of Defence had worked out was the optimum,' explains the CO of 1 Para. 'We were the first battalion to really settle down in that area and the same with other battalions in Londonderry. They had established a trust and then suddenly they had gone and the people found it very difficult to relate to a follow-on battalion. They tried but it wasn't the same. You can pass on contacts but you can never pass on friendship. So we lost the trust and by so doing we lost the intelligence, and that was one of the biggest set-backs.'

Almost six months of relative calm ended on 1 April 1970 when a company of the 1st Battalion the Royal Scots had to act as a barrier between Orange Lodge marchers and a crowd of stone-throwing Catholics on the edge of the Ballymurphy housing estate. 'This was not shooting,' emphasises the commanding officer of the Royal Scots. 'This was stoning, bottling, setting alight to buildings, a sort of havoc situation.' The old internal security that they had rehearsed for dealing with riotous crowds proved hopelessly inadequate: 'The internal security pamphlet talks about banners – "Halt or we fire if you cross this line" – and the man with the megaphone and the techniques of facing mobs and we initially felt that might be the way to do it. We were rapidly disillusioned because there was no way you could go into that sort of mode.' Shields, helmets and batons proved inadequate to the tasks: 'The rubber and the plastic rounds had not been developed. The protective clothing hadn't been either, so you found that soldiers were just keeling over, being hit with bricks in the face or hit with a bottle in the knee. You just couldn't face that. You had to withdraw.'

The next day the whole battalion was deployed in Ballymurphy and the Springfield Road to quell the continuing disorder. More than a hundred rounds of CS gas had to be fired: 'This was the time when the indiscriminate CS gas had to be used because there was no alternative. There was no point in standing there as an Aunt Sally and being bombarded. We would be wearing respirators but because of the vagaries of the wind, the gas wasn't necessarily able to be used properly and we had to be very careful about its use in so far as we were able, because it would billow off and end up in an old folks' home, perhaps, full of asthmatics.'

However appropriate, nothing alienated the minority community so effectively as the use of CS gas, which affected rioters and innocent householders alike. The Catholics could no longer regard the Army as their protectors and the Provisionals were able to capitalise on the growing friction. The honeymoon was over and the riots were on with a vengeance, as the Commanding Officer of the Royal Scots recalls:

> A report would come over the radio, 'There is a crowd gathering on the corner of . . .' That would be about six in the evening and the trouble would finish about three o'clock in the morning. And it would not, of course, be confined to one single area. It would spread itself across Belfast. There was never really a break from it because it was day after day after day. So what one had to do – and this was where I admired the soldiers so much – was somehow train them not to overreact, to maintain the principle of minimum force, which is so essential in these situations, to remain impartial and to impose the law within the law. I mean, it was very, very difficult – but they did it.

In Londonderry, too, a regular pattern of civil disorder became established, as Stuart Pollitt describes: 'You could set your watch by the public reaction. As the schools came out at around three thirty it'd start with a little bit of stone-throwing by the schoolchildren which would build up, you know, as the pubs turned out. It would come to a sort of semi-crescendo at about five o'clock, just pure stone-throwing, when they all knocked off for tea and to go and watch themselves, see how they had done on television. They would shout to you and say, "We'll see you at seven on our way to the pubs", you know. It was almost humorous and there was still a good rapport at that stage, funnily enough.'

Television and instant news reporting of the Troubles were already beginning to have a major impact, both in the coverage they gave of events as they unfolded and in the way Press reporting itself was exploited. No longer was the British Government able to control Press reports in the way that it had been able to do in a remote region like Borneo. 'In the early days the IRA won one or two notable victories by their handling of PR and the media,' declares a senior military figure. 'The military had always conducted its affairs with the understanding that there was a need to conceal what we were doing from the enemy. We'd never really come to grips with making the best use of the Press in a world where from the 1960s onwards the Press had become more and more powerful. They could get their news stories back to the television or radio stations or to their newspaper without having to send it through a military censor, so what one then had to do was to develop a capability of making sure that they got the right story.'

But the business of 'making sure that you got in there with the word before the opposition got in with his propaganda' was something that took time to develop. The commanding officer of a Royal Green Jackets battalion, which did two tours in Belfast in the early 1970s, recalls that whenever 'a violent incident occurred one was immediately assailed by the Press and the television, and whoever got in with the first story tended to be the person who was believed.' Attempts by the Army to present the facts were not always welcomed: 'I remember one afternoon when there was a riot outside the Springfield Road Police Station and the newsmen there were briefed by the leaders of this riot. I invited them into the police station to hear our side of the story. The television reporter, Trevor McDonald, agreed to come with me and was immediately set on, jeered and jostled and given a good dose of racialist abuse.'

Many soldiers believed that the very presence of a television camera and crew in a riotous situation only served to inflame the situation. What was more certain was that the rapid transmission of news on television or radio could itself affect events as they unfolded. The same Green Jackets CO remembers how 'on riotous evenings in the Upper Falls I found it necessary to move around the area with a small transistor radio tuned to the BBC in my flak-jacket pocket, so that I would have some warning of a change of mood in the crowds that might result from any particular news item.'

June 1970 saw the beginning of a new round of Orange Parades, leading to another bout of riots and pitched battles between rival mobs. In Belfast, in particular, many thousands of Catholic and Protestant families from the areas of mixed religions between the enclaves abandoned their homes and moved to safer areas, either because of direct intimidation or because they no longer believed the Army could protect their lives and properties. This had the effect of further diminishing the contact between the two communities as well as creating clear-cut no-man's-lands around each enclave, often made up of burned-out buildings. The enclaves themselves became more like ghettoes, introverted and strong in community spirit but more and more willing to give their allegiance to those who claimed to offer them leadership and protection.

It was not a happy environment for troops already suffering 'from lack of sleep and a disrupted personal life, from seeing those daunting mobs facing you, from seeing a comrade wounded, from being injured yourself. In fact, it was a very stressful situation sustained over a long period.' What compounded the stress still further were the conditions in which units like the Royal Scots were forced to live:

For my headquarters we were sharing a police station in the Falls
Road, several people to a room, with very little fresh air. We had
some temporary accommodation on the *Maidstone*, which had been
a submarine depot ship, but again packed like sardines. Companies
were in disused mills and I can remember a place called the
Mission, a former Mission House, which we had a platoon in. It
was an appalling place. Conditions for washing and so on were all
very difficult. It had had to be cobbled together. But that was
where we had to be, because it wasn't good enough being round the
corner, half a mile away. You had to be on the spot and able to
respond quickly. That was one of the keys to snuffing out riots, to
be there and to do it, just as a spring at its source can be turned by
a twig.

Being based at a police station meant that this commanding officer
was able to work closely with the local divisional commander, but
'police morale was very, very low' and intelligence a 'very scarce
commodity'. The process of building up an intelligence-gathering
machine had started but it would be many months before it could
become fully effective. At a higher level there appeared to be no
clear directive on how to pursue what was now taking on the
characteristics of a counter-insurgency campaign. The visit to Northern Ireland by a new Home Secretary who seemed to lack any sense
of urgency did nothing to instil any confidence in those who were
looking for guidance. He confounded one senior officer, who was
expecting to give the Minister a briefing of the situation, by falling
fast asleep the moment the officer began to speak.

Early in July, just as the Royal Scots were approaching the end of
their tour and looking forward to a much-needed rest, a further stage
in the escalation of the Troubles took place. 'One afternoon I was in
the police station when the divisional commander said he had some
information that there might be an arms cache in a house in
Balcombe Street, in the Lower Falls,' recalls their commanding
officer:

> Now the Lower Falls was still a 'no-go' area and the barricades
> were up. We had said that they would have to come down shortly
> and we had put in patrols but the barricades weren't down. We had
> some intelligence material and what the divisional commander said
> pretty well confirmed it so we decided to take a look. But knowing
> that this was a bit of a hornet's nest I took the precaution of
> standing by at the periphery three companies – a company of the
> Gloucesters, a company of the Duke of Edinburgh's Royal
> Regiment and a company of my own. Then with the police we

made up a joint patrol with my reconnaissance platoon who swiftly went in with the police in their vehicles – and radioed back to us and said, 'The house is full of arms and ammunition, but a crowd is already gathering and we will not be able to stay here for very long unless we get some reinforcements quickly.' Now, in fact, the place had really erupted. Buses were hijacked and driven into those little streets into the Falls that had not already been barricaded and in some instances set alight. It was astonishing how rapidly the whole thing rose up. The recce platoon, which had recovered a lot of weapons by this time, had to withdraw. As they were trying to get out they came across a mob and then there was a general fight. We were able to drive them off the barricades and clear it, but we decided that we couldn't handle the whole thing ourselves. Time flashed by and then, unusually, shooting started.

The GOC, General Freeland, and his Belfast Brigade Commander had seized the chance to mount a full-scale operation to clear the Falls: 'Here was an opportunity to get the barricades down and clean out the place in terms of arms and ammunition, so an operation was mounted, which just went flowing on through the next night. I don't recall off-hand how many battalions were used but four or five had to be brought in. A cordon-and-search operation of the Falls was done, house by house, and an enormous amount of arms and ammunition came out.' The Lower Falls was Official IRA territory, but it was the Provisionals who came in on this second night and took on the Army. Thirteen soldiers were wounded by gunfire, five by gelignite bombs. The Army returned fire, killing at least three terrorists while other casualties were believed to have been spirited out of the city and across the border. More than a hundred firearms were recovered, together with incendiary devices, explosives and thousands of rounds of ammunition.

In the opinion of the CO of the Royal Scots, the events of 3–5 July were 'a real turning point in the context of the recovery of arms and ammunition – but also in relations with the local population, because you cannot carry out an operation like that without damaging relations pretty badly.' A limited curfew imposed by General Freeland on the Falls, but lifted next morning at the request of the CO of the Royal Scots, only alienated the Catholics still further, becoming in popular and Press mythology a three-day curfew: 'In fact, it didn't mean anything because nobody was about on the streets anyway, but it was an emotive term and used as such.' The Unionists were jubilant, believing that the Republicans had been taught a lesson, but the real victors were the Provisionals, who were now able to argue that they were the true protectors of the Catholic community against the oppressive British soldiery. In June PIRA was said to have had less than a hundred activists in its ranks. Within six months that number had grown to about eight hundred. The split with the Officials was complete – and 'the gun and the bullet were going to be the solution to the problem'.

PIRA now began to prepare its forces for a terrorist campaign based on 'armed propaganda', by which, according to one officer who made a study of the subject, 'you use military action in support of your propaganda. That's to say, you kill people or blow them up in order to have a propaganda or public relations effect.' It organised its volunteers into so-called brigades and battalions along military lines, concentrating its strength in Belfast, where the Belfast Brigade was made up of three battalions each about a hundred and fifty to two hundred strong.

The British Army battalions also began to prepare for the worst: 'It was quite clear to us that, unless something was done politically, we were at the beginning of a major counter-insurgency situation – and we began to train for this eventuality.' In September 1970 the 1st Battalion of the Parachute Regiment returned to Belfast for its second Northern Ireland tour. The situation was now very different from what it had been seven months earlier. 'The feel of that city had changed dramatically,' states the battalion commander. 'The atmosphere was harsh and tense. They were all predicting that it was going to go on for very much longer and that bloodbaths were going to occur – and everybody was waiting.' While it waited the battalion trained:

> We trained extremely hard with firearms and many other skills
> and fitness training to make sure we were ahead of the game.
> Everybody fired almost every day on the ranges at Palace Barracks.
> We began to shoot more precisely in an urban environment, we
> began to listen to shots being fired in an urban situation, because
> buildings echo and create a different noise and you can't tell where
> the shot is coming from. And I used to say to the soldiers, 'What I
> don't want you to do is say, "Sir, there's someone over there
> shooting at me." I want to hear you say to me, "Sir, someone shot
> at me and his body is over there." That is what you have got to
> achieve.'
>
> They also learned to lift people in a riot. In the early days we
> were working by the book, where you got your shield and you got
> your baton and you put your helmet on and you stood there like an
> Aunt Sally and waited for the magistrate to come and declare a riot

situation. It was not like that now. I learned that you have to be positive and you have to be skilled if you were going surgically to stop this riot. In a riot you could feel this fear that generated the numbers. People would begin to get a feel that something was going on. They'd come out of their houses, they were curious, they wanted to know what was going on and so the numbers of people grew. But you couldn't afford to have large numbers of people out in a riot situation and so we trained every man how to make an arrest. We trained every single day and by the time we got on the streets they were exceptionally professional in this ability to arrest. We stripped off their armour, we stripped off all the heavy clothing and we formed snatch squads that could move quicker than the young yobbo.

By the end of 1970 PIRA felt it had a strong enough base in West Belfast to take its 'armed propaganda' into the streets – while units like the 1st and 3rd Paras were standing by ready to respond: 'We moved very much on to a war-type footing except that everybody was very strictly schooled in the use of what is now called the Yellow Card – that you were only to fire when someone's life was in danger.'

The New Year began with a spate of rioting in Ballymurphy, with petrol- and gelignite-bombing. Cars and buses were hijacked and set alight. Warnings went out to those still fraternising with the troops at discos or at other Army hearts and minds exercises to stay away or risk the consequences. In mid-January the Provisionals orchestrated a second outbreak of rioting in Ballymurphy, which continued for a week. Then in the first week of February the Royal Anglians began a cordon-and-search operation for weapons in the Ardoyne that set off another bout of rioting. Five soldiers were wounded in a burst of machine-gun fire, another three wounded by sniper fire. On 6 February a twenty-year-old gunner in the Royal Artillery was shot dead in New Lodge, the first British soldier to die since the Army had been called in to assist the civil power in August 1969. On the same night two terrorists were shot dead by the Army. Four days later a bomb intended for an Army patrol killed five civilians. The second British soldier to die was shot dead in Belfast on 15 February. So the fatalities began to mount up.

As a section commander in one of the Resident Battalions doing a two-year tour of the Province rather than one of the shorter, more intensive so-called 'roulement' tours of four and a half months, Stuart Pollitt had seen the tragedy unfold by stages, 'from the stoning, then the nail bombs, then the riots and petrol bombs, then the gunmen on the street, the snipes and ambushes, progressing all the time'. Soon it was the turn of his own battalion, the 1st Royal Anglians, to take casualties:

> I think the one that will stick in my mind most of all was a soldier I was talking to on the radio. It must have been a chance in a million snipe. He was sitting on his radio in a sandbag emplacement with a little slit for him to look out of, a form of observation post, when a round came straight through the slit and he was hit in the head. I remember him actually saying on the radio mid-sentence, 'I've been shot', although I'm convinced he was clinically dead. It just went dead after that. I reported it and said, 'Someone's been shot. I can't raise him', and then they got on the radio and reported that they'd had a contact. That was the first one we lost. It's very difficult to describe your feelings – anger, frustration, shock. I think it was the fact that he was a popular lad and a married man that brought it home, having to explain to the wife and seeing her face, seeing her leave the Province with the children. That was the difficult part of accepting it.

Chapter Thirteen

NORTHERN IRELAND:
Bullets and Bombs

ATO: Gentlemen, can I ask for cover, please? Can you watch the road on either side, OK? Just in case anyone gets anti-social.
(Radio interference as ATO approaches suspect IED[1].)

ATO: OK?

Asst. ATO: OK, sir.

ATO: Right, now what 'ave we 'ere, then? Oh, lovely! Yes, two detonators. Wait a minute . . . .
(Heavy breathing.)

ATO: OK. Right, there are two dets, in fact, red-red. There's a clock, there's some Frangex[2], bundles of it about the place. I'm just going to tie off . . . I can see that the dets are broken. Just a sec . . . .

Asst. ATO: Quite a pile, sir.

ATO: Hang on. There's still a lot of ANFO[3] about. Now I can't see the rest of the circuit. So we'll rip the bugger out, I think.

Excerpt from a radio transmission by an Ammunition Technical Officer (ATO) of an Explosive Ordnance Disposal unit defusing a car bomb in Northern Ireland in the early 1970s.

[1]IED – Improvised Explosive Device.
[2]Frangex – Commercial explosive produced in Eire.
[3]ANFO – Ammonium Nitrate (fertiliser) and Fuel Oil, home-made explosive used by PIRA.

By 1971 many of the more blatant injustices suffered by the Catholic community in Ulster had been removed and the Northern Ireland Government was itself being a great deal less obdurate in its dealings with the British Government. However, the reforms came too late to prevent the Republican cause from gaining considerable support from Catholics. In West Belfast and 'Free Derry' the two IRA factions were able to extend their authority in a way that brooked no opposition. Those who refused to co-operate were treated in the most brutal fashion. 'The nice guy who was hale and hearty when he spoke to you in the street could be a totally different animal in the backstreets,' explains an NCO who led a plain-clothes recce patrol in Belfast in 1971. 'I witnessed a punishment beating that was carried out on three children, two boys and a girl aged between eleven and fifteen, whose crime had been stealing from a gas meter in a public house. They had been brought into a Republican Club and the punishment was meted out by three rather large guys with billiard balls in socks who beat the children on the floor. The parents didn't complain, they were too frightened to. But to have to sit and watch that and to feel incapable of doing anything to stop it was terrible – and believe me, I was incapable. Any move on the kids' behalf would probably have finished up with me not being here today to tell the tale.' The same NCO was also made very aware of how good the Republican propaganda was when he listened to a cassette tape of ballads by a local group, which had been picked up in a raid: 'I sat down and listened to it one evening and, to be honest, it made me stop and think, because the Irish command of folk music is superb and they had a very clever way of putting over the romantic myths to the general public. I had to stop and take account of my situation out there. It was only the following morning, having listened to it a few times, that I realised how effective was that type of propaganda.'

Just as effective but far more deadly was the armed propaganda that the Provisionals began to wage from April 1971 onwards with the intention of so demoralising the general public as to make the Province ungovernable. This took the form of a bombing campaign: beginning with thirty-seven explosions in April, forty-seven in May, fifty in June and in July twenty explosions within one twelve-hour period alone that caused several million pounds worth of damage to shops and pubs as well as a number of civilian casualties. These were early days for the bombers, when they used mostly commercial explosive from Eire and scored several 'own goals' from premature detonations, but in this first year alone 1,022 explosions were listed.

The impact of the bombing campaign would have been infinitely more deadly had it not been for the sappers from the Royal Engineers, who provided search teams, and the Explosive Ordnance Disposal (EOD) units of the Royal Army Ordnance Corps. It was the job of the Ammunition Technical Officer (ATO) to respond to 'call-outs' at any hour whenever what was known in Army jargon as an IED (Improvised Explosive Device) was found. In 1971 the

ATOs and their support teams responded to over two thousand call-outs, a quarter of which entailed the making safe of IEDs. Every unit in Northern Ireland had its own appointment title used over the radio partly for convenience and partly for security. The bomb disposal men very quickly came to be identified by the call sign of 'Felix', although there are different versions of how that name came into being. 'It's argued that at one time it was going to be "Phoenix" after the bird that rose from the ashes,' explains one ATO, 'and in the early days in Northern Ireland lots of ATOs seemed to be around where there were ashes and flames. But the story told against the Army is that "Phoenix" was too complicated a name for the unwashed soldier and that it was misinterpreted over the radio or telephone as "Felix".'

As events soon showed, the ATOs or 'operators', as they called themselves, proved to be terribly vulnerable as they went about their business of making safe and dismantling IEDs that were not only lethal in themselves, but increasingly were armed with booby-trap devices of one sort or another. 'By the time I went to Northern Ireland two of my fellow officers who were on the same course as I was had been killed, blown up whilst dealing with a device,' remarks one of the earlier generation of ATOs, recalling the 'Stanley knife banzai days' when 'you got your own Stanley knife and a pair of secateurs, together with a handgrip and some tools and a demolition box.' But the high casualties suffered by the ATOs did nothing to discourage those who came after them: 'We all felt we had to do it. We had to chase the terrorist, push him into a corner. We had to get good court evidence, if for nothing else, then for our friends who had gone down. It was also a life-saving effort. Once a terrorist had placed a bomb something had to be done. That bomb presented a hazard to the local population and a terrorist, having planted a bomb, seems to think that, morally, he has handed the problem over to the security forces.'

Scientists and engineers from the Ministry of Defence worked long and hard to come up with more sophisticated equipment, including the development of remote-controlled 'wheelbarrows' from a first prototype built around a hospital wheelchair. But there was no way in which the ATO could ever completely avoid risking his life as he went about his work:

> My first tour was at a time when there was a lot of activity. Your
> introduction to the section was to join another team, regardless of
> your rank. So a new operator joined an experienced one and did
> some time with him before he took his own team out. With my

section we were very 'lucky' in that every operator seemed to get a live device on his first day, going solo, as we called it. And that first long walk with a real bomb at the end of it, which you only found out about after you'd rendered it safe, that seemed to take the pressure off. You know, you'd done one, and that gave you a whole different perspective. You've been there, you've seen it. Nobody can ever take that away from you – and that does take off the pressure. Although I don't remember the pressure coming from anywhere other than from myself. The troops on the ground were always very good. Never did they say, 'Felix, get a move on', even though they were perhaps being set up for a shoot or were having to deal with the brickings and the haranguings of the people at the edge of the cordon. It was always, 'Felix, what can we do for you?'

In the first bad years of the bombings rarely did the Alpha Teams, those on first call, find time to relax after dealing with one incident before being called out to deal with the next:

On that first tour the days seemed to be wet and dark, moving from location to location dealing with the devices. It smelt. There was the smell of home-made explosives, of bodies, of wet soldiers. If you were on Alpha Team duty you took over at about eight o'clock in the morning and you then went out and moved around the city centre and your brigade area going from suspect device to suspect device, ensuring that the cordon was right, ensuring that what safety precautions could be taken were and then, having completed your circuit, you started dealing with those devices that could be dealt with. Sometimes you couldn't deal with a device fully because a higher threat risk was given to you by brigade and you had to move to that one.

It could be a car bomb, it could be a cassette incendiary, it could often be to extract a body where it was suspected of being booby-trapped, or it could be to investigate the scene where a member of the security forces had been injured or, as happened to me once, to go and investigate it after one of the Saracens, the armoured vehicles used to move the security forces around, had been hit by a rocket fired from a rocket-launcher – and that was bad.

The team took their food on the street corners as and when they could. I seem to remember now that 7 RHA were a good unit to go to at lunchtime because their steak pies were the best and 38 Engineer Regiment had a very good relationship with East Belfast where the ladies produced lots of nice cakes, so that was a good place to stop at tea-time, and then the battalion up the road at

Andersonstown made excellent steak sandwiches. They were the highlights of bad days as it rained and the wind blew and you wondered whether you were on the ground to deal with a device or whether it was a set-up for a shooting. There seemed to be a break at about nine to ten o'clock, something to do with the patrolling pattern or the opposition going to their local shebeens. Then you'd go out again at eleven o'clock, probably worked around till three to four o'clock in the morning, then came back in, replenished and out again with first light and carry on. The days seemed to be like that and when you weren't on duty it was making and mending with the equipment and, of course, the paperwork. The reports had to be completed because the information had to go back to be assessed, to determine the trends of the terrorists and the best ways to counter them.

When supplies of commercial explosive began to run low the IRA made increasing use of home-made varieties, known as 'CO-OP sugar' and ANFO (ammonium nitrate fertiliser and fuel oil), which – quite literally – gave headaches to those who had to handle them: 'They had terribly distinctive smells that seemed to pervade everything. The constituents could give you the most horrendous headaches and after you'd rendered one safe and shovelled up this home-made explosive you went back to base, took your clothes off and just burnt them because some of the materials used to eat the clothes and boots away. We were never terribly confident about what it might be doing to our bodies.'

The experienced operator learned never to relax his guard: 'As the tour went on one got a feeling that one was getting better. You felt that you knew your area, knew the bombers who were working in it, and, hopefully, were more professional than they were. Maybe you had reached a plateau in your tiredness, but always there was this feeling, "Be careful, be careful, be careful," because folklore had it that if you were going to go down it was going to be either side of the couple of days you got in the middle of your tour for rest and recuperation. Either then or in your last couple of weeks when the days don't seem to go fast enough and you had to guard against cutting corners.'

Every EOD was potentially lethal and each operator could expect on every tour to face a number of situations where he had no option but to take his life in his hands. 'It's not uncommon for things to go wrong and that's when you must remain flexible in reviewing a situation,' explains one of a number of ATOs who won George Medals for gallantry in Northern Ireland in the early 1970s:

Initially when dealing with a device there is tremendous time pressure but after certain render-safe activities have been carried out then there is time for a fast but more considered line of action to improve the possibilities of a good render-safe. I remember once dealing with a particularly large car bomb on the interface between two hard areas. I took render-safe action and reached the stage where I thought it was relatively safe to go forward. I walked to the car and then started to get to the device and after I'd got a little bit done I found a second circuit that should not have been there. Then in answer to the question of the illustrious poet, 'What steps do you take?', it was 'bloody big steps' – back to the control point, where I reviewed my actions. But it was still there and something had to be done, and I remember being enthused by my Number Two, a particularly old and bold soldier who indicated that, 'You'd best get your arse back up there, sir, and carry on.'

The risk of death is something that every operator has to come to terms with. 'You tend not to think of dying yourself,' remarks a staff sergeant ATO. 'I've had a couple of times when it went through my head as I approached a big car, but if it does go it goes. I'm not going to know anything about it so there's no point in worrying about it. If a device is going to go I'd far rather it was a big car and you don't know anything about it rather than a small device that is going to remove a limb.' What was perhaps more of a strain to the Felix teams was hearing about other casualties. 'It seemed on the first tour as though every day somebody was hurt,' recalls one of the comparatively small number of ATOs who were available for duty in the early years of the bombings:

One used to listen to the local radio because the Army communications in those days were so cumbersome that it could be that the local radio would warn us of a suspect device before we were tasked. When notice was given that somebody had been injured either in a shooting or an explosion we had degrees of concern. It was, 'Please God, not an operator,' and then, 'Please God, not a member of the security forces.' It seems terribly callous but one was almost willing that it be anybody so long as he wasn't security forces, and that's how we felt. There was a deep sadness every time a member of the security forces got hit and with the boys in the bomb disposal, we thought very much about our friends who'd been hurt or killed. One had a cold rage, not a warm hatred but a quiet inner strength. We were going to do our job. We were not going to be beaten by criminals who considered themselves freedom-fighters.

For the married men in the bomb squads there was the additional strain of knowing what their wives were having to go through every time there was a reported casualty on television or the radio. One ordnance officer remembers 'an awful incident when the Press – despite advice to the contrary – put out that an ATO who had been based in West Germany had been killed in Northern Ireland. They didn't name the chap but there were only two people from our forces in West Germany working in Northern Ireland at the time. I got deputed to ring through to Germany to speak to the commandant of the depot in which both these particular soldiers were serving at the time. The commandant put the telephone down, looked out of his office window and the two wives were stood across the road waiting, and the poor man had to go out and say, "Mrs ——, would you please come in and see me." '

Set against the risk and the tragedy was the 'enormous satisfaction' to be gained whenever a lethal device had been made safe: 'It's a tremendous feeling when you've gone out there. You've tackled the suspect car and you've got a couple of beer barrels with explosives strewn around. You've got the timer unit and you realise just what you've done.' Every operator derived satisfaction from knowing that he had saved lives and damage to property and to some degree outwitted evil men for whom he nevertheless felt a 'healthy respect' because of their skills. 'It was always very satisfying to get to a device and disrupt that device before it went off,' declares an ATO who won a Queen's Gallantry Medal in the 1970s. 'You can then help in the collection of forensic evidence against the bomb-maker. And if you come across a new piece of terrorist technology then obviously you get even more satisfaction. On one occasion I was called to a small package in a toilet. I dismantled the package and at the second attempt I realised it was more than just a hoax package because I could smell the explosives. I could see a small box with a piece of circuit board in it, which turned out to be a long-delay timer. It was pretty rudimentary but it was the start of a more sophisticated type of bombing.'

It was the PIRA's belief that once the casualties among the security forces and civilians reached an unacceptable level the British Government would withdraw its troops and the Stormont Government would collapse. It is said that forty-five deaths among British troops – one more than the casualty figures from the Aden campaign – was the IRA target, achieved shortly before 'Bloody Sunday' in January 1972.

What the PIRA chose to ignore was the inevitable Unionist backlash. 'It took about six weeks for me to grasp the central political

The days of batons and CS gas: ABOVE A riot squad attempts to hold back the vanguard of a Loyalist march intent on proceeding into a Catholic area in early 1970; BELOW Marines of 45 Commando hold back a stone-throwing Catholic mob attempting to break up an Orange March along a Protestant-Catholic interface in Belfast, 26 June 1970.

ABOVE LEFT The face of the terrorist: An IRA gunman armed with a Thompson sub-machine gun in 'Free Derry' in the Bogside, Londonderry, April 1972; ABOVE RIGHT The face of the military: The commanding officer of a Royal Green Jacket battalion, West Belfast, 1972. BELOW After the battle: Belfast, autumn 1971. The company commander (right) of 'R' Company, 3rd Battalion, the Royal Green Jackets, listens to a local viewpoint with his sergeant-major and a section commander (left) in attendance. The experiences of the company and section commanders are chronicled in Chapter Fourteen

Two Greenfinch casualties: ABOVE LEFT Private Eva Martin, aged twenty-eight, was the first soldier to be killed in Northern Ireland, being hit by gunfire when her company base was attacked on the night of 2 May 1975. She was a schoolteacher as well as an UDR part-timer. ABOVE RIGHT Private Margaret Hearst, aged twenty-four, was sleeping with her daughter in a caravan at her home in South Amagh close to the border when she was murdered by IRA gunmen on the night of 8 October 1977. BELOW Armed propaganda: A paratrooper comforts a civilian casualty at the start of the Provisional IRA's bombing campaign in Belfast, on 20 March 1972.

Dealing with bombs: ABOVE A 'Felix Team' Ammunition Technical Officer makes safe a proxy car-bomb intercepted by the RUC outside Belfast, 1975; BELOW Royal Engineer Sappers clear sandbags from the Europa Hotel, Belfast, after the defusing of a bomb placed in the foyer, early 1970s. The hotel was repeatedly targeted by the IRA.

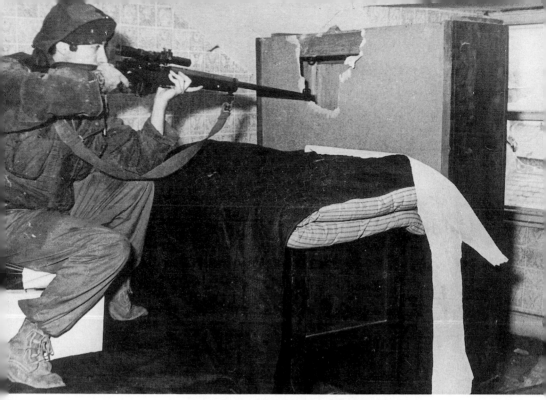

e intelligence war: obser-
ion posts, both known
l covert, were an impor-
t means of information-
hering, as were the foot
rols, with every soldier
ng as an intelligence-
herer. ABOVE A covert OP
nned by 42 Commando
Andersonstown; BELOW A
Commando foot patrol in
st Belfast, 1977, when the
st of the Troubles was
:.

Operating in bandit country: ABOVE A reconnaissance troop of 41 Commando after covert observation operations in the border area; BELOW A patrol of the 4th Battalion Ulster Defence Regiment being picked up by a Lynx helicopter in South Fermanagh. Both photographs were taken in the 1980s.

Police primacy: Since 1976 the Royal Ulster Constabulary has resumed its policing role with the Army acting in support. ABOVE Soldiers of 'C' Company 1st Green Howards pose with a member of the RUC after a week spent in trenches near Londonderry during joint RUC and Gardai border searches in 1988; BELOW An Army section provides an escort for the RUC in a Republican area of Londonderry, 1988.

The return to normality does not extend to certain areas of Londonderry and Wes Belfast, where foot patrols still have to face the threat of PIRA bombs and snipers. Th Bogside, 1988.

fact of Northern Ireland,' a Green Jackets officer recalls of his first tour in Belfast during this period, 'which is the nationhood of the Protestant people of Northern Ireland.' Every act of violence aimed at making the Province ungovernable hardened the attitudes of even moderate Protestants. The result was that 1971 witnessed the coming together of a number of banned paramilitary organisations such as the Ulster Freedom Fighters, the Ulster Volunteer Force, the Protestant Action Force and the Red Hand Commandos under the banner of the Ulster Defence Association, as well as the formation of breakaway Loyalist parties that regarded even the slightest concessions by the Unionist Government as a betrayal of the Union. The largest of these was the Democratic Unionist Party led by Mr Ian Paisley, a 'fanatic' as much loathed by the majority of British troops as any figure on the Republican side of the ever-widening divide. In these circumstances the removal of British troops was unthinkable. 'I always knew we were keeping two factions apart,' declares an officer who was an RSM on his first Northern Ireland tour. 'I think of all the good Irish people whom I've met and I dread to think of what would happen if the troops ever pulled out.'

It was now clear that there were going to be no quick solutions in Ulster and that until the political map altered the Army was there to stay. A new GOC, General Harry Tuzo, took over and announced that the days of 'pussy-footing' were over. Riots were no longer simply contained. Tough reserve battalions like 1 Para were sent in to break them up and to pull out the ring-leaders. 'I would be standing by with a lead company,' recalls their commander. 'If the thing got out of hand the brigadier would tell me to go in and sort it out. A very straightforward, uncomplicated order. I used to go in and do just that. I could put four hundred men into a company area and saturate it, and when you do that in a riot situation you can stop it immediately.' The attitude of the men themselves was equally forthright. 'I've always likened a soldier to a mailed fist,' declares a brother officer who was a senior NCO in the early 1970s, 'and you don't commit the mailed fist to a situation that could be politically sorted out and not sorted out by gunfire.' However, the soldiers were now committed and it was no surprise to them to find that those who had greeted them a year earlier as their saviours now regarded them as their oppressors:

> The feeling of hatred was intense among those people. They'd spit at you, they'd call you every name and shout, 'You are the Gestapo of the British. We do not want you here!' It wasn't just in the Catholic community. It could happen in both communities and, of

course, as this went on this great feeling of warmth in community relations which we had built up soon disappeared. And we began to feel it, too, and it was having an effect upon the soldiers. They had hardened themselves to it but they were living in a community which our soldiers came from, the same sort of backstreets. It was like their home town and then to find they were not welcome there was a harsh shock for these young eighteen-year-old lads, even though they were well trained. Particularly in some of the operations in the Falls Road when, for example, a body had to be buried and we knew they were going to make a ceremony of it. You were required by the rules of the game to have that body buried without a tricolour, without people firing over the coffin, and you were required to stand there and take the brickbats and I must admit that, on occasion, I felt very much like a Gestapo agent when we had to do this because you could sense the feeling on the street, the fear and the hatred, very deep. But the regimental system exerted itself. There was a pride in standing steady – steady the Buffs, you know. They didn't like it but they took it in their stride.

The year 1971 also saw the employment by the Provisional IRA of what was undoubtedly a very effective psychological weapon on the streets. 'We could handle the youths and the men, that's easy, but we were totally unprepared for the women,' recalls a Royal Marine officer who was then a lieutenant in 40 Commando based in Armagh:

I don't think anybody on their first tour in Northern Ireland will ever be prepared properly for that. Eyeball to eyeball confrontations with men are easy but it's very different when a woman who only comes up to your chest starts belting you with an umbrella, which seemed to be the favourite weapon, although I had a man on the 1972 tour in Belfast who was stabbed by a knitting needle in the groin. No matter how well you prepare people in training, it's very difficult to live with what the women say and do – for instance, being confronted by a woman who spits in your face. It's very difficult to be non-violent when violence is being perpetrated against you but that was exactly what we had to be and, frankly, I think the Marines' reaction was brilliant because they tended to laugh it off, which infuriated the women even more. But we found that the women were always the ones sent in to get close to us, to distract us so that the snipers could get set-up or the bombers.

What was just as demoralising at this period was that the foot patrols which went out into the Republican areas of Belfast and

Londonderry were in daily contact with men whom they now regarded as their enemies. 'One of the most frustrating parts of serving in Northern Ireland was the fact that you usually knew the enemy,' explains a section commander:

> You knew the villains within your patch and you passed them every day on patrol and they would actually speak to you. But having to work within the rule of law you couldn't turn round and say, 'Yes, we know you are up to something, yes, we have so many reports that you are responsible for that particular atrocity.' You had to actually catch them red-handed and nine times out of ten you could be almost there, you'd almost got your hand on his shoulder, but without the evidence you knew there was not a great deal you could do. Then you'd just got to put up with things like them quite happily walking past you and saying, 'How's your wife going to feel when you've got a small, round hole in the centre of your head tomorrow?' There's nothing illegal about that and you'd got to just grin and bear it, bite your tongue and give them the time of day. That was one of the hardest parts, knowing your enemy, knowing, but not being able to prove anything.

What the soldiers did not find so easy to take in their stride was that they had taken on the role of policemen in maintaining law and order in an emergency situation without any emergency powers:

> Constitutionally, the soldier is in Northern Ireland as an ordinary citizen, not with the powers of the police. There is no exceptional right for the soldier to use force against somebody except in the processes of arrest and that sort of thing, and in these he has less power than a policeman. And that individual soldier will stand trial for breaching those rules in a serious case exactly as somebody would if he was walking down Piccadilly and fired a shot there.

It was to let the soldier know exactly where he stood when it came to opening fire that the Yellow Card was introduced in 1971. It was to be carried on his person at all times and set out the exact circumstances in which he might open fire – and it was seen by some as seriously undermining their ability to fight back: 'You are constrained by the Yellow Card, so that you don't instinctively fire when somebody fires at you. You hold back, you think about the problem and think of the consequences if you get it wrong. That is not what you want to happen in war where a soldier has got to react immediately to a given situation, and so you have that difficulty.'

From a section commander's point of view, however, the Yellow Card was a restriction, but one that helped to maintain fire discipline:

> Unless you've identified a target there's no excuse or reason for returning fire. It's no good belting a few rounds in the general direction of where you think the shot may have come from. The sniper has got the advantage, because he knows you and you don't know where he is. But you cannot start putting any sort of covering fire in built-up and populated areas. Because you carry a weapon in the streets of Northern Ireland that isn't a licence, just because you've heard a shot, to open fire. So you've really got to be very, very careful, and you've got to identify the target as a gunman who is putting your life or members of your section's lives at risk before you can return any form of fire.

The law also limited a soldier's effectiveness in ways that he sometimes found hard to understand. 'We made an arrest one night after a shot had been fired,' remembers a senior NCO in the Royal Anglians. 'We stopped him and arrested him. He was lying on a black balaclava, which he claimed he'd tripped over. He was "only running away because he'd heard a shot". Very close by the weapon that had been discharged was found but that wasn't sufficient proof to tie to this guy. You needed to go to court with the right evidence and there wasn't an eye-witness to him squeezing the trigger. It couldn't be proved and he was free to roam the streets.' Many other soldiers experienced similar frustrations with a law that seemed insufficient to deal with an emergency situation that no British Government seemed willing to declare an official emergency. 'In those days the legal situation was such that it was made almost impossible for the security forces to be effective,' declares one Green Jackets officer:

> There was a well-known IRA activist, a woman whom we had arrested a number of times but had been unable to produce any sort of conviction. There was a hill with one of our posts at the bottom of it with two of our soldiers in it. She appeared at the top from what was obviously an artificially generated crowd with a pram full of explosives and set it off to run down the hill, obviously to hit the post and blow up the soldiers. She was well-known to the soldiers, they had binoculars and they could see her perfectly clearly. Fortunately, the pram hit a stone and tipped over and the detonators fell out and so the thing didn't go off. Now the soldiers were reporting this so it was heard over the radio and by absolute chance there was a Saracen [Armoured Troop Carrier] coming

round the back and the corporal in charge of it heard all this. With great courage he stopped, ploughed into this lethal crowd of about two hundred, grabbed this woman and dragged her fighting back into the Saracen. She appeared in court next day and there was an immediate dismissal of the case on the grounds that the corporal in the middle of this crowd had not specified to her the exact nature of her offence and the section of the act under which he was arresting her. In fact, what he had said was, 'You're for it this time.'

As far as this same officer was concerned, 'the single biggest problem I felt in Northern Ireland was the incomprehension by the senior ranks of the legal and constitutional position of military forces used within the boundaries of the United Kingdom.' Generals who had won their spurs in counter-insurgency wars fought under very different constitutional rules did not always appreciate that the situation was different in Northern Ireland:

> Some didn't seem to be able to grasp that the obstacle was our lack of police training. They'd been in places like Kenya and Malaya where there had been free-fire zones and so on. I remember going to an appalling conference with hundreds of people there when it was stated from on high that the main thing to improve our position in Northern Ireland was better shooting. What did we shoot at that time? About twenty-five terrorists a year, so if you'd increased your shooting ability by an amazing twenty-five per cent, what would you have shot – thirty-two people, perhaps. Did they actually think that a nation as courageous as the Irish would have been put off by those sorts of casualties? Until the generation who had been on the streets in Northern Ireland became senior officers themselves it was never grasped that, firstly, our lack of expertise in police matters to get convictions and, secondly, the lack of legal means to do so, were the main obstacles to effectiveness against terrorism.

In this officer's opinion it was not until 1973, when the Emergency Provisions Act and the Diplock Courts came into force, that the soldier in the street and in the court found himself supported by the law – 'and from that moment the Army became effective again'.

The security forces had begun their counter-insurgency campaign in Northern Ireland with the more familiar disadvantage of lack of intelligence, partly because the traditional intelligence-gathering apparatus had been virtually dismantled in early 1970 after the disarming of the RUC and the disbanding of the 'B' Specials. Many of these part-time policemen transferred directly into the newly-formed Ulster Defence Regiment as part-time soldiers but the direct link with the police was lost and with it a very significant tier of local community knowledge that took several years to rebuild. Another disadvantage was the initial reluctance of the RUC Special Branch to share information with the military. This was particularly frustrating for those now more senior officers who had served in colonial armed insurgencies and had seen at first hand the value of co-ordinating activities through such bodies as local Executive Committees. But Ulster was not a colonial situation and its problems had to be solved by means other than the application of drastic and draconian Emergency powers. So it took time for the civil and military authorities – to say nothing of the often extremely recalcitrant local political authorities – to learn to work as a team.

All these improvements came too late to stop what many in the British Army came to regard as the most serious political error made during the two decades of the Troubles. This was the decision – taken reluctantly by the British Government under pressure from Stormont – to order the Internment of some five hundred and twenty suspects whose names were on lists drawn up by the Special Branch. The operation was carried out by the Army and the police during the night of 9–10 August. Intended to 'smash the IRA', it had the opposite effect. Of the three hundred and forty-six men arrested virtually all were Catholics and only a minority turned out to have connections with PIRA or the Official IRA. The great majority of activists escaped the net and were able to orchestrate Republican elements in the community into an orgy of violence that resulted in thirty-four deaths.

For a unit like the Ulster Defence Regiment, which had begun to gain considerable popular recognition as a genuinely non-sectarian local force, Internment came as a major setback. 'In my company there were about twenty-two to twenty-five Roman Catholics,' remembers a UDR private soldier from Omagh. 'They made up about a quarter of the company for about the first year or so. In fact, we went on the first camp together and we had a joint service in camp which the local regular Padre took. That's something I look back on with good memories because it never happened again afterwards as Internment came on and the Roman Catholic element disappeared. It was not so much that they left voluntarily but they were really pressured out because they were living in communities and you can't live in a community and be at opposite ends of the local thinking, that's why.' Of the original number in the company about six or seven Catholics stayed on for another couple of years, 'but eventually they were pressurised to leave. There was an organised resistance against them. They were harassed, their families and their

children especially, by stone-throwers when they were ot
and so it was agreed that it made more sense for them to leave
stay. We go back to the age-old story that it's not popular ᵢ
Nationalist community to be a member of the government force
know a lot of people who would like to be members but it is nᴄ
realistic for a Roman Catholic to live in Northern Ireland and be a
member of the Ulster Defence Regiment. It's common sense, really,
and you cannot go against common sense.'

For the mostly part-time militiamen of the UDR everything
changed with Internment. 'On 9 August 1971 we were on a static
VCP [vehicle check point] when it was shot up,' remembers a
longstanding part-timer from Fermanagh:

> There was a ring of static VCPs round a border village and a car
> turned short of the VCP and drove back into the village. Then
> another car appeared and stopped short and the soldier who went
> out to intercept this car was cut down by a sub-machine gun. He
> was the first member of the UDR to be killed on active service and
> this changed the whole pattern of deployment of the UDR
> thereafter. Up to Internment Day no operational casualties at all
> for sixteen months and in the next sixteen months there was in
> excess of thirty UDR members killed, of whom eight were Roman
> Catholics. From that date till now I can say I was a friend of
> twenty-nine in this battalion who've been killed.

This was a pattern that was soon familiar to all those who served in
the Ulster Defence Regiment. 'My first platoon was drawn largely
from a Nationalist area and at least thirty per cent of my soldiers
were Catholics,' recalls a former officer in the UDR, now retired.
'For those living in Nationalist housing estates we would go and
collect them in civilian cars but the threat increased and increased.'
Some were simply told to get out, others received death threats in the
form of letters cut from newspapers. By the end of 1972 very few
Catholics remained in the UDR:

> One of the last to resign in my platoon used to walk from his house
> and be picked up at different spots but the threat became too great
> for him. He and his wife were very good Catholics and it was a
> tremendous strain on him to go to his place of worship and sit
> perhaps in the same church pew as someone intent on his
> destruction. Eventually, this guy came to me and said, 'Look, I
> cannot really do any more.' It would have been unfair to him and
> to his family to say, 'Stay on because we need people like you,' so
> we had to let him go. The very last Catholic was intimidated out

round about 1973. His son was shot by the Provisional IRA. I
remember it vividly because I was the one who brought him into my
office and told him – and then he resigned. I still see him, and we
talk and remember the old times when there wasn't the polarisation
that one tends to see now.

The autumn of 1971 following Internment became a new low for
the security forces. Catholics who had witnessed the Army acting as
the 'instrument of Internment' could more readily accept IRA claims
that it was an occupying Army and an instrument of oppression as
reinforcements brought the numbers up to 13,500 troops in the
Province. The British Army's authority was further undermined by
allegations of torture during interrogation that began to be reported
as men were released from Internment. Enquiries substantiated at
least some of these allegations and the Army lost more of the moral
high ground that it was never afterwards quite able to regain among
the Nationalist community, as one officer admits: 'There's no doubt
that starting with interrogation in depth – that disgraceful affair –
there was in certain units a good deal of petty bullying and roughing
up and that sort of thing. All this was a release of one's emotions and
did no good towards helping the outcome of the campaign. It gained
no worth-while intelligence and it produced a load of disgruntled and
disaffected local people.'

While most commanders exercised tight control over their men in
a way that still allowed them a necessary degree of aggression, a few
did not. 'It's very easy to misunderstand what toughness and strength
means in this context,' explains the same officer, who commanded a
battalion of the Royal Green Jackets in Belfast in the early 1970s. 'It
does not mean going out and releasing your emotions by breaking
windows, knocking people about and shooting indiscriminately.
That is always and inevitably counter-productive. What it does mean
is being tough and strong in terms of the extraction of intelligence
and getting subsequent convictions within the restraints of the law.'

But in this respect, as in many others, Internment had set the
forces of law and order almost back to square one. 'What you have to
remember is that Internment on 9 August 1971 had changed things
dramatically,' declares another Green Jackets officer, whose company was rushed over to Belfast in that same month as part of the
troops' build-up. 'Prior to Internment our predecessors could meet
known terrorists in the streets and talk to them daily without any
powers of arrest, detention or anything else. But the moment that
Internment was introduced all the known terrorists who had not
been arrested disappeared from the scene. The pattern of life

therefore was for them to be living under cover, mounting operations as and when they planned them, probably coming into the area to conduct them and then leaving the area and moving somewhere else. The police at this time were not active and so information was pretty sparse.' Indeed, a further direct consequence of Internment was the marked drop in intelligence as hitherto friendly informants ceased to co-operate with the security forces: 'We used to get names of known terrorists from brigade and sometimes the photographs of the people we were looking for, but we seldom got hard intelligence as to where they might be. It was a case of working out your own intelligence jigsaw for yourself and trying to piece the bits together to make a coherent pattern.'

Each battalion and company commander now had to set to in order to build up his own intelligence network within areas that were in many respects enemy-held territory: 'For nearly a year, between August 1971 and July 1972, the Army did not enforce the law in certain areas. They were called "no-go" areas, and it was astonishing that certain parts of the United Kingdom were put outside the writ of Parliament, outside the writ of court, outside the rule of law.'

Chapter Fourteen

NORTHERN IRELAND:
No-go

Someone's fired at you and you start dashing, crawling and rolling away, and you're asking if people have seen him. 'Where's the shot come from?' The heart's pumping and everything else, and you're looking round: Has anyone been shot in the section? No. Then you start trying to find where's it come from; do we move away, can we move away, all those sort of things. And it's just complete quietness. There's probably just one shot been fired at you, but in that split second you react as your training's taught you. You get down, you sort yourself out, you're all hot and you become part of a big rolling ball. That's when we earned our shillings, earned our pay, did what we was paid for.

One sunny Monday afternoon in August 1971 the hundred and twenty men of 'R' Company the 3rd Battalion the Royal Green Jackets were relaxing on an old airfield camp at Netheravon – 'we was actually playing cricket, an inter-platoon match with the ball being knocked around the place' – when they were summoned to a meeting by the Company Sergeant-Major: 'So we had guys in cricket gear, other guys who'd been out swimming, all in sporting kit, and the Company Commander duly told us to forget about our nice tour out in the Caribbean, because as of next Wednesday we were all going to Northern Ireland.'

'R' Company – a Representative company hand-picked from the remnants of the disbanded 3rd RGJ – was under-equipped and untrained for the job: 'We only had about fifty or sixty steel helmets and we were well down on rifles, radios, vehicles etc. In fact, we got our rifles on Tuesday morning and spent a hectic afternoon getting everybody down on to the range, and that, frankly, was the only training we carried out in the techniques and tactics of Northern Ireland. As it turned out, that was probably quite a good thing.' Arriving at Brize Norton Air Field on Wednesday the Company Commander learned for the first time that they were going to Belfast 'to be blistered on to another battalion'. This turned out to be the 1st RGJ, already deployed in the Lower Falls, Divis and Markets areas of West Belfast.

Late that same night the company arrived at what was to be its home for the next four months, Albert Street Mill, a disused Victorian warehouse in a back street off the Falls Road close to the Divis Flats complex that had been taken over for use as an emergency base at the start of the Troubles three years earlier. Here they took over the 'Penthouse Suite' on the top floor – 'up some eighty-eight steps' – where conditions were 'a bit cramped, about forty to a room' and the room that served as a joint Company HQ, Ops Room and Officers' and Sergeants' Sleeping Quarters flooded every time it rained.

On that same night some of 'R' Company's officers and senior NCOs went out with 1 RGJ to learn what 'clearing the Lower Falls' meant before settling down to a month's apprenticeship, during which they 'did the chores for the battalion, all the menial tasks like guarding bases, routine patrols and even some search operations in the relatively quiet city centre'. Then 1 RGJ pulled out, its tour completed, and much to its collective delight 'R' Company was ordered to stay on in Albert Street Mill and take over 'as our own parish' the Lower Falls and Divis areas of West Belfast. 'I was thrilled,' declares its Company Commander. 'The whole company went on a complete high,' reports a corporal who was one of its section commanders:

> Now we hadn't got our overlords, which was 1st RGJ, with us any more. Here we could now get our teeth into the job which they'd been doing and we could show our true colours. It was a damn good battalion area, the Lower Falls, without a doubt, the most exciting piece of Belfast. In the early 1970s anything that was going to happen from the IRA happened in the Lower Falls. It either started or it finished or it came from the Lower Falls. So here was a golden opportunity to go out there and do our soldiering and see if we could do a job as good as what 1 RGJ had done. That was the ambition, basically, of everyone and I think everybody from the company commander down to the youngest Rifleman all thought, 'Now's the chance to go out there and thoroughly enjoy ourselves.'

The area for which 'R' Company assumed responsibility was a small triangle of land just west of the city centre made up of two districts very different in character but both Republican strongholds:

There were the notorious Divis Flats – in fact, high-rise maisonettes in that there were two floors to each flat – with an outer corridor which ran round what was almost a spider's web of buildings. If you were fired upon from one spine of the cobweb as you were moving along the open corridor on another one it made it extremely difficult to get to the scene of the shooting. A very unfriendly area. Soldiers in there had to be prepared for constant and perpetual 'chi-iking' and indeed the rudest possible comments and, of course, you could only be at very close proximity to the locals. And then there was the Lower Falls, or the Reservation, as we called it, bounded in the north by the Falls Road and in the south by the Grosvenor Road – and through that ran the notorious Leeson Street. This was a totally different area of run-down terraced houses with small back-gardens behind them, each back-garden either butting on to the back-garden of the house in the next street or, alternatively, on to one of these dreadful little alleys, very narrow and very dangerous, where if you were caught you had no way of getting out. Again, an area of great hatred.

There was 'no police presence in that area at all'. The Lower Falls was 'predominantly the home of the Official IRA which reputedly had a battalion and three companies in the area and then another company operating in Divis. The Provisional IRA had one company in the Lower Falls and, it was thought, another company in Divis – although it's rather dangerous to try to equate these military terms to groups of terrorists.' Whatever their exact numbers, the two extremist organisations were now more than strong enough in men, arms and supporters to demand and command absolute obedience within their area. As in much of West Belfast, the Catholic population of the Lower Falls and Divis, was now living in a Republican ghetto, fast developing its own siege paranoia and turning inwards upon itself to offer total allegiance to the gunmen within that area. As well as punishing those who stepped out of line the extremists also took it upon themselves to deliver their own forms of justice upon those who transgressed the local codes. After the beatings and the tarring-and-featherings came the knee-cappings. It is reported that between 1970 and 1988 the Royal Victoria Hospital, just off the Falls Road, has dealt with fifteen hundred cases of knee-capping.

The Commander of 39 Infantry Brigade, responsible for operations in the Belfast area, was not one of those who advocated a softly-softly approach in dealing with the 'no-go' areas. 'Our Brigade Commander's policy was quite clear,' states the Commander of 'R' Company. 'There were to be no "no-go" areas in Belfast and there was to be a free flow of traffic throughout.' In three successive night operations 1 RGJ had cleared all the barricades that had sprung up with the introduction of Internment. 'R' Company intended to take the same hard line. In preparation, its officers, NCOs and Riflemen spent an intensive period debriefing 1 RGJ's outgoing company before they took over. 'The Company Commander saw to it that we made the most of these briefings,' remembers the Corporal Section Commander:

> We drank coffee, we had briefings, and we broke down what areas of responsibility were going to which platoon. And generally the next forty-eight hours was a lot of writing, filling out notebooks on various streets, looking at maps from the council, working out how many houses were in one street and generally what information was available, information left over from 1 RGJ, with each section commander breaking down the jobs to give each man a job. Eventually we finished up that every guy from the lowest Rifleman had got a job to do, and the way to do this was to say to people, 'Right, Johnson, your job is Macdonald Street. From now on I want to know who lives at every house, what colour curtains they've got, have they got a dug garden at the back, do they own a car, what colour, registration number, how many people live in the house – everything.' So everybody had a job to do all the time, updating his own information book, because later it became very apparent that you needed to know this information. If someone said to you, 'I live at 127 Macdonald Street,' then you called Johnson up, 'Right, who lives at 127?' 'Smith lives at 127.' So it was things like that, and that was the way you involved all the guys. It kept them switched on and they were always alert, looking for something new. Then on the Monday morning at about six o'clock Albert Street Mill doors opened and the first patrols went out.

After a couple of quiet days of small incidents – 'stone-throwing, petrol-bombing, blast-bombing and the like' – the tension began to build up as 'it became clear that there was going to be a battle of wills between the terrorists who wished to re-establish themselves in the company area and ourselves'. Then a Tarmac layer was stolen and used to create a barricade across the Falls Road, which became the starting point for 'R' Company's first serious test: 'This was their "Hullo to the Lower Falls", to find out how good the unit that's come in is, to let you know that this is where they live, this is their ground and they're top dogs. This is the time when you've got to go out there and say, "No. I'm afraid you're not. We're here for four months and this is how we're going to deal with it." '

'R' Company was duly deployed to clear the barricade and, according to its Commander, 'returned somewhat battered. The young Belfast teenager would make a very good cover point. He has a strong right arm and throws extremely well. I had a number of guys who'd been hit by stones, bricks, slates and who'd had to be stitched up and I was very conscious that there had been a major fault in my tactical handling of the situation. I sat down that night with a cold wet towel and started to analyse what I'd done wrong and it became quite clear to me that I had been far too defensive in my techniques.' The Company Commander decided it was time to go on to the offensive:

> I got the entire company together and I explained to them in detail where I'd gone wrong and I told them that they were now going to have to pay the bill for my mistakes. It was quite clear that there was now a major crisis as to who was going to control that area and that we had now to go out and face the music and assert our grip on the area. On 13 September in the evening therefore we deployed, initially as 2 Platoon and Company Headquarters. We dismounted in the Falls Road at the top of Leeson Street and we started to patrol down Leeson Street and the parallel streets. And very early on a not very brave gunman stuck his nose round one of the street corners and loosed a burst of fire at us at about fifteen to twenty yards' range. He didn't take careful aim and it just hammered into some of the buildings round about. This really was the sign I was waiting for and at that I brought the rest of the company out, two more platoons, one of which was mobile in armoured cars. We then started to patrol throughout the area with two platoons on the ground and the rest making sweeps round the back of the crowds to try and threaten any terrorists who wished to engage us with rifle fire.

The Section Commander was with his section in an alleyway when he heard the firing begin:

> Different gunmen were firing from different positions – I don't know how many – but barricades were quickly set up, cars were set on fire, people started arriving, young yobs with crates of Molotov cocktails started petrol bombing. I was looking straight up Cairns Street on to Leeson Street itself and there, at the junction, a barricade was being put up with these young yobs with petrol bombs and, as these Army vehicles were coming down, they were throwing them and setting them on fire – and to see a vehicle that's engulfed in petrol on fire, it looks pretty nasty. Now I should think these guys were about a hundred and fifty yards from me –

young guys coming up with a Guinness crate with milk bottles full of petrol with wads of rag hanging out the top, taking them and handing them to somebody else. One guy was standing there with a piece of wood that was lit or a cigarette lighter and they were actually forming a queue to light their petrol bombs and throw. And there I was laid down with seven guys all looking down over the sights of their rifles, looking at these chaps doing it, endangering people's lives, and not being allowed to fire. I came on the radio and asked for permission to fire and this was denied – and one looks back and thinks to oneself, why were we not allowed to open fire?

As the first platoon advanced down Leeson Street and came level with Cairns, it was joined by the Section Commander's platoon:

My platoon commander said, 'Right, I want you to take up the point section,' so we was now the front people and we'd gone about another thirty yards when we were opened fire on from down at the bottom of Macdonald Street. I think the first thing I did was to tell somebody that we'd been shot at. Then somebody said to me 'Bloody well shoot back then! Can you see him?' I said, 'Yes.' He said, 'Well, shoot back.' And that was it. I fired two rounds back at a guy behind a car who was about a hundred and seventy-five yards away. What happened then very quickly was a mob of people came into the road, so now the guy who did the shooting was masked by the crowd. They were actually giving him cover while he made his escape, knowing full well that the Army wasn't going to fire indiscriminately in front of a crowd. There was a pub nearby called the Bush Bar and when we arrived at the Bush Bar all the people came out – I mean, what's a bullet or two when you've still got a Guinness in your glass. This was their chance then to try and wrestle rifles off us and that sort of thing and throw their abuse and beer glasses. So they had their little nibble at us and then we'd gone the full length of Leeson Street and stood at the other end of the Falls fairly unscathed. We'd gone through it and every guy in that company had been under fire and it was finished.

After about three and a half hours the company returned to its base. 'Frankly, we were elated,' declares its Commander. 'During the course of those three hours we had been engaged by seven separate gunmen and we hadn't any casualties. There were two members of the opposition who were being patched up in the Royal Victoria Hospital – and I think we'd come of age. Certainly, I remember one of my platoon commanders who came into the little office that I used as my Intelligence Room shortly after we got back and threw himself down into a chair and said, "I've just grown up tonight." '

From then on 'R' Company kept up the pressure, with constant activity in the form of foot and mobile patrols: 'I like to think that we asserted a grip on the area which we were never to relax in the remaining three and a half months of the tour.' As part of maintaining its grip the company set out to make it quite plain to the gunmen in the area what their response to being fired upon would be. 'I laid down that never more than two rounds were to be fired at an aimed target by an individual,' explains the Company Commander:

> There were a great number of occasions during the following months in which we were shot at. There's a loud crack over your head and the echo in those streets makes it extraordinarily difficult to pick out where the shot's coming from. I was notoriously bad at it but quite a lot of the Riflemen, I'm glad to say, were a great deal better so that on almost every occasion on which we were engaged we 'returned fire'. When I say 'returned fire' I didn't mean a hail of automatic fire. I didn't want a mass of bullets screaming round the area with the risk of killing or injuring innocent people. But I did say to people that when they could identify the direction of the fire I wished one Rifleman to fire two aimed rounds. My reasons for applying this rule were really two. Very often on the streets there are masses of children and people moving around. If you get a reputation for being the sort of force which is going to return fire then when the gunman is out the children are taken off the streets. You could sense very often that there was about to be a shooting incident when suddenly the streets became deserted, so we were buying ourselves perhaps three or four seconds of warning that a shooting incident might be about to take place. Secondly, I wanted people in the area to know that we were tough and professional and were going to return fire, because I felt that might have an effect upon the terrorist. Perhaps one or two of the less experienced terrorists might be a little jittery on the trigger and perhaps not so accurate.

This policy certainly seemed to work. During its entire four month tour 'R' Company only sustained three injuries from gunfire: two Riflemen who were grazed by snipers' bullets and a third who suffered a shattered thigh bone. Another feature of 'R' Company's procedure that was quickly established was its patrolling routine:

> One platoon was responsible for guards and fatigues and for the general running of the base for twenty-four hours. On the second day they would be the mobile patrol platoon responsible for vehicle

patrols throughout the area and in support of the third platoon on foot patrol. On the third day of their cycle therefore they would be the foot patrol platoon. In addition to that routine there was also the business of what we used to call the 'five o'clock knocks'. We used to get lists of suspects whom Special Branch were keen to see and we would therefore have to go looking for them. We would sit down and work out all the various connections between the various families and we would then go visiting those houses, usually sometime between midnight and six o'clock in the morning in the hope that the target concerned might be there and in bed.

Backing up the three platoons was a small group known as the 'Burglary Squad', made up of clerks, signallers, storemen and others from Company Headquarters whose duties kept them confined to base during the daytime but who did not want to miss out on the company's outside activities. Unlike the other night search and arrest teams who worked on information, the 'Burglary Squad' went out on random searches, working its way quietly through 'the many yards with which the Lower Falls abounds' in its quest for hidden arms and weapons, with considerable success.

However, of all the Riflemen's duties none was more physically and mentally demanding than the foot-patrols, when section strength patrols of eight Riflemen went out in small groups of four or five into the local area, usually staying out for not more than two hours at a time. Here a great deal of responsibility rested on the shoulders of the platoon and section commanders:

The moment that you go out there and you actually set foot into a place like the Lower Falls, everyone knows it within seconds. In those days when you come out it was dustbin lids clattering on the floor. Once one woman did it, another woman did it, then another, then a group of women, until the whole of the Lower Falls is covered with a crescendo of crashing dustbin lids, and that goes on all the time. And you have to remember that if you're out on patrol for two hours in that area – you might be going out to check something out, a car, perhaps – when you go out there there isn't one soul in that area who speaks to you. Everyone you pass basically thinks bad of you. They lean on the doorways, they throw water on you, they call you names, and that's from the moment you set foot in there till the moment you leave. When you leave the dustbin lids stop.

And that's what you have to work in all the way through. You couldn't say to anyone, 'Excuse me.' If you said anything to them they just ignored you. And you'd be there leaning on the gatepost

244 WAR AT HOME

in the alert position, observing, trying to cover someone else going across and people would come and stand deliberately in front of your weapon to stop you covering a comrade. So for four months you were basically switched on from the word go. At no time could you ever switch off, because you weren't out there looking after yourself, you were looking after someone else. If someone else was moving you was covering him. You had to make sure that he got to the other side of the road and then when he got there it was your turn to move and someone would cover you across.

Everywhere you went was basically near enough at the double. It was up, down, into the fire positions – and you soon realised the fire positions to take. It was not advisable, for instance, to lie behind a breeze block, because bullets pass straight through them. Tuck yourself right round the corner of a wall, get yourself as low as possible, don't stay in the same place for very long, move your fire position, get somewhere else, make sure the guys in your section are moving. Every day we would find something new. Guys would say, 'There's a different way of doing this' and it was passed on very quickly. It's very easy to set a pattern, so your mind has to work all the time, 'Right, we will drive in this time and get dropped off in the middle of Leeson Street, we will walk in from the north of Leeson Street, let's start down another street and walk into Leeson Street.' Trying to break the pattern up all the time, trying to be on top of the job. There is no chance out there for individuals, you have to work as a complete section in everything that you do. The man who's at the front knows that he's the scout, he covers forward. The man at the back knows he covers the rear. The radio operator knows that he is never more than an arm's length away from his commander because we might need some assistance, we might need that radio very quickly. Everyone covers one another, it just becomes second nature and after a while you get to a stage where you don't even know you're doing it. You just do it, because, don't forget, we had to patrol Leeson Street or wherever maybe five hundred times in four months.

Attempts by the Company Commander to build bridges with the local community, as his predecessors had done only two years earlier, proved hopeless:

I cannot pretend that the atmosphere was one of anything other than total hostility – except on one occasion when a rumour spread around that the Protestants were going to come into the area and take out the Roman Catholic population. Quite suddenly for a period of about twenty-four to forty-eight hours we really became quite popular, people spoke to us and almost accepted we were there to protect them. I did form a considerable rapport, I like to think, with the local priest. He was a very nice man and a sensible one but, as he made clear to me, he had his community and if he was to hold their respect he could not under any circumstances be seen to favour us in any way, and I entirely understood that. However, there were other priests in the area with whom I had dealings and, well, to say they were less than friendly would be being unreasonably kind.

In an effort to encourage contact I opened up one of our garages as a youth boxing and football club. I thought that perhaps if some of the locals would like to come and use up some of their energy hitting one another and kicking a football around, they might well have less energy for throwing things at us. And this lasted very well for several weeks but then the IRA said this was quite unacceptable and the young boys were refused permission to come and it simply dried up.

The active involvement of the women of the Lower Falls both in protecting the IRA as vigilantes and as trouble-makers in their own right – 'shouting, screaming, throwing things, doing everything they could to frustrate our operations' – was something that every Rifleman in the company had to come to terms with. Only very rarely were the soldiers able to score a point off these formidable women:

One of their more amusing techniques was that they tried to frustrate our night time operations by calling all the women out on the street. On every corner there was a sentry-party consisting of two women with a whistle and a dustbin lid, and our arrival in the area would be greeted by the blowing of whistles and the banging of dustbin lids, so that in a very short space of time hundreds of women were out on the streets shouting and screaming at us. We learned very quickly that although they had this excellent stand-to procedure they didn't have a stand-down procedure and the area used to bubble for at least three-quarters of an hour after we'd gone. So we decided that we would teach them a lesson.

On one particular night I sent out five patrols in vehicles to five different parts of the area and immediately the dustbins went and the whistles blew and the women started shouting and there were crowds of them running from corner to corner round the area. No sooner had we seen that they'd deployed than the Riflemen jumped back into their vehicles and came straight back to base. An hour later they went out again, just after all the women had gone back to bed. So we had them out again and we kept that going for three nights until nobody in the area was getting any sleep at all. In fact, we got to the stage when some of the women sentries were so fast asleep on their street corners that the Riflemen could go up to them and tap them on the shoulder and say, 'Hey, shouldn't you be banging your dustbin and blowing your whistle?'

This situation was finally put to an end by the Company Commander going to the local priest and asking him to point out in his Sunday sermon that if anybody wanted any peace and quiet they should 'stop this stupid business and leave us in peace – and indeed that came about'. The Riflemen also demonstrated that they, too, could employ psychological pressure if the situation demanded it, as when the activities of a notorious IRA militant were successfully curtailed:

She was always one of the planners and never one of the operators but she was behind a great deal of the aggravation in the area. Well, one day three of my corporals came to see me and said, 'Look, we've been giving K . . . a bit of a run-round lately and we think she's about to complain. Every patrol which has gone past her front door has banged on the door and asked for the time. We just put on a silly smile and just say, "Excuse me, madam, I wonder if you could tell me the time." She's taken to shouting and screaming at us and I should think we've been doing that now about ten to fifteen times for the last three days and we think the moment has come to bring you in on the act, sir.' So I went out with the next patrol that evening and went round to K . . .'s house and banged on the door and she came and muttered some marvellous oaths at me. I waited until there was a pause and I said, 'Look, I really came round to say how grateful I am to you for the help that you've given my Riflemen in telling them the time.' And then I slightly changed my tone and said, 'Now, if you felt on the other hand that you'd like to move out of the area and not come back for three months,we'd all be delighted' – and I'm glad to say she did.

However, this was by no means the end of 'R' Company's troubles with the Republican women of the Lower Falls. About halfway through their tour an incident occurred that was to set their relations with the local community at an all-time low. 'We had a company operation which basically was to go out and search a house in the Falls,' recalls the Section Commander. 'One platoon was to do the inner cordon, one was to do the outer cordon and the third was to do the search.' The Corporal himself was with the search party and was about fifteen minutes into the search when shots were fired outside that were 'very different from shots I'd heard in Northern Ireland. The self-loading rifle is a high velocity weapon and when you fire a high velocity weapon in the closed streets of somewhere like the Lower Falls it's like a cannon going off. These shots were low velocity but the next thing I can recall was high velocity shots, the SLRs being fired.' His Company Commander takes up the story:

> After circling the area for some time a civilian car had driven into the street we were operating in. I'd tried to stop it by putting an armoured vehicle across the road at the bottom and it had avoided that, driving up on to the kerb and roaring down the street. I remember, particularly, jumping out trying to stop it and rather stupidly raising my hand and then realising that this was not the place to be and taking a very fast nose-dive into the nearest doorway. The car went on up the street and as it was going out the other end the back window was broken and two or three shots were fired. Of course, a car careering at speed down a street is not an ideal platform for firing from accurately and the shots missed any of my Riflemen. But three Riflemen returned fire and engaged the car, which duly crashed.

Before any soldiers could reach the crashed car a crowd had assembled, preventing them from reaching its occupants. Meanwhile, the Section Commander had run out of the house on to the bottom of the street: 'Then a taxi came out of the crowd and down the street and voices shouted, "Stop that taxi! Stop that taxi!" So one or two of us duly stepped out like an English bobby with his hand up, whereas the taxi obviously didn't want to stop, clipped me and threw me across to the side of the road and sped away.' An ambulance was summoned and it was then discovered that two dead passengers in the back seat of the crashed car were women, both of them apparently dressed in men's clothes. No weapon was found, nor was the driver of the car ever located.

For 'R' Company and for its Commander, especially, the next twenty-four hours took on something of the quality of a nightmare:

> I found myself virtually accused of murder and that was probably the low point of my own morale. I knew we had every justification for opening fire. Frankly, at four o'clock in the morning on a darkened street in the rain in Belfast you don't stop to ask what somebody's dressed in, nor indeed what sex they are. If somebody shoots at you you return fire. The difference was that my Riflemen fired very accurately and the other side didn't. But at lunchtime on that day I was required by Headquarters Northern Ireland to attend

a Press conference which turned out to be a somewhat hostile
affair, initially about fifty reporters and then later during the
afternoon about three or four radio interviews and three or four
television interviews, and the line being taken by the Press was
unfriendly, to put it mildly. Now when your life has been that of an
ordinary soldier and quite suddenly you find that you're item one
on the radio and television news and you're headlines in the
newspapers the next day it's something of a cultural shock.

The line taken by most of the Press and the media was that the
soldiers had shot two innocent women and 'the fact that forensic proof
was provided within twenty-four hours that one of the women had
used a firearm a short time before she was killed was totally
overlooked.' To the distress and anger of those who knew what had
taken place, the IRA made maximum propaganda out of the incident:

> We were 'murderers', and all we'd actually done was our job. It
> was 'Two women murdered in Belfast by the Army' in the local and
> Irish papers. It was just horrendous. And that particular case went
> on for as long as ten years, I think, going backwards and forwards
> to say in court in Northern Ireland what you had heard that night,
> to stand there in the witness box and be told that you had never
> heard two low velocity shots, that you weren't qualified to know the
> difference between low and high velocity. And they weren't very
> good days to go to court at all, because you've got all the family
> looking at you. If there's an adjournment you walk out of the court
> into the foyer and they glare at you, spit at you, make gestures at
> you.

As to the innocence of the two women concerned, it was perhaps
significant that a local Republican newspaper devoted seven and a
half columns of IRA death notices to them in which it was made clear
that one of the women was a senior officer on the command staff of
the Women's Provisional Wing and the other a Volunteer.

Following the Lower Falls shooting incident the whole area
'boiled' and 'one got the feeling that the gunmen had been given a
three-line whip to shoot a Rifleman'. The Company Commander's
response was to take all the foot patrols off the streets and to
concentrate instead on intensive patrolling in armoured cars. Unable
to find easy targets the local gunmen turned their attentions on the
neighbouring Army units instead, sniping at them from across the
Falls Road boundaries, injuring three soldiers and missing several
others. In fact, this redirection of their mischief was to continue to
the end of 'R' Company's tour. Both the Scots Guards to the north

and 3rd Queen's to the south suffered casualties, while the Riflemen in the middle remained relatively unscathed: 'One really felt that the Riflemen were now on top of the business. The gunmen seemed disinclined to tussle with us. At the same time our successes started to increase markedly.'

Among those who played a major role in building up these successes was the young Corporal Section Commander, who made several unusually spectacular arrests during the course of his first tour. The first of these began as a matter of pure chance but its conclusion was entirely due to good judgement and decisive action:

> We were out on a mobile patrol, two armoured cars patrolling around the Lower Falls. We drove up Leeson Street from Grosvenor Road and on the left-hand side two hundred yards in front of me were three characters standing next to a car with a passenger door open. We were going reasonably slowly but you can't hide the noise of an armoured car and these three guys looked up and saw the Army vehicle. One guy, he jumped behind the driver's wheel, one guy bolted into the house and one stood there with a package. He threw it into the back of the car, slammed the door and ran off across the road and down a street. The car came towards us for about ten yards and then turned right and raced off into Grosvenor Road, which is quite a busy main road. For a fraction of a second I thought, 'Right, what do we do now? Do we go after the guy who's gone into the house, the guy who's gone down the road? No, we'll go for the vehicle.'
>
> So we quickly turned left and as we turned we saw the car turn left on Grosvenor Road. Then we had a bit of luck because there were traffic lights on red. There were already cars ahead so he was really trapped, he couldn't get across the traffic lights. By now we'd got the armoured car doing about thirty-three mph and breaking the sound barrier, just about, and I'm thinking that when we get level we'll jump out and nab him. But the lights went to amber and then green and things started moving forward. We were still doing the maximum speed so I said to the driver, 'Bugger it, ram him!' He looked at me and said, 'Do you mean hit him?' and I said, 'Yes, ram him!' So we swerved quickly, hit him in the side and rammed him across the road.
>
> I started sending guys to various positions to give us cover and then as I walked towards the car where the guy was sat there, I suddenly thought, God, what if he's just been buying fish and chips and that's what's in the back, or the week's shopping? I asked the guy to get out of the car and as I opened the back door I was saying

to myself, 'Please let it be something. How am I going to explain this?' I opened the door and there it was – the smell straight away was marzipan. It was a bomb. And the guy just looked at me and said he hadn't got a clue how it had got in the back of the car, that it wasn't his car, he'd borrowed it. And later on through the intelligence system we heard that we'd done quite well. We'd got a guy quite high up the ladder and in possession of ten pounds of explosives. So that really was a good feather in our cap.

However, success against the IRA was undoubtedly hampered by the paucity of information: 'We didn't have great intelligence in those days. We knew the ardent Republicans but as to the organisation of the IRA you might have the names of one or two but basically it was a jig-saw puzzle. You wouldn't find the Commander of "B" Company Lower Falls Provisional walking down your street. He probably wasn't even in the area for months, he'd have his minions carry out the orders and they were the people we were getting, the minions.' But just occasionally the big fish did get caught:

I stopped a guy one night, about one o'clock in the morning and asked him to tell me where he lived, what his name was, where he was going and so forth. He answered me and said his name was . . . and he lived at such and such an address. The name rang a bell and I got on the radio and asked our Ops Room for what is known as a 'P check'. They sent a message back saying, 'Hold him' and that shortly a vehicle would be on its way and they'd arrest him. So we were waiting and then all of a sudden a door opened and two women came outside and switched a light on and saw the Army and this guy. Within two minutes the place was just pandemonium. Every door was opened, every light came on, upstairs, downstairs – it was just like Blackpool illuminations – and they all came out on the street. Now I did not know who this guy was, but these people did not want us to take him away. The next thing that happened was guys were being hit by brushes, water thrown on them and dustbin lids thrown at them and eventually in all this messing about that was going on this guy got away.

Returning to Albert Street Mill with his section the Section Commander heard who it was they had let get away: 'I had stopped an IRA Company Commander in the street that night and we'd lost him. To the section that was just rock bottom. We'd had the guy and he'd got away from us. Terrible.' However, that was not to be the end of the story:

Two and a half months later I was stood in an alleyway on Falls Road with three other guys, black faces, soft shoes on. We'd been on a night search and having a hunt round, checking through waste ground and outside sheds, when I saw, walking down the road on the other side with a woman, the guy who'd got away from us two and a half months earlier. I said to one of the guys, 'Come and have a look at this. Can you remember who that is?' He said, 'No.' I said, 'Well, that's the guy who got away from us that night.' I'd already said to myself that there was no way this guy was ever going to get away again and when he came level with me I stepped out and placed the muzzle of my rifle along the side of his neck and said, 'Stand still!' Then we bundled him from the road into a house and laid him down on the floor in the front room and we sat on him. Then I got on the radio and told them where we were and that we needed picking up and it had to be pretty quick. We took him back to Headquarters and the Company Commander came to see me and said, 'Who have you got?' and I told him. That guy told the Company Commander that the very night he was stopped two and a half months earlier he had left the area and went down to the south of Ireland. This very Saturday he had come back to spend the weekend with his wife – and he has to bump into the very soldier that had sent him away two and a half months ago.

However, such moments of supreme satisfaction had to be set against the many tedious hours put in as Riflemen like the Section Commander fulfilled the dual role of soldiers and policemen:

Everything that happened in the street you dealt with. You're an arresting officer. You charged him, you handed him over to the RUC, who did all the necessary paperwork, but you were the guy who stood in court and told them what you'd seen, why the guy was there, what you found. Now on some days there was that much happening you could actually arrest five different guys. That's five times you've got to go to court. It got to the stage where you didn't want to do the guy yourself. I mean, you had to get someone else to arrest him, because if you hadn't your whole life would have been for ever appearing in the local Belfast courts.

As far as the Corporal Section Commander is concerned, his first Northern Ireland tour was essentially 'a section commander's or a soldier's war, a little war that *they* fought, because they were in the street all the time. It was their war, the guys on the ground, not the guys who sat up in headquarters.' But to the Company Commander: 'counter-insurgency operations are, as far as my experience is concerned, really a company commander's business. In Northern Ireland platoon commanders were out on the ground a great deal of the time but the pattern of operations was directed by the company commander and larger incidents were commanded by him.' So it is very much a matter of viewpoint.

In terms of satisfaction, however, both men share the opinion that their tours together as section and company commander respectively, first in the autumn of 1971 and then again a year later also in the Lower Falls, represent the supreme periods of their military careers. 'This probably sounds awful,' says the former Company Commander [later a brigadier before retiring from the Army to take up farming], 'but when I look back upon my entire Army service I don't think there's much doubt that the most stimulating and most demanding – and therefore the most satisfying – time was when I was a company commander in Belfast. When you're with a gang of people with some shared experience, which actually puts your life at risk, then you build a degree of rapport, of mutual respect which far transcends rank or anything else, and which is deeply personal and very lasting.' The former Section Commander, who became the first soldier to be awarded the Distinguished Conduct Medal in Northern Ireland, agrees:

> My time as a section commander and as a platoon sergeant, that has been the Army for me. Those times there in Northern Ireland, nothing ever has come along that's made me think, 'Well, this is better.' Nothing's been better, because I was a guy on the street, I saw everything happen around me, I had my own little command, everything. Now it's someone else's problem, there's other section commanders on the street, it's their turn to have their moment of excitement. Those basic thrills of being there on operations, they're no longer available to me, so you live on memories. We have a reunion every year, you bump into guys and you talk about things that happened eighteen years ago. And you still talk about the same things but we never get fed up of listening or talking about them.
> That was the peak of my Army career, being a corporal in Northern Ireland and a young platoon sergeant, without a shadow of a doubt.

After this tour the Company Commander was also decorated for gallantry, receiving the Military Cross. One MBE and three Mentions in Despatches were awarded to other members of 'R' Company, probably the largest number of awards made to a single company on one tour in Northern Ireland.

'R' Company handed over the Lower Falls to the incoming battalion at 3 p.m. on 9 December 1971. At 3.45 p.m. the new company in Albert Street Mill sustained its first casualty.

Chapter Fifteen

NORTHERN IRELAND:
The Intelligence War

The improvement was so effective, so dramatic that the area was totally dominated by the end of 1975. On the 1972 tour we had three people killed in the battalion and some others seriously injured, but in 1973 and 1974 we had one soldier shot in the arm, which did show that the area was totally dominated by my battalion. I would say that we knew an enormous amount about the Provisional IRA and we got very good at the business of low-level intelligence. You couldn't predict what was going to happen but you would know within one or two days of an incident who had done it and why. However, the feeling we had was that we were not solving the problem, we were merely containing it.

Over in Londonderry the situation at the end of 1971 was quite different from that which existed in Belfast. The Creggan and Bogside were to all intents solidly Nationalist. Army movements in 'Free Derry' provoked such hostility that they were scaled right down. 'I noticed there a total difference,' remarks a senior officer whose battalion did tours in both towns. 'The kid gloves were on when you were in Londonderry. You were much closer to the border and you were in a community which would react very violently indeed, as they did later.'

All marches had been banned since Internment but a number of civil rights' marches took place without provoking any preventative action by the authorities. Encouraged by this, the Northern Ireland Civil Rights Association announced that it would hold a big march in Londonderry on 30 January 1972. The Army decided to allow the march to proceed so long as it remained within the Catholic areas and it remained peaceful. But to deal with any breaches of this order the 1st Battalion of the Parachute Regiment were brought over from Belfast, where they had been acting as a Reserve Battalion for some fifteen months. The reasoning behind this decision was that they were the most experienced unit in Northern Ireland. They were also the toughest, having become extremely skilled at the task for which they had been specially trained, which was to go in hard when a riot got out of hand and break it up. Whether they were the right troops for Londonderry is questionable. However, they were sent in – and the result was 'Bloody Sunday'.

The organisers of the march had let it be known that they wished to avoid confrontation with the Army but, inevitably, confrontation followed when hooligans in the crowd began stoning soldiers. One of the latter recalls listening to radio reports as the march got under way: 'The initial report was a crowd of about four hundred, which was quickly corrected to four thousand, and we then deployed round the outskirts, denying them access to the city walls. Within about ten minutes we had another report that the crowd was about 40,000 strong, which was quite formidable. We did expend some CS gas and turned them back at just about every point until the march finally reached the Rossville–William Street junction – where the firing broke out. Then you could hear the sporadic firing.'

As the Paras climbed out of their 'Pigs' carrying their batons a section was fired upon. Its response was immediate – and irreversible: 'All you've got then to do is react. You don't sit and wonder about it, you go like a well-oiled machine. Sometimes that's right and sometimes that's wrong but you can't stop that immediate reaction from taking place – and if you ask anybody who was at Bloody Sunday, "Would you have acted any differently?" the answer has got to be, "No, you *can't* act any differently." '

A focal point of the firefight that followed was Rossville Flats where 'a guy on the corner of Rossville House opened up on us with a Thompson'. Fire was returned and the man was seen to fall. Other gunmen were identified and fired at as the Paras skirmished through the Flats. When the firing was over, thirteen young men aged between eighteen and twenty-six were dead, none of them soldiers. But initial feelings of elation among the troops at what they thought was a 'huge success' slowly turned to disquiet as more and more bodies were collected: 'Watching the bodies coming in to the car park, you know, at the end of Craigavon Bridge, with the bullet holes in them, I think that really brought it home. They were shipped off as quickly as possible to the hospital but we couldn't send them all in one ambulance. I remember a body had to be removed to the riverside while an ATO removed a nail bomb and blew that up on location, because obviously you can't send somebody to hospital with explosives in his pocket. People weren't talking, everyone was shocked at the outcome of the day.'

Both among 1 Para and others who were on the streets that day there are many who believe that the marchers were infiltrated by a number of inexperienced and not very well-armed gunmen who tried to take on the Paras and suffered what was in military terms a disaster, many of their dead being taken over the border to be buried in secret. 'I'd have put the body count at thirty – not thirteen,' declares one experienced soldier. In the event, however, Bloody Sunday was portrayed to the world as a massacre of innocents by soldiers who had run amok. Delays in collecting forensic evidence and the decision to use only one simple explosives test – which showed that nine bodies carried heavy concentrations of lead – did nothing to clarify the rights and wrongs of the matter. 'Whoever got in with the first story tended to be the person who was believed,' declares a battalion commander. 'The prime example of this was "Bloody Sunday", where the Government side made no comment. The terrorist side made full comment, although inaccurate, and was believed.'

'Bloody Sunday' set the tone for 1972, the worst year of the Troubles to date, with violence piled upon violence. 'In our first six weeks,' recalls the same battalion commander, 'in an area of two square miles we had, I think, over two thousand shooting incidents and simply uncounted numbers of bombs. I myself got blown up on a bomb, but it was fired by milliseconds at the wrong moment. There were two Land Rovers and it was detonated between the two. The only person who really suffered was the driver of the second Land Rover who lost quite a bit of his right arm. It was a very, very violent time.'

Violent deaths among civilians, service personnel and police alike soared. The bare statistics for 1971 were sixty-one civilians killed, fifty-four known terrorists and forty-eight soldiers. In 1972 they climbed to two hundred and twenty-three civilian fatalities, ninety-eight terrorist, one hundred and twenty-nine military (including twenty-six members of the Ulster Defence Regiment) and seventeen RUC deaths. As this violence escalated above what a British Government minister described as 'an acceptable level' more troops were brought in: 'Northern Ireland was moving at a hell of a pace at the time. Fifteen to twenty units were deployed over there which for four months at a time meant an enormous percentage of the Army were perpetually on the go to and fro.' In March 1972 the Stormont Government was prorogued and replaced by Direct Rule from Westminster, creating a brief lull before the IRA once more went on to the offensive.

Among those who suffered their share of casualties was 40 Royal Marine Commando on its four-month tour of the New Lodge, a small

Catholic enclave just north of the City Centre in Belfast, in the summer of 1972. 'During that tour we lost three Marines killed and we had several badly injured,' states one of its Company Sergeant-Majors. 'The situation was such that a whole Commando unit was required to contain an area as small as the New Lodge, which was something like five or six streets wide. To put all those troops in there now would look extremely strange.' In the summer of 1972, however, it was a matter of sad necessity: 'During our tour we had what was to become known as "Bloody Friday" [21 July] when seventeen bombs went off in Belfast, of which twelve were in 40 Commando's area.' Most of these bombs exploded in the city centre, killing nine people and injuring more than eighty women and children. A month earlier, on 24 June, the hundredth British soldier had been killed.

In 40 Commando the first fatal injury took place in July on the same day in which a new troop commander joined them as a reinforcement:

> I took over my troop and an hour later I had a man killed, Marine Allen, the first Royal Marine to be killed in Northern Ireland. It was a classic incident. A five- or six-pound blast-bomb was placed at the back of a building to draw the troops. When it went off, the first three men round the corner were Marine Allen, myself and my signaller. As we ran round the corner into Unity Square from Upper Library Street about five rounds from an Armalite were fired from across the square and Allen fell hit through the head, dead before he hit the ground. The signaller behind me got hit in the elbow. I was unharmed.
>
> The man who did the shooting was a man named Jesse 'Blueboy' Kelly, who was seen but then disappeared. Three days later he returned to Unity, was sighted by one of the patrols and cornered in a house. We went in with three troops and had to fight our way through the crowd with riot shields and batons to reinforce our four-man patrol, who were very bravely holding the people out of the house. We then got the vehicles in and went inside to make the arrest. Sergeant B— and I went in and there was a lot of shouting from upstairs by 'Blueboy' like, 'First man through the door gets killed' etc. But, in fact, when we actually went through the door he was hiding behind a chest of drawers whimpering and he'd defecated and wet himself in fear, because he was convinced we were going to shoot him out of hand.

Kelly was arrested but in the absence of any solid evidence linking him with the shootings four days earlier he was never charged with the murder of Marine Allen: 'He was interned as being a member of the IRA. He escaped from Longkesh dressed as a monk on New Year's Eve 1972 in the fog and in the summer of 1973 in East Belfast he was shot dead by 42 Commando. He opened fire on a patrol and they shot him dead. So there is justice.'

Living and working on what was virtually a war footing, units like 40 Commando worked their men in shifts round the clock that rarely allowed them more than six hours' sleep within a twenty-four hour period. 'The most you ever got in one lot was three to four hours, but we learned to cat-nap,' reports the same Troop Commander. 'You'd sit in a chair with all your gear on, ready to go, and shut your eyes and you were out. Then somebody would just touch you on the shoulder and you were up and away. You got into the habit of it, no problem.' Suprisingly, breakdowns were very rare: 'There was no question of people cracking-up under the strain because we were far too busy. That sounds rather ironic but it's true. There was never a question that we weren't doing something that was vital and as a direct result the motivation level was very high and crack-ups were non-existent. What's interesting is that in my next tour, the "cease-fire" tour in 1975, there *was* a tendency to crack-up and people did feel the strain because there was virtually nothing to do. The less you do the more you worry.'

But tiredness did inevitably affect efficiency, even on the four-month 'roulement' (short) tours that were now becoming the norm for every infantry battalion and Royal Marine Commando to take in its stride. One Green Jackets company commander from this time remembers returning from accompanying a patrol and being told off by his leading scout:

> After the patrol had been debriefed I used to sit down in my little intelligence room and this marvellous chap called H— used to come in. We'd put down our rifles and then he would nip off and get a Thermos of coffee and some sandwiches and we would sit and talk, usually for about an hour or two because he was tremendously good at intelligence. This time, however, he just stood looking at me until I said, 'What are you waiting for, Corporal H—? Go on off and get the Thermos!' But he just stood looking at me and then he said, 'It won't do, you know.' And I said, 'What won't do?' He said, 'Five times this evening on patrol I saw you yawning. Now how the hell do you expect the Riflemen to keep sharp if they see the company commander yawning? It won't bloody well do and I hope it won't happen again, and I'll now go and get the coffee.'

By the summer of 1972 the situation had become both militarily and politically intolerable and it was decided that the 'no-go' areas of

West Belfast and Londonderry had once and for all to be cleared and law and order restored. To the intense irritation of some soldiers – 'it was extremely frustrating to know that we were going to stand and watch the IRA weapons leaving New Lodge' – but in a deliberate move to avoid civilian casualties, the IRA were forewarned that a massive military clearing operation was about to take place. Then at four a.m. on 31 July, Operation 'Motorman' was launched, involving a total of 21,000 troops drawn from over twenty-seven different units – including four Royal Navy landing craft which transported Royal Engineer bulldozer tanks up the River Foyle.

'Motorman' was an outstanding success and, in the words of the commander of the Spearhead Battalion which headed the operation in Belfast, a 'turning point' in the Troubles, although its most impressive feature for him at the time was the astonishing way in which companies, squadrons, platoons, troops and batteries were 'all mixed up together and working. You'd take someone else under your wing or hand out your people and more and more people did swap companies and things. We all got very much better at operating with other people and out of this came an ability to accept other regiments in a way that had not often been the case before.'

A memorable example of this mixing of units took place soon after 'Motorman' when the troops were called out to prevent a Loyalist march from crossing the river from East into West Belfast:

> Three of my four Royal Marine companies were working with various battalions in the western half of the city, but to deal with the march I needed seven companies, and they came from the Queen's Regiment, the Queen's Own Highlanders, the Scots Guards, the Royal Artillery and the Life Guards. I had agreed a route with the organisers and I was standing with three or four of my team on the bridge across to the city centre watching for the marchers to pass about a hundred yards away. To our horror, at the point where they had agreed to turn left, the head of the march instead came straight towards us – and not one of the organisers was in sight. It was a mighty close-run thing getting enough soldiers to join us and hold the bridge.

With the Colonel was one of his company commanders, who remembers 'this snake of thousands, very ordered, marching very well towards the bridges. The Colonel went up to them to persuade them not to move across those bridges and indeed they did stop. I won't say it was frightening but one was anxious because there were only a few of us standing there and this huge crowd of disciplined, very determined people – it wasn't Cypriots or Indians or whatever –

our own people, a number of whom were ex-servicemen.' What they were witnessing was, in fact, the 'rise of the Ulster Defence Association', which was to become the bane of the British Government over the next few years. It exercised its very considerable political muscle as an umbrella organisation, linking various Loyalist paramilitary groups, to block and frustrate moves towards power-sharing, which might otherwise have weaned many Republicans away from the 'Stickies and the Provos'.

As far as these two Republican organisations were concerned, 'Motorman' was a disaster. The saturation by the security forces of the Catholic districts of Belfast and Londonderry had forced them to relinquish control of the ghettos – which allowed the Army to move into a different phase in its campaign.

That long-term in-depth intelligence was the key to success in counter-insurgency was now accepted thinking in the Army and the Ministry of Defence. But whereas in 1970–71 intelligence-gathering had been largely unco-ordinated, with the emphasis very much on short-term, tactical intelligence, now it was being applied across the board at every level and with full support from Army Headquarters and above, 'so you were building up sources and methods of intelligence-gathering, using the best computer technology devices you could obtain. It's not a thing you can instantly do but the speed with which the Ministry of Defence supported us in the field was remarkable.' So speaks a Brigade Commander. 'The way corners were cut was superb. Things that would normally take years to develop – money was put into them, they were developed, produced, delivered and put into service in record time.'

Backed up by Army Intelligence at Brigade Headquarters linked to RUC Special Branch and CID, and with a second source of information to draw upon through the local RUC Divisional or Sub-Divisional Headquarters, a new battalion coming in to take over an area on its 'roulement' tour had far more to work with than units in earlier tours had ever done. The battalion's Intelligence Officer (IO) now became very much a key figure, with his own staff of intelligence operatives made up of a number of senior and junior NCOs usually headed by an experienced Warrant Officer. He and part of his team would precede the incoming battalion as part of the hand-over process, inheriting all the known details of the terrorist ORBAT (Order of Battle) together with mug-shots of every identified extremist or suspect to line the walls of his Briefing Room.

A senior NCO who returned to Northern Ireland in 1973 after a two-year absence found the change in attitudes quite remarkable, with an awareness that it was now 'an intelligence war in which every soldier was part of an intelligence machine. The people above had realised that troops weren't just there to walk down the streets and be shot at, and the soldier on the ground had realised that he was not there just to patrol on the off-chance of catching a terrorist. That was what by this stage was taking place in Ulster.'

This was not an isolated opinion, as an officer who served as a Battalion IO confirms: 'I started as an Intelligence Officer in 1973 in Belfast and it was clear straight away that information-gathering had improved out of all recognition since the previous tour in 1972 when I had been a platoon commander. The sources of this information were being efficiently handed on from battalion to battalion from tour to tour. The Army had got its act together.'

While Military Intelligence and the RUC concentrated on long-term intelligence, at battalion and company level the emphasis was still very much on short-term, tactical intelligence. 'A primary consideration was the safety of your own people,' explains the Battalion IO. 'This to some extent affected the attitude you had towards intelligence-gathering and the use you made of the intelligence you gained.' Nevertheless, the gathering of information and the use to which it was put had reached a new level of sophistication. 'Intelligence is getting to know people,' declares a company and battalion commander who worked out a 'four-phase intelligence campaign' for his second and third tours. This began with a general intelligence-gathering period followed by a second phase with the emphasis on specific information: 'Here we identified certain families who seemed to be of significance in the area and we kept watch on them.' Regular weekly meetings were held in which every scrap of information was pooled and analysed. This was followed by phase three in which contacts were cultivated: 'By about halfway through the tour I hoped we would know specifically who the leading terrorists in the area were and then try and find them, for which you've got to get the right contacts who will tell you where to find them. And then, of course, comes phase four when you launch into the major offensive itself, when you're able to target people exactly and, with luck, arrest them. And this is really how it turned out.'

To supplement ordinary patrols, units operated specific intelligence-gathering patrols which went out in the guise of ordinary ones or operated in plain clothes driving unmarked cars. In the same way, overt Observation Posts (OPs) established at key strategic points such as high-rise flats were supplemented by hidden OPs set up wherever they would be placed, often in derelict or burned-out buildings but sometimes in more dangerous locations, in the hopes that they would not be spotted by the opposition. 'These were set up on what we knew were the blind spots of the overt OPs,' recalls an officer who was then a senior NCO in charge of an intelligence-gathering section. 'They were extremely covert. They were inserted by various means, either with patrols or through cars or by more sensitive means. They were able to get themselves into position with night observation devices and allowed to remain there for probably not more than two days and they had to protect themselves.'

In an urban area the chances of these hidden OPs being discovered were considerable. One officer recalls an occasion when the cover of one of his best ones was well and truly blown: 'I managed to secrete an observation party of two in the roof of a house which was, in fact, occupied by an old couple and unfortunately during the night the ceiling of their bedroom gave way and they were joined in bed by two Riflemen, who then had to explain what they were doing there.' But more serious incidents did take place when OPs were identified and attacked, as the senior NCO who led an intelligence section remembers well:

> One OP was in the Funeral Parlour of the New Lodge Road, which was set up when we knew people were marching in and out of the New Lodge Road. It became known to the locals and the IRA decided to attack it. My two people inside were quite badly shot up by an Armalite rifle. One had been shot through the throat and we had to go in and extract him in the middle of the night. I remember trying to jump over the Funeral Parlour's iron railings and being impaled on the spikes on the top of the railings, but we got inside and rescued the senior NCO. I remember in the dark putting a field dressing on one side of his face where there was a wound, moving the field dressing to the opposite side where the blood was still coming out, and then realising that there was an entry and an exit wound. Happily, he lived and subsequently has been back to the Province on duty.

Intelligence-gathering through patrolling and observation could never be enough in itself. 'It all turns on inside information,' declares a Lieutenant-Colonel who was particularly successful in these comparatively early days of the intelligence war. 'Never mind patrolling or shooting. That sort of thing will not make any difference. At the end of the day there's only one way to win this sort of campaign and that is to get yourself good informers. There's no other way.'

These informers came in all sorts of different forms, many of them supplying intelligence without being aware of the fact that they were doing so. This was largely made possible by what was known as 'screening', which had now become a standard feature of security measures in Northern Ireland. This entailed the questioning of large numbers of people picked up by the security forces on what often appeared to be a random basis. Although such a measure fell a long way short of the harsh steps employed in earlier counter-insurgency campaigns, screening was an undesirable curtailment of civil liberties in the Province, however reluctantly introduced and however necessary. But set against this weakening of civil rights was the undoubted fact that screening protected genuine sources of information because it was done on such a large scale that the extremist organisations were no longer able to threaten and intimidate all those who had been questioned.

Screening made possible the development of pools of informants in ways that would otherwise have been impossible, as the former Battalion IO explains:

> Once that information comes in the IO and his intelligence sections will try and pick out the more important from the less important. They may then ask the companies on the ground to bring in certain people for further questioning. Now sometimes these people will come in and give answers, which they themselves don't think are significant but are in fact significant, so those are the people who give information unwittingly. Very few people will just sit there and say nothing. Then there are the people who come in and give information – the next level up, as it were. These aren't part of the PIRA or Official IRA or of any of the Protestant paramilitary organisations, but are actively trying to help the security forces for a range of motives, either because they are against violence or out of a sense of fair play or for some other reason. Then the next stage up – and obviously you try and target these people – were those who were actually involved at a low level. And a surprising number of these people were prepared to give information – and when I say surprising, I mean in terms of the consequences for them if they were caught giving it. These people gave information for a range of motives but it was always important to identify that motive and if possible work on that. Finally, you would get the next level up from them, people who were heavily involved. Again, there would be a range of motives as to why they were giving information but quite often it could be because they had been caught and they were worried about being locked up for a long period of time or they thought you knew much more about them than you were disclosing.

This particular Battalion Intelligence Officer had 'a hundred and twenty active sources on our books' on one tour in a city area in the early 1970s:

We would work with them in terms of meetings, bringing them in, trying to see what information they had after certain incidents, trying to see what information they had had after action we took like, maybe, raiding four or five houses or lifting people. They would come back with a reaction from the area to what had happened. The main reason they gave information was the sheer exhilaration, the sheer excitement of talking to people who had real power within their area. They were able to talk to us and see something happen. The connection to them was tremendously exciting and that is why they gave information more than any other reason, for them to feel they had this exhilarating position of power. There was also to some extent an identification with us. You felt with some of these people that they personally liked you very much and there were one or two of these people who wanted to come and join the Army. These people became participants in the whole information-gathering business and they would actually co-operate with you in setting up ways of obtaining more information. Very often we had to rein them in. They were doing things that endangered themselves and we had to say, 'No, you can't do that because you might compromise yourself.' The IRA was terrified of these people and spent a tremendous amount of time trying to work out who they were, which is why we had to deal very carefully with these people. Obviously, our list of these people was kept very confidentially and with great regard to their personal safety, both from a moral point of view and also because it would have been completely counter-productive to jeopardise them in any way.

People volunteered information or became informers for the most surprising reasons. 'There's people's vanity you can play on by implying to them that they are very unimportant and that you've been told you've got to interview them for form's sake, and it's not difficult by what has been described to me as the "unremitting pressure of doing absolutely nothing" to get people trying to convince you how important they are.' Unexpected kindness and humane treatment could also play its part in winning over suspects when they were brought in for questioning. 'The first thing they always got from us was an enormous fry up,' declares one company commander of this period. 'I used to go and sit and talk to them while they were eating and I used occasionally to throw a name in and see what the reaction was. I remember one man who when I mentioned a particular name went scarlet. I got nothing more out of him but that was the first indication I had that I was on to the Mr Big in the area. Then as time went by I got more informants and as a result of one of these informants we were able to arrest the leader.' Sometimes remorse could win a suspected terrorist over. One of the hundred and twenty listed informers referred to above was an IRA man who had been appalled by a particularly brutal IRA bombing: 'A young fellow who has seen young girls being shovelled into body bags from a restaurant is moved by this and must ask himself, "Is this right?". He was basically a moral man and eventually, after long talks, felt that the course that the IRA was taking was the worst possible thing for the Catholic population and that the IRA was doing more harm than good and he turned round and gave us information on things that we had no idea were going on.'

Another informer on the same list was there for rather baser motives, as the Commander of that battalion describes: 'I remember one IRA man who thought he should have been the next company commander for a particular IRA company, who, because he wasn't promoted, gave us information in order to have the person who had been promoted moved, so we hauled this guy in. Believe it or not, he again wasn't promoted so he shopped the next chap. He then eventually got promoted and so we hauled *him* in and I remember quite clearly his indignant little face and him saying, "But you never gave me a chance!" '

Among the best informants, however, were those who were caught in the commission of a crime which could be used as a lever against them: 'Your most powerful weapon is when you get in a boy of, say, twenty, and he's been found with a smoking bomb in his hand and you say, "Right, we'll just sit for five minutes." Silence. Then you say to him, "Well, if you go down to prison for, let's say, ten years, that's those five minutes multiplied by however many times it is to make ten years. You're going to have to sit through that. Can you face that? Now if you want to avoid that, help us." ' This was the situation that the battalion commander was able to use to advantage in turning an IRA man who became his most valuable operator:

> We arrested a man who was driving a stolen car. I knew he was an
> officer in the local IRA company but I also knew that he was pretty
> small fry and that he wasn't detainable under the terms for
> detention which were then being applied. In the course of an
> interview with me I made it clear to him that if he was handed over
> to the police he would be locked up for having stolen a car. The
> second option was that we could turn him loose. Now the local IRA
> leader was a particularly unpleasant man and I knew of an occasion
> when an operation had gone wrong and the man responsible had
> been made to hold on to a red-hot poker. I therefore said to this

man that if we turned him loose he would undoubtedly be accused of joy-riding in a car which had been stolen for operational reasons and he would be punished. I asked him to imagine what sort of punishment he might get and I even named the person who had been made to hold on to the red-hot poker. I suggested that perhaps a knee-capping or even a head job might apply in his case. And then I offered him a third option, which was to work for us – and he thought that was the best.

This was at a time when the RUC presence in the Republican strongholds was still minimal, so the turned IRA man was moved into an Army base:

This lasted for about a week until I persuaded the authorities that he should actually live in my company lines. We cut his hair, we shaved his beard off, made him look a bit more reasonable and initially he never left our base. When people were brought in from the streets he would see them from behind cover and tell me whether they were of interest or not. As time went on I used to take him out on patrol in the back of an armoured vehicle so that he could identify people as we drove around. Of course, when you remove somebody from circulation it does look suspicious unless you have some way of filling the void, so it was arranged that he should be 'moved' to West London from where his post-dated letters were sent to his girlfriend with the story that he was working on a building site to keep away from the area for a bit. He was with me for about six weeks and proved to be invaluable.

For the Battalion IO, too, his biggest success came from an IRA informant:

A vehicle with two hundred pounds of explosives had been brought into our base by a very alert corporal and his section, along with the two people who had been driving it. Their first excuse was that they were joy-riding and that they had just picked up this vehicle and it happened to have explosives in the back. However, one of the two people was found to be a senior explosives officer in the Provisionals and was thought to have been involved in the —— bombing so various senior people came in to question these people. This first person gave very little information and the second person, who was not so involved, adopted the same posture to begin with. They spent several hours with him and then at about 1 o'clock in the morning I went to see him very much as somebody going in just to have a chat with him off the record after the interrogation. I remarked that he would be going down for about fifteen years and it produced a great shock in him.

I then said, 'The other person says that you are primarily to blame and that he had nothing to do with the explosives.' This produced a totally shocked response from this person and he asked me, 'Well, what can I do to improve my position?' Trying not to show too much interest I said, 'Well, what you'd have to do is to show how that other person was actually involved in some way.' Quite amazingly, he then started giving me lots and lots of information on the other person, his techniques, some of the incidents he'd been involved in, all new information that we'd never heard before. This went on for about five hours until daybreak. Then everybody came into the base and that was the end of the interview – and he then said, 'One last thing. There's another seven hundred pounds of explosives in the Funeral Parlour.' I said, 'Well, thanks very much,' not expecting to find anything. We sent a section out and they discovered another seven hundred pounds of explosives in the Funeral Parlour. That was very satisfying.

All this gathering together of high-quality intelligence allowed the soldiers out on the street to act more and more in an offensive rather than a defensive role. 'We started to get major successes,' remembers a soldier who was then a section commander:

We weren't going out to arrest one man at one house, we were going out to arrest ten men. Before, in the early days, to find something you had to nose around and look for it. You had to open the shed door and lift some sacking up and maybe find guns and ammunition. Now we were being told where to look – 'Go to such-and-such a place and you will find such-and-such a thing' – and lo and behold, we went there and we found. You weren't finding just five pounds of explosives. You were finding sacks of explosives in places that you wouldn't think of looking in – 'Go and dig up the concrete coal bunker and underneath it are weapons' – things like that. The IRA were getting better, because don't forget, they had their own intelligence – but the British Army was getting better quicker.

By the end of 1974, the Provisional IRA had been so weakened by arrests, detentions, arms and explosives finds and infiltration by informers that it was a broken force in the urban areas. At Christmas PIRA announced a truce that was followed by a three-month suspension of what it termed 'military activities' while it reconsidered its position in the light of the failure of its urban insurgency campaign

– for failure it undoubtedly was. 'The IRA had taken a tremendous hammering and were licking their wounds after the successes of the security forces,' asserts a Royal Marines officer who was a troop commander at the time and one of many who objected to the ceasefire being accepted by the authorities. 'The ceasefire merely gave them all the time in the world to rearm, retrain and refinance. They had lost a large proportion of the old, hardcore professional operators both to the jail and to the graveyard and they needed a chance to train the next generation. Up to battalion level all the officers were saying we should not allow this. Our perception at grass-roots level was that the politicians at that time were making a decision we abhorred.'

Whether or not this was a fair judgement to make, the fact was that senior figures in the terrorist organisations were allowed to go about their business with impunity:

> We had an incident in Andersonstown where ——— ———, at that time the Number Three in the organisation, was seen. The company commander immediately surrounded the house and sent a deputation to the door and told him that his number had come up and he was under arrest. Then we were ordered to leave him because of the ceasefire. Now that man should have been arrested. He was a known murderer and a known terrorist but because of the terms of the so-called ceasefire which we held at that time, he was allowed to go free. I thought that was invidious and so did the unit. It caused a fairly major morale blip in the unit's feelings.

Whether a chance to destroy the IRA as a guerrilla force really was missed in 1975 seems doubtful. However, the urban war had been lost and with it the IRA's only possible hope of demoralising the Protestant majority or the Government into accepting a British withdrawal from Northern Ireland in the interests of peace. Indeed, the attitudes of this majority had actually hardened, with growing support for Loyalist groups like the UDA and its many splinter groups which once again frustrated British Government moves towards power sharing.

As for the IRA, pressures within the two wings resulted in the formation of a splinter group, the hard-line Irish Republican Socialist Party (IRSP) and its military wing, the Irish National Liberation Army (INLA). Their tactical response to the crisis brought about by the security forces' infiltration of their ranks was to abandon their grandiose military formations and to set up in their place small terrorist cells, known as 'active service units', which could operate independently of one another. In terms of strategy they extended their campaign to the British mainland, beginning with the Guild-ford, Woolwich and Birmingham pub bombings in August and November 1974 in which twenty-five people were killed and more than two hundred injured. They also made a partial withdrawal into the countryside of Northern Ireland in order to develop a dual urban-rural campaign that would allow their activists to take advantage of the pro-Republican border areas such as South Armagh as well as the refuge of the border itself. This now became 'bandit country', offering a new challenge to the security forces to which they were quick to respond.

Chapter Sixteen

NORTHERN IRELAND:
Twenty Years On

At one stage it was news, you know: 'Soldier Injured, Blown-up, Lost a Limb'. But now you seem to get page 5, in little print, 'Three Soldiers Killed', and page 1 is 'Pregnant Panda'.

I always thought in those early days of community relations that the humour in Ireland, the warmth, the genuineness of those people in the streets where you could sit and drink tea and eat lovely warm cakes and scones with nice, friendly human beings, normal people in any city, I thought that that warmth and humour would eventually win through. But it hasn't been like that.

As police statistics show, the IRA was never again able to raise its terror campaign to the level of 1972. In 1973 the casualty figures were half what they had been the year before, as were recorded shooting incidents, which fell from 10,628 to 5,018. The decline in violence continued, falling to two hundred and thirty-seven shooting incidents and a hundred and forty-eight explosions in 1985, the lowest figures since the start of the Troubles in 1969. In that same year, 1985, there were twenty-five recorded 'security situation' deaths among civilians (including known or suspected terrorists), a very far cry indeed from the four hundred and sixty-seven violent deaths recorded in 1972. However, 1985 also saw the deaths of twenty-nine members of the police and security forces, of whom no less than twenty-three were from the ranks of the Royal Ulster Constabulary. The IRA was acknowledging the existence of police primacy, which had been reintroduced as official policy in 1976 but had now become a reality. The Army had returned to its proper role of supporting the police rather than acting in their place, as it had been forced to do in the early 1970s.

From 1975 onwards a slow, painful recovery had begun in the Province. That same year saw the gradual phasing out of Internment without trial, so removing one of the IRA's main propaganda points. Soldiers returning for a second or even a third tour of duty noticed the difference straight away. 'What was dramatically obvious to me was the return to normality,' asserts one soldier, speaking of 1976. 'Both in Londonderry and Belfast, which I'd left in 1972, there was a return to civil order. You could drive through those areas that in 1972 were very sensitive and made the hackles of your neck stand on end. I spent some time in Londonderry on R&R [rest and recreation], going to the shops. The police had resumed their control of searches before you went into the big department stores and this was a great step forward from the times of 1972.'

The 'return to normality' was only relative, however. The people of Ulster had learned to live with the Troubles: 'The fact that you see soldiers in the streets, the fact that people will be stopped on the street and have their handbags searched doesn't actually bother the average person in Northern Ireland now.' It was also true that 'the problems don't touch the vast majority of people in Northern Ireland, Catholic or Protestant.' A degree of control had been regained whereby the violence was being contained by the police and the security forces, only occasionally boiling over into upsurges associated with a particular PIRA-INLA-Sinn Fein propaganda drive such as the Bobby Sands hunger-strike campaign in 1981, but otherwise confining itself for the most part to single acts of terror, each one an outrage and a tragedy, but infrequent and dispersed enough and yet constant enough to become integrated into the Ulster scene as the Troubles became increasingly institutionalised.

From the mid-1970s onwards the main focus of these acts of violence shifted away from Belfast and Londonderry, the chief population centres: 'The fight seemed to have developed out towards the country,' remarks one soldier of this period. It seemed to him that 'they'd driven most of the terrorists out to the areas commonly known as "bandit country", down in South Armagh and along the Enniskillen borders'. The counter-insurgency campaign had reached a new phase.

The Ulster countryside with its rolling wooded hills, its patchwork of small fields and hedgerows and its narrow lanes was a haven for terrorists, difficult to patrol and ideal for ambushes and quick getaways. Many of the part-time soldiers who had joined the Ulster Defence Regiment lived in these country areas and it was they who now became prime targets for the PIRA.

The Ulster Defence Regiment had been raised specifically to support the regular forces, consisting originally of seven battalions, one for each of the six counties and one for Belfast. In 1972 another four battalions were raised, bringing the total numbers up to about nine thousand men, nearly all part-timers who combined an ordinary day-time job with several hours of soldiering a week, usually at night and at weekends, when they performed guard duties, manned road-blocks and vehicle check-points (VCPs) and carried out patrols. They were never used in crowd-control duties nor deployed in such sensitive areas as Londonderry, West Belfast or the border areas of South Armagh, which remained – as they do to this day – the preserve of the touring Regular Army battalions.

The majority of the men who made up the first generation of UDR soldiers were drawn from very much the same background. 'It has always been a fact of life in Fermanagh that we have had to provide security for the country in which we live,' declares one old soldier, a farmer from the border area who had previously served in the Ulster Special Constabulary for twenty-two years before it was disbanded: 'My father served in the Royal Irish Constabulary in the 1920s and subsequently in the RUC. I had a brother in the 'B' Specials, two brothers who served with the Army. My ancestor came over with King William's Army in 1689 and it has always been a tradition in the Enniskillen area to provide and join the security forces.' He and other part-time soldiers became marked men, learning to live with the constant danger of 'assassinations, booby-trapped vehicles and landmines underneath the culverts in the road' as they went about their business. 'My details have been found in a house south of the border,' he admits. 'I haven't told the family because it would serve no useful purpose.'

Another of his fellow soldiers in the same battalion also lives close to the border in an equally vulnerable situation. 'My home of —— has suffered a lot from the terrorists,' he reveals:

> A lot of good fellows who joined the UDR because of their sense
> of loyalty, built themselves up, became better people in the
> community, were then wiped out by a terrorist who uses this as part
> of his excuse, with local people doing the targeting and then passing
> it back to the PIRA. Personally, my own family has suffered a wee
> bit too much from the terrorist. I've lost a brother, a fitter in a local
> factory, who on leaving his work was caught up in a queue and took
> fourteen bullets. That was the end of life for him. Then a nephew,
> trying to build up a life for himself, who built himself a new
> bungalow that he occupied for a month before he lost his life. I
> could go on because there's quite a few others, not just immediate
> family, but within my family all the same.

For men like this, drawn mostly from long-settled, rural, working-class communities, the issue of why they joined and why they stayed in the UDR was a very straightforward one. 'This is my country and

I'll fight for it,' is how one part-timer puts it. 'My son has to grow up in it, my whole family, and I will not be browbeaten by anybody, I don't care who they are.'

It was the men in these border battalions of the UDR who took the highest casualties. In the two UDR battalions in Tyrone only thirteen of the fifty-nine soldiers killed in terrorist attacks between 1971 and 1988 died on duty. All the rest were murdered off-duty, in most cases as they went to or from their homes at night. 'Only twenty per cent of the members of the Ulster Defence Regiment who have been killed have been killed while in uniform,' confirms a now-retired senior officer who himself has survived two assassination attempts:

> The most dangerous times for anybody in the regiment is when you're leaving home or going home. I developed a routine in which as I was going home in my car I used to douse the lights and go along the narrow lane with the engine merely ticking over. When I got to within thirty or forty yards of the house I would turn the lights full on and accelerate forward, at the same time holding my pistol, which was loaded with the safety catch on, and both windows open.
>
> There was one occasion when I followed this routine and put the headlights on to discover a figure wearing a balaclava and carrying a rifle standing in the lane about thirty yards in front of me. I was faced with an alternative. Either I could open fire with my pistol, which was probably reasonably accurate up to about thirty feet, or I could douse the lights and reverse like hell along the lane. I chose the latter category and got away. I then drove like hell to the nearest police station. They turned out two patrols immediately, we came in on foot – bear in mind it was five o'clock on a very still morning – and as we worked our way along the lane we heard a car start up about a mile off and accelerate away very quickly. They had brought in a helicopter but unfortunately it arrived about three minutes too late, otherwise we would perhaps have been able to follow the car concerned.

This officer is a company director who had joined the UDR in 1971 'out of sheer frustration. Everything I saw and valued in Northern Ireland was disintegrating before my eyes. That's what drove me into it. It wasn't sectarianism or Unionism. I objected to terrorism emerging on either side. A terrorist is a terrorist, be he Loyalist or be he Nationalist.' Now that he has retired from the UDR – and still a terrorist target, since no less than forty people have been murdered after they had retired or ceased to belong to the UDR – he feels he can speak more frankly about the 'most enormous guts' of the UDR part-timers:

This is one point that cannot be stressed enough to those in the rest of the United Kingdom who cannot possibly appreciate what it's like to be on duty twenty-four hours a day and to be a target twenty-four hours a day. You're doing your civilian job but at any time somebody could be coming up behind you. It certainly never really dawned on me until I left the regiment what the effect of my joining had been on my family. My daughter was aged ten when I joined and from ten to eighteen she never knew what normal life was at home. The blinds were drawn at night, she couldn't answer the door, we had alarm systems, we had an intercom. There was one occasion on which a gun battle actually raged outside the house while she and my wife were lying on the floor not knowing what was happening – and I think that if medals are to be awarded they should be awarded as much to the wives and families as to the men concerned. It's only when you come to other surroundings that you suddenly realise you've been living a totally unnatural life for a very long time. It took me a year before I could sit in a pub with my back to the door.

The same officer fiercely rejects the charge so often made by Sinn Fein and others that the UDR is a sectarian force created to oppress the Catholics. To prove his point he cites an incident that took place in the mid-1970s:

It was a night when absolutely all hell broke loose. I should have been in the Ops Room but they required every mobile they could muster out on the ground so I gathered together what we had left, a storeman corporal and two young recruits who came from what one might describe as a fairly hard-line Protestant area. To cut a long story short, we captured a gunman that night after a car chase. We arrested this chap, we had him charged and handed over to the police and it turned out he was a member of the Ulster Volunteer Force who was waiting outside a pub to assassinate a Catholic barman. When I got back to Headquarters again I talked to the two young recruits. I said, 'Right, what's your reaction? This chap's a Protestant and you're both Protestants.' And one of them turned to me and said, 'Sir, a gunman's a gunman. It doesn't matter a damn where he comes from.'

As well as its male volunteers the UDR also began in 1973 to recruit women soldiers, initially 'for the purpose of searching women and children under ten and also for administrative and clerical duties'. Their role was a non-combatant one and, as it is today, they were given no weapon training and forbidden to carry arms.

They very quickly came to be known as 'Greenfinches', a name that originated from the signals appointment title given to them in radio code: 'The title came from a signals instructor who was attached to us and that's the name by which we have been affectionately known ever since.'

One of the first women soldiers to join is now an officer, who remembers all too well her motive for enlisting in the UDR: 'I joined in September 1973 after a close relative had lost both her legs and an eye in a restaurant bombing.' At the start she and the other recruits found themselves up against considerable hostility from some of the older soldiers in the regiment:

> I remember my first night on duty, when the sergeant-major lined us up and said he didn't like women, he didn't want us and would we stay out of his way, which we duly did for the first few months. But we worked hard to prove ourselves and then they realised we were actually quite good operating radios; the female voice came across very well on the net. Being very methodical, we were extremely good at working in intelligence cells collating information, and being instinctively nosey, we were also very good at searching women and searching cars. So then the sergeant-major eventually let us go out on patrol, and it evolved from there. We were then allowed to go on search operations, area searches, house searches, doing the scribing at vehicle check points. So we earned the respect of our male colleagues very quickly.

However, there were real problems over safety that had to be overcome when the Greenfinches started patrolling alongside the men: 'When we first started going out with them they were very protective and we very quickly learned that in order not to be a liability we had to get our heads down and keep out of the way.' Initially, this was not made any easier by the regulation requiring them to wear skirts: 'It took about two years to convince the hierarchy that we really needed trousers on patrol, not skirts. Sitting out in a vehicle at three o'clock in the morning in the snow and the ice and the rain we had to remain warm if we were to remain agile. At one stage they issued us with beautiful pantaloons, black with white lace round the bottom, but they still didn't keep the cold out.' One young Greenfinch was wearing a pair of these when her patrol came under fire: 'They were given the order to take cover and in attempting to scramble over a barbed wire fence she got her bloomers caught. A big burly sergeant came to assist her but she wouldn't let him touch her bloomers. Her modesty overcame her fear.'

However, the fact that the Greenfinches were non-combatants and carried no weapons did not prevent them from being in the firing-line – and taking casualties. 'We have had four Greenfinches killed, two on patrol, one in her base and the fourth murdered at home,' recalls the Greenfinch officer:

> I can still remember when Private Eva Martin was killed in an attack on the company centre in Clogher, County Tyrone, on the night of 2 May 1975. She was on duty and had just had her identity photograph taken by her husband, who was also in the UDR, when the base came under attack. She was racing down the stairs past a window when she was hit in the head and tumbled down the stairs into the arms of her husband. The spirit of the girls came to the fore then because the next duty night every single girl in Private Martin's company reported for duty. We had two others killed on patrol. Jean Leggett was on mobile patrol in County Armagh when she was shot in an ambush in April 1976. Heather Kerrigan was blown up on patrol in County Tyrone in July 1984.

The killing of the fourth Greenfinch casualty was the most savage. Twenty-four-year-old Private Margaret Hearst lived with her three-year-old daughter in a caravan in the garden of her parents' home in a border village in South Armagh. On the night of 8 October 1977 PIRA gunmen burst into the caravan and raked it with automatic fire, killing the mother first before firing on her daughter in her bunk bed – but fortunately, failing to injure her.

Traumatic as these casualties have been for the men and women of the Ulster Defence Regiment, their determination to go on soldiering remains as strong as ever: 'People ask why we continue in the regiment after all the heartbreak we've seen but, of course, the memory of all those extremely close friends who have been killed by terrorism and have given their lives in the cause of democracy and to protect other people, that is an extremely big factor in why we carry on.' Nowhere is this determination stronger than among the remaining Catholic three per cent of the UDR, as one such Catholic, now a Greenfinch welfare officer, testifies:

> The fact that I'm a Catholic doesn't worry me as far as my own personal security is concerned. Obviously, we've got to take extra and stringent security precautions but those of us who remain have no intention of leaving. One of the main reasons I joined was to show that not all Catholics were in the IRA. People on the mainland get the impression that every Catholic is affiliated to or sympathises with the IRA and it's just not true. I thought it very, very important that I stood up to be counted.

For her courage she and her family had to put up with years of intimidation from both sides of the sectarian divide:

> I lived on an interface between the Loyalist and the Catholic community. Being on the Loyalist side of this interface my children played mostly with the Protestant children. This worked out okay until they had a fight or a squabble and then the children would be called names like 'Fenian' or 'Taig' and they would come in crying and saying, 'Mummy, so-and-so has called me a Fenian or Taig. What does it mean?' As the children got a wee bit older and started to understand, this began to play on them. They didn't go out as often, just stayed in the house with each other. On top of this the Catholic side of the community had harassed us over a period of years. They too would call out to the children 'Orange lovers', 'Prod lovers' and all the rest of it. As well as that we were constantly attacked. The house was bombarded with stones, bricks etcetera, with new windows having to be put in morning, afternoon and night, as well as the verbal abuse – and the children took it very badly. I personally would have stuck it out because we were the last Catholic family that was left on the Loyalist side and I'm afraid I'm very stubborn, but I had the children to consider and for their safety's sake I had to move.

As the IRA regrouped in the border areas in the mid-1970s UDR off-duty soft targets and patrols came increasingly under attack. 'We were doing "eagle" patrols,' remembers one UDR part-timer of an incident that took place in this period:

> We were being landed by helicopter, four of us, two regulars and two part-timers. All the incidents seemed to happen close to the border then so your hair would stand on the back of your neck a little when you were patrolling there. You were afraid, but it had to be done. On this occasion we were caught on the road very close to the border in the open. It's hard to explain but once the enemy fires on you and you get down out of the way then you feel you're both equal. We fired back and one of them was injured but, of course, they got away. At that time they wouldn't allow us to carry anything more powerful than a semi-automatic rifle, so the terrorist knew he could attack us and get away.

This situation began to change as the Army developed new tactics for dealing with the terrorists in 'bandit country', combining the latest technical surveillance aids with the skills pioneered by special forces units in Borneo, Oman and elsewhere. Only when hostilities have ceased can the remarkable story of these largely covert operations be told in full for, as a senior military commander explains, 'one of the reasons why these operations are so effective is that they keep the terrorists guessing and uncertain'. However, it is on the public record that the Special Air Service Regiment has had a major role to play, and that many other units have also been involved in this most skilled and arduous form of counter-insurgency warfare – the Royal Marine Commandos among them. 'We had freedom of access everywhere in South Armagh,' remembers one Royal Marine officer of his tour in South Armagh in 1976 as the commander of a special reconnaissance troop. 'We were tasked entirely by Special Branch who in South Armagh were second to none, and that took us into a whole new world.' Part of their surveillance work involved inserting their men into hidden close observation posts – including four such covert OPs in the very heart of the IRA's stronghold – 'which proved conclusively that Crossmaglen was not bandit country'. Such hidden OPs were manned continuously, often for weeks on end, with the observers being changed every few days:

> We only had one or two occasions when operations were compromised, usually through children, which is not a bad track record. And we did start to get problems halfway through the tour with blokes going down with malnutrition because we were so close to those whom we were observing that we couldn't cook. In one instance we were in an attic where the guys used to take with them little polythene bags of cold food, one bag per day, and one large flask per day. But by the fourth day the flask was starting to get a bit lukewarm. I had one guy get pleurisy, several went down with very bad influenza but they all refused to stop soldiering.

Only one particular target defeated them: 'This was a public house where the only way we could observe the target was by standing up to our necks in water. We did the reconnaissance in black immersion suits standing for twelve hours in the river and when we came out we said, "No more", because there was no way we could have defended ourselves if we'd been compromised, even though we had back-up teams.'

In this officer's opinion the 'unsung heroes of Northern Ireland have got to be the people who do covert operations. Those guys are really what's holding the terrorist down. The fact that you don't shoot a terrorist is, frankly, an irrelevance. The fact that they believe you could be there is sufficient to stop them operating.'

'Holding the terrorist down' or, in another officer's words, 'keeping the level of violence at as near an acceptable level as possible – if there is such a thing', is what the security forces have been engaged in from the mid-1970s onwards. For them, too, the Troubles have become an institution, a set feature in their military careers. 'We go there for a limited number of months,' remarks the former commanding officer of a county regiment:

> We put everything we can into it for the time we are there, working fourteen, fifteen, sixteen hours a day and then once you leave and move on to your next posting you forget about Northern Ireland. Then someone says to you, 'It's time to go back to Northern Ireland', and the first question you ask is, 'Where?' And then you switch on. Then for months before you read, you study, you train and, hopefully, by the time you get there you are ready to play a small, modest part in a very sad situation.

For one much-decorated senior NCO the pattern seems endless, without any hope of it being broken: 'You know when you're on tour that this is never going to be the last tour you're going to be on. We're never going to solve it this tour. We're going to do something, but we're going to come back here next year or the year after. We're getting better at everything we do all the way along the line, but we still have these major disasters that we can never foresee.' A more senior soldier, now retired, believes that the cycle will continue until the terrorists are beaten. 'The Army will be in Northern Ireland for ever,' he declares, 'until the terrorists give up hope of winning. Now they have no hope of winning because of the military might and determination of the Protestant people, but they haven't faced that yet and they have been given many of the wrong signals.' His solution is more policing of the border: 'The first signal that must be given to the terrorists that the party is over is controlling physically our frontier with the South.'

Others would disagree. 'We're always looking for initiatives to beat the terrorist on the border,' declares a Royal Marine officer who has worked his way up through the ranks and has distinguished himself in a number of military operations in Northern Ireland. 'However, in my opinion, it would never ever be a military victory on the border. It's an exceptionally good training area with a good enemy to work against, but we all know it's not going to be a military victory. It's going to be a political victory, with the local community doing its own policing and its own problem-solving.'

An officer in the Parachute Regiment – who has also worked his way through the ranks – takes much the same view, coloured by his own experiences, which include being blown up by an IRA bomb:

> The young soldier of today looks forward to his first two or three tours purely for the experience, if you like, but thereafter it

becomes more and more hateful the more tours one does, because one can see the utter futility of the whole exercise, with nothing for the people of Northern Ireland to look forward to. The situation is kept on-going by the fanatics of both sides and never the twain shall meet, it would appear, though it is certain there is no military solution to Northern Ireland – and everyone must know the only solution to Northern Ireland is round the table.

But while the politicians fail to agree the soldiers have to continue to 'hold the ring', all too aware that their presence is an unwelcome one to many. A delicate balance has had to be struck between keeping terrorism in check and not treading too heavily on the civil liberties of both communities:

> If you operate within the context of minimum force in a civilian population you have to be exceedingly careful. You have to have proper intelligence with which to seek out and pursue the terrorist. You have also to minimise the damage you would do to normal people living their normal lives, and it is very difficult to strike the right balance. That is one of the dilemmas of operations in a part of the United Kingdom. We did have more powers in the early days than we have now in terms of stopping, arresting, questioning and entering houses, which were all taken away because it was judged to be too much of an intrusion into the lives of people living in a democracy.

On 14 August 1989, the twentieth anniversary of the decision to commit troops to the streets of Northern Ireland was marked by a brief spell of intense media interest in the Province but by only sporadic and somewhat half-hearted rioting in West Belfast and Londonderry. Tight policing based on good intelligence had succeeded in frustrating a number of planned IRA operations. For all the Press attention there was no accompanying political re-evaluation of the situation.

In those twenty years there have been almost three thousand deaths arising out of the security situation – rather less, in fact, than the total number of fatalities from road traffic accidents in Northern Ireland over the same period. These deaths, which include four hundred and nineteen British soldiers killed, are only a part of the Ulster tragedy. Twenty years of conflict have polarised the two communities. Sectarianism paralyses provincial and local government, with such concerns as education, housing and health being run by government quangos rather than by elected bodies. The local economy has to be propped up to the tune of £1½ billion per annum, with the policing of Ulster swallowing up another £500 million.

To date, £500 million has been paid out in compensation while terrorism itself has created flourishing spin-off industries in law and order and rebuilding. Despite a variety of initiatives such as the Industrial Development Board, Fair Employment Legislation and the Make Belfast Work programme, unemployment in Ulster is twice as high as it is in the rest of the United Kingdom, with Catholic unemployment two and a half times higher than it is among Protestants. Half of those who are in work are employed by the state. Yet injustices have been removed, housing conditions have improved, employment prospects look set to rise, all the indications are that the extremists are losing ground to the moderates.

As for these extremist organisations and their paramilitary wings, their ability to terrorise has been greatly curtailed – but they remain powers to be reckoned with. On the Loyalist side proscribed organisations like the UVF, the UFF and the PAF have largely degenerated into criminal syndicates, limiting their violence to protection rackets and the occasional sectarian killing – while always remaining capable of reorganising themselves and bringing havoc to the Province if the Protestant supremacy is ever seriously threatened.

On the Republican side, the combined forces of PIRA and INLA are said to have been reduced to less than three hundred members, with perhaps another thousand active supporters who provide them with safe houses, transport, look-outs and other back-ups. These hard-core terrorists have lived with violence for most of their comparatively young lives. A soldier who was first in Ulster in 1969 remembers 'a young lad of about eleven years old with stones in his pocket whom we lifted [arrested] following a lot of stoning at about two o'clock in the morning. He was taken to the police-station, his parents were called and he got the summary clout round the ear-hole and was taken home.' When seen again on a later tour thirteen years later 'this guy was about twenty-four years old and allegedly one of the top gunmen of the area. From the age of eleven he has seen nothing else. He has grown up within the ranks and become very professional.' This is a pattern familiar to every experienced soldier who has ever served two or more tours in Northern Ireland. And just as the Army has grown more proficient at countering terrorism so these terrorists themselves have developed: 'The calibre of guys has changed. It's no longer your local IRA man in the street at Number 24. We've got IRA men now who are doctors or bachelors of science. They're now very well organised. Some of them are very professional in what they do – and they live for their cause, without a doubt.'

So long as 'evil men' seek to enforce their will on the people of

Northern Ireland through the bomb and the bullet, the Army believes it has a role to play in the defence of that community: 'If you ask the average British soldier if he wants to pull out of Northern Ireland he would tell you, "No". If you ask him the reasons, he will say to you, "Because of all the good people that are in Northern Ireland". Terrorism is created by a few people and it will be defeated, and at the end of the day it will probably be defeated by those young section commanders out on the streets – allied, one hopes, with a political solution.'

Until that political solution is found there can be no real conclusion to the last chapter of the 'Savage Wars of Peace' which form the subject of this book. Just when that conclusion can be written is anybody's guess. In the meantime the British Army will continue to act as it has always done, holding the ring for the politicians – and offering only its own reflections. 'Certainly I don't as a soldier see any military solution to Northern Ireland,' declares an officer who speaks for all his comrades-in-arms. 'But then I don't think soldiers are in the business of seeking solutions. They're in the business of buying time while others provide the answers. The worry with Northern Ireland, as I've seen it, is that you can't force people to love one another. Until there is a degree of the sort of trust which I feel about being a soldier existing between civilians living in Northern Ireland I can't see a solution.'

Until that last chapter can be written the last word must go to a young Warrant Officer, an ATO in the Felix team, describing his feelings as he attended the aftermath of a terrorist killing at Ballynahinch, County Down, in April 1987:

> I can remember one very cold, wet morning when we were called down to a small RUC station. Two RUC officers leaving in a vehicle had been ambushed from the graveyard opposite. I remember looking down at my feet where the blood of one of the two RUC officers was running off the pavement, being washed away by the rain. It was running down underneath my feet and disappearing down the drain, and to see somebody's life-blood flowing away down a drain made me think long and hard about what was going on across there – and how cheap life is out there.

Index

For reasons of security, not all the names of the interviewees who appear in the book have been attributed.